A SINISTER GIFT

AN ELENORA BELLO MYSTERY

JACINTHE DESSUREAULT

Demiurge
Underground

Legal deposit – Bibliothèque et Archives nationales du Québec, 2021
Legal deposit – Library and Archives Canada, 2021

ISBN 978-1-9994431-2-2 (paperback)
ISBN 978-1-9994431-3-9 (ebook)

CHAPTER ONE

Was there ever a good circumstance for anyone to go to court?

On this bleak and freezing early February afternoon, Elenora Bello sat on a wooden bench in the third row on the prosecution's side of courtroom number three. Next to her, attorney Jean-Philippe Gendron sat stiffly, his breathing shallow. Despite his sharp dressing, the man, who was used to being on top of things—especially in a courtroom—looked like a lost boy. Elenora's heart ached for him.

As a social worker with the police, she went to court regularly with a victim or a witness to soothe their worries and put them at ease. But since she couldn't turn off her sense of empathy, she inadvertently absorbed her fair share of second-hand stress and anguish.

When a trial went well for a client, it brought her and them great joy and relief, a sentiment that some justice had been restored. But heartbreak, grief, and desperation were also frequent and devastating outcomes, regardless of the efforts made.

Elenora was used to accompanying unfortunate and disoriented souls from early on, from their first moment of crisis when the police had to intervene to break up a fight or a psychotic episode, to answer their call for help, or to take their statement. She listened to them, calmed them down, advised them in their decisions to get help or press charges.

More often than not, she felt like she made a bit of a difference in their life somewhere along the way, sometimes nudging them into changing the course of a severely broken path, helping them take a better, healthier direction. Sometimes leading them to forgiveness or redemption.

She made herself available to them and guided them as much as they would let her. It felt like a privilege to her, especially when someone asked her to help them face an abuser, always an excruciating experience for a victim.

Today was such an occasion.

Jean-Philippe Gendron's long fingers fidgeted against his thigh. He was a bundle of nerves under his cool facade.

How torturous it must be for him, Elenora thought and hoped he would heal regardless of the trial's outcome.

She put a gentle hand on his upper arm, and he took a deep breath. She offered him a sympathetic smile. He forced his lips to smile back, but his eyes betrayed his apprehension. She knew he had owned this very courtroom countless times. But today, she also knew there was no amount of confidence he could summon and no amount of acting he could do to feel like it was just a normal Friday.

Jean-Philippe Gendron himself was not on trial, but he was about to face the man who was, a man who had robbed him of his childhood and killed something inside of him a long time ago.

Father Albert Callahan.

The man sitting in the accused box.

Pushing eighty, the priest was frail and had the looks of a doting grandfather. Listening to the current testimony from one of his other victims, he appeared confused, shaking his head gently, as if he could not believe what he was hearing. Like this could only be a big mistake.

Jean-Philippe's fingers stopped fidgeting and balled into a fist. Elenora squeezed his hand to make him aware of how tense he was. He relaxed, but whispered sharply, "The bastard's gonna lie through his teeth. I just know it."

Elenora nodded. She, too, suspected the old man was putting on a show. A convincing one. And she knew that Jean-Philippe's main fear was not the embarrassment or uneasiness of admitting, in front of a room full of colleagues and strangers, that this man had sexually abused him when he was young. What he feared most was that the monster would get away with it, and he was afraid of how he'd react if that happened.

"You're doing the right thing," Elenora whispered back to him.

"I know." His gaze flicked to the ceiling. "I just hope my mother will forgive me."

"If she had known, she would have understood."

"If she had known, it would have destroyed her."

Father Callahan had been present in Jean-Philippe's life, not only at church when the lawyer was a choirboy but also at home when his mother became ill. The priest was there for her while she was on her deathbed. He helped give her a peaceful and dignified death.

Jean-Philippe had confided to Elenora that he was

ambivalent about testifying against the man and telling the world about his true nature. He felt it would diminish what the priest—as monstrous as he was—had done for his mother. And that this would somehow tarnish her memory.

Elenora understood where he was coming from and how torn he was. "Nothing will ever take away what that man did right for your mother," she assured him. "Nothing can take that away. But he needs to be brought to justice for what he did to you and the other boys and to prevent him from striking again. I think your mother would understand."

Elenora's words had seemed to settle something in Jean-Philippe. His initial reluctance vanished, and he became determined to turn the page and help seek justice for everyone involved in the class-action suit.

And here he was, about to put himself out there against Father Callahan. Vulnerable and ready to bare his soul in front of his abuser. He shut his eyes and took in another deep breath. When he opened them, there was a new resolve in his gaze. His composure looked solid.

He was ready.

Elenora couldn't help feeling admiration for this kind of courage in the face of evil.

A shiver went through her, and the most jarring thing happened: she felt a spark at her core, as if a bright light, a heatwave radiated inside of her. Like a miniature, internal big bang.

What the hell was that?

It didn't feel like a gastric issue. Still, she thought about what she had for lunch. She and a colleague had gone to a new brunch place with cutely named items on the menu. Elenora had chosen the *Rays of Sunshine* breakfast—a plate loaded with home-style potatoes and fruit with two sunny-side-up eggs in the middle, surrounded by strips of bacon strategically placed around the eggs to mimic sun rays. But unless there was anything radioactive on the plate, and as funny as it'd be to think the plate's name was literal, she couldn't see what could have caused this eerie disturbance inside of her.

Having recently turned forty, she hoped she was still a little young to have hot flashes.

As her mind tried to find a plausible explanation for the bizarre warmth still dispersing through her, she felt a light touch on her left arm, where no one had been sitting.

The touch was quickly followed by what felt like a hug. Someone was hugging her arm.

She turned and was surprised to see a young girl smiling at her. Her appearance was striking, pigtailed hair so light as to appear white and eyes of a deep, blueberry-like blue. She appeared alone and unbothered by the cold, adult surroundings of the courtroom. What was this kid doing here?

Before Elenora could ask the little girl if she needed help, she felt a tug on her other arm. The judge had called Jean-Philippe to testify.

"Wish me luck," he said to her in a poised voice.

"You won't need luck. You have the truth on your side. And my admiration." Elenora knew that the truth didn't always win in court by a long shot, but she meant it.

He gave her a nod and stood tall, ready to go into battle.

Elenora's gaze followed him for a moment before she turned her attention back to the little girl.

But the little girl was gone.

The court adjourned late in the afternoon. When Elenora emerged from the courthouse, darkness had already fallen, and the freezing air had become even more biting thanks to the merciless gusts of wind. She decided to take a cab instead of walking or waiting for the St-Laurent bus to travel the few long blocks to her small office at her downtown precinct.

Jean-Philippe had given a strong and heartfelt testimony and she felt proud of him, but she was also glad that the trial session was the last thing on her schedule for the week. That meant she could wrap up some paperwork while basking in pride and contentment before calling it a week.

In the quietness of the short, toasty cab ride, Elenora's mind went back to the little girl in the courtroom. Had she been real, or had she imagined her?

The kid had seemed real, and Elenora thought she couldn't have dreamed the touch on her arm. She was engrossed in Jean-Philippe's plight, and the touch had made her turn. How could it have gotten her attention if it had not been real?

Elenora thanked the driver and headed inside the station, her thoughts drifting back to the child again. She had a clear mental picture of her, like an afterimage engraved in her memory. Almost as if she knew her. Could she have met her before?

She considered the possibility and almost went through her past case files. But she met few young kids in her line of work, and they were all so memorable to her, she would have known instantly if she'd encountered this striking little girl before.

And if she had, given that the child couldn't have been more than four or five years of age, this would have happened recently.

How very odd.

"Busy figuring out the toppings?" A familiar teasing voice made her look up. Her husband, homicide detective Tom Madigan, was standing in the doorway with a smirk on his face.

Friday night was restaurant delivery night at their house, usually pizza. Elenora and Tom were both decent cooks, and most of the time she didn't mind cooking—unless she finished work late and cooking meant having to eat late and fast while exhausted. But she also deeply appreciated those times when she didn't have to prepare food. Man, did it ever taste good when she didn't have to make it.

She smiled at Tom's ribbing and reached for her cell phone, holding it up. "Caller's choice! I got my finger on speed dial," she teased back.

His smirk turned sheepish. "Well, the good news is...you get to pick whatever you want tonight."

Elenora wrinkled her nose. This meant he had to work late.

"I'm sorry," he said.

"Not your fault. I'll see if Pierre's available. It's been a while." Pierre Deveraux was a retired detective who had been in Elenora's life and a father figure to her ever since she was a young girl and had lost her father in a freak car accident.

"And if he's not, I'll grab some takeout on the way home," she added. The precinct was within a stone's throw of just about any type of food, from fast to fancy. Finding something to eat was never a problem.

Tom rapped his knuckles a few times against the doorframe. "Sounds good. Try to have a cozy evening, okay? I love you."

"Love you, too."

<hr>

"There should be red wine in the fridge," Elenora said to Pierre as she left the kitchen to meet the delivery man at the front door.

Pierre took out plates and cutlery for the two of them and set them down on the table. Elenora waltzed back into the room with two large pizza boxes—one vegetarian and one *all dressed*. She was counting on leftovers.

"D'you want some?" Pierre asked, holding a wine glass in one hand while his other rested against the glasses and mugs shelf.

As Elenora was about to answer, the face of the little girl in the courtroom flashed in her mind, and a funny thought dawned on her: could she be pregnant? With a girl?

Is that what the weird internal fireworks had been?

She didn't remember ever reading about women feeling anything specific, let alone spectacular, the moment they'd conceived. But somehow, she had a strange feeling this might be the case for her. And the timing added up: they'd made love two nights earlier, so it was a possibility. A very odd one since they'd tried to conceive unsuccessfully for ages. If she were pregnant now, it would be a pleasant yet daunting surprise.

"Wine shouldn't be a matter of life and death. I apologize for the pressure," Pierre joked.

"Sorry about that. I think I'll pass." *Just to be on the safe side.*

"Any news to share?" Pierre gave her a suspicious look. Even though he was no longer a cop, he was still unnervingly observant.

She was tempted to share with him her bizarre gut feeling and what had happened at the courthouse, but she caught herself before going down that rabbit hole with him. For years, Pierre seemed to have been waiting for—expecting even—something extraordinary to happen to her, when all she ever wanted was to live a normal life.

"Too early to tell?" Pierre read into her hesitation.

"I'm just tired. It's been a long week."

"All right."

Elenora spent dinner and the rest of the evening obsessing over the little girl—and what this strange incident might mean for her—while trying to take part enough in the conversation so that Pierre wouldn't feel the need to grill her. Good thing that his favorite TV shows were on, and as they watched them together, it allowed her to remain away from his scrutiny.

She might be pregnant, and that made her giddy. She wanted to tell Tom but feared she would sound crazy. And if this turned out to be a false alarm, like several times before, it'd be cruel to get his hopes up.

She decided to keep this unfounded news to herself for now and hope for the best.

CHAPTER TWO

Pierre would never forget that deadly, late November night thirty-seven years ago in a mountainous part of the Mauricie region, when he first met a young Elenora, who was only three years old at the time.

The little girl and her family were driving home late at night along a sinuous road on a high embankment next to the St-Maurice River. Back then, lumber companies used the wide waterway from spring to fall to send logs cut by lumberjacks down the river to paper mills in towns settled downstream. The river was deep and its current powerful, ideal for this kind of activity.

The Bello family car was traveling down a deserted narrow road. The temperature had dropped, leading to intermittent freezing rain. Patches of black ice covered the pavement in random places, and now a dusting of snow added a layer of difficulty to the already treacherous road conditions.

The car had skidded a few times since they'd left a gathering in a neighboring town. Martin Bello, Elenora's dad, was a cautious driver and took his sweet time to reassure his wife Muriel, Elenora's perpetually anxious mother.

Snow started to fall more heavily, and visibility reduced even further. However, it wasn't the snowstorm that would lead to tragedy but a deer appearing in the middle of the road.

Upon seeing the animal, Elenora's dad yanked the wheel just in time to avoid hitting it. But this course correction and the hairpin turn ahead brought the car right onto a patch of black ice at an unforgiving angle.

The car careened and hit a boulder by the side of the road, sending the vehicle spinning down a hill. Elenora's dad struggled to regain control, but it proved impossible.

Muriel's screams and the curious swaying of the car woke up Elenora, who had been asleep on the back seat. Before her little mind could process what was going on, the car plunged down a cliff and landed in the icy waters of the river, piercing through the thin layer of ice that had barely started to form at the surface.

A group of hunters playing cards in a nearby cabin heard the accident. One of them phoned the authorities while his friends rushed to the scene.

As a member of the Québec provincial police in charge of that territory, Pierre was dispatched to the scene. When he arrived, one of the hunters was fishing Muriel out of the water. She was barely conscious, her lips a deep purple from the frigid water, and her savior carried her to the cabin to warm up.

Moments later, another hunter brought Martin out of the river. Unlike Muriel, he was pronounced dead, no matter the effort to revive him.

Pierre would never forget that night, not only because of the man's death and the woman who had barely made it, but mostly because as paramedics did CPR on the man, a little girl—Elenora—showed up at Pierre's side.

Where she had come from would always be a total mystery to him. Her clothes and her hair were damp, and she shivered softly, supporting the theory that she'd been in the car when it plunged into the river. But none of the hunters had seen her, let alone saved her. How could a child so young have escaped by herself from such an extreme scenario unscathed?

Her collected demeanor, given the circumstances, also felt eerie to Pierre. He whisked his jacket off his back and wrapped it around her tiny shoulders. He scooped her up and jogged them to the cabin.

"What's wrong with my daddy?" Her little voice bounced along with Pierre's feet hitting the ground.

"That's your dad?"

Elenora nodded. "Where's my mom?"

"She's in there. You're gonna see her in a minute. And we're gonna get you warmed up, okay?"

At the sight of her daughter, Muriel broke into uncontrollable sobs, holding on to her in a tight grip while a paramedic attempted to examine the girl.

Pierre was itching to ask Elenora how she had escaped from the car, but he gave the grieving mother and daughter some privacy first and went back outside, where the other paramedics slipped the gurney with Martin Bello's body into the ambulance.

Pierre soon felt a tug on his sleeve and startled to see Elenora at his side, his enormous jacket engulfing her.

"What happened to the little boy?" she asked him.

"What boy? Do you have a brother?" Alarm took over Pierre. *Please, let there not be a dead child in the river.* Elenora's mom, despite being deeply in shock, had not mentioned a missing son.

"I don't have a brother," Elenora replied with a small frown.

"Then who's the boy?"

"The boy in the field at the bottom of the river."

"The boy in the field at the bottom of the river?" Pierre repeated, puzzled. He thought she must have misused the word "field"—the most logical explanation. But the thought of a "boy at the bottom of the river" in itself was distressing enough, and if there was a boy down there, he sure as all hell wasn't alive by now. What horror had this little girl seen?

"Was he...asleep?" he tried, not wanting to ask her bluntly if she had seen a dead kid.

Elenora frowned again. "He wanted to play with me."

"He wanted to play with you... What did you tell him?"

"I told him I had to go. It's past my bedtime."

"And then what happened?"

"I think he was mad at me."

Back then, Pierre was a young bachelor who seldom interacted with kids, both at work and in life in general. He couldn't help wondering if conversations with three-year-olds were always this maddening.

"What makes you think that?"

"He pointed at me with mean eyes."

"He pointed at you with mean eyes?"

Elenora nodded matter-of-factly.

"And then what happened?" Pierre asked.

"I came here."

"You swam from the bottom of the river?"

She looked at Pierre like he had said the silliest thing. "I'm not allowed to swim without my floaties."

Pierre massaged his forehead. The child's words made little sense, and yet she seemed to be telling the truth. It must have been the trauma talking.

"I see..." Pierre had rarely been this perplexed in his life. "We'll see what we can do about the boy."

Pierre never found out who the mystery boy was—or found the body of a boy, for that matter. A team of divers had combed the bottom of the river extensively to find him, unsuccessfully. Pierre had also phoned around to find out more about the Bello family, but there was no boy to be found.

CHAPTER THREE

"Good morning, sweetie, and Happy Valentine's Day!" Tom said, entering the bedroom with a latte in one hand and a red rose in the other.

Elenora stretched in bed, a smile lighting up her face. "Oh, that's lovely." She took the mug and the flower and inhaled both of their enticing perfume. "Thank you."

Tom slipped back under the covers and gave her a tender kiss on the lips.

She put the coffee and the rose down on her nightstand before opening the top drawer and retrieving a small, gift-wrapped box. "I've got a surprise for you too." She handed him the box.

He quickly unwrapped it, uncovering a box of After Eight chocolate mints. "My favorites!"

She chuckled. "Every chocolate out there is your favorite."

"Anything wrong with that?"

"Absolutely nothing."

Tom made a mock frown and shook the box to guess its

weight. "Hmm. The plastic wrap is missing, and this sure feels light for a full box. Have you eaten half of it already?" he teased.

"God, no. I wouldn't eat what's in there."

"Oh?" Tom's brows shot up with curiosity, and he opened the box. There was a pregnancy test stick in it, with a little plus sign announcing it was positive.

"Happy Valentine's Day, daddy," Elenora said with a big grin. Her courthouse insight that she was pregnant turned out to be true, whether by fluke or otherwise, whatever *otherwise* would mean.

It took Tom a moment to register what this meant. "For real?" His eyes were twinkling.

"For real."

"When did you find out?" he asked quietly, as if he couldn't yet believe the news.

"I took the test late last night before bed. I tried to stay awake until you came home to surprise you, but I fell asleep."

Tom looked at her with so much love in his eyes. "Come here." He pulled Elenora into an embrace, nestling his head into the crook of her neck. "That's such wonderful news. I'm so happy." He pulled back. "Though a bit bummed I'm not getting chocolate..."

She slapped him playfully on the arm. "Want me to take it back?"

He moved the After Eight box away from her, well out of her reach. "No way in hell."

She laughed.

"How are you feeling?" He resumed his embrace.

"Very happy. And not feeling sick yet. So, very happy." After a pause, she couldn't help adding, "I think I saw her."

But the moment the words escaped her lips, she regretted it. There was no way to tell Tom about her vision without sounding like a loon or making him freak out if he believed her.

Or both.

"Who?"

Now she didn't have a choice but to give him something and hope she didn't dig herself into a deeper hole. "Our daughter."

"We're having a daughter?"

"I think so."

"Isn't it a bit early to know?"

"Not for a gut feeling, apparently," she replied with a light laugh.

"And your gut's often right, so I won't be betting against it."

He kissed her. "What is she like?"

"What do you mean?"

"You said you saw her. What does she look like?"

Dammit.

"She's beautiful and has light hair." She didn't say "almost white" on the off chance he'd remember that detail and their daughter did turn out to have white hair, as unlikely as it was since they both had dark hair. Elenora's was a deep brown bordering on black, a few shades darker than Tom's.

"Her face is round, like mine, and she has blue eyes." She should stop talking now, keep her predictions vague.

"I'm sure she'll be lovely no matter what she looks like," he said, amused, not taking her seriously for a minute.

"You *do* dare question my gut!" she feigned offense, happy to have dodged a bullet.

He kissed her again. "Can we start sharing the news? Or should we wait to be on the safe side?" he asked.

She suspected he was dying as much as her to tell the world, but erring on the side of caution was probably wise.

He must have read her mind. "Okay, let's wait. It won't be easy, but that sounds best."

Elenora nodded. "Pierre will figure it out, so we might as well tell him. But just him." Her face darkened. "And my mom. It's not like she's gonna understand what's going on or remember."

"Or tell anyone," Tom added softly.

Elenora snorted to cover a pang of bitterness. "Right. And, on the bright side, we can break the news to her as many times as we feel like."

Tom hugged her again and didn't let go for a long time.

"Mom, you're going to be a grandmother. We're going to have a baby. Isn't that the greatest news?" Elenora held her mother's hands in her own. Her voice was warm and tinged with cautious enthusiasm. She knew better than to expect a reaction from her mother, but saying out loud that she was pregnant filled her with joy. She could at least savor that.

Her mother had never quite recovered from the shock of the accident that took her husband's life. Back then, despite being struck with grief, Muriel Bello had managed to keep taking care of Elenora by herself for a while. But her mental health deteriorated, and she became distracted and distant. At times neglectful. Often uncommunicative. It became more and more apparent—to both Pierre and the staff at

Elenora's school—that the mother's state of mind was worsening and that her daughter would need external care.

Muriel soon ended up as an in-patient in a psychiatric ward, and Pierre helped find a good home for Elenora. She was placed with a loving older couple he knew well. He kept in touch with the new family throughout the years, as much as his hectic career as an investigator allowed, becoming a steady and reassuring presence in the girl's life. The bond between him and Elenora grew strong, and she soon considered him a father.

In the past decade, Muriel's mental health had further declined, and she was now heavily medicated. She was too deeply gone into her own world to react to anything happening outside of her or move much of a muscle, let alone have an opinion on something. She never gave any sign that she understood or was even aware of anything happening around her, that she even knew who her own daughter was. But even so, whenever they visited, Elenora and Tom interacted with her as if she knew they were there and could hear them, especially since there was no hard evidence confirming that Muriel could no longer be reached.

"Elenora thinks it's a girl," Tom added, with the same restrained enthusiasm as Elenora's.

The moment he said the word "girl," Muriel's fingers bunched into a fist and a sharp expression flashed in her eyes.

Both Elenora and Tom noticed this very unexpected response. But before they could interpret it, Muriel's fingers relaxed and went back to being limp, her gaze as dull as ever.

"Mom?" Elenora asked. "Is there anything wrong?"

No number of questions and no rephrasing got anything more out of Muriel, leaving Elenora and Tom perplexed. The rest of the visit was painful, filled with awkward silences and small talk.

"Do you think she disapproves?" Elenora asked Tom bitterly as they drove back home.

Tom took a while to answer. "How could she disapprove, sweetie? Perhaps she wishes she could be there for you and the baby, and this reminded her that she's trapped. She's going to be a grandmother. And yet, she'll never be able to truly be one. If she's conscious but unable to express herself, it must be overwhelming and very frustrating for her."

Elenora suspected he was playing devil's advocate to make her feel better and wanted to believe he was right. She often reflected on how tragic and unfair it would be if her mother was in fact aware, if her soul was trapped inside a prison of bone and flesh, unable to communicate with the outside world, no matter how hard she tried. A lonely onlooker of her own existence.

While that prospect was gut-wrenching, so was the thought that her own mother might not approve of her daughter having a baby, let alone a girl.

"Perhaps we should see this microscopic reaction she had as a good sign," Tom tried. "An awkward sign, for sure, but still a sign that she can hear us. That she's trying to tell us something. We've been wondering all these years. What if this is the beginning of her emerging from her current state?"

"Right." Elenora was not convinced of Tom's theory, but she clung to his positive outlook to put an end to this sense of unease and disappointment that had been punching her in the gut since her mother's odd response.

Maybe Tom was right. Maybe this was a positive sign.

Even though something about it didn't feel right.

CHAPTER FOUR

Montréal, 1847

Twenty-seven-year-old Rolland Carmichael was a tall drink of water with the tortured looks of a romantic poet. He was used to provoking two strong types of reaction: either a sneer and stink-eye combo from the men he beat at card games, especially when he took a small fortune from them, or intensely lustful stares from women of most ages—and the occasional man as well.

However, this was the first time he had received a sneer and stink-eye special from a woman. But there was no mistaking that the sharp eyes of Mrs. Penelope McDowell, a well-off and elegant, self-entitled piece of work, had been shooting angry daggers his way all evening from across the room.

"What have you done to poor Mrs. McDowell?" Rolland's good friend Charles Ferrier asked him, hiding a smirk behind a sip of sherry. They stood drinking lazily by the roaring fireplace in the dining room, slightly apart from the soirée in full swing in the next room.

"Nothing. Absolutely nothing, I assure you," Rolland replied. *And that is why she is so irate*, he thought to himself.

Two days earlier, Mrs. McDowell had summoned Rolland under a false pretense to her mansion in the old part of town and thrown herself at him, trying to, at first, entice him—then badger him—to accept a very lucrative, indecent proposal. Rolland had to turn her down. Not only did she have a reputation as a high maintenance busybody—a trait Rolland avoided like the plague to keep his intimate services discreetly under the radar—but her aggressive behavior and refusal to take no for an answer had turned him off beyond a point of no return. He even had to use force to extricate himself from her and fight his way out of her house.

Rolland had some pride, but mostly rules to protect himself. While he was a risk-taker at the card table, he didn't like to gamble too much when it came to biology and angry husbands. His first rule was to get involved mainly with widows and spinsters of a certain age, preferably past child-bearing years. As a fan of every female form, he didn't mind that they could be his mother or grandmother even, nor did he care much about their looks. Aside from the money, the appreciation he received for showering them with attention was hard to beat. He understood that there was no age too old for wanting to be desired.

These women knew and honored Rolland's wishes to not get romantically involved past some friendly tenderness. He was a businessman, and the deal was physical. His clientele was fiercely independent of mind and wealth, and the arrangement suited them just fine.

In his personal life, Rolland was also not interested in young ingénues looking for a husband, knowing too well he wasn't a good catch nor husband material. His romantic activities with older women allowed him to scratch an itch while leaving his mind and heart in peace, and his life devoid of unnecessary drama. As long as he kept away from the likes of the devious and repulsive Mrs. McDowell.

"She seems to think otherwise," Charles fished again.

Rolland gave Mrs. McDowell a sideways glance. She still looked intent on getting his attention and making him pay for refusing her. He would have to watch his back, as the woman was capable of anything.

"Care to share what she's thinking?" Charles was getting desperate to know.

Rolland didn't take his friend's bait, sucking on the inside of his cheek to suppress a laugh. As a gentleman to his core, he was determined not to kiss and tell—or in this case: not kiss, fight off, reject with as much decorum as possible, and tell.

A tray of hors d'oeuvres appeared between him and Charles. They each picked one at random. Rolland surveyed the variety, knowing he would likely bring some leftovers home.

"Thank you, Adam," Charles said to the servant, dismissing him with a kind nod.

They were in Charles's family mansion on Beaver Hall Street, filled with the city's business elite. Most of the wealthy businessmen Rolland played cards with were here at the swanky gathering. Soirées at the Ferriers were always sought-after events, and tonight was no exception. Everyone was dressed in the latest fashion, including Rolland, despite the very modest world from which he came and in which he still lived most of the time.

Rolland was ten years old when his mother died of scarlet fever, leaving him to fend for himself and take care of his then seven-year-old brother, Rory, whose health had been fragile from birth. Their father had been killed in a construction-related accident when Rory was a baby.

Rolland was a strikingly beautiful child, and he took advantage of his looks as a beggar and an errand boy to get money from richer urban dwellers, while Rory, who was more of an introvert and amazing with his hands, made custom furniture for clients or to sell at the market.

Growing up, the Carmichael brothers were not rich, but they looked after one another and usually managed to have enough food to eat and keep a roof over their heads. It helped that they'd inherited the little wood house in the Faubourg St-Laurent their father had built. It was tiny and drafty, but it was home for the two boys.

Once Rolland reached adolescence, he became a favorite of higher society ladies, who came up with ridiculous reasons to employ him, mostly so that they could have him around. His presence in those circles allowed him to meet his good friend Charles, whose family took an honest shining to him.

Charles's father, who only had one son and felt outnumbered at home on the gender front, had been too happy to take Rolland under his wing. He taught him countless things, including how to play cards, and Rolland proved particularly talented at strategy and reading his opponents. He soon was invited to join the men's card games.

Rolland quickly realized that while he could shark the men with his eyes closed, it was a greater payoff to play the long game and not alienate powerful men, his cash cows. So, he would pace himself and win big only when he needed to.

"Ah, there they are," Charles exclaimed, looking at a group of young women in their early twenties decked out in opulent evening gowns.

"Your sister has new friends?"

"Indeed. A new friend and one of Miss Hargrave's cousins, I believe. Let's introduce ourselves, shall we?"

Feeling Mrs. McDowell's death stare boring into him, Rolland followed his friend toward the group of young ladies. He already knew Ophelia Ferrier, the youngest of Charles's sisters, whom he considered his own sister. Next to her stood her best friend Millicent Hargrave, who Rolland also already knew, and two other young women. One had dark auburn hair and the straightness of her posture suggested she could take on the world all by herself. The other one...

Rolland's eyes fell on the other girl, and everything else in the room ceased to exist. She was beautiful, but there was more to her delicate presence that attracted him to her. A mysterious charisma. He felt a twinge of trepidation at the thought of making her acquaintance—a first for him.

The group of young women was engrossed in a lively conversation. As Rolland and Charles approached, the women noticed them and stopped talking, sneaking glances at them. "I gather Mr. Carmichael must be near," Ophelia said before turning, a smirk appearing on her lips.

"Good evening, ladies. We apologize for the interruption. I am Charles, Ophelia's only and favorite brother. And this is my good friend Rolland Carmichael. We are pleased to make your acquaintance."

Charles gave them all a bow, and Rolland followed suit,

his eyes lingering on the young lady who had caught his attention.

"Rolland, you already know my good friend Millicent. And this is Miss Barton, her cousin," Ophelia said about the girl with the fiery hair and disposition. She gave him an amicable smile.

"Miss Barton. It's a pleasure to make your acquaintance." Rolland kissed her gloved hand.

"And this is Miss Deschamps," Ophelia said of the intriguing girl.

"Delphine," Miss Deschamps added.

Delphine. What a pretty name.

"She and her family recently moved here from Québec City," Millicent volunteered.

"Delphine..." the name caught in Rolland's throat before he kissed her hand awkwardly. Their eyes met, and her gaze held his, showing an assurance and a boldness that took him off guard. Feeling an inappropriate flush of heat come over him, he let go of her hand and looked away. His own reaction puzzled him, and he couldn't tell whether this was good or bad. He did feel rather thrilled and alive, but perhaps it was the sherry.

"Dear sister, you seemed to be discussing a passionate topic before we rudely interrupted your lively exchange," Charles said.

Rolland knew this was a prompt for Ophelia to either resume the topic at hand and include him and Charles in the conversation or tell her brother to go check on Mary in the kitchen, her way of dismissing the boys. If she chose the latter, Charles would apologize and propose a new, irresistible topic as an attempt to muscle himself into the discussion, unless he didn't feel like being a part of it. Rolland prayed his friend didn't mind mingling with the group.

"We were discussing the literary merits of the recent works of American writers compared to penny dreadfuls," Ophelia said while still giving Charles an eye roll.

"Emerson's essays? Hawthorne's tales?" Rolland surprised himself. He didn't think his mouth had enough saliva left to produce a sound, let alone clear and coherent words.

"You've read Hawthorne?" Delphine inquired, delighted.

"I have. I think he is a fine storyteller." His eyes stayed on her until he reached the limits of propriety.

"Though not as fine as Alcott, if you ask me," he added in a conspiratorial whisper, making a show of looking over his shoulder at the sea of gentlemen present, as if worried they would question his manhood should they hear he'd been reading a female fiction writer. He turned back and offered the young women a knee-weakening smile. They all blushed to various degrees.

"We lived in New England for a while," Miss Barton said boldly. "I might be impartial, but I think it's a hotbed of interesting ideas and activities."

"I agree. Please tell us more about your experience," Rolland asked with genuine interest.

As part of his efforts to blend into high society, aside from wearing the trendy garments his brother Rory made for him, Rolland was a big reader of everything he could put his hands on, both for his own enjoyment and to keep up in conversations with businessmen and educated women. He enjoyed wit and was disappointed whenever discussions in educated circles turned out dull or ignorant, barely better than those he suffered through at the tavern, where he sometimes played cards with drunken, newly arrived European immigrants.

While Miss Barton talked passionately about Boston's literary and artistic scenes, Rolland made an extraordinary effort to not stare at Delphine, despite his interest in what was being said. Their gazes occasionally crossed. Was she struggling to keep her eyes off him, too?

"What do you think of Poe?" Rolland asked Miss Barton. Something about her made him suspect she might enjoy a good blood-curdling tale.

"I think he's a delight," she replied, faking an innocent smile.

"You mean a delightful menace." Ophelia shuddered.

"I once read him before sleeping, and I will never make that dreadful mistake again." Delphine's voice was full of self-derision, making the group laugh.

"Nevermore?" Rolland retorted with a cheeky grin. He got an amused smile out of her, and once again, she held his gaze. Direct and intense.

Right there and then, he wanted to know more about this girl. He wanted to know everything.

"There you are, my dear," a male voice announced, making Delphine's smile twitch. It was a subtle movement, but Rolland caught it. A lanky young man wedged himself between Delphine and Ophelia. He acted good-natured and confident, but his body language suggested something unpleasant was lurking underneath the sugar-coated exterior.

Rolland straightened his posture and took a sip of sherry. The man was already scrutinizing him.

"Delphine, will you introduce me to your friends?" the man said, barely hiding a hint of irritation.

Delphine forced a pleasant smile and flatly declared, "Everyone, this is Mr. Leopold Christie."

When she didn't continue, he prompted her, "And…?"

"And Mr. Christie is the heir to his family business."

Once again, she added nothing else. Rolland guessed she was doing this on purpose, out of displeasure or to get a rise out of him. Likely both in this case, judging from Mr. Christie's impatient reaction.

"And fortune," Christie added for her. "And Ms. Deschamps forgot to mention the best part. Or perhaps she's already shared the good news that she is betrothed to me."

"Our fathers thought we would be a judicious match," Delphine justified coolly, at the limit of impertinence.

A slight malaise traveled through the group. As a gracious hostess, Ophelia chimed in, "We are honored to have you here tonight, Mr. Christie. I am Ophelia and this is my brother, Charles. Welcome to our home."

Christie took Ophelia's hand and kissed it with a flourish. "It's my most sincere and honored pleasure to make your acquaintance, Miss Ferrier." He turned to Charles and gave him a perfunctory nod. "Mr. Ferrier."

Christie's gaze snapped back to Rolland. "And you are?"

Rolland knew what would happen next. It was tedious and always the same, him being identified as "romantic rival number one." A threat. To the fiancés he encountered in the presence of their beloved, he always appeared a threat.

"This is my good friend, Rolland Carmichael," Charles said. He too was used to this aggressive charade toward Rolland, and he always put himself in his friend's corner.

"Ah. And what do you do, Mr. Carmichael?" Christie

puffed himself up, confident his opponent couldn't beat him in that department.

It doesn't matter what I do, you will discount me regardless of my answer. 'What do you do?' was always the inevitable second question, and Rolland never tried to embellish the answer. There was no point in it. He didn't care to impress strangers. His small circle of friends knew who he was and accepted him for it, and that was all that mattered.

But tonight, in front of Delphine, who looked mortified of Mr. Christie's presence and ready to go hide in the butler's pantry, Rolland wished he had something impressive and grand to retort, to put the insufferable man in his place. And impress Delphine. Which was a bad thing. He'd never wanted to wish he could impress a woman, especially one with romantic ties, and he certainly didn't want to start now. This could only lead down a dangerous path.

"Mr. Carmichael is a businessman in several trades," Ophelia said on Rolland's behalf. "A valuable contact within the business community. He is a bridge between the rich and the poor. Which I find admirable." Her voice dripped with pride as she listed Rolland's more proper business activities.

Rolland worked hard to support his artisan brother and find homes for his products, but the brothers were also community-minded and helped those less fortunate than them whenever they could. But even with hard work and frugal living, it was often a challenge to make ends meet when Rory's medical issues flared up. The cost of medical care and medication took a serious toll on their finances. This was where Rolland's more lucrative extracurricular activities of card sharking and bedsheet warming made a substantial difference.

"Hmm," was all Christie replied to Ophelia's glowing portrait of Rolland. A little smirk of disdain appeared on his lips, dismissing his imagined rival as a man worth anything.

His predictable reaction didn't faze Rolland at all. If anything, he couldn't help responding with a slight smirk of his own, which destabilized Christie, and momentarily wiped the arrogance off his punchable face.

Christie grabbed Delphine by the arm, making her wince. Rolland stiffened and his right hand balled into a fist, ready to intervene. His temper could be short at times, and few things got under his skin faster than a brute being rough with a lady.

Rolland felt Charles's hand on his upper back, telling him not to engage. In his youth, Rolland often had to defend himself, and his fighting style could be described as scrappy. While he rarely itched for a fight nowadays, the desire to react in the face of injustice could easily resurface.

"It's late, my dear. I will escort you home." Christie's tone left no room for Delphine to argue. Before she could reply anything, he was already pulling her away.

Rolland watched them leave and caught the desperate glance Delphine shot him over her shoulder.

That glance would forever be seared into his memory, despite him not wanting to welcome the effect this young woman had on him.

He cursed in his head.

Rolland left the soirée earlier than he usually would have with a bag of leftovers. The odd resentment he felt after meeting the sweet Delphine and her unsavory fiancé, coupled with Mrs. McDowell's unrelenting stare, had worn him out, and he needed fresh air.

Despite lazy flurries, the late March night was mild enough that he politely declined Charles's offer of a ride home in his family's carriage in favor of walking. It was only a twenty-minute walk from the Ferrier mansion to Rolland's modest home.

The first half of the route was on well-maintained cobblestone streets, but once the rich part of town was behind him, the roads became rougher and less maintained, in the image of the common dwellings lining them and their inhabitants.

Rolland didn't mind the change of scenery. He was as appreciative of the beautiful architecture of the rich neighborhoods as he was of the atmosphere of hard work and bootstrapping ingenuity that permeated the poorer parts where he lived.

His world.

Along the familiar walk, the snow-muffled sounds of the city took a back seat as Rolland tried to figure out what had happened to him earlier that evening and why the fresh memory of Delphine was already haunting him.

Why her?

Why now?

What was it about her that made him feel so confused? What made him wish she'd been the one to proposition him instead of the awful Mrs. McDowell?

A wave of desire washed over him. How he would love to...

No. He couldn't entertain such a thought. She was engaged. And even if she hadn't been, he had nothing to offer her.

He would have to forget her, the sooner the better. And he hoped that she and her intolerable fiancé would not become regulars at the Ferriers. He hoped their paths would never cross again.

As he neared his home, it surprised him to see a faint light glowing from one window. What was Rory doing up at this hour of the night? His brother was an early riser and usually in bed by now.

Entering the house quietly in case Rory was asleep, Rolland took off his boots and went to investigate the source of the flickering light. It was coming from Rory's workshop in the back. His brother was not the type to leave a burning candle unattended. He was responsible to a fault about every aspect of his life and well aware of the flammability of the wooden structure of their home. A house fire was the last thing they needed.

Approaching the doorway of the workshop, Rolland spotted a pair of legs on the ground. His heart skipped a beat, and he rushed inside the room.

His brother lay unconscious on the floor next to his stool and workbench.

Rolland checked for a pulse. It was weak, but thank God, there was one.

"Rory?" He touched his brother's face, caressed his cheek, and checked for bumps on his head. "Rory?"

Rory's eyes fluttered open. "Is it morning?" he mumbled, confusingly taking in his surroundings.

"You must have fainted while working."

"I must have."

"You were working late?" There was a hint of accusation in Rolland's tone. He couldn't help being protective of his brother and couldn't stand it when Rory unnecessarily pushed himself to exertion, something he would do way too frequently if it were entirely up to him. Rory felt guilty to impose such an important financial stress on them, and if he had a say, he would work himself to death every day to make up for it. Fortunately, Rolland was usually around to force him to pace himself.

"Help me up," Rory said.

Rolland gave him a hand, and Rory teetered to a standing position. He struggled to remain upright but pretended like everything was fine.

"Let's get you to bed," Rolland said.

Rory didn't argue, and they trudged up the stairs to a tiny room with a tiny bed. It was barely bigger than a closet, but both brothers had their own closet-sized bedroom, which they considered a luxury.

"We lost the Mulbrays," Rory blurted out. "Fernand came by after you left. The shop was closed this morning when the workers showed up. It won't reopen."

The Mulbray brewery was a family business that had brought a sizable amount of carpentry work to the Carmichael brothers. Losing their business was a major hit for them, as it would also be for the many other families who depended on the brewery for their survival.

Rolland let out a groan. Would this awful evening end already? He didn't think he could take any more trials or bad news. "Did you tell him we'd find a way to help?"

"I did."

"Good. I will call on him tomorrow and see what the needs are."

Rolland was already thinking of the new Beaulieu bakery, how they seemed open to bartering. Perhaps he could help with bread-making in exchange for a few loaves for the families in need. That wouldn't be much, but that'd be a start and help keep their fellow workers from starving while they got back on their feet.

"Good night," Rolland mumbled to the room, his brother already asleep.

He went to get the candle that was still burning on the workbench and headed back upstairs to his room with it, his mind revving. If only Mrs. McDowell wasn't such a...

Ugh.

He shouldn't even entertain the idea. In what world would he be able to take the handsome sum of money she was offering him without retching? What could he possibly do to pleasure her without his body betraying him, broadcasting loudly and clearly that he would rather be cleaning up a gallows platform than touching her?

That wouldn't go well, now, would it?

Rolland let out a long sigh of frustration. Why couldn't this new offer have come from someone else?

Rory barked a nasty string of coughs, reminding Rolland that his brother's health was steadily getting worse.

And they had lost the Mulbray account.

They could really use Mrs. McDowell's money.

Rolland reached for the candle, and his eye caught a mouse silently scurrying across the hall. He blew on the flame and the room went dark. The rodent could no longer be seen.

What if he didn't see her? Didn't have to look at her? Pretend she was someone else? Like Delphine?

Delphine...

Could he think of Delphine and distract himself enough if he and Mrs. McDowell were in pitch-black darkness?

The woman would have to remain quiet, too. That'd be ideal but unlikely that she'd accept these kinds of conditions.

Another parade of coughs from the other room made his blood pressure rise a little more.

What if he could convince her to wear a bag over her head as some kind of naughty game?

A blindfold?

Perhaps *he* could wear a blindfold.

And stuff his ears with something to not hear a peep from her poison-laden tongue.

As Rolland drifted into an exhausted sleep, he took the resolve to make things work. He'd put his pride aside and crawl back to the rich hag on his knees if he had to.

Pride was yet another thing he couldn't afford.

CHAPTER FIVE

Montréal, present day

Every time Elenora set foot in courtroom number three, she couldn't help searching for the little girl.

She had not seen her again since that one time, but she was convinced that her presence—her *apparition?*—was tied to her becoming pregnant, that the girl was her future daughter. Even if that made no sense or was even possible.

Being in the room never failed to remind her of the pregnancy milestones that she reached in this very room—coincidentally? Like the first wave of nausea that had hit her as the jurors of the class action suit against Father Callahan read their verdict, as she heard the lenient sentence awarded to the undeserving old monster.

That alone would have been enough to cause a fair amount of disgust in anyone, but Elenora also received some unwelcome help from her changing hormones. She squeezed Jean-Philippe's hand in solidarity and told him she'd be right back. She rushed out of the room and barely made it to the ladies' room in time to unload the contents of her stomach.

On a much more joyous note, there had been the first baby kick during an assault trial.

And the first "belly wave" at a nasty murder trial.

Bad timing on this one.

A terrified witness was giving the audience a gory depiction of what he'd seen when Elenora felt the skin of her belly stretch considerably and move in an undulating motion.

What was baby Aubrey—her and Tom's chosen baby girl name—up to?

This is so awesome, Elenora thought as a collective gasp of horror traveled through the courtroom in reaction to a disturbing detail of the murder.

And then, what could only be a minuscule body part pushed outward and distended Elenora's stomach in one spot, as if a tiny heel were trying to break free from her stomach, *Alien*-style.

Elenora rested her hand over the small protrusion, caressing it at first and then trying to grab it for fun. The adorable little thing receded, and another wave coasted along the outer wall of her stomach.

The feeling was astonishing and delightful, and Elenora had to make a considerable effort to contain her excitement out of respect for the drama playing out in front of her in the courtroom. Despite the urge to shout to the world about this wonderful thing that was happening to her against a backdrop of human greed and cruelty. Despite wanting to bolt out of the room to catch a cab in the hope she'd reach Tom at the station fast enough for him to experience this miraculous occurrence with her.

Thankfully, the belly wave happened again—and often—since that first time in the courtroom. Elenora was able to savor those moments and share them with Tom, Pierre, and even her mother—though there was no telling if Muriel was aware of anything. But on the off chance, Elenora included her mom as much as possible, despite her still being incarcerated in the prison of her own mind and not giving anyone any more signs of sentient activity since that one eerie reaction when Elenora and Tom had announced the pregnancy to her.

Overall, the beginnings of Elenora's pregnancy had been fairly idyllic. Pretty much everyone in her life—other than her mother—had welcomed the news with joy. Pierre couldn't wait to be an honorary grandfather, and her colleagues at work pampered her.

Elenora often got lost in thought, imagining all the things she and Aubrey would do together, the songs she would sing to her, the books she would read to her, the baking and crafts projects they would do when Aubrey was older.

Fortunately, morning sickness had become manageable after the close call at the courthouse, and for a while, the smell of coffee, of all things, was the primary cause of it. How could one go from finding an aroma so delicious and salivating over it to getting instant nausea at a faint whiff?

The first trimester was a dream. The second one took a slow turn into a less pleasant territory. At night, Elenora started having intense dreams. The early, delightful glimpses she had of Aubrey made way for visions of a darker nature, complete with physical side effects.

At first, the dreams were mostly abstract, though still stressful. Feelings of uneasiness woke her up during the night and lingered until morning. She'd wake up with stiffness in her hands, concluding she must have made fists while sleeping. Tom also pointed out she was grinding her teeth more and more. That explained the sore jaw.

By the third trimester, the nightmares had turned into more concrete scenarios. One recurring dream was simple: her little girl walking away from her. Elenora would try calling after her, but she had no voice.

On the surface, it seemed innocuous and typical of a dream, but Elenora would wake up with a nagging sense that something was wrong. She couldn't put her finger on it, but the feeling of angst was real and overwhelming.

She would then recall her dream, Aubrey walking away from her, and she'd wonder if there was cause for concern in real life. Was her body trying to tell her there was something wrong with her daughter? Was she too old to have a healthy child? Was she not taking the right vitamins? Eating the right foods? Eating bad foods?

Or was this a premonition of things to come when her little girl was older?

Would Elenora lose her?

On one hectic morning, when the alarm had failed to go off, and they were crazy late for work, Elenora intercepted Tom coming out of the shower to tell him about the recurring dream. The timing was awful, but she sensed she was this close to losing her mind from anxiety and needed to tell Tom on the spot. Pregnancy panic attacks had zero regard for timing, or life in general, and waited for no one.

Thankfully, Tom had a bottomless well of patience. He listened to Elenora as he toweled himself off and went around the room to fish his socks and underwear out of the top drawer of his dresser, then headed to the closet for a shirt and pants.

"Perhaps it's the pregnancy hormones playing havoc on your emotions," he tried after she gave him all the details. "They've been real assholes. I wouldn't put it past them."

These hormones were indeed powerful—and assholes at times, for sure—they certainly did a number on the mother. She knew this. She had read about this and experienced it first-hand, too. How could she not have suspected hormones from the get-go? They had a ridiculous impact on her memory already—how many times had she stared into the fridge, her mind blanking, wondering what the heck she was looking for? They were now affecting her nights and judgment, too. Simple as that.

"The anguish you feel is clearly real," Tom added, "and I don't want to undermine what you're feeling—you know that. But perhaps this pregnancy-related anxiety is par for the course? I mean, becoming a mother must be one of the most daunting things in life, and perhaps your subconscious is trying to work some things out before the little one shows up."

Tom put a hand on Elenora's protruding belly and lowered himself to whisper to it, "Hey, cutie, try not to give your mama a hard time, okay? She needs her sleep. And her sanity."

Elenora rubbed Tom's shoulder. Could she possibly love this man any more than she already did? He stood back up and kissed her.

"Do you think it has anything to do with the fact I kinda lost my mother when I was young?" Saying the words gave Elenora some perspective. Perhaps the dream anxiety was related to her situation with her mother, a situation she would not want to see repeated for anything in the world.

"That would make sense."

It would.

Tom glanced at his watch, reminding them both they had to get their show on the road, but instead of rushing them out of the room, he opened his arms and pulled Elenora to him.

"I wish I could feel those awful feelings for you, but since I can't... Perhaps look at it this way: does worrying about the dreams produce anything concrete?"

"No." She knew where Tom was going with this. She used the same line of reasoning with her clients to reassure them.

"Is it something you can control?"

"No. I don't think so."

"Then, is it useful or productive to worry?"

"No." She smiled, feeling better now. "And point taken. I know the rest of the song. We're gonna be late."

"We're already late. And we can't change that fact by worrying either." He smirked.

"Thank you."

"Anytime. Now let's go back to obsessing over onesies, playpens, and other non-anxiety-inducing baby stuff, shall we?"

***

Expressing her concerns to Tom had soothed Elenora.

Briefly.

The dreams—nightmares, really—came back with a vengeance.

They became more intense and jumbled and oppressed her with a convincing feeling of drowning.

Countless times, Elenora woke up breathless and gasping for air in the middle of the night, eyes wide with panic, her heart threatening to jump out of her chest. Her arms flailed, and her hands desperately grabbed at anything they could hold on to, often getting a death grip on Tom—his arm, shoulder, face—startling him awake.

Calming herself down from those dreams was a colossal challenge, and even Tom's usually effective reassurance took a long time to kick in.

She often rushed to the window, desperate to feel some fresh air on her face. Into her lungs. Bring her heart rate down.

Those nights were traumatic and deeply disconcerting.

Why would she stop breathing? Was her asthma worsening? But Elenora was used to mild asthma attacks, and this felt like something else.

She went to see her doctor, who thought it was likely hormones. Or something neurological combined with hormones—Elenora didn't catch all of it, just that it should soon go away on its own.

Thankfully, as the doctor had predicted, the drowning nightmares and associated panic attacks eventually subsided.

Only, they made way for an equally disturbing vision.

Of a little boy.

In a field.

At the bottom of a river.

CHAPTER SIX

Montréal, 1847

Ever since he had met Delphine at the soirée, Rolland's mind kept returning to the memory of her, distracting him greatly. He was not used to having a woman on his mind, especially one who was way off-limits for him.

If he had some money and had not slept his way through a sizable number of bedrooms and boudoirs, he'd be one of the city's most eligible bachelors. But he couldn't change past actions nor the harsh, immutable realities of his very modest birth.

Still, he couldn't help wondering what could have happened had he met Delphine under better circumstances.

If he had money.

If he was of better breeding.

If he was a normal man.

If he was worthy of her.

He liked picturing a full, loving life with her. Adorable children. Dogs. Reading side by side in front of a fire on cold winter nights and having stimulating discussions. All the lovely bits of daily life he was not meant to ever have with a woman, beyond the initial thrills of seduction and carnal desire.

This fantasy made his heart ache.

No matter what he thought or might yearn for, he wasn't good enough for her. He'd never be good enough for her. He was a poor prospect for any young lady of good repute.

He was tainted goods.

But meeting Delphine had provoked such a visceral reaction that it made him wonder if there was such a thing as kindred spirits. Otherwise, why would he feel such an odd and strong pull toward a total stranger?

If kindred spirits existed, he never thought he'd meet one of his own. At his age, Rolland thought he'd seen and experienced just about everything there was out there for him to see and experience.

Maybe he was wrong.

But could fate be so cruel as to destine a lovely creature such as Delphine to a no-good man such as him? There had to be a mistake, if only for her sake.

Each time these thoughts crossed his mind, Rolland inevitably concluded that his attraction to Delphine, even if due to fate, was pointless and should not exist. He should not give in to this treacherous impulse. Even if he was consumed with desire for her, he had no intention of ruining her, so it was just as well that she was already betrothed. Rolland might have been a huge flirt, but he wasn't a heartless man.

And thus, every time he went down this mental spiral, he would strengthen his resolve to steer clear of her to avoid tempting fate. Even if deep down he ardently wished he could see her again.

At worst, he would limit himself to thinking about her, even if that tortured him.

Perhaps someday Rory would be in better health and Rolland could save enough money to move to another town to start anew, where his background and reputation didn't precede him.

But what were the odds of him ever finding another woman like Delphine, for whom starting over would be worth the effort? He felt like she was the only woman for him.

And he couldn't have her.

"Mr. Carmichael!" a feminine voice called from behind Rolland.

There must have been another man named Carmichael since Rolland didn't know anyone in this remote part of town, aside from the male shopkeeper where he was headed.

"Mr. Carmichael!" the voice insisted.

Rolland turned and was astonished to see Miss Delphine Deschamps walking at a fast pace to catch up to him. What could she possibly be doing—on foot, nonetheless—in this desolate neighborhood? Was she lost?

"I thought it might be you," she said.

She seemed delighted to see him, and all the fantasies Rolland had entertained about the two of them rushed through his mind. He wondered if he was blushing like a young bride because it sure felt like he was. But it didn't matter. He needed to get his composure back quickly before letting any of his inappropriate feelings show.

"Miss Deschamps. What an unexpected delight to see you again." He barely managed to keep his voice steady. Gentlemanly and appropriate. Careful not to let her know how much he meant those words.

"And you too, sir." She offered him her gloved hand.

Rolland took it and gave it a gentle kiss, his eyes lifting to meet hers. He doubted he could hide the fire he felt in his gaze.

Amazingly, she didn't look away. In fact, there was a similar intensity in her eyes that was hard to miss.

The whinnying of a horse pulling a carriage in the dirt street broke their trance, and Rolland let go of Delphine's hand. "Please forgive my impertinence."

"There is nothing to forgive," she replied with a smile.

"May I accompany you to your destination?" He offered her the crook of his arm. She took it and glanced around, searching. She opened her mouth to say something but stopped herself. She straightened her posture and looked Rolland in the eye. "*This* is my destination."

Rolland gave the street a quick scan, searching for a clothing shop or another such business that would have attracted Delphine to this part of town, but they were standing in a stretch of the road that only had common dwellings.

Before he could ask her about her destination, she said, "I was hoping we could further discuss literature. I very much enjoyed our talk the other night, before..."

Before her boorish fiancé forced her to leave? The words were on Rolland's tongue, and judging from the grimace that briefly distorted Delphine's lovely face, similar words might have been on her tongue as well. Rolland guessed she hadn't been too happy with the other man's interference.

A woman with a mind of her own.

His type. He had suspected she had an independent streak when they first met, and *this*—her reaction and her standing right there in front of him in a seedy part of town—had to be a confirmation of it.

He was in so much trouble.

"It was a lovely conversation. We appear to have *literary* affinities," he said carefully.

"We do, indeed."

They shared a moment in silence, oblivious of the fact they were hogging the sidewalk and the other pedestrians had to maneuver around them. Rolland allowed himself to soak in this wonderful moment until he got elbowed by a man walking by.

The stranger took in his height and blurted an apology, probably more to avoid ruffling his feathers than out of being genuinely sorry. Rolland made nothing of it and acknowledged the man's apology with a nod.

After an awkward pause, Rolland said to Delphine, "So. Here you are..."

"Yes."

"In this neighborhood."

"Yes."

One of his brows rose. "To...discuss literature?"

"Indeed. Since we are here..."

"With me?"

"As improper as it may sound, yes." She sounded confident.

Rolland's mind raced, trying to make sense of this unexpected conversation, afraid to reach the wrong conclusions and give himself false hope.

"How can a chance encounter be improper?" he tried.

"Shall we walk?" she asked, changing the subject. He followed.

"I have not seen you at the Ferriers lately," she said.

"I have not been."

"Do you plan on being there again soon?"

He didn't want to tell her he had no intentions of going to Charles's soirées knowing that she would be there. That would be playing with fire. But now that she was standing next to him, stirring a deep turmoil in his body and soul, and if she wanted him there—as bizarre as the notion sounded—he had to reassess.

But did she truly want him there? Or was he reading what he wanted between the lines? And even if she did want him there, why him? Her circle of friends seemed well versed in literature and other topics of interest. Unless literature was just a pretense, and she craved his presence as much as he craved hers.

But surely she knew they could not mingle with one another, and especially not under the watchful, twitching eye of Leopold Christie. Rolland knew the kind of man he was and that he would not allow her anywhere near him.

Rolland's life was complicated enough without the need to make things even more challenging. One of the main reasons he didn't do romance.

"I'm afraid I shouldn't," he finally admitted in a strangled whisper. The way she looked back at him, she understood what he meant. And she didn't hide her disappointment.

She was disappointed that she would not be seeing him.

Her disappointment made Rolland's insides flip with joy and churn with dread. If their attraction was mutual, this was at once the most wonderful and the most atrocious news. How could he avoid her now that he knew she longed for his company?

"Then I guess we will need to rely on chance encounters," she said softly.

"If only these were reliable," he replied, resorting to humor to mask the pain.

A wry little smile tugged at the corner of Delphine's lips. "Chance can always be arranged."

⁂

Chance could indeed be arranged.

A week later, Delphine "bumped" into Rolland once again in another sketchy part of town. His initial bafflement delighted her, as did his surprised reaction when she confessed to bribing a street kid nicknamed Young William, to keep her updated on Rolland's business whereabouts, so that she could conveniently organize these "chance" encounters, far from their shared social circle.

From the start, Rolland knew these clandestine meetings weren't a good idea. But the intoxicating way he felt when he was with Delphine clouded his judgment. And thus, he agreed to meet her secretly in various industrial and seedy parts of town to spend time together while avoiding the risk of being seen.

Their affection for one another grew fast, as they had much in common beyond their mutual attraction. Their trust in each other also grew, and Delphine even dared to confess how deeply unhappy and horrified she was about her situation with Leopold Christie. It was an execrable arranged marriage as far as she was concerned, and she would do anything to get out of it.

To lighten the mood, Rolland joked he was free to elope with her on any Wednesday afternoon.

The jest and sentiment behind it made her laugh and smile. But what started as a joke quickly evolved in them talking about eloping as a feasible plan.

They would leave everything behind, and with Rory in tow, they would head out west to Ontario and go to Cornwall, or Kingston even, to put enough distance between them and Delphine's family, at least until her father accepted her new —and chosen—life.

Despite knowing this could only be a fantasy, Rolland had never been so happy in his entire existence.

CHAPTER SEVEN

"I saw the boy in the field." Elenora's voice was heavy with disbelief.

Pierre's silence on the other end of the phone conveyed the same level of bafflement. And he was rarely at a loss for words.

"I saw the boy in the field, Pierre. What the hell does that mean?"

"You saw him where?"

"In a dream. Last night."

"Okay. Do you think it was just a dream?"

That was the first thought that had crossed her mind when she'd woken up at four a.m. and the disturbing memory of the dream was fresh.

"It felt different from just a dream. More like the first insight I had of Aubrey, but this time, I was asleep."

Elenora had eventually told Pierre about her pregnancy hunch since she knew he'd be open-minded about it. He often hinted at having encountered things that were hard to explain during his career, though he'd never volunteered any concrete details. He'd been fascinated to hear about the little girl Elenora had seen in the courtroom and her knowing that she was pregnant with that kid. He had no idea how that could be, but the whole thing captivated him.

She'd made him swear to keep it a secret from Tom. She felt bad about keeping anything from her husband, but while he, too, was curious and receptive about all the things, he was also prone to worrying about her. There was no point in weirding him out over an anomaly. Her pregnancy was stressing him out enough as it was.

"Okay..." Pierre let out a long breath. "What did you see, exactly? What happened?"

"It felt like I was reliving a memory, like I was brought back to the bottom of the St-Maurice River. I was standing on the riverbed, observing. I could see my parents' car sinking from above, and one of the hunters struggling to open the car door to rescue my dad, who looked unconscious. Already dead."

Elenora's voice was steady as she told him what she'd seen. Being so sleep-deprived and hormonal, she expected to be emotional when describing the scene out loud and the sight of her dead father—even if this was not an actual memory—but she felt detached.

"Once the hunter swam to the surface with my dad, I heard a sound behind me. I turned, and I was no longer in the river but in a field. In the mountains."

"In winter?"

"No. Summer. And there he was. A blond boy of about five years old, I'd say. His clothes looked old."

"The eighties weren't the height of timeless fashion."

"No. Much older than that. *Little House on the Prairie* kind of old."

"Oh."

"Yeah."

Elenora had seen the show as a kid and wondered if perhaps the memory of it had influenced that part of her dream, along with decades of Pierre asking her if she'd ever seen a little boy. Throughout the years, whenever they had the "accident conversation," Pierre would casually mention something about a boy in a field, no doubt to see if it would jog her memory. But she never had anything to say.

When she was fourteen, she asked Pierre why he kept mentioning a boy to her, and he simply shrugged. "Just curious. Just something someone said." He then changed the subject and never mentioned the boy again.

"He was staring at me. His gaze was very intense for such a small kid. Unnaturally so. There was something deranged about it." In all her years of intervening with people in distress, Elenora had seen her lot of intense, deranged stares.

"And then he asked me, 'Are you having fun yet?' in the creepiest voice." Goosebumps emerged on her forearms.

Pierre grunted. "And then what happened?"

"And then, it felt like I got sucked out of there, and I was standing in front of you, on the shore of the river, at the scene of the accident. That part was in winter. You gave me your jacket."

There was another moment of silence before Pierre asked, "Did you say anything to me?"

"I asked you about the boy in the field at the bottom of the river."

"What did I answer?"

"You asked me tactfully if he was asleep."

Elenora heard a soft gasp from Pierre. She guessed he must have said this to her in real life. And he'd never pronounced these words to her.

"Perhaps this dream jogged my memory of our first encounter. Perhaps it was just a buried memory and nothing more."

Elenora tried to rationalize the dream, but she wasn't convinced there was anything rational about it. Its eerie vibe felt so real, along with her sudden, crystal clear remembrance of Pierre's words.

And why now?

"Perhaps." Pierre sounded just as unconvinced as she was.

His brain was no doubt revving and trying to make sense of her words. This was a decades-long puzzle that had been a lifetime obsession for him.

"What's your take?" she asked to fill yet another silence, despite knowing that if Pierre had a take, there wouldn't be a silence to fill.

⁓

Are you having fun yet?

The creepy little boy's taunting words had echoed in Elenora's mind all day and once again now, as she waited for Tom to meet her at the obstetrician's office. Today was an ultrasound day, which was supposed to be joyful.

Are you having fun yet?

The unnerving words were hard to forget. They kept

Elenora on edge, wondering what the creepy kid meant. They sounded like a veiled threat of ugly things to come.

She shouldn't let words in a dream get under her skin like this. She knew better than to let that happen.

Are you having fun yet?

Elenora looked at her watch. Tom was running late. If only he were here to distract her.

She leaned forward to pick up the worn baby magazine at the top of a pile on a side table in the waiting room. The magazine was three years old, and the advice headlined on the front page was old news to her. It felt like she'd already read about every pregnancy-related fact out there more than once.

Are you having fun yet?

Ugh.

Get out of my head, little twerp.

She was tired. Exhausted from lack of good sleep. That was the reason she had this irrational voice in her head taunting her, nothing more than that. She knew the devastating effects of bad sleep and stress and shouldn't forget it.

She needed to find a way to deal with this insanity and nip it in the bud. She couldn't let a dream interfere with her enjoyment of her pregnancy. She wanted to cherish every moment and make great memories. She couldn't let a little creep ruin her life.

Are you having fun yet?

Elenora tried to take a step back and analyze her situation objectively. Fact: she was hormonal. Fact: she had been sleep-deprived for weeks. Fact: Tom had suggested she take some time off from work to rest. He said that her health and well-being were a priority and that they would manage money-wise if they had to. Cut down on restaurants and whatnot.

But she had refused his offer. Work kept her grounded and nicely occupied. Everyone at the station knew about her situation, and management was being sympathetic and accommodating. She could always take a nap in her office if she felt the need.

But that was before, when things had still seemed kind of manageable.

Now, she felt like things were degenerating quickly and getting out of hand. She couldn't let things get out of hand. She wasn't thinking clearly, and she couldn't afford to not think clearly. She'd make mistakes.

For her sake, the baby's and even that of potential clients, she should ask to be assigned to administrative work and stop tagging along on patrol, refrain from intervention work, including the seemingly lighter cases. Interventions were a mixed bag of situations—she never truly knew ahead of time what shade of human distress she might end up dealing with. Until she got there. And even then, she never knew when a surprise twist would hurl itself at her.

She couldn't risk gambling with other people's lives.

The upside: admin work would take some stress and pressure off. She'd be forced to slow down. Maybe she'd sleep better.

"Elenora?"

She looked up from the magazine she'd been mindlessly leafing. Nurse Sandra's eyes found her, and her face brightened.

Elenora stood up, dropped the magazine back on top of the pile, and went up to the nurse.

"How are you doing today?" The woman's cheeriness was welcoming.

"Hanging in there," she said, injecting good humor into her voice. "Yourself?"

"Pretty well right now, but ask me again later. My son's taking his driving test this afternoon. So, either we'll be buying ice cream to celebrate, or we'll be buying ice cream to drown his sorrows."

"Sounds like fun. I can't wait to experience that."

"Two words: public transit," the nurse chirped while consulting Elenora's file. "Speaking of fun: an ultrasound today! Is Tom coming?"

"He's running late. I hope he'll make it on time."

"Well, you're in luck. Dr. Poitras is running a little late herself. And I'll keep an eye out for Tom. Let's see what we can do."

"Thank you, Sandra. That's awesome. *You're* awesome."

"Just doing what we can." The nurse pointed at the recliner bed in the ultrasound room. "You know the drill. Do you need help—"

Elenora answered by getting on the bed by herself.

"Great. Just make yourself comfortable. The doctor should be with you soon, and I'll be on the lookout for your husband." The nurse closed the door behind her.

Elenora looked around the room. A variety of medical equipment filled the floor. Diplomas and baby pictures hung on the walls. What was Tom doing?

She checked her phone for a missed text or voice message.

Nothing.

She wished she weren't there all by herself right now. As

an older, expectant mom—with what some still called a "geriatric" pregnancy—every ultrasound made her a little nervous. She couldn't wait to have a confirmation that the baby was fine, that everything was still progressing normally. To hear a regular little heartbeat. Sleep deprivation was not helping with her nerves. She seriously had to do something about that.

Are you having fun yet?

"UGH! Really!?"

A knock at the door made her jump. Tom stuck his head in. "So sorry I'm late. Did I miss anything?"

She beamed a smile of relief at him. "You didn't. All good." Things were all good now that he was there.

"It's always exciting, isn't it?" he said as Dr. Poitras came into the room. They exchanged greetings, and the petite, thirty-something woman perched herself on a stool before glancing at Elenora's file.

Before long, the ultrasound machine came to life and its wand did its magic, revealing little Aubrey on the monitor.

"She's gotten bigger," Tom whispered in awe.

The machine picked up the baby's heartbeat.

SHWOOOSH,   SHWOOOSH,   SHWOOOSH, SHWOOOSH.

It sounded like an alien message hailing from a foreign galaxy. An underwater galaxy at that. A hypnotic sound that also reminded Elenora of being submerged. Like when she was at the bottom of the river, before the little boy appeared in her dream.

The bottom of the river. Where she would have died had she been down there for real. Pierre was right to be puzzled as to how she had survived if she'd been in the river.

SHWOOOSH,   SHWOOOSH,   SHWOOOSH,
SHWOOOSH.

Are you having fun yet?

Elenora's chest tightened, and she became hyper-aware of her jagged breathing. Was a panic attack looming?

SHWOOOSH,   SHWOOOSH,   SHWOOOSH,
SHWOOOSH.

Movement caught her attention. She looked down and saw water pooling on the floor, its level rapidly rising. At this rate, it would fill the room in no time. She wanted to turn to Tom to alert him but was frozen in place. Smiling in awe at the monitor, he was oblivious.

Are you having fun yet?

Elenora's lungs struggled to let in enough air. She felt a tear rolling down her cheek.

"Heartbeat's good." Dr. Poitras's declaration brought Elenora back to reality.

She took in a sharp breath, her lungs finally letting air in. Glancing around the room, down at the floor, she saw no sign of water.

She had imagined it.

So, add hallucinations to the list? Just what she needed.

"Are you okay?" Tom whispered to her, his hand wiping her cheek. Was she crying?

"Tears of joy," she quickly volunteered with a weak smile and wanted to add, "And of relief, stress, sleep deprivation, hormones, and dread."

She didn't fool Tom. "You're on a roller coaster, sweetie. It's normal."

Deep down, she knew it was normal.

But was she?

Elenora's nightmare that night reached a new level of alarm.

At first, all she perceived was a heartbeat against sheer blackness. She felt it pulsing in her abdomen. It had to be the baby's.

She tried to tune in to its rhythm, and the heartbeat became audible to her ears. Faint at first, but then increasing in loudness.

Its speed also increased, becoming faster and faster.

Until it became overwhelmingly quick and loud in Elenora's ears, as if bouncing around invisible walls, manifesting in surround sound against the darkness of the dream.

The heartbeat was urgent. Anxiety-inducing.

Pain shot through Elenora's jaw. The sharp and sudden ache spread throughout her body, and she clutched her abdomen to protect Aubrey.

Strobing flashes of light unveiled parts of a man running, stealing her focus away from the pain. The flickering light made it hard for her to see him well, but she felt compelled to watch him, to study him as much as she could.

He looked disoriented and terrified. Like he was running for his life away from something horrific.

His fear seeped into Elenora and became her own. His heart was beating out of his chest, the sound echoing in her own ears, and she felt her throat constrict, making it hard for her to breathe.

She could hear his strained and uneven breath. It matched her own.

Streaks of blood escaped from the corners of his mouth.

She felt another sharp pain along her jaw, and a warm liquid poured out of her own lips.

The stranger fell to the ground, clutching his throat, as if being strangled by invisible hands. Elenora braced herself for her own fall. But it didn't come. Instead, she felt paralyzed. Forced to watch the man's demise while feeling it, life draining out of both of them.

She tried to go help him, but none of her muscles would so much as twitch. She was utterly powerless.

The heartbeat sound stopped cold, and the man ceased to move.

She felt water wet her bare feet. She glanced down and saw a torrent of water rushing around her ankles.

Reaching her calves.

Her thighs.

The water level rose quickly, and she was stuck in place.

And then it came. Ever so faint, but she heard it.

Are you having fun yet?

Elenora woke up, letting out a guttural scream.

Good thing the windows were closed, or she would have alerted the entire neighborhood.

"Ele!?" Tom gasped, adrenaline pumping. "Are you okay? Is it the baby?"

Elenora was shaking. It took her a while to realize where she was. Going through these horrible night terrors nearly every night, she should be used to them by now. But this time, she was even more disoriented than before. This felt new.

More serious.

More real?

Tom's arms gathered around her, and he rocked her

gently. "You're gonna be okay," he whispered. "I'm here for you."

Elenora nodded, mostly for Tom's benefit. Putting him through these sleep-disrupting ordeals over and over was unfair to him, and she felt bad for waking him up all the time, and now for triggering his fight-or-flight response. He didn't deserve this, but she didn't know how to make it stop.

How she wished she could make it stop.

"I'm so sorry," she muttered.

"Shhhhhh. There's nothing to be sorry about, sweetie."

She felt tears pooling in her eyes. "It felt so real," she blubbered.

"What did?" he asked softly.

The stranger's pulse. His labored breath. His sheer terror. His agonizing pain. Life draining away from him. From me.

"Tell me what felt real, Ele."

She didn't know what to say. It had felt so real. In fact, it still did—her jaw, throat, and chest still ached as if actual pain had been inflicted on her. Her ears were ringing, and her heart still beat way too fast.

"I'm here with you. You're safe. You're not in danger," Tom whispered.

Not in danger. The dream had felt exactly like danger. Like she was in danger.

Was this it? Was this a sign, some cryptic message from her subconscious telling her she was in danger?

Did her subconscious know something she didn't, just like it had known about her pregnancy?

A wave of alarm surged through her, and she felt Tom's arms tighten around her.

But why would she be in danger?

Surely it would have to be work-related, the only environment in which she might have angered someone enough for them to seek retribution. But who?

Things had been rather serene lately, and she couldn't think of anyone angry with her who was either loose on the streets or on the verge of being released from prison. Still, she would go through her files at work and see if she could identify a threat.

And then she'd tell Tom, and he could keep an eye out. Protect her and the baby.

As dreadful as it sounded to know someone out there might want to harm her, this felt like a step in the right direction. Like something tangible at last, something over which she could have some control, unlike the night terrors. Tom was a brilliant investigator and would find that person and stop them. And perhaps this would put an end to the nightmares.

Elenora took a deep breath and let out a sigh of relief.

"Thank you. I think I'll be fine now," she said.

Tom shifted them back to a sleeping position, his protective arm resting over her expanded waist. Feeling safe, she drifted back into sleep.

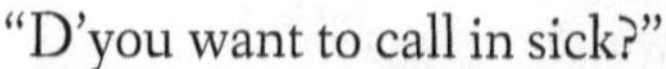

"D'you want to call in sick?"

Tom looked up from his laptop as Elenora entered the kitchen. He was eating breakfast and looked rested, considering. She suspected she didn't look nearly half as good as him, but she felt better than she thought she would after the mental ride she'd been on mere hours earlier.

The curious pain she had suffered in her body after the nightmare was mostly gone. She was a little stiff, but that was barely noticeable. If Tom had suggested she take the day off right after the nightmare, she would have considered it. But now that she felt okay and had a mission to find out who might be after her, she didn't want to delay taking action.

"No, I think I'm good." She gave him a genuine smile.

"Yeah?"

His piercing gaze bore into her in lie-detecting mode. She must have been convincing because he soon went back to his laptop and pieces of toast.

Elenora prepared herself a bowl of oatmeal with chunks of banana and walnuts. She understandably felt tired, but her new goal gave her strength. She couldn't wait to put an end to these nightmares and move on.

Once that was done, she'd go on the baby shopping spree she kept postponing to clear her mind of any remaining darkness and get back on the right foot. And then schedule a massage to release tensions and the probable foot and back pain a trip to the stores would likely give her.

As she carried her breakfast to the table to join Tom, the image on his computer caught her eye.

It was the picture of a man.

The man who had died in front of her in her dream.

CHAPTER EIGHT

Montréal, 1847

Rolland came to awareness, and waves of agony assaulted him on all fronts.

A sharp pain shot through his abdomen, his throat, and his skull. Searing pain along every inch of his skin heightened with the equivalent of an infinite number of paper cuts. Every one of his limbs felt beaten to a pulp by a grindstone.

A metallic taste—blood, no doubt—coated his mouth. His tongue felt around, and he noticed that several of his teeth were either loose or gone. The thought of a bloody mouth with dangling teeth revolted him, and he would have retched had he not felt too weak to even do that.

He tried to open his eyes, but they were swollen and crusted shut.

He felt panic rising, but he battled the unhelpful feeling and squashed it. What he had to do, right now, was think.

Think and try to get some help.

A breeze caressed the fresh wounds on his face, so he

knew he was not trapped inside. His raw hands painfully felt pavement. He must still be in town and not abandoned on a country dirt road.

He listened to his surroundings, and beyond the stillness —it must have been the middle of the night—he could hear the clopping of hooves in the distance. He smelled enough putridity in the air to confirm, once again, that he was in the city.

If he were outside, like it seemed to be the case, and not in the middle of a deserted area, someone would eventually stumble upon him. If he could stay alert long enough to hear them coming and convince them he was not dead—he suspected he looked closer to a corpse than a living being— then he stood a chance of making it to a hospital.

And then what? Did he even stand a chance to heal from all this, whatever this was? What could possibly have happened? He racked his brain, trying to find his most recent memories.

He was walking home late at night after a poker game at the tavern with a handful of newcomers from Ireland and Britain. His mind was on Delphine, and his game was off.

He must have been the victim of a sneak attack, maybe from a gang of hoodlums, and left for dead in a ditch. Rolland doubted a single man could have carried on such a vicious attack. Not impossible but improbable. So, a concerted effort by a group of persons.

The newcomers at the pub didn't seem to know each other very well, and it had been every man for himself. He couldn't picture them being so vehemently mad at him as to want to kill him over cards. Not tonight, anyway. None of them had lost big to him.

The person responsible for such an attack had to have had a deep hatred of Rolland and want him out of the picture.

Like a filthy rich, lustful woman who felt slighted or a filthy rich man finding out Rolland had secretly been seeing his fiancée.

"With whose wife did you sleep?" Rory asked under his breath, more for the universe's benefit than his brother's. He was sitting on a wooden chair by Rolland's hospital bed.

You know I don't sleep with wives, Rolland wanted to retort, but each syllable that had passed his lips so far had demanded an excruciating effort and a matching amount of pain, so he let his baby brother vent his frustration on him instead of answering his rhetorical question.

As Rolland had hoped, a baker from a nearby shop had rescued him. He was in a gutter, unconscious, when his rescue took place, and Rory had relayed to him all the information he knew. The good Samaritan thought Rolland was dead at first and didn't want the kids who sometimes played in the alley to stumble upon a mangled corpse, so with the help of his assistant, they started to transport Rolland's inert body to the back of his bakery, intending to inform the authorities.

Fortunately, as they'd lifted him, Rolland emitted a hair-raising groan, which had scared the bejesus out of them but also convinced them to seek medical care. Now here he was, on the third floor of the Ursulines Hospital, hanging by a thread. But conscious at least.

"I told you these...questionable activities of yours wouldn't end well," Rory muttered again.

He knew very well that Rolland's questionable activities made his own medical care possible. But while Rory was immensely grateful to his brother for making such a sacrifice for him—and often mentioned with great angst how he could never, ever repay him—he was still uncomfortable with the means Rolland had adopted to get the money. Despite Rolland's frequent reassurance that it was all fine and good for him, that he enjoyed himself most of the time and would say cheekily that it was for a good cause, Rory wished his brother didn't have to stoop so low.

It dawned on Rolland that with the awful physical state he was in, he was probably nowhere near going back to the ladies. Not anytime soon, anyway.

If ever?

What if his face and body didn't heal well?

Judging from Rory's violent reaction, the few times Rolland had asked for a mirror and his brother's quick refusal to comply—with horror and sadness painted across his face— Rolland had quickly concluded he wasn't a sight for sore eyes. More like a sight causing sore eyes.

Most of his body was wrapped in bandages like an Egyptian mummy, save for his stinging and burning face. His few remaining teeth would have to be removed for him to get dentures, the only workable solution. His cheeks felt hollow, and his face must have looked like it was on the brink of caving in.

The ladies might never seek him out again.

The thought painfully sunk into Rolland. He'd never been the vain type, and he cared little about his looks past the fact they allowed him and Rory to stay afloat. But this way of earning might be compromised, certainly for now and perhaps for good. The thought was horrifying.

Rolland had no problem with the notion of finding honest work, but he knew, having searched high and low throughout the years, that very few types of activities within his grasp could pay well enough to cover Rory's expensive health issues.

And now, add to that the looming medical bill from the Ursulines Hospital for his own extensive issues that surely would be astronomical.

It would probably destroy them.

Rolland groaned in his mind, careful not to move a muscle. What the hell would they do?

He must have looked distraught because Rory let out a deep sigh and changed his tone dramatically.

"I apologize. You don't need grief from me. I just feel so powerless. I so wish you had seen whoever did this to you."

"Del...phi..." Rolland wanted to spit out his theory about Delphine's fiancé being behind the attack.

"Delphine knows you were attacked. I sent Young William to give her the news. I will tell you when I hear from her."

Rolland's heart twinged at the thought of Delphine finding out about what had happened to him, at the pain she would endure knowing how much he was suffering.

Would she suspect her fiancé of being involved? And if so, would she want to leave town with Rolland and Rory even faster?

Rolland's mind whirred. God forbid Leopold Christie would also find out about their plans. Or perhaps he already knew, and that was why Rolland was in a hospital bed? What if the monster took his anger out on Delphine? Punished her for betraying him?

That sorry excuse for a man had to be stopped.

Rolland mustered all the energy he could to get out of bed and go rescue Delphine from danger. But all he managed to do was move his arms and legs slightly. The good news: he wasn't paralyzed. But that was pretty much it.

"Her fi...an...cé..."

"I don't think her fiancé would care to know about you, Rolland," Rory said. His face changed. "Her fiancé. Of course."

Rory was the only soul who knew about Rolland's and Delphine's secret relationship and plans, in part because he was included in said plans, but mostly because the brothers didn't keep secrets from one another.

"He must have paid a group of thugs," Rory reasoned.

Rolland managed a slight nod.

"We should leave town the moment you are well enough and watch your back in the meantime. The next time he attacks, you might end up in the basement of this fine medical establishment."

Rory's suggestion that Christie would send Rolland to the morgue if he got a second chance only stoked the hatred and fear consuming him that the mad man would turn on Delphine before Rolland could even do anything about it.

"I wonder if Delphine realizes how much you're saving her life by taking her far away from that nefarious man."

Delphine had confided in Rolland that Christie was short-tempered and might have a violent streak. That ugly trait had now been confirmed loud and clear, and if that man could do this to him, Rolland couldn't bear thinking what kind of abuse he'd be capable of dishing out on a spouse over a lifetime. The unbearable thought made him shudder.

Rory stood up and walked around Rolland, his eyes surveying him as if to evaluate the state he was in and how long he would take to heal. He stretched and resumed his sitting position by the bed.

"If we could leave before winter..."

A soft gasp caught their attention, and their gazes turned toward the entrance of the room, where Delphine stood, gracefully in shock.

Rolland's eyes met hers, and he saw a sheer look of horror in her eyes. She looked on the cusp of fainting.

"Miss Deschamps. How marvelous of you to have come," Rory said.

Delphine didn't answer or even acknowledge Rory's greeting. Her eyes remained glued to Rolland's battered face and body. Her hand lifted to cover her mouth.

With a hopeful voice, Rory added, "He will heal. Please come in."

Delphine ignored the invitation and stood there, staring.

Rolland could read a slew of negative emotions in her eyes, the worst one being revulsion. He thought she would have looked at him with compassion—or at the very least some kind of pity—and a shred of hope that he would stop suffering and be well again soon. And that she would be by his side, supportive during his convalescence.

But she seemed to feel the opposite. Not only was he frightening her, but he was scarring her for life. Offending her delicate sensibilities. Revolting her.

The way she was looking at him told him she felt better off staying with her fiancé.

She would soon confirm these dreadful thoughts running through Rolland's mind.

After an insufferably long moment, Delphine broke the stare and faintly said, "My mother will wonder where I am."

She turned around and walked away, leaving Rolland behind with a broken heart.

Both aghast in their own way, the brothers listened to the receding sound of Delphine's heels clicking against the floor, echoing down the corridor.

The clicks became sharper and faster as, they guessed, she picked up the pace. Until it sounded like she was running.

She ran away from me, Rolland thought.

"It is an awful lot to take in," Rory tried diplomatically. "Give her time. She will come around. She loves you." He looked like he wanted to believe his own pacifying words.

But Rolland hadn't seen or sensed any love from Delphine just now. What if she didn't love him anymore and would never love him again?

And then it hit him—hard—like a dagger through the remains of his shattered heart, the thought that perhaps she had never loved him at all.

Perhaps, like the countless others, she had only loved his looks.

Perhaps there was nothing else of him worth loving.

CHAPTER NINE

Montréal, present day

Elenora wasn't the type to lie and especially not to Tom, who could detect a lie a mile away on a foggy night, anyway. But when she recognized the man from her nightmare on his computer screen that morning, she was unable to candidly tell him the truth.

What could she possibly say? "Oh, my God, honey, I've seen this man die in my nightmare last night. Small world."

As much as she'd love for Tom to reassure her and tell her there was a logical explanation for this impossible coincidence, she couldn't say anything. This couldn't be a mere coincidence. And there was something very wrong with her.

She stood behind Tom, staring at the man's face over his shoulder, searching for answers. How could she have seen this man, a total stranger, in her dream?

In her mind, he had been attacked and had died. And now, here he was, in trouble. The file labeled him as missing. Perhaps he was already dead or, at the very least, in danger.

Odds were he wasn't just sipping a latte in a different Starbucks than his usual one.

It dawned on her maybe it was this man and not herself who was in danger, like she had concluded earlier. A selfish relief washed over her to think she was not a target, along with a feeling of guilt. But if she could foresee someone else's grisly misfortune, the notion was still profoundly disturbing.

Was that a premonition she'd had? Was she psychic now?

It was one thing to have an adorable gut feeling about being pregnant. It was an entirely different ball game to foretell another person's death.

Or maybe she was just losing her marbles, like her mother had. Maybe she was genetically predisposed to losing her sanity.

The thought gave her vertigo. What if this was happening, and she too would pass this—whatever *this* was—down to her own daughter?

What if she got committed before she could even meet her and take care of her?

Was getting pregnant a huge mistake? What had she done?

"You used to date him or something?" Tom's teasing voice cut through her manic thoughts.

"Hmm?"

"You look enthralled and appalled."

"No, I don't think I know him." This was partly true. "How old is this case?"

Perhaps this was not a fresh case, and she'd seen this missing notice before. Her subconscious could have latched onto the image of the missing man. A logical explanation. A glimmer of hope surged—

"He was reported missing this morning."

Crap. So much for hope.

"Who is he?"

Perhaps the man was a realtor with his face advertised in newspapers or on bus shelters.

"Dr. Réginald Haché. A plastic surgeon."

"Hmm."

Elenora sat at the table with her breakfast. If she kept hovering over Tom's shoulder, staring at his screen, he would launch a Spanish inquisition. She started eating, feeling his gaze on her. He had this look of when he tried to understand something that didn't quite make sense.

"Perhaps I should cut back on the maple syrup," she said, pointing at her oatmeal, to change the subject and get him off her case.

"Can't go wrong with that, I suppose."

He went back to his breakfast and laptop, while Elenora's mind returned to the man. A plastic surgeon might have advertised his services or been interviewed on TV. It sounded like a stretch, but that could explain why her subconscious knew of him.

But the timing of dreaming of a stranger mere hours before he was reported missing and possibly in danger was truly uncomfortable.

What did this mean, and what was she supposed to do with this most likely unreliable information?

The station sometimes received so-called tips from so-called psychics, and while they did their due diligence and humored the "enlightened ones"—as Tom's cop partner, Alexandre Bélanger, liked to call them—to Elenora's knowledge, none of these tips had ever been true or of any use.

Was she herself an "enlightened one" now?

If she was and Alex found out, what would he think of her?

And what about Tom? How embarrassing it would be for him to have an "enlightened" wife. He'd become a laughing-stock at the precinct.

"His face rings a bell, but you can't put your finger on it, is that it?"

Once again, Tom's voice brought her back to reality. Of course he wouldn't let her odd behavior go so easily. She nodded to him.

"I bet he owns a private practice and they advertise. It might be where you've seen him," he volunteered.

"That would make sense." She liked that Tom thought this, too.

He stood up with his plate. "You don't need one more thing to worry about, Ele. So, unless you've seen the man being abducted or have anything concrete that could help find him, there's nothing you can do. So, don't lose sleep over it, okay?"

He kissed the top of her head. Hopefully, he didn't hear her gut churning.

— ❧ —

Unless you have anything concrete...

There's nothing you can do...

Don't lose sleep over it...

She spent the car ride with Tom and most of the morning with her mind racing to figure out what she could do to help the missing man, even if it was a futile endeavor.

Tom was right.

Unless she had hard facts to contribute, what she'd seen and experienced in the middle of the night was utterly useless. Even if she called the station's tip line anonymously, what could she tell them? "The plastic surgeon will die or is already dead."

Thanks so much for calling!

Not.

Ugh.

Aside from an urge to scream, she had absolutely nothing.

In the precinct's kitchenette, Elenora dumped a packet of sugar into her decaf tea. She really ought to cut down sugar in tea as well, but she was stressed and yearning for a sweet, warm drink. Besides, cutting down on sugar might help with stress, but it would add another challenge to her to-do list. And couldn't cutting too much sugar too fast lead to withdrawal? She didn't need one more thing to mess with her hormones and emotions.

She stirred the sugar in the hot tea and added milk.

Hormones.

Stir. Stir.

Damn hormones. They clouded her judgment, controlled parts of her, and drove her crazy. They screwed with everything.

What if her brain, flooded with pregnancy hormones—compounded with sleep deprivation—was just playing tricks on her? Had made a false connection?

What if the man she saw in her nightmare looked like the plastic surgeon but was a different guy, who also happened to have wavy dark hair? After all, she didn't get a good look at the man in her dream.

She took a cleansing breath and tried to remember the nightmare objectively, without panic.

She focused on recalling the man. She reminded herself he had dark, wavy hair. The image that popped into her mind was that of the man on Tom's laptop. She shook her head and put the milk back in the fridge.

She wrapped her fingers around her cup of tea and let the warmth soothe her. She'd try a different approach and concentrate on the elements of the dream instead.

She thought of the unsettling heartbeats growing in volume. The jagged breathing. The terror. The pain taking over her body. The blood.

She shuddered. She really had a hard time with blood.

The image had been so vivid. Still, she forced herself to visualize the blood coming out of the man's mouth. Another massive shudder went through her as she pictured red liquid trickling from the corner of his lips, but she couldn't see more of his face. As if she was trying to force a memory that didn't want to be recalled. Or that had been erased.

This was bizarre and frustrating.

"There you are." Tom's partner Alex stood in the kitchenette's doorway. Built like a quarterback, he filled most of the frame. His stature and demeanor, coupled with his permanently stoic expression, were intimidating. But Elenora knew the tough exterior was there as an armor to protect his sensitive and wounded soul, as it often was the case with people who had experienced trauma.

He reached inside his jacket. "Tom wants you to see this. He said it might reassure you."

He showed her a picture of three people in lab coats mugging for the camera.

"The ad Dr. Haché's been using. He's plastered half the town's media with it. Tom says you might recognize it."

Elenora and Tom's hunch was right, and she recognized the man and the publicity shot.

A rush of relief went through her as she studied the missing man standing in a power stance in the middle of the picture, arms crossed and legs apart. The few times she'd seen this picture, she thought that he looked like a poster boy for mansplaining. He was flanked by two female colleagues, each with a more modest attitude than his. The man's expression suggested he was used to posing and liked to be seen. He was moderately handsome, his wavy hair tamed and his face clean-shaven.

In the picture on Tom's computer, the man had a short beard like in her dream, and his hair was slightly disheveled. The laptop picture had been taken outside of a professional context. Likely by a friend or a family member. He looked considerably different, which was the reason Elenora couldn't place him.

But in her dream, he had a beard...

Then where had she *seen* him with a beard?

Elenora reached to take the picture from Alex to get a closer look. As her fingers made contact with it, images from the dream rushed back inside her mind.

She saw the man's face clearly now: his scruffy beard. His battered face. His eyes bulging. The blood trickling at the corners of his lips.

This time, though, his mouth opened, and a handful of bloody teeth came out of it.

Elenora gasped and her fingers let go of both the picture and her tea. The mug crashed to the floor, spilling its content.

The scraping sound of metal against linoleum jolted her back to consciousness.

"Ele? How about you sit down?"

Alex took her elbow and guided her into the chair. He crouched in front of her, looking concerned. "Are you all right?"

She noticed the spilled tea and made a move to clean it up. He put a hand up in front of her. "Leave it. Gary will take care of it. Are you all right?"

Was she all right? She didn't know.

Those teeth...

Elenora felt a shooting pain going through her gums. She touched around her jawline. The pain was gone as fast as it had come.

What in the living fresh hell?

"Elenora?" Alex wanted an answer.

"I might need to see a dentist," she said, hoping it wasn't too much of a lie.

Alex burst out laughing at her apparent non sequitur. He looked relieved. "Not your favorite thing?"

"It's right up there with getting a root canal," she said dryly.

He let out another laugh. "You scared the crap out of me. I thought your water had broken or something."

"No, but I still wet the floor." She snickered, staring at the spilled tea.

"Yes, but that's easily cleanable and won't result in a premature baby."

"Good point."

Alex stood. "Want me to go get Tom?"

"No, thanks. I'll be fine."

"You sure?"

"When in doubt, blame it on hormones. They're determined to make me look crazy."

"You look more sleep-deprived to me than crazy. I'll send in Gary," he said as he left.

Elenora waited a moment and whipped out her phone, sending Pierre a text. *Meet me for lunch?*

CHAPTER TEN

"What do you think it all means?"

Elenora had asked Pierre to meet her at the Fish & Ship, a restaurant near work specializing in seafood. Tom hated fish, the smell of fish, and anything that tasted like fish, so she knew the chances of him waltzing in during her chat with Pierre were microscopic.

She had spilled all the crazy beans to Pierre. As she expected, he listened intently to all of it. He was always keen on the gory details, both figuratively and literally. Ever since he'd retired, nothing and everything was fair game for a little investigating. Golf never became his thing.

"I think this means that you are special, like I've always suspected."

"You mean, a euphemism for *not normal?*"

"Please don't ever think that."

"My mother is *special* too..." A bit of sadness coated Elenora's words.

Pierre studied her for a moment. "Is that your worry? That you're like her? That you'll end up like her?"

"Isn't that where I'm headed?"

Pierre finished chewing and swallowed his bite of seafood poutine before answering. "I think that what you're going through is traumatic, like what happened to Muriel, sure, but I think the similarities end there. I don't think she has special powers."

Special powers? What Elenora was going through felt more like a distressing, insanity-inducing, life-destroying aggravation than a special power. Was there such a thing, anyway?

"You think I'm some kind of psychic?" She couldn't believe she even said that out loud. Her eyes skated over the neighboring tables to make sure no one had overheard her.

"I don't know," Pierre said. "Factually, if we recap, you've had a vision about a little girl that convinced you on the spot that you were pregnant—"

"We could call that a hunch."

"One mighty hunch. So, first a vision while awake. Then last night, this very concrete nightmare about a man who turns out to be missing. In real life. So, that's another vision, but this one while asleep." Pierre held up two fingers, building his case.

With resignation, she added, "And then, I touched his picture and saw even more."

Pierre uncurled a third finger. "Another vision, yes, and I would guess some kind of special tactile sensory ability."

Tactile sensory ability?

"I think that one's important because it suggests you might have some control over it, as opposed to the visions in your sleep."

"How so?"

"As in, you touch something, and a vision comes to you. But if you don't touch anything..."

"Hmm." She liked the sound of that, the possibility of having some control.

"And let's not forget the little boy at the bottom of the river who's now showing up, and your clear recollection of a conversation we had thirty-seven years ago and that no one else knew about. Surely that's worth two fingers." Pierre's five fingers were spread out.

"You can stop with the fingers," she groaned.

"You can't argue with fingers," he said before honoring her request and putting his hand down.

"So, what should I do now that your fingers have established how doomed I am? Convince Tom to bring me to the guy's house and his operating room so I can sweep my hands along every surface for clues, like the psychic, human-equivalent of a sniffing dog?"

"Well, that'd be a start..."

Elenora raised a brow—he couldn't be serious.

"That'd be ideal but highly impractical. I recognize that." He said around a mouthful of food. "Nora, I can appreciate the weird predicament you're in and the inability to be straightforward about it."

"Thanks."

She stabbed a piece of broccoli and ate it. Her baked salmon plate was flavorful, and she was eating more than she thought she'd be able to, considering the circumstances.

"You know what gets to me, aside from the debilitating fear this whole situation is causing? And aside from hiding this from Tom...?"

"You still haven't told him?"

"No."

"Do you intend to?"

"I dunno. Not yet. I'll see. I mean, what if this turns out to be nothing, and the plastic surgeon turns up alive? I don't want to freak Tom out over nothing. He's got way enough stress with work and me being so hypersensitive all the time. He's a real saint, putting up with me as it is."

Pierre opened his mouth to argue but reconsidered. He pushed some fries around his plate before saying, "That's understandable and your decision... So, what's getting to you?"

"The feeling of powerlessness to do anything. It's as if I were facing a jumper and knowing that he's about to jump and knowing that I could talk him out of jumping. But I'm being prevented from acting, from doing anything at all."

"And then some macho asshole arrives at the scene and pulls rank, telling you to take a hike?"

That got a slim smile out of Elenora.

"Yeah. I mean, what's the good in having this weird info if I can't do anything about it? It's killing me."

"I understand the feeling."

"I know you do.

"It might feel like you've hit a dead-end but be patient," Pierre advised. "You've had a new clue just a few hours ago."

"Yes, but a useless clue. Bloody teeth don't sound like a slam-dunk piece of information. It probably just means the guy's getting tortured, right now, as I'm enjoying lunch. Good luck finding him based on that useless insight."

"I hear you and feel your frustration. But sometimes, a seemingly useless clue can become important."

Elenora shook her head. "I don't know how you used to do this and not go crazy."

"Who says I haven't gone crazy?"

"But not as much as me, I bet," Elenora said self-derisively.

"You're my favorite crazy person. Don't you ever forget that." Pierre pointed his fork at her, a strand of cheese from his poutine stretching and dangling.

"So, you think a handful of bloody teeth might mean something? Other than the guy getting beaten up? You think this clue might help us find him?"

Pierre shrugged. "I don't know. I'm just saying you shouldn't dismiss it. Perhaps whoever's on the case—"

"Lagacé and Monroe."

"Okay, so perhaps Lagacé and Monroe will find the guy dead and looking just like you saw him, and that will be it. No more, no less. But your mind emphasized bloody teeth. It fed you the image in a separate vision. It might mean more. Concretely or abstractly."

"You mean like a symbol?"

"Yes, it could be a symbol. Perhaps the missing guy got into a fight with a bad dentist?"

Elenora couldn't help a snort.

"You know what I mean."

"I know."

They ate in silence for a moment.

"Is there such a thing as a tooth fetish?" Elenora mused out loud. "Maybe we need to look for a dentist, like you joked, or someone who likes teeth? Have you ever come across a tooth-related crime?"

"In a crime involving torture, yes. But as a fetish... I can see a disturbed mind collecting teeth as a prize."

"What about a dentist gone off his mind? Ever arrested a dentist?"

Pierre pondered for a moment. "Not from memory, but I could ask around. Ask Tom to look into that too."

She groaned. "And have him run for the hills when I explain why?" Elenora dropped a hand to her belly. "In case you haven't noticed, now's not the best time to break up my marriage."

Pierre frowned. "You know he wouldn't do that to you."

Deep down she did.

"Again, it's your decision..." Pierre said. "But, if you told him, it might freak him out, puzzle him for sure, but he'd understand. If you gave him a chance and a bit of time to process. He's not an asshole."

"I know he'd eventually understand, but he'd worry sick, and I'm already worrying him so much and making sure he can't have a good night of sleep with those stupid nightmares."

"Right, but if you shared these worries with him, you might overcome them together and both of you might get better sleep. You need Tom on your side, not on your conscience."

Pierre's words sunk in.

"Right."

The server showed up and reached for their empty plates. "Was everything good? Any room for coffee or dessert?"

"It was delicious. Can I have the bill, please?"

"Sure can. I'll be right back."

Pierre waited for the server to be gone before saying, "I'll inquire about cases, including cold ones, related to dentists and dental torture, fetish, and what-have-you."

"And people selling teeth? Is there a black market for that?"

"I don't know, but nothing ever surprises me. I'll add that to the list."

"Thanks."

Pierre was on board and would help her navigate through this nonsense. If there was one nugget of a clue out there that might help, he would patiently comb through everything until he found it. He never met a haystack he didn't like.

A thought crossed her mind. "If you find something, let's not provoke a wild goose chase. If we feed Lagacé and Monroe far-fetched leads related to teeth, we might derail them and cost them precious time, no?"

"Sometimes a chase is necessary to catch a wild goose."

"Yes, but we don't know there's any validity to my insights."

"And we don't know that there isn't either. How about we assume there's legitimacy to what you're seeing and sensing, and at least give it a try? Of course, we'll evaluate any lead we find before suggesting them to anyone. This beats having nothing and doing nothing."

The server came back with a portable payment terminal and offered it to Pierre.

"What if you tried welcoming your gift instead of trying to repress it or running away from it? When Aubrey first came to you, you had no preconception..." Pierre hovered his card over the machine until it beeped.

Elenora reached for her purse as he thanked the server and put his credit card away.

"Thank you. You both have a good day now," the server told them with a smile.

"Thank you." Elenora returned the smile before turning to Pierre. "How much do I owe you?"

"On the house."

"It's always on the house with you."

"Unless we're at *your* house. You feed me all the time."

"All right, but you'd tell me if I was taking advantage of you, right?"

"Sure thing. But that'd never happen."

They both stood up, and he helped her put on her coat. "Look," he said. "I'm obviously not in your shoes, and perhaps I would want to run too if I was. So please don't think I'm trying to pressure you or tell you what to do."

"But you're right. And it doesn't change the fact that I need to tell Tom and come to terms with what I can't control."

"See where that leads?" He gave her a supportive smile.

She let out a long sigh. "Yeah. See where that leads."

It would probably lead either to hell in a handbasket or to a room next door to her mother's.

That night, in bed, Elenora rehashed her conversation with Pierre over lunch and her insights into the case of the missing plastic surgeon.

She had decided to follow his advice and give it all a fair try on the off chance that anything could help find the missing man before it was too late. If she was going to suffer through this weird premonitory power regardless, it might as well be for something.

She closed her eyes, forcing herself to visualize the visions. The same mental barrier she had experienced earlier in the kitchenette at work seemed to keep her away from clear memories.

She wished she could see the damn teeth again. See if there was something special about them. They had produced such an effect on her, past the obvious shock of seeing bloody teeth falling out of a dying man's mouth. Perhaps Pierre was right to think they might hide a clue.

What did the teeth mean?

Restless, she slid out of bed, trying to not wake Tom up. She padded down the stairs to her laptop she'd left on the living room coffee table.

In a Google search, she entered *dream meaning teeth* and the words *falling out* appeared as a predictive search option. Apparently, she wasn't the only one concerned about this gross imagery.

One of the top results suggested that dreaming about falling teeth could be related to death or a personal loss. So... having seen the death of the missing man, were the teeth a sign that the guy was indeed dead? As in, "Call off the search party, folks, it's a lost cause"? Or did it mean a deep personal loss for Elenora, like a relationship? Were the teeth foretelling marriage trouble for her because she was keeping this whole insanity from Tom?

Ugh. Was this a cosmic middle finger?

Another Google entry suggested the dream could represent anything from self-esteem issues to worrying about aging to money problems, to a rebirth, to regretting saying something mean to a loved one or an enemy, to being unable to ask for a raise at work... It could mean anything, and everything, *and* the kitchen sink.

How helpful.

Thinking about the kitchen sink, Elenora felt a pang of hunger and headed to the kitchen for a midnight snack. She hesitated between grabbing a handful of grapes, a piece of cheese, or...ooh, chocolate cake!

Over the weekend, Tom had helped their neighbor Ian move some heavy pieces of furniture, and his lovely wife Aïsha had insisted on making them a decadent chocolate cake with hazelnut ganache. She used to work in a bakery and was an amazing baker in her own right. There was no way they could have turned down that cake.

The baby moved as Elenora's eyes lingered on the cake, and she took it as a sign. She agreed with Aubrey that cake sounded good, and since Tom had little self-control when it came to food, who knew how long this scrumptious leftover would last in the fridge.

She went back to her laptop with a slice of cake and a glass of milk.

A result from the search caught her attention: someone had asked if the dream meant one was pregnant. It led to an article from a parenting magazine that explored how dreaming of falling teeth could be linked to stress and the apprehension of becoming a parent.

"Huh." Could it be all it was? Her stress and insecurities? It would be so delightful to be able to believe that. If only she could buy it.

She let out a deep sigh before taking a bite of cake.

Dammit, she realized she was so consumed in her quest to find an answer that she wasn't savoring the delicious dessert, and it was almost all gone.

She stopped looking at the screen and devoted her attention to eating the rest of her slice mindfully, the small plate resting on top of her stomach. She caressed her belly underneath it with her free hand.

"Your mamma's not always the brightest bulb, you know. She almost wasted this piece of cake. She needs to lighten up before you show up. Are you enjoying the cake? Or are you back to sleep?"

She waited a moment to see if Aubrey would answer her question. When she didn't feel any movement, she put the now empty plate down on the coffee table and dove back into the web.

She came across an article about how, in the Victorian era, some people's teeth exploded out of the blue. It turned out chemicals used to make early fillings might explain this weird and gruesome mystery. But to this day, no one knew for sure.

Elenora felt grateful that, at least, she wasn't dealing with visions of teeth exploding out of people's mouths, like a dental version of *Scanners*.

She shuddered.

A quiet shuffling noise made her look up, and she startled as a dark silhouette came her way.

"It's just me, love!" Tom said, holding up his hands. "You shouldn't be watching horror films in the dark at this hour."

"I'm not!" she giggled. "You know I'm so not."

"Then what are you doing?" Tom spotted the empty plate with the dirty dessert fork on it. "Hey, was that cake?"

"Maybe."

"Seriously?" He headed to the kitchen.

Elenora debated whether to close her search and pretend to have been working on something else. But that would be unnecessarily deceptive, and she was already extremely uncomfortable with the secret she was keeping from Tom.

Should she tell him now?

Would now be a good time to unload the truth? She might feel better, but she'd ruin his enjoyment of his piece of cake.

She could tell him she was dreaming about teeth. That was true and would unveil nothing impossible to believe. She could tell him about that part, just not the whole thing. Yet. That might be a way to ease toward the truth.

Tom came back with a plate, though he had already eaten half his piece on his way back from the kitchen. He plopped himself down on the couch next to Elenora.

"D'you have a bad dream?"

"I dreamed about teeth falling out of a mouth, and I'm trying to find out what that means."

Tom leaned toward the laptop screen and read about the mystery of the exploding teeth. "Wow. Nasty. Is that what you dreamed about?"

"Oh, no. Thank God, no."

"Okay, good. Then why are you reading this? You won't be able to go back to bed. I mean, I'm gonna have nightmares, and I'm not even the squeamish one in this relationship."

Elenora reached for the laptop screen and closed it. "You're not wrong."

"Did you find out anything helpful?"

"Not really."

"Are the teeth still worrying you?"

Elenora pondered his question for a moment. "Supposedly, dreaming about falling teeth can mean a plethora of things. So, I'm not specifically reassured. Let's say I'm puzzled."

"Puzzled is better than scared shitless, isn't it?"

"Yes."

Wanting to cut the conversation short before she said too much, she leaned in for a hug, her belly in the way. Tom met her halfway, and they hugged as much as physically possible. "Thank you for being there for me."

"I'm glad to be there for you. You ready to go back to bed?"

"Yeah. You need your beauty sleep."

He chuckled. "Always. And thanks so much for sharing that sweet imagery of exploding teeth." He grimaced.

"I'm always happy to share the joy."

As they headed up the stairs, Tom's cell phone rang from their bedroom. He ran up ahead of Elenora to go answer it.

When she entered the room, he was getting dressed in a hurry.

"They found Dr. Haché, the plastic surgeon. He's dead." He shot her a bewildered look. "And you won't believe this: his teeth are missing."

CHAPTER ELEVEN

Montréal, 1847

The moment he was able to drag himself out of bed, Rolland took his leave from the hospital to stop adding to the small fortune in fees he had already incurred.

From the time of the beating, it took two solid months before he went from being a badly scarred, useless bag of torn muscles and broken bones to a slightly less scarred, useless bag of slowly healing muscles and bones.

Being home idle drove Rolland crazy from the moment he set foot back in the little wooden house he and his brother came close to losing. As he'd suspected and feared, the hospital bill could easily have made them destitute had it not been for unexpected help. Various neighbors and business acquaintances the brothers had helped over the years came out to support them, to give back and lend a hand. They helped pay the hospital fees and ensured the brothers would be fed and kept their house while they regained their footing. Rolland would never forget their generosity.

Charles and his family also chipped in. In the past, other than soirée leftover food (which would be a sin to let go to waste), Rolland had been too proud to accept handouts from his friend. This time, Charles imposed his help and insisted that Rolland let him take care of him, at least until he was better. He made it clear this was non-negotiable. Rolland didn't have the strength to argue and was beyond grateful for Charles's friendship and compassion.

He was also deeply touched that Charles's sister Ophelia frequently visited him and that she was not afraid to look him in the eye, despite his disfigurement. While most people (himself included when he came across a mirror) diverted their gaze when they looked at him, he saw no horror or disdain in her eyes as she offered him support and encouragement. This was one of the small gestures that helped him heal the most.

Rolland went back to playing cards for money as soon as his fingers were strong enough to hold cards steady, without tipping his hand. His healed nose was slightly crooked, and his face had nasty scars that seemed to never get better. In fact, they looked as fresh as on the night they were carved into his flesh and gave him a hardness he didn't have before.

His off-putting appearance made it impossible for him to play again in his old circle of upper-class businessmen, and he had to limit himself to playing in taverns with commoners. His people.

It was hard to find other players at first, as his new looks made him seem lethal, but he soon became a local legend. Like a repulsive circus curiosity, he started to attract weirdos looking for a thrill by playing against him. The money would be nowhere near as good as in the past, but it was a start.

Hence, little by little, Rolland's life went back to a new kind of normalcy, his body aching a little less every day.

But two things would be permanently broken: Rolland's pulverized heart and his self-esteem. He erected a metaphorical wall around the former to contain the shattered bits. With the exception of his loyal brother, he vowed never to let anyone make him vulnerable again, and this new resolve toughened him.

As for his self-esteem, the fact that Rolland was no longer a pretty boy didn't hurt him as much as the fact his ugliness was a constant reminder of Delphine's unexpected and devastating rejection. Every time he passed a mirror, his reflection reminded him he was nothing. He hadn't even been worthy of her giving him a chance to heal.

He wasn't worthy of her support.

Of her love.

Of love.

That spoke volumes as to his worth as a man, he figured. He should have been left to die in that gutter, like his attackers had no doubt intended.

But then, as if on cue, Rory's fragile health would act up, reminding Rolland that he couldn't just leave his brother fending for himself. And with that reminder, he'd find the strength to soldier on.

Past the loss of beauty and his legendary attractiveness, Rolland's face presented another serious challenge: getting dentures.

Dentures were expensive, and Rolland asked Rory to help him find a solution that would prevent him from accepting any more charity from Charles or other people. He needed a way to earn his new teeth.

Rory found a dentist willing to take on Rolland as an apprentice and lend him a set of fake teeth to wear while he'd learn to make his own. This solution suited Rolland. While he was still physically weak, he looked forward to having a goal to occupy his time and his mind and not feel so useless.

Rolland's denture-making days started brutally. The dentures he was lent were an inelegant, clunky contraption held together with piano wire. They gave him headaches, hurt like hell to wear, and made his gums and the delicate lining of his mouth bleed from the constant friction. Thankfully, he took them out at night, but enough damage was done during the wearing hours to ensure nights of continuous pain.

Not only did Rolland look monstrous and had pain and headaches from the nasty device, but his speech was also barely better with the dentures than with no teeth at all. There was no way he could live like this.

With the dentist's blessing and in the name of advancement—his own and that of the other poor victims stuck wearing such monstrosities—he endeavored to find a way to better the dentures, to refine them.

He made some headway in the pain mitigation department, but alas, the results from an esthetic standpoint were always as grotesque.

There was one faint light at the end of the tunnel, however: Rolland discovered he had excellent fine motor skills and a talent for precision and detailed work. That could only come in handy, and he even envisioned perfecting himself and working in dentistry.

He could also see himself doing more hours at the Ursulines Hospital morgue, a place where he did some work. He was missing twelve teeth for his own set of dentures, and to save money, he struck a deal with the hospital to get a set of acceptable, compatible teeth from a cadaver. Rolland had insisted on the term "acceptable". He had to have some standards.

In return for getting teeth, Rolland performed various tasks at the morgue, from cleaning the premises and the equipment to helping move bodies and providing other forms of needed help. He discovered an interest in anatomy and was allowed to watch during autopsies.

He was a quick study, and with his dexterity, he even started lending a hand. He found the work fascinating and was keen to think this could be another interesting way to make money if he could keep learning.

At first, Rolland had found the place macabre and unsettling, but he eventually grew accustomed to most sights, smells, and states of the human body, from pristine to advanced decay. His stomach churned less frequently. What got to him the most was learning about the folks who ended up on the tables in front of him and their demise. Some had a touching story while others had gotten their comeuppance. He often wished he could have helped those with a tragic ending.

He also felt satisfaction when he assisted the doctor performing an autopsy and they found answers that helped render some justice, return some balance to the world. This had to be his favorite, along with the fact that being around mangled corpses and people accustomed to seeing ghastly things, he felt less self-conscious, like he wasn't always the scariest-looking thing in the room.

Rolland's prayer for finding a good set of teeth was answered after a few months of work at the morgue when a battered dead man was brought in. He had given up the ghost on his way to the hospital inside a horse-drawn carriage. He'd been in a brawl, and his body was beaten to a pulp.

When Rolland and his fellow worker Raymond went to collect the freshly deceased man from a carriage waiting outside, he thought the guy looked familiar. He reminded him of this rough immigrant from England with whom he had played cards the week before at the Russell Tavern. The card player was a small and stocky bloke with distinctive tufts of blond hair, and he'd flashed a gold tooth a few times when gracing the other players with a scowl.

Rolland pushed the lifeless man's lower lip down with his thumb, uncovering a gold tooth that matched the card player's, confirming his identity.

"Oliver something..." he mumbled to himself.

"You know him?" Raymond asked.

"I think I played cards with him recently. The entire time he seemed angry. Itching for a fight."

"Then it sounds fitting with his character that he would start a brawl."

Rolland nodded. "If only he had known the outcome. Poor sod."

It occurred to Rolland that he, himself, could have been sucked into that brawl had he not been at the morgue that night and wondered if he would have survived another round of beatings.

Fate was an odd thing.

Shrugging off the thought, Rolland inspected the rest of the man's teeth. He cared little for the gold tooth itself—it had monetary value, of course, but the hospital would no doubt not let him keep it anyway. Rather, the other teeth seemed in particularly good shape and a good match for his own jaw.

"Are these the ones?" Raymond asked with enthusiasm.

"Very possibly."

Rolland tried to remember his brief encounter with this Oliver fellow to guess what his lifestyle might have been like, gathering any hint of whether the man's teeth were right for him.

At worst, he could always make another set of dentures later should they prove to be in a worse shape than they looked, but he liked to do things right the first time.

He recalled that the man had not been very talkative while playing cards, doing more scowling than talking.

Would wearing this frustrated man's teeth make him scowl, too?

Rolland's amusement at the thought didn't last long. Now that he had little to smile about in his life and that his facial muscles might never heal properly, scowling might very well be his new default expression, too.

The thought depressed him to no end, but he refocused his mind on the task at hand and the fact he had found his new teeth. Perhaps they would somehow make his mouth less painful. That alone would be a reason not to scowl.

If there ever was one night when Rolland should have stayed home, it would have to be that one late October night. Rory was out of town on a business trip in Sherbrooke, and Rolland felt excessively lonesome and restless.

To distract himself, he'd lined up the foreigner's teeth with his own on the kitchen table and was contemplating them all for the nth time. They blended in well with his—that part was good news—but a sense of uneasiness bothered him. He was close to reaching his dentures goal. He had planned to start working on them the next day, and that should have rejoiced him.

Before he'd got these remaining teeth, he had entertained the hope that his life would get back to normal. Maybe having some of his own teeth back inside his mouth would erase everything awful that had happened and destroyed his previous life. His livelihood. Everything.

But now that he was getting closer to this goal, he feared that the little white sticks before him would not bring him the big positive change he craved after all.

He felt deflated.

Depressed.

If he was to wallow in despair, he might as well go to the tavern and make some money playing a few rounds. Have a drink or two.

Two drinks became three, and then four. Rolland stopped counting. His mind felt sharp enough to keep track of cards, and with each drink, he felt slightly less awful. So, what was the point of keeping count? Rory wouldn't be there to put up with his pitiful state when he got home, anyway.

The rest of the night became a blur. Rolland thought he

won some rounds and lost a few. He wasn't certain. The only thing he was certain of was that he'd stopped caring. Most of the pain—both physical and emotional—was mostly gone, and he was basking in his current delightful lightness of being.

The warmth and fuzzy feeling followed him outside into the chilly fall night as he left the tavern—or had someone instructed him to leave? That part wasn't clear.

But it didn't matter. He enjoyed the wind on his face and the prospect of crawling into bed as soon as his wobbly walking pace would allow.

On the opposite side of the street, a rowdy bunch of men appeared from an adjacent street.

Normally, when in a non-inebriated state, Rolland avoided being seen in public, taking the less-traveled streets and keeping the hood of his cloak firmly in place over his head to hide his face.

But tonight, he didn't care to stick to side streets and shadows.

A gust of wind brought down his hood, uncovering his head and face. A streetlamp shed an unflattering spotlight on his already unsightly features, making him look even more freakish than he was.

The men across the street gawked and jeered at Rolland, catching his attention.

He squinted at them, unsure what they wanted with him. He was about to keep going on his merry way when his eyes landed on one man staring and smirking at him.

Leopold Christie, Delphine's smug fiancé.

The bastard who had done *this* to him.

The recognition cut through Rolland's drunken gaze and hit him in the gut. If he had reasonable doubts before that this evil brute was behind his attack, the brute's arrogant smirk and amusement of the scene confirmed his guilt in the matter. Rolland would have no more doubt.

The brute's mocking eyes were glued to Rolland. Not only had he destroyed his life, but he was also laughing at him.

Anger fought through the sluggishness of the alcohol and rose inside Rolland's chest. If only he could make the vicious coward pay for what he'd done.

One man of Christie's posse took a few steps in Rolland's direction, but a passing horse-drawn cab cut off his path, nearly hitting him.

Christie grabbed his minion by the arm, telling him not to bother. He led his men away without giving Rolland another look.

Once home, Rolland tried to drink himself to sleep, but the street encounter had twisted a knife into his wounds, and he couldn't help rehashing his rival's smirk, his unmistakable air of victorious contempt.

Rolland wished he could wipe the man's arrogant smirk along with the rest of his pretty face. An eye for an eye. Have the despicable man find out how much it hurt when Delphine and the whole world looked at *him* with disgust.

Delphine would never look at Rolland ever again.

Unless he could work a miracle with his new teeth...

Rolland dragged himself out of bed and staggered to the kitchen table where his treasured loose teeth were laid.

He picked one up at random and examined it.

How could he better the dentures?

Could he set the teeth differently?

If only he could skip the unwieldy bases or make them more delicate. The result more elegant. And lose the damn piano wires...

The roots of the teeth were intact. What if there was a different way to make them stay put?

In a moment of drunken folly and desperation, Rolland wondered why the teeth couldn't simply be implanted back into his gums. The holes might still be there, underneath the newly healed surface. And at worst, he could make new holes, his intoxicated brain reasoned.

If he shoved the teeth into his gums hard enough, perhaps they would stay in.

It would be so marvelous if they stayed in.

Would they stay in?

There was only one way to find out.

He brought a front tooth over his lower gum and poked it around, searching for a hole. Perhaps he should do this in front of a mirror. God forbid he'd put a set of molars in the wrong place. If he looked bad now, there was room for making things even worse. That would not be a good move.

He went to fetch a small mirror and propped it up on the table. He sat down and took a swig of whiskey to dull his gums, anticipating pain.

Bracing himself for pain.

What if this worked, and he looked more like his old self? What if Delphine fell in love with him again? Hope washed over him, and he brought the tooth to his mouth. With the mirror's help, he guided it to a suitable spot.

Thinking of Delphine smiling at him in adoration, he pushed the tooth inside the sensitive gum tissue.

Pain shot through his mouth, and he felt some resistance. But as the root of the tooth pierced the gum, releasing blood, it felt like the tooth took over and dug its own way down. Back into its intended place.

Rolland was taken aback. He must have dreamed this.

He took hold of the tooth to wiggle it, but it didn't budge. It felt solidly in place.

He studied it in the mirror and couldn't believe how much it looked perfectly in place, as if it had never been elsewhere than nicely set in his mouth.

Hmm.

Rolland tried the same process with another tooth.

And another.

Lo and behold, they all did the same thing. They all obediently planted themselves into his mouth, all in a row and in the right places, like a neat little garden.

Blood trickled out of the corner of his mouth, but he barely noticed it or the pain, totally lost in the fantasy of the day when he'd be healed, and Delphine would come back to him.

He'd have to act fast before she tied the knot. He'd have to find a way to get rid of the scoundrel. Get him out of the picture before it was too late, and she made the biggest mistake of her life.

What could he do to prevent this disaster?

What should he do?

Rolland's mind raced, and he felt warm. Feverish?

The room started to spin. His body went limp.

And everything went dark.

The next morning, Rolland woke up with his mouth and head aching so unbearably his hangover barely registered.

He tried to remember the night before, and it felt like a feverish dream, followed by one huge, wicked nightmare. Did he go out to the tavern and get drunk for real?

Before he could remember all the odd details of the night, it hit him how badly he'd tossed and turned all night, dreaming that Delphine's fiancé was on the autopsy table in front of him, and he had *carte blanche* to do whatever he wanted to him. The rest of the dream was cryptic, punctuated with vivid images of a scalpel cutting through flesh and teeth being pulled.

That last image prompted Rolland to move his tongue around his mouth, and he felt teeth.

He must have fallen asleep with his dentures in, maybe the reason for the dream. He slid his fingers inside his mouth to investigate, but there were no dentures to pull out.

Rolland dragged himself out of bed, and the room spun a little—he caught the corner of his dresser to stabilize himself.

He stumbled to his mirror as fast as his balance allowed him to. The sight awaiting him astonished him. His jawline looked normal.

How could this be?

As he inspected the teeth in his mouth, memories of him implanting them came rushing back. He remembered, and it made sense. Yet, it also made no sense. If there was a way to stick teeth back into one's mouth, surely someone would have caught on to that fact by now.

This felt suspicious. And insane. If only Rory was back so they could figure out what was going on. In the meantime, until his brother's return, Rolland would keep busy to distract himself from the rising feeling of uneasiness.

As he got dressed, a fuzzy memory of his near encounter with Christie and his gang came to him. The man's smirk and Rolland's feelings of anger and inadequacy overwhelmed him.

He wondered if someone else also ever had the desire to take that arrogant smile off the man's face. Surely there were other men out there who had been abused by the guy.

Images of Rolland's nightmare flashed again in his mind. Pliers extracting teeth from a bleeding mouth. A scalpel tracing a clean line around the contour of a dead man's face.

Rolland shook his head to rid himself of the gruesome images. He should eat breakfast and prepare himself for the day. Focus on work. The nightmare would eventually fade and leave him alone.

He headed to the kitchen, and Christie's taunting sneer popped into his mind again. A sickening feeling assaulted him as he neared the porcelain basin on the counter. He suddenly knew what he'd find at the bottom.

A bloody scalpel and a pair of pliers.

He recalled a hazy memory of him washing blood off his hands. He felt like he had, at once, done something awful and yet hadn't. Had he been a witness?

With a growing sense of foreboding, Rolland went back to his bedroom. He kneeled and reached for the small chest under his bed, in which he kept a few things of value.

There was blood smeared on it.

With his heart beating in his ears and his hands shaking, Rolland lifted the lid and came face to face with a bloodied mask of flesh.

He had an idea whose face it once had been.

The smirk was definitely gone.

CHAPTER TWELVE

Montréal, present day

The shocking news of the missing plastic surgeon found with his teeth gone echoed in Elenora's mind.

"I can't believe the man's teeth are missing... Like in your internet search... Isn't that the weirdest coincidence?" Tom shook his head while putting on socks. As homicide detectives, he and Alex had now inherited the case.

Elenora forced a faint smile at his observation. "It is."

"While we're at it, you don't happen to know who the killer might be?" he asked her dryly.

Elenora's heart threatened to jump out of her chest. She couldn't wait for Tom to be out the door. She was juggling so many thoughts and emotions, so keeping up a calm facade was the last thing she was able to do well right now.

Tom stood, gave her a quick peck on the cheek. "You gonna be all right? You look a little pale."

As soon as you're gone, yes. "Yes. Go!" She shooed him out of the room.

The moment she heard the front door close, she texted Pierre on the off chance he wasn't asleep. Insomnia was rarely a blessing for anyone, but her phone rang a moment later, and it comforted her to no end.

"So, they found him without teeth..." Pierre said after she told him the news.

"Yeah."

"Wow. That's just...that's just wow, Elenora. It's so amazing that you knew!"

Give it to Pierre to find a silver lining in the darkest of places. She felt like this was anything but amazing.

"Where did they find him?"

"At a construction site. A total fluke, apparently. The evening crew was wrapping up when a piece of machinery broke a water main or something. They had to dig to do an emergency repair, and that's where they found the body. Buried underneath. It shouldn't have been found. It should never have been found. But the flood had to be dealt with."

"A flood... You knew about the water too."

Elenora had been too dazed by the missing teeth detail to make a connection with the flood. Pierre was right. She had seen and felt water, too. Two elements she had gotten right. One element too many to be a coincidence. Again.

Another concrete proof that her visions weren't just a product of her imagination.

"Do you think they will go away?"

"What, the premonitions?"

"Yeah. Now that they found the man. I haven't seen the killer. It's not like I can help."

She hadn't seen the killer. Perhaps there was hope that this was it. The end of it.

Pierre remained silent on the other end of the line longer than she would have liked. "You know how much I wish I could tell you this is all over... Would you like me to come over?"

Elenora thought about it. As reluctant as she was to be alone with her thoughts, she really needed time by herself to process everything.

"Thanks for the offer, but I should go back to bed. Tom might not be long."

"Okay, well, don't hesitate."

"Thanks for being there, Pierre."

"I'm happy to be there."

Elenora slipped back into bed, overwhelmed.

She worked on steadying her breathing, trying to anchor herself to the present, to reality, to calm herself. She put a hand on her belly and tuned into the baby, who seemed at peace. Probably asleep.

Little angel.

Count your blessings.

She had foreseen her pregnancy. Out of the blue. *That* had been a wonderful thing. Perhaps her gift was not entirely awful. Perhaps she would see other beautiful things from time to time.

Okay... Reframe your thoughts, focus on the positive.

So, what had happened? What did she know?

Other than predicting her pregnancy—which had been awesome—she had seen a missing man and his death. Or rather, she had seen mostly vague or symbolic clues about his death as opposed to, say, a clear picture of where he'd been buried. Her visions didn't come with Google Maps directions.

Those clues had been gruesome, unhelpful, and more frustrating than anything, but she had been right, and who was to say future clues wouldn't be helpful?

Future clues. Ugh.

Future clues would mean having more visions. She dreaded seeing more clues, no matter what they were.

But there was no benefit in dreading something that hadn't happened yet. Perhaps the next time—if there was a next time—she would conveniently see the killer's address written in black and white and save the day. Easy peasy. A girl could wish.

Thinking of all sorts of non-scary and blood-free visions she could have to help catch a murderer or help solve other crimes, her mind drifted to sleep.

Elenora dreamed she was shoveling dirt alongside construction workers. Her shovel hit something hard. She moved dirt aside with the metal tip of her tool and unearthed a blue piece of fabric.

The missing man's shirt.

With the man still in it.

She shoveled more dirt aside and uncovered his pale face with dried blood at the corner of the lips.

She crouched next to him and moved his lips apart with her fingers to see if his teeth were missing.

They were.

As she ran fingers along his bare lower gum, she felt transported to a different place. A room with heavy stone walls. Dungeon-like.

She heard a clanking sound and searched for the source. She saw a tall young man bent over a stainless-steel table, on which a body was laid. As if he was performing a medical procedure of sort.

She took a few steps toward him to get a better look.

With a set of pliers, he yanked a tooth out of the corpse's mouth and dropped it into a metal bowl, making the clanking sound again.

The young man had a full head of unruly black hair, with the occasional curl. He wore an apron over clothes from a long gone past. Regency-era fashion, perhaps?

As if sensing Elenora's presence, he lifted his head. His eyes found hers. His gaze was piercing, coming from light blue eyes. Two important and bright red scars marred his face, one along each cheek.

Elenora gasped, jolting herself awake. "It's him!"

"Who?" Tom asked, half-asleep but springing to a sitting position, ready to kick someone's ass.

It was the crack of dawn, and soft light filtered inside the bedroom from around the blinds. Elenora was confused, struggling to reconcile what she had just seen with reality. Oddly, despite the tension from the dream, she wasn't entirely filled with dread. A part of her was curious and wanted to understand and know more.

Tom rubbed her back and asked softly, "What did you see?"

"The killer. I saw the killer," she said. Secrecy and reason be damned, this was too important. She had a face. Finally, something to go on. To help.

"Which killer?"

"Yours. The man who killed the plastic surgeon."

"Okay... What did you see?" Tom asked patiently. Was he believing her or humoring her to calm her down?

"I was digging near the water main at your crime scene, and I unearthed Dr. Haché. And then I opened his mouth, and his teeth were missing, and when I touched his gums, I ended up in a dark room with stone walls. Like an old basement. And this creepy young guy was doing an autopsy on a man, pulling his teeth out. And he looked at me."

The realization that the killer had seen her sent a chill through her. "Oh my God, he saw me!"

"Shhhhh. It's just a dream, Ele. I'm so sorry. I shouldn't have told you about the crime scene. I should've known better. I'll be more diligent in keeping these things to myself, okay? I didn't mean to freak you out."

"I already knew about the plastic surgeon, Tom," she said, resigning herself to come clean. She had started to spill some beans; she might as well dump the entire bag. And Tom was now in charge of the investigation. She wouldn't have to call the anonymous tip line and pray for someone to take the information seriously.

"What do you mean?" he asked, frowning.

"Please promise not to have me committed."

"What? Why would I ever have you committed?"

She could tell he was struggling to hide his amusement. He was nowhere near understanding the gravity of the situation.

"Please promise."

"I promise."

"You remember how I knew we were having a girl?"

"Yes. That was an impressive guess."

"That was more than a guess. I'd seen her in dreams, and I even knew the exact moment I became pregnant."

Tom frowned again.

"I've dreamed of the plastic surgeon too. I've seen him die in my mind. His teeth fell out of his mouth, and there was water everywhere..."

Tom's expression was now hard to read, but he was no doubt trying to process this strange information.

Elenora went on. "And then tonight you told me he'd been found dead, without teeth. Because of a broken water pipe. Water. Like I've *seen*. And now I just saw the man who killed him. We can't ignore this. I'll look at mugshots. He has scars on his face. And dark hair. Pale blue eyes. Do you want to write this down?"

"Okay... So, it sounds like your dreams are...realistic? Honestly, I'm not sure what other conclusion to reach. What makes you think the man you saw in your nightmare is the killer?"

"Because when I touched the dead surgeon, I saw the young man with scars yanking teeth out of a cadaver. These have to be clues. Just like the water and the teeth were clues. Even though I wasn't convinced back then."

"But how do you know these weren't just coincidences?"

"Trust me, I fervently hoped these visions were all just coincidences. That they meant nothing. But obviously, they do. And I can't ignore them anymore, like I wish I could."

Tom gave her a tender look, one that suggested he really, really wanted to believe his adorable but very, very hormonal and sleep-deprived wife.

How could she prove to him that this was real? What could she say to convince him?

Give him a detail I couldn't know about. Something from the construction site.

She had unearthed the dead man in her dream. Her shovel had touched—

"Was the victim wearing a blue shirt when you saw him tonight?" she asked Tom with confidence.

He reached for his phone on his nightstand and searched through the crime scene photos.

"Yes. But a lot of men wear blue shirts, Ele. I don't want to sound insulting, but perhaps that's just a good guess."

She racked her brain for another detail. She closed her eyes, moving dirt in her mind, unearthing more of the blue shirt. For some reason, this time, the memory cooperated.

"There's a logo on his breast pocket, though the shirt is too dirty for me to see clearly..."

She kept her eyes closed as she spoke, afraid to let the memory slip if she opened them.

"The top button is missing, probably from a struggle... There are marks around his neck from strangulation. That's how he died, choked to death."

The image faded, and Elenora opened her eyes.

Tom stared at her, stunned.

"Please don't freak out," she asked in a small voice. "I'm so sorry I didn't tell you earlier. Please don't think I'm crazy."

"I don't think you're crazy, but I don't know what to think. There has to be a logical explanation for all this."

"I've already had this conversation with myself and with Pierre, and we both concluded there are no logical explanations other than me having visions."

There.

The "V word" had been said.

She took a cleansing breath.

Tom's face fell. "You talked to Pierre about this? You told him but not me?"

"Pierre already knew about some weird things, and he always seemed open to crazy...paranormal stuff." She spat out the last two words with great pain. "I thought he was the least likely person to think I was crazy. That's all. I love you, Tom. Please don't think I chose Pierre over you."

He ran fingers through his hair. "First, please stop thinking that I think you're crazy. Gimme a chance here. This is a lot to process."

"I know."

"What do you mean Pierre knows about weird things?"

Tom already knew the "official" version of the car crash that had killed Elenora's father, so she told him about the bizarre circumstances of her survival and the little boy at the bottom of the river whom she had started to see recently. And how Pierre had waited for so long for her to remember.

Tom couldn't possibly look any more baffled even if he tried, as something dawned on him.

"Your internet search... You knew about the teeth last night before I even got the call."

Elenora nodded.

"How?"

"That's one of several questions that have been keeping me up at night."

His face darkened, revealing more hurt. "And you didn't trust me enough to tell me about any of this? About what you were really going through?"

"Of all the upsetting things I just told you, this is what upsets you the most? It's not a matter of trust, Tom. This is so far out of left field, what's happening to me. There's no how-to book for me on this!"

After a moment of fuming and staring into space, Tom got out of bed and grumbled, "I need to shower."

"I'm sorry I didn't tell you earlier," she called after him. "Believe me. I'm scared shitless."

He turned and acknowledged what she said begrudgingly before closing the ensuite bathroom door.

His reaction stung, and Elenora hoped he would come around sooner than later. Try to see her side of it. On the bright side, she did feel lighter now that she no longer had to keep anything from him.

The bathroom door reopened, and Tom peeked his head out, looking contrite. "I'm sorry I'm upset. You know how it gets to me when you're hurt, and I can't do a damn thing about it. I can't help feeling pissed off that you went to Pierre instead of me. I'm glad you talked to someone who believes you and loves you. And I'll get over myself. Just allow me to stew in the shower for a moment, okay?"

She gave him a smile. "Okay."

"When I come out, we'll go over what you know, and we'll try to figure things out, all right? Together, we'll figure things out."

CHAPTER THIRTEEN

Montréal, 1847

"Pull as hard as you can, and don't worry about hurting me," Rolland instructed Rory.

Hesitantly, Rory shifted his position and tightened his grip on the pliers secured around a molar on the right side of Rolland's mouth. A bead of sweat appeared near his hairline. Playing amateur dentist was not high on his list of preferred hobbies.

He grimaced and pulled.

Rolland felt his brother's attempt at a vigorous tug before the pliers slipped and sent Rory flying backward.

"Ugh! I swear I'm trying!"

"I know. I felt it."

Rolland let out a sigh of frustration. When Rory had come back from his business trip, Rolland had shown him the incredible, miraculous state of his teeth and told him everything that had happened in his absence, including how he feared he might somehow be indirectly involved in Leopold

Christie's demise. Christie had been declared missing the day after Rolland's grisly discovery and had yet to be found.

It might have been early to conclude the man was dead, but it was hard to believe he could be alive somewhere out there without a face.

Roland had a strong, sour gut feeling about this one.

After hearing Rolland's impressions, Rory had reached the same conclusion as him: the teeth from the dead foreigner in his mouth must be cursed.

And thus, as a priority and despite the expected physical and emotional pain, the teeth had to go, even if that was the ultimate disappointment when they made Rolland's face look and feel so much more normal and free of pain.

If their price was for Rolland to turn murderous, it was too much of a raw deal for him to keep them. The teeth had to go.

But apparently, the teeth didn't want to go.

"I'll try again," Rory said with determination, barely hiding his feelings of revulsion.

Rolland held out his hand for the pliers. "No. Allow me."

Rory didn't argue and handed him the tool.

Rolland had already tried yanking the teeth out by himself when he first thought they were cursed, but to no avail. He suspected this time would be no different, but it was worth a try before hopping into a cab and heading to an obscure part of town to ask some backyard butcher to take his best shot. If he could avoid such a trip, he was all for it.

A trip to three different sketchy "dentists" yielded no better results. The damned teeth were there to stay, which meant the brothers would have to leave town before a chamber pot hit the proverbial fan. There was no sensible way to explain how the teeth were staying put in Rolland's mouth, and too many people knew about his dental issues for them to simply not notice the obvious difference or dismiss the fact he no longer needed dentures, starting with the denture maker he worked with and his colleagues at the morgue.

If he and Rory stayed, it was only a matter of time before Rolland was questioned and accused of being in cahoots with the devil over the teeth. He would become a pariah and be burned at one metaphorical stake or another, be it by the church or the good people with wagging tongues.

Still, it was a huge endeavor for the brothers to move away from what they had known all their lives. Rolland and Rory considered every possibility, but all of their options ended with them selling their home, packing up their meager belongings, and heading to a new place to start over. It was the very plan they had entertained with Delphine, except without her, though Rory insisted that heading to Kingston was out of the question. Should anyone ever find Leopold Christie's body and his murder be traced back to Rolland, Delphine might think of Kingston.

So, they settled for Toronto, a much bigger city, which would allow them to keep an even lower profile than in Kingston.

Worried he might unconsciously hurt Rory, Rolland had first suggested to exile himself while Rory stayed in Montréal, at least until he could figure out what was going on and get this madness under control. He would find work and send money for Rory's medications and have Charles check in on him.

But Rory refused, pointing out that if Rolland's subconscious wanted him dead, he would have acted by now. Rory was so frail, and even more so compared to his healthy brother, that Rolland didn't need to sneak up on him while he slept to kill him—especially when one quick blow to the gut would do the trick.

Also, if Rolland was indeed involved in Leopold Christie's murder, the dead brute had provided Rolland ample motivation to strike back, to get back at *him*.

Rolland desperately needed his brother by his side, so he didn't argue with his logic, though he made Rory promise to let him go should he feel dark urges take over him. He also made it a habit to cuff one of his legs to his bed before sleep so that, should he get possessed in the middle of the night, Rory would get a fair warning to flee or a fighting chance if he foolishly decided to confront him.

Some cold comfort, but better than nothing.

As they packed and prepared to move, Rolland had time to reflect on what was happening to him. He no longer needed dentures and looked closer to normal. He felt a guilty gratitude for this improvement in his awful appearance, while never able to shake the thought that he might have had something to do with Christie's grotesque end.

But what had truly happened? Was it really because of the teeth? And was the devil involved as Rory thought?

Rolland got the impression he might never get answers and live the rest of his life with a crippling sense of remorse and dread, knowing he had taken a life.

Did he curse Delphine's fiancé by thinking ill of him?

Delphine...

How was she coping with Christie being gone? Truth be told, if there was one good thing to come out of this appalling, senseless event, it was the fact that the ignoble man could no longer hurt Delphine.

Delphine...

Did she think Rolland had anything to do with his disappearance? Would she, someday, ever look at him with less repulsion in her eyes?

Pain twisted his heart. He didn't need to torture himself any more than he already was, but he couldn't help it. Perhaps Rory was right when he said that by leaving Montréal, Rolland would probably never see Delphine ever again and could truly start to heal.

Rolland wasn't sure what healing meant anymore, but he wanted to believe that the future would be less bleak and kinder to him than the present and recent past.

Perhaps Leopold Christie's death had been a one-shot deal with the devil and Rolland would never be involved in another person's death, other than helping perform autopsies.

The thought that he would never quite escape death hit him and brought a grim smile to his face. But it wasn't so much death as murdering that distressed him.

Distress...

He realized that he'd been in a constant state of distress since his beating. In contrast, before that tragedy, his life had been relatively serene. Recovering serenity was what he should strive for. Being at peace with himself and grateful for what he had.

How hard could that be?

For the next two years, the brothers lived in relative anonymous peace in Toronto.

For some cruel reason, Rolland's scars never healed, always looking fresh, and hair didn't grow near them, so not even a beard could hide the marks. His face was still too scary for any work requiring him to be seen by the sensitive public.

Fortunately, he soon found work at the morgue of a nearby hospital, quickly making himself indispensable and continuing his quest to learn more about anatomy, hopeful that someday he might know enough to help Rory's health beyond throwing money at his issues. If only he could find a way to heal him. Rory now did light carpentry work, even as his health steadily declined.

The brothers were constantly on the lookout for triggers and symptoms in Rolland. Luckily, no more killings happened.

However, Rolland's patience with Dr. Harris, Rory's quack doctor—the only so-called doctor they could afford—was wearing thin as the man kept recommending suspicious miracle treatments and medications advertised in newspapers that claimed to cure everything yet seemed to do nothing but deplete their meager savings.

As far as Rolland was concerned, the dubious medicine man was letting his brother perish. He was scrambling to find a better doctor when Rory was struck with a lightning-fast fever that claimed his life before Rolland could fetch more competent help.

Rory's death devastated Rolland and was the last nail in his emotional coffin. To protect the fragile remainders of his destroyed self, he decided he would no longer allow himself to feel anything.

The day after Rory's passing, Rolland forced himself out of bed to go to work so he could afford a decent funeral for his brother. Oddly, his knuckles were sensitive, and he noticed the skin on his hands was split in a few places, as if he'd been in a fistfight.

He had a bad feeling about this.

As he headed to the morgue, the chilly November morning compelled him to put his hands in the pocket of his cloak. His fingers brushed against some kind of elongated little rocks. Only, he knew they weren't rocks.

He pulled his hand out and retrieved a handful of teeth.

What had he done now?

He kept walking to work, his heart beating in his throat, expecting the worst.

Sure enough, the cadaver that landed in front of him moments later was the quack doctor.

And his teeth were missing.

CHAPTER FOURTEEN

Montréal, present day

"What if this traumatizes the baby?" Tom asked with gentle concern as he maneuvered the car around a double-parked sedan. He cursed the navel-gazing driver for worsening the already thick rush hour.

Tom's question hit Elenora in the gut. She'd been obsessing over doing everything right for the baby, feeling a tremendous responsibility on her shoulders to make sure this little human would come into the world in the healthiest state possible. To suggest she might be doing something damaging to that crucial mission felt like a blow despite her understanding of Tom's concerns. Deep down, she knew he wasn't trying to give her a guilt trip, and that helped. But still.

"You don't think I haven't thought of this?" she blurted out with an ounce of bitterness. "I'm not in control of anything, whether I choose to act or not. But perhaps acting will put an end to this ordeal faster. If we solve the case, it's less exposure for the baby."

After a moment, Tom nodded reluctantly.

"But...the morgue? You know how sensitive you are. You can hardly stomach the sight of blood, Ele. Seeing a cadaver—scratch that, *touching* a cadaver—what is that gonna do to your state of mind and well-being? Once you see a dead body, you can't unsee it."

"Tom, I've already seen the dead body. It's already seared into my brain. But if I remain complacent, like I've been, knowing I could have helped prevent—"

"You weren't complacent. You didn't have enough to go on."

"Perhaps not then. But maybe I will soon, if I do this."

Since breakfast, they had reviewed Elenora's visions of the dead plastic surgeon, and Tom had quizzed her from every angle, trying to grasp what was happening to her and how her insights could help the case. Since the visions had already occurred, they might as well try to milk them and get answers out of them.

Elenora could tell he was making a tremendous effort to keep an open mind and wrap his brain around what was going on. It was no easy task. She'd been experiencing this strange and impossible situation for longer than him, and she still didn't know what to make of it, let alone accept it.

Things had gone relatively smoothly until she asked him to see the dead man's body at the morgue. She wanted to touch his bare gums like she'd done in her latest dream, hoping it would reveal more clues.

Tom had lost his shit over the idea, to put it mildly.

Elenora had argued it could only help, and they had nothing to lose. Tom had countered that it could scar her for life. Her and the baby.

So here they were.

"Nobody can possibly know if this could affect her," Elenora said. "I wish there were an online parenting forum where I could ask if touching a cadaver for clues could have a damaging impact on my developing daughter."

Elenora's angst was palpable, as was the tension in the car.

She let out a huff. "Maybe I'm just being selfish and want to feel in control, but—"

"You're the last person who could be accused of being selfish."

"Well, tell that to the truckload of guilt that keeps running me over."

They drove in silence for a while, both staring ahead at the minivan in front of them with the faded bumper stickers. A drizzle of rain fell on the windshield, making the day grayer.

Tom grabbed her hand and squeezed it. "Ele, I'm processing as fast as I can. I mean, that's one hell of a curveball. And I'll admit I'm still very freaked out..."

She squeezed his hand back. "*I'm* still very freaked out."

"I'm sorry you're going through that. And I'm sorry you felt like you couldn't tell me. I wish I'd been there from the beginning to support you, so you wouldn't have been freaking out all by yourself."

"Thank you for trying to understand and your willingness to freak out with me."

"Hey, it's just the foundation of any healthy relationship..."

She squeezed his hand again.

"What are we gonna tell people?" he said. "Will *they* understand?"

"Can we…try not to tell anyone? At least not Alex? Not yet."

Tom groaned. "Alex. Yeah. That might not go over well."

"An understatement."

"I don't know if we can hide the morgue visit from him. Hopefully, we'll be quick. I'd send him on an errand, but he'd get suspicious *and* pissed off for being treated like an assistant. I'm starting to appreciate how hard it must've been for you to keep this a secret from me."

"It does require some mental gymnastics." Elenora felt a chill and fiddled with the heating controls.

"What about the killer's clothes? You said they were old. Like from another era?" Tom asked.

"Correct."

"Perhaps he's an actor."

"The killer?"

"Yeah. Perhaps that's a clue."

"Huh."

"I'll give Renaud a description and ask him to look into period plays and films in production right now that might fit the bill. Get headshots."

"Okay. And when he asks why?"

Tom thought for a moment. "I'll tell him it's an anonymous tip."

Elenora nodded. That could work.

"What about the dungeon room I saw? You think that was a theater? A movie set?"

"Anything's possible."

"Could Dr. Haché have disfigured a patient, and then the patient chose revenge over a refund?" Elenora asked in a whisper as she and Tom headed to the morgue in the basement of the police station. The corridors were empty, their colleagues busy elsewhere. Still, she didn't want to be overheard.

"That's a plausible scenario."

"The scars I saw on the young man's face...a two-year-old could have done a better job."

"Maybe Haché even butchered the killer's face on purpose, to get back at him. But that sounds like a stretch."

Tom loved to use Elenora as a sounding board. They spitballed theories, and their only rule was to not censor whatever idea came through their minds. They never knew what thought might lead to a deduction, a crucial connection between clues.

"Or maybe he was not a very good plastic surgeon to begin with. But that too sounds unlikely. Especially with his marketing budget," she said.

"Though there are complaints of botched surgeries lodged against him."

"Some specific types of surgeries? Or he just happened to have bad days?"

"Maybe he was impaired some of those times. Drugs or alcohol. I'll ask Renaud to look into these possibilities. Vengeance too."

As they approached the morgue, Elenora's pace slowed. Damn jitters.

"How are you doing? You can still change your mind. At any time, all right?"

"I'll remember that."

"I'll go see if Carl's ready. Why don't you sit down a minute?" Tom pointed to a bench near the morgue's entrance. While driving to the station, he had called Carl, the morgue's tech, to tell him they'd like to see the plastic surgeon and ask if he could please cover up the body except around the mouth. It was typical of Tom to be this thoughtful on a regular day, and with Elenora pregnant, he went even more out of his way to shield her from any discomfort. She beamed him a relieved smile when Carl agreed and didn't question their request.

Tom came out of the morgue with a mask and a small jar of menthol cream.

"Here. Put some under your nose. With the mask on top, that should help with the smell. Everything's all set and Carl's busy in his office, so we'll have some privacy."

"So, all I have to do is not psych myself out?" She smeared some menthol over her upper lip and put on the mask.

"That would help."

They entered the room and headed to an autopsy table on which a covered corpse was laid. As expected, only the mouth was visible.

Tom handed Elenora a pair of gloves. "You think you'll be able to see something with these on?"

"Your guess is as good as mine," she said, putting the gloves on.

She approached the body, her gaze locked on the lifeless lips in front of her. A shudder went through her, and she reminded herself that time was of the essence. They had a killer to catch and colleagues to avoid.

Just do it.

She brought her fingers to the lips and parted them gently, trying to repress a wave of revulsion threatening the stability of her stomach.

She shuddered again. Good thing her morning sickness days were long over because this would have been utterly unbearable.

Her fingers landed on the man's destroyed gums, and she closed her eyes, expecting a flood of images. Instead, she saw nothing but darkness.

Hmm.

She trailed her fingers along the gums and a faint, blurry image appeared in her mind. Was it a desk?

She forced herself to concentrate to see better. It did look like a wooden desk, and she could tell there were objects on it, but her vision was too fuzzy for her to see what they were.

This was frustrating.

Elenora opened her eyes and yanked one glove off.

"You sure?" Tom asked.

"Does it matter?" She brought her naked fingers back to the dead man's mouth.

It's just a mouth.

Upon contact with the lower gum, the vision rushed back inside her mind, but vividly this time. She let out a gasp.

Tom said something, but his words sounded muffled, and she didn't catch them. Deeply invested in capturing her vision, she focused on the wooden desk in front of her. It looked like an antique.

On top of it were various kinds of knick-knacks, some

that looked like artifacts from a long-gone past, mixed with pens, and notebooks, while other objects could have come from a dollar store.

Elenora felt compelled to open the top drawer. She reached for the knob, wondering if she'd be able to open it. Her fingers went to grab the tiny piece of metal, but all she felt was thin air. Still, the drawer opened—no doubt her mind, her will, at work. This baffled her, but there was no time to be baffled.

She turned her focus to the content of the drawer: a pile of papers. She reached for them, willing herself to pick them up and shuffle through them. Once again, her fingers didn't feel the documents, but they still ended up in her hands.

There were restaurant menus, from the top ones being recent to others dating from around the time home deliveries must have started.

Then, handwritten letters. "Dear Mr. Carmichael—"

Mr. Carmichael.

Some letters seemed to date from a long time, judging by the yellowness of the paper and the fancy handwriting. The ink blotches.

Elenora kept looking through the pile, searching for a first name.

Mr. Robin Carmichael.

Robin Carmichael! She had a name!

Could she also find an address?

She looked at the next envelope—Mr. Roy Carmichael, P.O. Box 53.

Roy.

Hmm.

Okay. So, two Carmichael men.

She kept going through the stack of letters. It produced two more first names: Rory and Rolland.

Robin, Roy, Rory, Rolland.

Four Carmichael men?

Four generations of fathers and sons? Brothers? Cousins? Who lived here and when?

Every letter used a postal box with the same number—P.O. Box 53—in either Montréal, Toronto, or Kingston. And the dates on every missive had been blacked out with ink. To cover tracks?

Elenora put the letters and restaurant flyers back in the drawer and opened the other one.

It yielded a single photograph, a daguerreotype picturing two young men, one of which looked very much like the intense-looking guy with the two huge scars. Except this man's face was flawless. He must have been an ancestor, a dead ringer for the killer.

She gently put the picture back in the drawer and lifted her gaze to look around.

Where was she?

Dark gray stone walls. The same dungeon-like basement she had seen before. This time, she noticed an arch at the corner of the wall ahead of her with a stone staircase leading up.

The rustling of clothes attracted her attention. She turned and froze.

Behind her, across the room, the tall young man stood, his back to her.

The killer.

This time, he was looking at himself in a mirror. Beside him, an assortment of tools laid on top of a small table.

He picked up what looked like a scalpel and brought it to his face, to one of the scars. His steady hand stopped before reaching his skin as his gaze shifted and caught Elenora staring at him in the mirror's reflection.

Time stood still as they took in each other.

The man frowned and pivoted to face her, scalpel still in hand. Surprise flashed briefly in his pale blue eyes before they became impossibly cold. And he started toward her.

Elenora wanted to scream, but no sound came out.

The man was approaching fast, an ugly mask of rage on his face. The scalpel pointed straight at her, ready to stab her.

She recoiled, bracing herself for a painful impact. A current of icy air went through her instead.

A pair of hands clutched her arms from behind.

"You're okay," she heard Tom whisper in her ear.

Elenora blinked and found herself back in the morgue, panting. Her heart caught in her throat.

Tom wrapped his arms around her. "I got you."

She hung onto his comforting presence. Her ears were ringing, and she swayed. Was she on the verge of fainting?

Just as her legs went limp, she heard a metal scraping sound, and a chair materialized behind her. Another pair of hands guided her to sit on the chair.

"What in tarnation are you two up to?" a man's voice asked.

Alex.

CHAPTER FIFTEEN

Alex was the king of knee-jerk reactions. He was the kind of guy who said no before even hearing the question.

Elenora understood it was a defense mechanism in reaction to past trauma. Under his gruff, bear-like exterior, his sense of empathy was off the charts, and he often absorbed a good emotional dose of other people's problems, especially when it concerned someone dear to him.

Once he'd found out about Elenora's new hair-raising situation and the turmoil she experienced, she expected him to blow his top.

And that moment was now.

"How long were you standing there?" Elenora asked, avoiding his puzzled stare.

"You mean, 'How little can you tell me about having your fingers down a dead guy's throat and still get me off your back'?" There was a hint of teasing in his voice. Perhaps he sensed her distress and was trying to lighten up the atmosphere. Typical Alex.

But Elenora's face remained grim, and he picked up that something serious was going on. His face fell a little.

She looked at him to evaluate his mood. He seemed receptive, but there was no good way to say what she was about to say, to not make it sound dreadful and demented and not set him off.

"This is really fucked up, Alex. I don't know if you'll be able to understand."

She was about to add that she didn't want her problem to affect him but stopped herself as it dawned on her: this was affecting *her*, and she couldn't control his reaction when she could barely control her own. She didn't have the emotional bandwidth to coddle him—which he hated anyway—and shield him from a problem that wasn't his. It was *her* problem, and for her to even own it was overwhelming enough. She could only be honest with him and hope that with time, he would come to understand. Or at least recognize the fact she was dealing with something impossible and give her a break.

Tom put a supportive hand on her shoulder.

"How about you try me before giving up?" Alex asked gruffly.

He crossed his arms over his massive chest, readying himself for what was coming, but despite his defensive posture, his expression still seemed open to giving her a chance.

"All right. Then, please listen to everything before—"

Elenora's phone rang. She started toward her purse, but the glove on her left hand reminded her that her fingers were coated with death and she shouldn't touch anything.

"I'll get it." Tom was already reaching for the purse. "It's Pierre. Should I let it go to voicemail?"

Pierre knew about Elenora's visit to the morgue, so of course he was eager to know how things had gone.

"Just ask him to hold a minute," she said on her way to the sink, aware of Alex's hawk-like gaze on her. "Actually, please put him on speakerphone."

Tom hit the speakerphone button and held the cell up as Elenora came back, drying her hands with a paper towel.

"Hey, Pierre," she said.

"Hey, Elenora," Pierre's voice filled the room.

"Good morning, Pierre," Alex said.

There was a brief pause. "Alex, how are you?"

Alex threw an uncertain look at Elenora. "Doing good, I think. Yourself?"

"You know how tough retirement is," Pierre chuckled, though he was barely joking in his case.

"I can only imagine," Alex retorted.

There was another pause, which Elenora interpreted as Pierre wondering if he could speak freely in the presence of Alex.

"I'm about to lift the veil, Pierre. So, it's all good."

"Are you sure?" Tom asked her.

She glanced at Alex and met his eyes. "There's no time like the present."

"Okay, then, but don't forget Carl." Tom jerked his head toward Carl's office. The door was open a crack.

Elenora took the cell from Tom, brought it close to her lips, and dropped her voice. "Pierre, d'you have a pen and paper?"

Tom and Alex both reached for their pen and notepad.

"I'm all ears," Pierre said, following her lead and lowering his voice.

With her eyes on Carl's door and without so much as a preamble to Alex, Elenora recounted what had just happened when she touched the plastic surgeon's gums. Every little detail, from what she found in the desk, to being able to move objects without feeling them, to the young man with the scars looking at himself in the mirror, about to mutilate his own face with a scalpel. And then him rushing at her with the sharp tool.

As she spoke, she could see Alex at her periphery and couldn't help wondering which part would make him explode. But he stood still, his gaze glued to her phone and his face bunched up in growing confusion.

When Elenora finished talking, Pierre said, "Wow. Nora, do you realize how terrific this is?"

When she didn't answer, he toned down his enthusiasm and added, "Okay, so, I'm sure you guys will look into those Carmichaels and the postal boxes, but I'll see if I can find anything on my end too. I'll get back to you if I find anything."

"Thanks, Pierre. Talk to you soon," Elenora said before hanging up.

"All right, let's get to it," Tom said with excitement in his voice and pride in his eyes.

"This is a prank, right?" Alex's face now wore an expression of disbelief on top of his initial confusion, which wasn't entirely gone. He knew Elenora and Tom were not the types to pull pranks.

"Alex, you have no idea how much I wish this was a prank," Elenora said, looking around the morgue and shivering. "I'll tell you the rest in my office."

"Good idea," said Tom. "I texted Renaud the names and

addresses. He's gonna look into it. Great job, Ele."

"Did you tell him it was another anonymous tip?"

"No. But I can see that the "anonymous tip" angle will only go so far before it starts to sound suspicious."

"A contact of mine has found instances of the four Carmichael names linked to the postal boxes in Montréal, Toronto, and Kingston," Pierre announced from the speakerphone.

Elenora, Tom, and Alex sat in her office, listening to him.

Just moments before, Elenora had told Alex everything that had been going on with her since she became pregnant, and he was still recovering from her insane-sounding information dump. He had listened to her without interrupting, an impassive expression on his face. She suspected he was struggling to cope with the weirdness she was throwing at him while keeping his temper in check. It was unclear whether his absence of reaction was a good or a bad thing.

Was he bottling up her words now to explode later?

This put her on pins and needles, but she reminded herself that how he dealt with her hardship was up to him. She could only give him a chance, like he asked, and hope for the best.

Once Elenora was done talking, Alex said, "Okay..." in a flat tone.

Okay.

That was it. But with Alex, the words unsaid often meant just as much as those that made it past his lips. Sometimes more. The fact he hadn't fled the room or wasn't ranting about the situation being ridiculous spoke volumes. Was he willing to try to understand, no matter how painful or impossible the situation must have seemed to him?

And now, before he'd had much time to digest Elenora's brutal news, Pierre was throwing even more shit on top.

Again, Alex was listening intently. He must have been making a herculean effort to be attentive to what the retired cop's contact had found out. No doubt his strong sense of duty to do his job right and help the case was forcing him to remain on board of Elenora's crazy express train across loony town.

"The Montréal postal box is still active, but it's tied to a street address that's currently a vacant lot," Pierre said. "Maybe the address existed when the box was first rented and thus was never questioned, or maybe a fake ID was used. That is unclear."

"What name is it under?" Tom asked.

Elenora was relieved to see him at ease discussing this surreal lead, and she loved him so much for it.

"Roy Carmichael."

"And the other boxes?"

"They're no longer associated with the name Carmichael." They heard the shuffling of papers over the cell's speaker. "The Toronto one now belongs to a Clark Chen, and the Kingston one to an Alyssa Boyer."

"Does the Montréal postal counter have a security camera?" Alex said with gritted teeth, drawing surprise from his colleagues, who didn't expect him to take part.

"It does. And while it's not specifically aimed at the postal boxes, it's picked up three visitors to Box 53 in the past six months: two different young men and one woman. We can't see them clearly, but neither man seem to match the one Elenora saw. And they all look a little rough. We think they might be street kids running an errand for Carmichael."

"Okay, let me get this straight... Your source has had the time to find and watch six months-worth of footage in the past half hour?" Alex asked, developing a facial tic.

"My source has mysterious ways to work efficiently," Pierre replied. His answer did nothing to take away the *wtf* frown on Alex's face.

"This latest Montréal Carmichael doesn't want to be caught on camera," Tom mused, focusing on the clues at hand and ignoring Pierre's cryptic reply.

"Looks like it."

"So, he's cautious. Might have something to hide."

"The fact all those Carmichaels bothered to have a postal box tells me he might not be the only one with something to hide," Pierre said.

"You think we might be dealing with several generations of sketchy people who've been watching their backs since the first one got the ball rolling?" Alex asked.

"That's a possibility."

Judging from the excitement in Pierre's voice, Elenora could picture him being so happy to have a brand new, shiny puzzle to solve.

"Do we know who the first one is?" Tom said.

"Rory Carmichael rented the very first box in Toronto in 1847. And then almost a century later, the Montréal box was transferred to his name in 1945."

"You mean, to another Carmichael named Rory. So, we have five Carmichaels, not four," Alex mumbled.

"Actually, it's possibly the same Rory..." Pierre replied.

Alex made a face at the phone, like he must have heard Pierre incorrectly.

"What makes you say that, Pierre?" Tom said.

"My contact has a theory that this Rory might be one and the same. Call it a hunch."

Alex choked on his saliva. "Who the hell's your contact?"

"My contact is one who requires a very open mind," Pierre retorted.

"I don't even know what that means, and I'm afraid to ask." Alex shook his head. He caught Elenora's gaze, and she gave him a sympathizing smile. This was still not a prank.

"Did you get anything else?" Tom asked Pierre, reviewing his notes without questioning the latest leap of faith being asked of him.

"No, that's pretty much it for now," Pierre said. "I'll email you the screen grabs from the security camera even if they're not great. And the list of names and dates we got for the postal boxes."

"Perfect! Thanks so much, Pierre, and please thank your contact for us," Tom said.

"Will do."

The line went dead, and silence filled the room. Alex stared blankly at his notepad and ran fingers through his hair.

Tom stood up and lifted his empty mug. "Anyone care for a refill?"

"I'm good, thanks." Elenora put a hand over her mug. If she got a refill, she'd be peeing until next week.

"Alex?" Tom asked, jerking his partner to attention. "Coffee?"

"Sure, why not," he replied absentmindedly. Tom nodded and left the room.

"I hope you're not mad at me for not telling you earlier," Elenora said to Alex with a note of worry.

He shook his head and asked softly, "You really see those things?"

"I do, yes."

"I should've known something wasn't right."

"How could you have known?"

"In the kitchen, the other day, when you touched the picture, there was something weird about your eyes."

"Really? How so?"

"Well, it happened so fast, I thought I'd imagined it. But it looked like your irises went paler, a very light shade of gray. Almost white. When you said you needed to see a dentist, I almost suggested you see an ophthalmologist too."

He offered her the ghost of a smile. It was on the tense side but a smile nonetheless. She'd take whatever he could offer her.

"Hmm. I wonder why that is, the color change."

"I'll pay more attention to your eyes next time you're in a trance."

"In a trance. That sounds so woo-woo." Elenora became weary, and Alex noticed.

"The whole thing does... Hey, I won't pretend to understand any of it—and to be honest, it's scaring the crap out of me—but if any of this helps catch a killer, I'll do my best to shut up and be on team woo-woo. Okay?"

"Thanks, Alex. That means a lot." She gave him a smile.

"I just saw André down the hall," Tom said, returning with two coffees. "Would you be up for trying for a sketch, Ele? We don't have to mention a specific case."

"You mean I wouldn't have to tell him I've imagined the

guy?"

"Yeah, that."

They met with the sketch artist moments later, but what sounded like a great idea became an exasperating dead-end. Past the scars and the tortured, cool blue eyes, Elenora tried hard to recall the young man's facial features she had seen so vividly in her mind. But she couldn't communicate them to André, who patiently waited for her input.

He tried coaxing details out of her from various angles, but Elenora struggled. The same memory blockage she had experienced earlier was happening again, even though she had seen the man clearly earlier in her vision at the morgue. Her memory was usually fairly good. And once again, it was as if something was deliberately clouding her mind.

But that sounded like a bad conspiracy. Could it be the hormones? A bad case of mommy brain?

She sighed. It was probably the dang hormones.

She apologized profusely to André for wasting his time, and once she, Tom, and Alex were out of earshot, she asked to see the picture of the dead plastic surgeon again, the one she had reacted to. Perhaps touching it would trigger the same vision again or some new information if they were lucky. They headed to Tom's desk for the picture.

No matter how much she tried to concentrate, the photo yielded nothing this time, except a very faint trace of memory of the previous vision in the kitchenette.

"You've given us some great information, Ele. There's no sense in driving yourself crazy," Tom said to her.

She leaned into him. She knew he was right, but she wanted to make sure not to leave any stones unturned. "Okay. I'll stop. But first, I'd like to go back to the morgue."

CHAPTER SIXTEEN

Touching the cadaver's gums again yielded nothing but irritation and cringing.

Desperate to trigger more clues, Elenora went off-script and roamed her fingers away from the dead man's mouth, to exploring the rest of his face. She felt along his jawline, and even headed down his neck, where he had allegedly been strangled.

But she got nothing.

How could she have had such clear and intricate insights mere hours earlier, and now nothing?

She let out a groan.

Tom's voice got her attention. "How about you take a break, and we investigate the crap out of what we have?"

"Yeah, don't hog the case," Alex said in jest.

Elenora headed to the sink to wash her hands, realizing how far she'd roamed her bare hands over the dead man's body. The thought sunk in, and she shuddered. *Gross.*

"I'll let you pick the toppings tonight," Tom said to her with a big grin to distract her.

"It's gonna be vegetarian, I can tell you that." She wondered if she'd ever be able to eat meat again. Especially cold cuts.

"You guys having pizza tonight? Vegetarian's right up my alley."

Vegetarian was the last thing up Alex's alley. He must have really wanted to join them. And since Elenora was still so grateful for his willingness to accept her new reality, she'd be happy to have him around for dinner.

She beamed him a smile. "You know where we live."

Elenora did a follow-up on a few case files and then read up on identity disorders for the rest of the day. There was something irregular in the killer's gaze that kept coming back to her.

In her line of work, she had encountered many deeply troubled individuals and cold-blooded killers with murderous eyes. She had seen the young Carmichael with and without a glacial look in his gaze. In some brief instances, she could swear there was a sliver of humanity in them.

A tormented vulnerability.

The difference between the two gazes was jarring.

Could the killer have dissociative identity disorder, which could explain this significant contrast?

Elenora felt a headache coming on and was delighted to see it was almost five o'clock. She was tired and her feet were swollen. Heading home and having some food would be a welcome break. She would dump her theory on Tom and Alex, and they could run with it if they saw fit.

It turned out that Tom and Alex had exciting discoveries of their own to share with her over dinner. They had also invited Pierre to join them.

"Ready to hear this, Ele?" Tom started. "Better hold on to your hat. Renaud went through the newspaper databases and found a similar murder in Kingston, a strangled truck driver missing all his teeth, back in 1965."

"And Pierre's *contact*," Alex couldn't help a hint of sarcasm shine through his enthusiasm, "found a Robin Carmichael in Kingston in 1965."

"So, a similar murder by another Carmichael?" Elenora asked.

"Looks like it," Alex said. "Which got us wondering: what if the killer from the sixties killed other people?"

"So, you dug deeper."

Tom nodded. "Much deeper, yeah. That brought us to another similar murder in Toronto. This time, another doctor but—wait for it—in 1849. And there was another murder in Montréal two years earlier, in 1847. A young businessman. Both were strangled, no teeth."

"Actually, the Montréal victim was missing a face, too," Alex added, tearing a huge bite of pizza from a slice dangling from his hand.

Elenora grimaced.

"According to census records, there were both a Rolland and a Rory Carmichael in Montréal in 1847," Pierre jumped in.

"Here. Take a look at the postal boxes owners and the murders." Tom slid a piece of paper with a handwritten list in front of Elenora.

1847(Leopold Christie, businessman), Montréal, no postal box but Rolland C. and Rory C.*

1849(Dr. Gerald Harris, physician), Toronto, Rory C.*

1849, Kingston, Robin C.

1877, Montréal, Roy C.

1902, Toronto, Rolland C.

1945, Montréal, Rory C.

1965(David Leland, truck driver), Kingston, Robin C.*

1965, Montréal, Roy C.

Now (Dr. Réginald Haché), Montréal, Roy C.—same name since 1965*

"So, four murders with similar M.O.s? And all by Carmichael men?" Elenora asked. "Like there might be a genetic component?"

"Or they have a fine copycat killing tradition passed on through generations. You know, keep the craft alive." Alex snickered.

"That sounds...troubling. Has such a thing ever happened before?" Could they be facing a World Guinness Record in the psychopathy category?

"Not that we know of," Tom said with a wide, excited grin. Alex and Pierre also had matching ones. Elenora couldn't bring herself to share their giddiness.

"What about the fact that only the first victim was missing a face?"

"The missing face suggests that one death might not belong with the others, I'll give you that," Tom answered. "Flukes are possible. But what are the odds of two murders with a very specific M.O. being totally unrelated...? Especially back then?"

"So, for now, you assume they're related, and the first murder simply had a variation for some reason. Like the original killer getting carried away as a first-timer?"

"Exactly. Maybe at first they intended to collect both teeth and faces but realized it was too much work. Either of these procedures alone must be time-consuming, and unless the victim's face meant a hell of a whole lot to them, perhaps they concluded it wasn't worth the trouble. Ultimately, they chose to make their statement with teeth. And their murderous descendants or fans stuck to that motif."

Fascinating, in a macabre way. The psyche of highly disturbed individuals coming to light during murder investigations always intrigued Elenora, especially when they suspected a serial or a copycat killer.

What made these people tick? What influenced their insane methods and made them crave for order and meaning within the immoral act of taking a life?

Elenora reached for another slice of pizza. "Well. Let's hope the latest Carmichael doesn't have kids."

Elenora stayed awake well past midnight, wondering about the mysterious Mr. Carmichael and the haunting tortured look in his eyes. There had to be a story behind those eyes, when he didn't come across as a ruthless killer with a chilling stare.

Her mind kept going back to the blade he had brought to his face. Was he self-mutilating? Had he scarred his own face?

If he hadn't caught her staring, would he have added

another gash to what she guessed had once been a handsome face? Was he inflicting himself bodily harm to numb the pain inside? To make himself pay for something?

Hurting others and himself?

Who are you, Mr. Carmichael?

CHAPTER SEVENTEEN

Montréal, present day

Leaning over his kitchen counter, Rolland stared into space, lost in thought while waiting for the kettle to boil. Before the plastic surgeon's unfortunate demise, it had been over fifty years since the last time the evil inside Rolland had taken over him.

Back in 1965. In Kingston.

Rolland was convinced that back then, his sense of outrage had triggered the ill-fated killing of the truck driver by his own unwilling hands.

It had happened late at night, after an evening shift at the hospital morgue. He was eating peacefully by himself in a diner when he overheard the two men at the table behind him one-upping each other over macho crap they had done. One of the two brutes gloated about beating up his wife to remind her who was boss.

A fit of blinding anger had taken over Rolland before his mind went blank.

The next day, in the local newspaper, he read about the offensive truck driver having been found dead in a dark alley, his teeth missing.

Rolland flexed his fingers and understood why his hands were sore. His stomach churned. He couldn't believe this shit was happening again. It had been well over a century since he'd dispatched the charlatan doctor who'd let his brother die. He had finally come to believe this kind of trouble was behind him.

Wearily, Rolland went through his coat pockets and, sure enough, felt teeth. He prayed his fingerprints wouldn't be found anywhere on or near the body. Damn modern technology. New worries to contend with.

Rolland toured a bunch of eateries to get rid of the evidence, flushing a few teeth in each toilet until he ran out of teeth. The incriminating little things would end up scattered in the river and, hopefully, they'd be impossible to trace back to him if some of them ever surfaced.

Rolland had gone home and prepared to move. He'd waited a bit before telling his employer he was moving to not raise suspicion. And he headed to Montréal instead of Toronto. He missed the place like crazy. Coming back to his hometown had proved good for his soul, and he lived in relative peace during the fifty-plus years following his return.

The previous time he'd lived here was after World War II, where he'd been active in the medical community. That had been a time when everything was paper-based and taking pictures was still a luxury few could afford. Back when he could easily remain a ghost.

This time around, shaken from the truck driver's murder and with technology making leaps and bounds, he chose to skip employment altogether so he could remain under the radar as much as possible. After centuries of being thrifty, saving the bulk of his paychecks, and stock-piling old—and highly collectible—currencies, he was independently wealthy and could afford to live a modest, uneventful life. Undetected and without provoking the darkness inside of him.

And this had worked for decades.

Until now.

Until he had met Anna at the homeless shelter where he volunteered from time to time to keep a shred of contact with humanity.

Luminous, wonderful Anna.

Rolland didn't think he'd feel so strongly for another human being ever again, let alone a woman. He had tried so hard not to let that happen. But Anna had lovingly wormed herself into his life and his heart without a warning.

He had let it happen, and now all hell was breaking loose. His own hands had taken another life. And why? Because he wanted Anna to want him? Was it his desire to be loved that had triggered the evil in him this time? Was he not allowed to be happy at least once more in his miserable, never-ending life?

Perhaps that was the goal of his nefarious inner douche, to keep Rolland guessing and despondent until the end of time.

Asshole.

The asshole nestled within his soul—assuming he himself still had a soul—was no doubt once again responsible for yet another murder. But its motive was unclear.

The shrill noise of the kettle whistling nudged Rolland back to this side of reality, enough for him to absentmindedly pour water over loose tea in a blue ceramic teapot. While the tea steeped, he decided to peel a handful of potatoes to go with the chicken already in the oven. The repetitive motion of the potato peeler brought his mind back to the questions rattling around his mind.

Why had the arrogant plastic surgeon turned up dead?

The man had infuriated Rolland, sure, but nothing like the truck driver, or the quack doctor, or Christie had. Was annoyance all it took? Was he really this ridiculously hair-triggered?

As far as he could tell, after decades of mulling it over, rage had been a common denominator in his killings so far. But this time, he hadn't raged over the man or wished for his death. And plenty of people had gotten under his skin before and had all survived.

This felt like something else. Like it had much more to do with his renewed wish to get rid of his scars than full-blown rage.

Then, if so, was the reason for his latest killing as shallow as his desire to look less scary for Anna? Had his selfish want triggered the beast?

Over the past centuries, Rolland had tried to fix his scars himself, studying various types of surgical techniques as they became available. But none had been successful. Or rather, some had shown promise at first, but then the scars had reemerged.

Eventually, he gave up and resigned himself to living with the scars. He didn't care much about the red marks aside from the fact they prevented him from blending in and made him memorable. Unless he used makeup, which he did occasionally.

Through time, he experimented with a variety of products to cover the scars. And while makeup helped conceal the deep redness of his marks, it took several coats to smooth their protrusion, which only made him look a different kind of weird when seen up close. Still, caked-up overuse of makeup proved useful for the odd trip in public, where it was good enough to fool security cameras and distracted cashiers.

But all in all, it took him a fair amount of time to look just as grotesque, so it was a good thing he seldom went out. The only time he didn't bother with this charade was when he volunteered with the homeless on the streets. He blended in just fine with this accepting and weathered clientele.

But recently, with Anna in the picture and today's promising scar revision surgery procedures, a new hope had bloomed inside Rolland, and he'd been willing to throw a lot of money at any competent plastic surgeon willing to help him on the black market. It would have to be outside of any system that could risk exposing him—and this included patient databases.

So, he'd kept his ear to the ground until he found the right man for this hush-hush job: one Dr. Réginald Haché.

Rolland cubed the peeled potatoes, careful not to cut himself as recollections of the unnerving meeting with the plastic surgeon late one night in an alley flooded his mind. They had agreed to meet in a decrepit part of town mostly populated by old factories with boarded-up doors and broken windows. Both men wanted to keep this lucrative, clandestine deal a secret.

The doctor had asked him to enter the alley from a specific point next to a defunct fur coat shop. Rolland already believed that one could never go wrong by erring on the side of paranoia and welcomed the extra precaution to make sure they weren't seen together.

The covert meeting had gone well, considering how brash the doctor had been. Rolland was sure Haché would turn down the deal. But after studying the scars with disdain, the man surprisingly accepted to do the procedure.

While the man's superior attitude rubbed Rolland the wrong way and even made him consider walking away, Rolland was in a hurry to get rid of the scars, so he bit the bullet. He agreed to having the procedure done discreetly after hours in a confidential location.

Rolland thought that, with his face improved, he might get out of the friend zone with Anna. The prospect elated him, and that was the last thing he remembered thinking as he left the alley. He suspected he blacked out right after that.

And he knew too well what that meant.

Rolland dumped the potato chunks on a baking sheet and drizzled them with olive oil. He added some salt, pepper, and fresh twigs of rosemary before sliding the sheet in the oven. A delicious aroma of roasting chicken escaped and spread through the kitchen.

He enjoyed the homey feel as he poured himself tea in a dainty teacup he'd bought at Morgan's at the turn of the previous century. He kept room in the cup for a few fingers of gin.

Obsessed with finding answers and solutions, he'd recently turned to the bottle to help numb the emotional pain and anxiety, just enough to take the edge off. Good thing he'd remembered to hit the liquor store a few days earlier. He hadn't drunk in ages, and the idea of uncorking an 1890

Château Margaux just to keep a buzz going was an additional layer of pain he didn't need.

He took a sip of his little helper, eager to head to his laptop to hit refresh on the news sites and check his security camera feeds.

Back in 2002, when the movie *Panic Room* came out, Rolland had such a room built in the basement of his home and a camera system installed outside at his front and back doors. Since then, he had the cameras upgraded to nearly invisible models, and they were linked to his laptop and cell phone to alert him if someone showed up on his doorstep.

Should the police ever come visit, this would allow him to evaluate the odds of fleeing undetected. If he could, he would escape the city on the motorbike he kept stashed in a nearby indoor parking lot and head to a small cabin he had in the Laurentians.

If there were cops at both doors, he would scurry down to the basement and hide in his secret room.

With Dr. Haché's death, he visited it recently to restock the mini fridge, recharge his e-book reader, and make sure the room was ready to welcome him.

It crossed his mind that perhaps he should head out to the cabin for a while, but that would mean going away from Anna and technology. The cabin was rustic and would make him vulnerable. A sitting duck. It was best used as a last resort.

He made a mental note to upgrade the cabin should this shitshow miraculously blow over.

Boozy tea in hand, Rolland checked the camera feeds and the various alerts on his laptop and was at once reassured and antsy that nothing new came up. He hated being kept in the dark. How long would he have to put up with the unsettling suspense of nothing happening?

The evolution of technology and scientific discoveries had been both a blessing and a curse. Rolland's spiffy surveillance system should have brought him some peace of mind and allowed him to sleep better at night, but the arrival of a little thing called DNA in forensic science in the 1980s had made him a lighter sleeper.

He just couldn't win.

Rolland took a sip of his spiked Earl Grey and moved to his living room to perch himself on the wide, well-cushioned arm of his favorite armchair by the window that afforded him an excellent view of the street below. Even though he'd lived to see the neighboring houses being built, he never tired of admiring their architecture from a long-gone era, of which he was slightly nostalgic from time to time.

His view was also convenient for keeping tabs on his neighbors and avoiding them so that they wouldn't notice he didn't age. Rolland usually left and entered his house through his backdoor to avoid being seen. He inevitably bumped into people occasionally, but he wasn't about to put in even more time fiddling with makeup to age himself just to go for a stroll.

There was only so much insanity he could handle in his life.

Luckily, in the past two decades, there had been a high turnover of residents and an influx of hipsters and young professionals who barely had time to be home.

As if to prove his point, Rolland spotted a mover's van parked a few doors down the street. He made another mental note to keep an eye on the new residents of 3827.

He took a chug of tea-flavored gin and wondered what would happen to his place if the police caught him for the murder of Dr. Haché. Would a moving van show up to empty the house of its priceless antiques when someone realized who and what he was, while he'd be left to rot in jail for eternity?

This line of thinking didn't help the sour feeling that had taken residence in his stomach since the morning after his meeting with the plastic surgeon and had been around as a tormenting reminder ever since.

Memories of the atrocious morning of Haché's death surfaced. Rolland waking up, feeling groggy and noticing his fingers were sore. Finding a handful of teeth in his pant pockets. Wondering if he should start wearing garments without receptacles...

He'd sighed. Yet again, he would have to find a good way to get rid of the bloody little things, and then he would have to pack—

Wait.

He couldn't move to another town. Not this time. If he did, he'd be leaving Anna behind.

His heart had sunk lower than ever before in his excruciatingly long life. He couldn't run this time. He couldn't just go away for a fresh start. The thought of losing Anna was too much to bear. He needed her.

What if he didn't have to leave? What if there weren't enough clues out there to lead the authorities to him?

Rolland had been racking his brain to remember and figure out if anything could tie him to the plastic surgeon's death. With the truck driver mishap in 1965, technology was far less advanced than nowadays, and it had been much easier to get away with murder.

The good old days.

Rolland scoffed at himself for even thinking that before his mind went back to rehashing his problem at hand. First and crucially, had any security cameras caught him together with the dead man?

At their meeting, he didn't think so, but he couldn't be entirely sure. After the murder, who knew how careful or sloppy his despicable puppet master had been. Though it had taken over sixty years for Leopold Christie's body to be found, so he had to give it some credit.

He grimaced at that thought, too.

Dr. Haché's body had been found at a construction site around the corner from the alley where they'd met, and Rolland assumed his amoral alter ego had been smart enough not to parade a cadaver around, and thus there was a chance that no one or any electronics had either seen or captured the deed.

Rolland combed online news sites and the internet for any new information about the crime and the victim—scrubbing his web search history afterward each time despite using a VPN connection to cover his suspect sleuthing—but he couldn't find anything other than the news of Dr. Haché's disappearance and, later, a very brief update on the body that had been found. Nothing about suspects or persons of interest.

Whatever the police knew, they weren't sharing, and that drove him crazy.

Would he have to bolt and go into hiding?

Bolting was the last thing he wanted to do. But what

other choice would he have if the police found clues that led them to him?

Rolland brought the cup to his lips and found it empty. Why was his life like this? He got up and headed to the kitchen for a refill.

He couldn't help fantasizing and imagining scenarios where he'd have his life back, free of crushing murder-related worries, and where he'd no longer look so damn scary and repulsive. What had he done that was so terrible to deserve such a cruel fate?

And why could no number of attempts at redeeming himself make any difference? Why couldn't he free himself of the evil gripping him inside?

If only there was something he could do to rid himself of that nasty, soul-sucking abscess.

***

Rolland went to bed with a fever that night.

And then a brilliant idea shone through his advanced state of delirium. He would find someone to help him get rid of the festering asshole within him, and he'd be free, once and for all, to take charge of his fate.

Surely he could find an expert to address his issue on the internet.

At the very least, he hadn't tried an exorcism in decades. Perhaps there were new modern techniques. If he got rid of what damaged him on the inside—the obvious barrier to any progress—he could then proceed with working on the damage on the outside.

And even better, he could stop living like he was always one hair away from setting off a goddamn apocalypse.

And best of all: he wouldn't have to leave town. He could be with Anna.

This was a great plan.

This was a foolproof plan.

An evil-proof plan.

CHAPTER EIGHTEEN

Elenora woke up to the sound of Tom getting dressed behind her on the other side of the bed. The room was still dark. She peeked at the alarm clock on her nightstand. It was barely six a.m.

"Aren't you off today?" she mumbled, half-asleep.

It was Saturday, and like Elenora, Tom usually had weekends off, unless a pressing case demanded overtime. While catching the plastic surgeon's killer was a priority, Tom had done what he could with the meager clues they had so far, and a weekend team was scouring through every database for every R. Carmichael in the city, the province, and beyond. So technically, Tom could take a break. But knowing him, he wanted to catch the guy as soon as possible for the population's safety and his very pregnant wife's sanity.

"I'm just gonna go touch base."

"I've heard those words before. That means I'll be eating dinner with Pierre," she teased him.

"I thought you liked Pierre," he teased back and kissed

her. "I'll try very hard to be back well before dinner, 'kay? Call me if there's anything."

She waved him away and drifted back to sleep. Soon, she found herself floating down a dark corridor. She noticed a light ahead that soon materialized as a cozy fire in a fireplace.

The dancing flames cast a warm and lovely glow around a pretty room, allowing Elenora to take in her surroundings. Judging by the decor, furniture, and heavily floral wallpaper, the room was stuck in the past.

Lying down on a couch—upholstered in another loud floral pattern—was an elderly woman. Her long silver hair looked messy with fever, and her face was ashen and waxy. Beads of sweat pearled across her forehead.

Elenora approached the woman and sensed overwhelming physical pain but also, beyond the pain, a feeling of peace and gratitude. Kneeling by the woman, she opened her mouth to ask her if she needed help, but as before, no sound came out of her. She tried to touch the woman's arm to get her attention, but this time, despite her will to touch, her fingers went through the stranger's arm.

Elenora could only observe.

She felt a presence next to her. A manly silhouette appeared and kneeled beside her. He was shrouded in darkness, and she couldn't get a good look at him. But she saw his hands reach for the dying woman. They landed on either side of her face, cradling her jawline, before traveling down her neck.

Was he about to kill her?

A vague sense of unease pooled in Elenora's gut, but it vanished before it took hold.

The man took the woman's hands into his own. The

woman's eyes fluttered open, struggling to look at the man. He leaned toward her and kissed her forehead.

She struggled but managed to look at him for a few heartbeats—her gaze filled with adoration—before the light of consciousness dimmed and left her eyes.

The man brushed fingers along her face and gently closed her eyes. His shoulders shook with quiet sobs. His facial traits appeared, and Elenora recognized him.

Mr. Carmichael.

A tear welled at the corner of his eye and fell down his face along one of his scars. Elenora felt the man's pain tearing him inside but also a surprising amount of love.

"You will always be in my heart, dearest Delphine," he whispered.

Elenora woke up, disoriented. It took her a moment to realize she was crying.

Why was she crying?

She felt a deep sorrow as the dream reappeared in her mind. Not in a violent way like the previous, horrifying premonitions. Bittersweet, like there was a tenderness about the vision amidst regret.

Was it simply a dream? A good, old-fashioned dream?

Or was her mind extrapolating Mr. Carmichael's humanity by making up a scenario, wishing to find a sliver of good inside a monster?

Or maybe it was a different kind of premonition. But if so, had this woman's death already happened, or was it about to?

Elenora splashed cold water on her face to bring clarity to her fuzzy mind. If it was a premonition, what did it mean? The overall feeling of love and serenity didn't suggest murder. The woman seemed to die in a loving circumstance. Unless Carmichael had poisoned her, which was a possibility. But Elenora had felt no animosity at all. Could it have been a mercy killing?

And who was this woman? His grandmother, perhaps?

Tom came back home an hour later and found her drinking tea in the living room, still pondering the dream.

She told him about it, and he texted Renaud, asking him to look for a Delphine Carmichael just as Elenora's phone rang. It was Pierre, asking if she and Tom were home. He'd be dropping by soon with a surprise.

The doorbell chimed five minutes later. Tom got the door, and Pierre went straight to Elenora to hug her.

"You look well," he said to her.

"I actually got some sleep, if you can believe it. It's amazing how big a difference a bit of sleep can make."

"Your trip to the morgue worked wonders?" Pierre teased.

Elenora made a sour face at the thought before turning her attention to Tom, who was leading a young woman with a long mane of auburn hair into the room. She seemed confident and easygoing.

"Elenora, I'd like you to meet my good friend Serena," Pierre said.

His "good friend?" Was that code for "love interest?" Elenora couldn't remember the last time Pierre had made time for romance, but the woman looked quite young for him. In her late twenties, she'd guess. Several decades younger than the retired detective. Being a sugar daddy wasn't usually his thing, not that she wanted to judge.

"Elenora, it's such an honor to meet you at last. Pierre told me so much about you." Serena sized Elenora up appreciatively.

"Nice to meet you too, Serena," Elenora replied, intrigued.

The visitor's gaze dropped to Elenora's stomach, and she waved at it. "Hey, girl! High five?" She brought a hand up close to Elenora's baby bump.

Elenora's surprise at the young woman's odd greeting deepened as she felt Aubrey move in response and saw a tiny limb poke underneath the surface of her stretching belly.

"Good enough, little miss," Serena acknowledged the baby's response. "Foot waves are adorable and way underrated."

Elenora glanced between Serena and Pierre, speechless. Tom looked just as baffled.

"Serena is an original and independent spirit," Pierre declared without hiding his amusement.

"That's a Pierre euphemism for excusing my cuckoo behavior. Not the first time or the last. We do go way back."

"How *way back*?" Elenora couldn't help asking.

As if reading her mind, Serena said, "Let's just say that I'm much older than I look."

Pierre snorted. "Yes. Serena is not what she seems... On that topic, please keep her visit quiet. She has accepted to help us, but her help is a little...above my 'pay grade,' if I can put it that way."

Tom narrowed his eyes at Pierre, trying to catch the full meaning of his drift. "Of course," he said, unsure. "Can I offer you something to drink, Serena? Coffee? There's a fresh pot."

"Coffee would be great. Black. Thanks."

"One black coffee coming up. Have a seat," Tom said, making a sweeping motion at the couch and armchairs in the living room. "Pierre? Coffee?"

"Smells good. Yes, please."

"So, Serena, you are here to help?" Elenora said.

"Yes. To help you get an image of our mystery man on paper," Pierre said, sitting in an armchair while Elenora and Serena both chose the couch.

"She's a sketch artist? But Pierre, I told you it didn't work with André, no matter how hard I tried," Elenora admonished Pierre before turning to the young woman with a sheepish look. "I'm so sorry, but we're wasting your time. I can't seem able to remember his face enough."

Serena and Pierre both looked undeterred.

"Nora... Like you, Serena has special skills. It's worth a try."

"Based on what Pierre told me, it sounds like something's interfering with your memory, like casting a veil over it." Serena reached for her steel blue messenger bag and retrieved an electronic tablet and a stylus pen. "I'd like to try something. May I?" she asked, pointing at Elenora's hand.

Uncertain, Elenora gave the young woman her hand.

Tom came back with two steaming mugs and put them down on the coffee table before settling in an armchair near his wife. His eyes landed on Serena holding her hand.

"Close your eyes," Serena said to Elenora.

"You want me to think about him?" Elenora asked.

"You don't need to think about him." Serena's voice was

warm and inviting. "Actually, picture a black square. Darkness. Let me guide your mind."

Elenora obeyed. She felt a tingle in her hand, like a mild electrical current going from Serena's hand to her own. The tingling made its way up her arm, a feather-light tickling like a string of marching ants crawling over her skin.

She felt it go all the way up to the back of her neck, penetrating her head and spreading around her skull. The feeling wasn't unpleasant, just unexpected.

Slowly, from the canvas of darkness in her mind, a part of an earlier vision emerged: the young man looking at himself in the mirror with the scalpel near his face, his eyes catching Elenora's.

She heard a soft gasp from Serena, and the mental image began to move. The man turned, briefly offering his tortured look. His face hardened, and coldness filled his eyes. He started toward Elenora, scalpel raised and menacing.

Like before, Elenora couldn't help bracing herself. She felt a hand squeeze, and her mind went blank.

"Got it!" Serena let go of Elenora's hand, the sudden movement prompting her to open her eyes.

The young woman picked up her stylus and made a move to draw on her tablet, but then she stopped and lowered the pen. "You know what? I won't even pretend. Pierre said you're already way down the rabbit hole. So, let's skip the theatrics."

She turned her tablet around to show Elenora, Tom, and Pierre what was on it: the very images Elenora had seen in her mind, playing like a video, from beginning to end.

Tom's face paled with horror and disbelief as the young

man's expression became more threatening. "This is what you've been seeing, Ele?"

Stunned, Elenora took a moment to nod.

He stood in front of her and pulled her up to him in a fierce hug. "I'm so sorry. I didn't think it was...this terrifying."

"I'm all right, Tom. I'm getting used to it."

"I know I've said this before, Nora, but what you see truly is mind-blowing," Pierre said, his eyes still on the tablet. "All of this is outstanding. How did you do that, Serena? That's one heck of a trick."

"Yes, how did you do that?" Elenora freed herself from Tom's embrace to face Serena with interest. The magnitude of what had just happened hit her, and her knees weakened. She fell back on the couch.

"What Pierre meant to ask is 'How did *we* do that?'" Serena clarified. She, too, looked impressed by what was on her tablet. "To be honest, I was just hoping to get a few details from your mind. I never expected such a clear picture, let alone a full clip. This is mind-blowing, even to me. You are powerful, Elenora. That much I can tell."

"But how did you do that, concretely?" Tom had not yet recovered from his shock, either. "Mind reading? Are you a mind reader?"

"Kind of. But not entirely. Like, I can't just read people's minds. In this case, there was a connection between Elenora and me that allowed me to capture very specific images. I wish I had a more factual answer about the mechanics of it."

"Hmm." Tom looked away, pondering.

Elenora guessed he was trying to calm himself with answers. Her brain, too, was swirling with questions, struggling to explain how Serena had extricated the images out of her. She had mixed feelings about the young woman's extraordinary ability and imagined this was how Tom and Alex must have felt when they learned of her own insights.

Tom pointed at the tablet. "So, this is our guy?"

"Yes. It would appear so," Serena confirmed.

"Did you get anything else? Like a location on him?" Pierre asked.

"No. This is all I got."

"And that's one hell of a start," Pierre pointed out supportively.

"It is. I'll send the images to my colleague, see if she can read more into it." Serena's fingers danced around the screen of her tablet.

"Can I do the same?" Tom asked before frowning. "Well, I understand a video like this would raise too many questions among my colleagues, but perhaps I could get a still image, so they know who to look for?"

Serena weighed her words. "I guess a still image for your immediate colleagues would be okay if they keep it internal. But I would strongly warn against broadcasting a picture of this man at this moment."

"We don't want to spook him?"

"That, and possibly more. It's early for me to reach this conclusion, but if he's ever located, it might be best if neither your colleagues nor civilians approach him, let alone confront him."

"Okay, then, what do we do?"

"If you find him, my colleagues and I will take it from there," Serena said matter-of-factly.

Tom's frown deepened. "I understand this man is danger-ous, but—"

"Allow me to explain, detective. Pierre told me you retraced three other similar murders and theorized it might be a copycat. Correct?"

"Correct."

"And with Elenora seeing the four Carmichael names when she read Dr. Haché's body, you think there might be several generations of Carmichaels involved, with recycled first names?"

"Also correct."

"It might even have occurred to you that a psychopathic gene could've been passed down from one generation to the next, and different Carmichael men committing each killing?"

"Indeed."

"That's a dead end."

Tom's eyes darted to Elenora and then to Pierre, perhaps to see if they, too, were trying to follow Serena's bold assertion.

"I admit the intergenerational gene theory is far-fetched, but why should we discard it right off the bat?" Tom asked.

Serena took a moment before answering, as if enjoying the anticipation she was building.

"Because I know for a fact that this man—" She held her tablet showing a clear still of the killer from Elenora's mind, "—is Rolland Carmichael, and I think he committed all the murders that we know of so far."

Tom and Elenora gave Serena matching stunned looks. Pierre seemed just as stunned as them, but an amused smile appeared at the corner of his lips.

"All right, Serena," Tom said. "I'll ignore the fact that the suspect would have to be well over a hundred years old, and

I'll play. What makes you think that?" Past his obvious skepticism, Tom looked genuinely intrigued to hear Serena's explanation.

"Because I know Rolland Carmichael personally, and I suspect the devil has something to do with all of this."

CHAPTER NINETEEN

Elenora, Tom, and Pierre stared at Serena with dropped jaws.

"You didn't see that one coming, did you, Pierre?" Serena let out a giggle, reinforcing her college schoolgirl appearance.

Pierre grinned widely and shook his head like this was the best, most unbelievable thing he'd ever heard. "I sure didn't." His smile vanished. "D'you think it's like what happened to Tim?"

Elenora gave Pierre a *who-are-you?* look. "Who's Tim?"

"An old childhood friend of mine. I'll tell you all about him on the next rainy day," he replied before turning back to Serena to hear her answer.

"I don't know yet if it's a possession or some kind of curse or some other phenomenon. But hopefully, we'll find out soon."

Tom reached for his notepad and a pen from his pants pocket and asked her in a professional tone, "Okay, so, what's your theory? And how do you know this guy?"

"All right. Deeper down the rabbit hole we go. The last time I saw Rolland Carmichael was in 1847."

"1847? As in one, eight, four, seven?"

"That's right. 1847. A great year for Emily Brontë and typhus."

Tom scribbled something in his notepad and kept his eyes on the page. Elenora could tell he was wondering if Serena was messing with him and was patiently waiting to see where this was heading.

Serena kept a calm and serious countenance, giving no indication that she was messing with them. "I might as well address the elephant in the room," she said. "I can do much more than the occasional mind-reading trick. Essentially, I'm a witch." She let that outrageous bit of information sink in. "And I don't mean that as a euphemism for *bitch*," she added.

Elenora took a moment to react. At first, she thought Serena was joking, but her deadpan look, combined with the serious expression on Pierre's face, convinced her it was no joke.

And then Serena's words echoed in Elenora's mind and she grasped their meaning. She was a witch.

Of course she was a witch.

It was the only way to explain how she had captured her thoughts so well and effortlessly.

This woman sitting next to her was a witch. Elenora herself might be some kind of psychic. And their prime suspect might be immortal and possessed.

Had the world entered an alternate reality?

Elenora was barely getting used to the undeniable fact there was something abnormal about her, and now she was in the presence of someone claiming to be a witch, who also claimed to have met their murder suspect nearly two centuries ago...

She felt faint and leaned her head back against the couch, closing her eyes, willing for the unpleasant feeling of dizziness to stop.

"I'll get you some water," Tom murmured, touching her arm before he stood up and headed to the kitchen.

"Nora?" Pierre said softly to get her attention.

"Hmm?"

"I know it's a lot to take in, but there's no need to be anxious about Serena. I've known her for a long time, and I've seen firsthand the fantastic work and all the good that she does."

Elenora opened her eyes to look at him.

"And it's not like she goes around throwing spells at people," he added with a smirk.

Elenora accepted the glass of water from Tom and focused on the coldness of the glass to anchor herself to reality. Or whatever was left of it.

Tom sunk into the sofa next to her. He slipped an arm around her waist and held her. "How is any of this possible?" he asked, his keen gaze on Serena.

"You mean, how is it possible that you can believe that your wife has supernatural abilities—which she indeed does—but can't conceive that someone else might have some too?" Serena answered dryly. She did have him there.

Tom groaned and scrubbed a hand over his face.

Elenora murmured to Serena. "Pierre's right. It's a lot to take in."

"I know. Especially with everything that's happened to you recently," Serena sympathized. "And I'm not unveiling myself to you both for shock value. Now that you are pursuing Rolland Carmichael, you will encounter far scarier truths. You might as well get the disbelief out of your systems now."

Tom put his professional façade back on. "Thank you for putting your trust in us." He cleared his throat before adding, "May I ask how you knew the suspect nearly two hundred years ago when you seem way too young for that?"

"You mean this?" Serena ran a hand up and down in front of herself regarding her youthful appearance.

Tom nodded. "You're what? In your twenties?"

Pierre answered for her. "There's vampire blood in her lineage. And while she's not immortal, she ages very slowly."

"So, you've been in your twenties for a long time?" Elenora's curiosity took over.

"Not quite. My current appearance is just a glamor. I'm kind of middle-aged now, but I find that making myself look younger makes me seem less threatening. And people have lower expectations of me. It comes in handy."

To prove her point, she morphed into a more mature woman. Her auburn hair had strands of silver, and she was just as strikingly beautiful. Her spunky attitude was intact too, and she seemed even more assured than before. A woman not to be messed with.

"I think it suits you either way, but I see what you mean," Elenora said with awe.

"There's also a practicality to it." Serena morphed back to her younger self. "I've recently begun a new cycle. New last name, new IDs, a new place smack downtown—I love that condo! And right now, my neighbors think I'm a kid in her twenties, and they'll see me age for decades or for as long as I want without them questioning who I am."

"So, you stay like this all the time?"

"Most of the time. There are some rare occasions when it's convenient to adapt my physique to a different look."

"Like when you helped bust that child trafficking ring," Pierre volunteered.

"Exactly."

The thought of someone busting a child trafficking ring spoke to Elenora. She could see some of the unique possibilities Serena's abilities offered and understood better what Pierre meant when he said she did a lot of good. Centuries-worth of knowledge and experience in the unsuspected body of a child was a prime example. As far as undercover work was concerned, this was really impressive.

But as fascinating as Serena's unusual situation was, there must have been some negative aspects to living forever.

"What about family? Are they still around or are you all alone?" Elenora couldn't help asking.

Serena seemed touched that Elenora would even think to ask this. "My twin sister's alive and well. And we're pretty close. Our parents died in the 1950s. So, that's old news. I have a few cousins here and there. We keep in touch on social media. And..." Her words trailed off, as if she was hesitant to say more.

"You have me," Pierre said, teasing.

Serena let out a little laugh. "I sure do, and you're the best." The friendship and connection between the two of them were palpable, even though the fake age difference on the outside was still jarring.

"Do all of your friends know about your abilities?" Elenora asked.

"I might be an extrovert, but I'm pretty selective when it comes to friendship. But yes, my other few friends know."

"So..." Tom said, emerging from a thoughtful silence. "If I understand correctly, Rolland Carmichael somehow doesn't age—can't wrap my brain around that one just yet. D'you think he did cycles like you to be invisible? Assuming different Carmichael identities and moving around? Or are there actual relatives involved in the murders?"

"I really think it's just him. He only had one brother —Rory."

Tom flipped through his notebook. "The same year and location as the murder of the first doctor."

"Indeed. And probably related."

"Does he have vampire blood like you? Is that how he's still around?" Pierre asked.

"Not that I know of. In the 1840s, as far as I know, he was human through and through. And other than his natural magnetic charm, I didn't pick up on any particular gift. But something must have happened to him since then to explain why he's popping up in Elenora's mind in connection to a murder that just happened."

"Did he have those facial scars back then? Was he prone to self-mutilation?" Elenora asked.

"He didn't have the scars, no, and I don't think he had the temperament to mutilate himself. I remember him as an easygoing and lovable guy. One hell of a looker, too. It's a shame what happened to him."

"You mean him turning murderous?" Tom asked.

"That, of course, but also the fact he got beaten up by a

bunch of thugs and left for dead. Possibly where he got the scars and what triggered all this. My sister and I were in New York when the beating occurred, but we were still in touch with our cousin Millicent and her friend Delphine and—"

"Delphine?" Elenora perked up. "Was she his grandmother?"

Serena frowned. "No, she was a young woman Rolland seemed to fancy. What makes you ask that?"

"I saw a woman named Delphine who seemed close to Rolland, but she was much older. It must've been another Delphine."

"What did you see?" Serena asked, intrigued.

"I saw her die, and Rolland was by her side."

"Did he kill her?" Pierre asked.

"Not explicitly, and I don't think so. He seemed to have a great deal of affection for her."

Elenora offered her hand to Serena. "Would you do that trick again and see what I saw?"

"That's a marvelous idea," Serena replied, reaching for her tablet.

"Are you sure?" Tom's eyes were full of apprehension.

Elenora put her other hand on his knee. "Yes, dear. There's nothing to fear from this one."

Once again, the two women held hands. Elenora closed her eyes and relaxed her mind, focusing on the color black. She felt the tingles go up her arm, and before she knew it, she was transported in the pretty living room, just as before, witnessing once more the touching scene of Delphine's passing. She felt Rolland's agony. His feelings were unmistakable.

When she returned to reality, she felt a tear on one of her cheeks. Serena's eyes were glassy, too.

"Did you feel that?" the witch asked Elenora, looking befuddled.

"Yes."

"It's astounding that you can feel a vision so clearly."

Elenora nodded. Serena was right. It was rather astounding.

"But much less so when the vision is evil and terrifying," Tom added, rubbing Elenora's back.

"Of course." Serena gave her a sympathetic smile.

"Did it capture...?" Pierre was sitting at the edge of his seat. Serena checked, and Elenora's vision had once again miraculously translated into pixels. They watched the clip. The emotions were palpable.

"It's the Delphine I knew, and it looks like he truly did love her. We wondered if it was a crime of passion," Serena said.

"What do you mean? You think he *did* kill her?" Tom said, confused.

"Not her. The oldest similar crime you found? Leopold Christie? He was Delphine's fiancé. A proper asshole, if you ask me, and she didn't want him—it was an arrangement."

She shuddered. "You couldn't pay me enough to put up with that backward shit ever again. Anyway, we suspected Leopold was the one responsible for the savage assault on Rolland, and that Rolland had retaliated in kind."

"So, we have a motive for the first crime. What about the other ones? The Toronto doctor two years later?" Tom updated his notes, eager for more. "Could he have been a rival? And the truck driver in Kingston? All crimes of passion?"

Serena shook her head. "No idea."

"But then we have our plastic surgeon, who was single and gay." Pierre pointed out. "Unless Carmichael is bi?"

"Let's not discount that possibility. But the plastic surgeon's death might have to do with his scars. Perhaps he wanted them taken care of, but things went wrong?" Tom said. "Elenora thinks Carmichael might have been a disgruntled client of Haché's after a botched surgery."

Serena's phone chimed with an incoming message. "Speaking of the scars..." She turned to Elenora. "I sent your first vision of Rolland to my sister, and she was able to find this, thanks to the scars pattern."

"She already found something?" Tom glanced at his watch and shook his head with incredulity.

"Claire-Lune's fast," Pierre said.

"And let's be honest, she also has tools and abilities that give her an edge," Serena added to soothe Tom's dismay.

Everyone leaned in to see a black-and-white picture on Serena's phone.

"She says it was taken at the Royal Elizabeth Hospital shortly after the Second World War."

The picture showed a handful of fresh-faced doctors in white coats, posing in front of two rows of patients lying in hospital beds.

"This is Rolland, right here." The man she pointed to looked unquestionably like Rolland, his scars in clear view.

"He became a doctor?" Tom asked, incredulous.

"Possibly a surgeon. This unit had burn victims and other poor men who came back mangled from the front."

Tom rubbed his temples. "So, our guy is part devil, part saint. He might have an interest in surgery past his own cosmetic issues. This might affect his latest motive. And he might have killed that other doctor in Toronto back in 18—" He scanned his notes. "1849. A medical rivalry perhaps? And then there's the truck driver from the 1960s. I don't suppose he also took up an interest in trucking?" Tom's voice was part serious, part sarcasm. He asked Serena, "I should have asked this earlier, but, with your powers, is there any way to just locate the guy?"

Serena smiled. "As you can imagine, we've already tried that."

"Yeah, of course. I didn't mean to sound offensive."

"No offense taken. Under normal circumstances, we might've been able to find him. But in this case, whatever is ailing him seems to run interference. It's cloaking him, some-how. And God knows what else it can do." Serena's words lingered in the air, and she stood up. "It's been lovely meeting you two, but I'm afraid I must get going."

Elenora, Tom, and Pierre all stood up as well.

"You've been very helpful, and we appreciate your help immensely," Tom said.

"My help was possible thanks to Elenora's spectacular findings and abilities." She smiled at Elenora.

"Now we just need to process this baffling information and make sense of it. Would you object to me bringing my partner Alex up to speed?" Tom asked.

Serena glanced at Pierre.

"Alex is a trustworthy skeptic," Pierre said.

"Ooh! My favorite!" Serena said with a hint of an eye roll. She turned to Tom. "That's all right, then. And good luck with your skeptic."

"Any advice for us, other than not to engage with Carmichael?" Tom asked.

"Keep digging like you have been. Let's keep each other informed. We'll find a way to get him." Serena paused, debating with herself. "Not to freak you out, but I suspect he's extremely volatile. Much like an innocent bystander strapped with a terrorist's bomb. He's not in control. If you encounter him, please call me right away, and do not confront him. I can't stress this enough."

Tom and Pierre nodded, understanding the gravity of the situation.

Elenora's mind was stuck on the picture Serena had painted of Rolland, comparing him to the hostage of a terrorist. Like he was wearing a metaphorical bomb and wasn't in charge. Was he aware of this? And if so, was he living in constant terror of it going off?

"What will happen when we get him?" The concern in Elenora's voice stemmed as much from the fear of the situation as from her finding herself caring about the man's fate.

"When we get him...we'll find a way to deal with him." Serena sucked in a sharp breath. "And pray for the best."

"That bodes well," Tom muttered.

"Will he need to be killed?" Elenora asked, dreading the answer.

"Hopefully not. But we don't know how much of *him* is left."

Judging from Serena's grimace, she must have thought the odds were not in Rolland's favor. Elenora knew that not everyone was redeemable, but it still bothered her they might not be able to give this man a fair chance. "He seemed to love Delphine. Perhaps there's enough of him left."

"I don't doubt he loved her. But that was a long time ago. People change. Especially when they're possessed."

"So, you *do* think he's possessed..." Pierre said.

"Odds are good." She hugged him before heading to the front door.

Elenora accompanied her, wishing for more time to talk with her. She had so many questions.

The most pressing one escaped from her lips as Serena zipped up her trendy high-heeled boots. "Will my new abilities affect my baby?"

The witch considered the question. "I don't know enough about your case to know for sure, but I can tell you that witches have healthy babies all the time."

Elenora felt a torrent of relief. Her little Aubrey might be safe. While she had tried not to dwell on it, the question had been killing her slowly. If anything were to happen to her little girl because of her, she didn't think she could ever forgive herself.

"Is there anything I can do to control the visions?" Elenora asked softly.

"You mean stop having them?" The corner of Serena's lips quirked. She was good.

"Yeah," Elenora admitted.

"Well... I don't have a definite answer for that either. Dreams seem to be the hardest to control. But with visions when you're awake, if you identify the triggers—and don't hang out in morgues—that might help." She said this tongue-in-cheek and got a smile from Elenora.

"Yeah. The morgue part shouldn't be too difficult."

Serena finished buttoning her long black coat and stepped outside. She went down a few steps before stopping. "Hang in there, okay? I'll try to help you find answers, but I can't promise anything. Just know that you are not alone."

"Thanks."

Elenora waved to the woman as she headed to her car and returned inside, where she found Tom and Pierre looking grim.

"Alex called. A woman and her young daughter have just been reported missing," Tom said.

"Is she a plastic surgeon?" Elenora asked, her heart skipping a beat.

"No."

"Then it might not be Rolland." She couldn't help being hopeful. If only they could find him before he committed any more crimes.

"It might not be him. But the missing woman is the owner of a witchcraft store."

CHAPTER TWENTY

Rolland woke up to a bizarre whisper that sounded like a little voice asking for breakfast.

Damn fever.

He touched his forehead to gauge his medical state. His skin seemed to be back to a normal temperature now.

He heard the voice again—clearly, he was not dreaming, fever or not. The voice came from behind him. He rolled over and found himself nose to nose with a wide-eyed four-year-old girl.

"Hi, mister. I'm hungry."

Even though she spoke plain English, her words and presence took a while to register for Rolland.

His mind raced. He vaguely remembered a crazy dream in which he had found on the internet a woman claiming to be a jack-of-all-trades in the occult department. He had a fuzzy recollection of a car ride in the night. And of carrying a sleeping child in his arms.

Huh...

"Say, cutie, what does your mommy do?" Rolland asked in his softest voice.

"She's a witch."

Rolland stiffened.

The girl went on. "And she sells key chains with black kitties. I like those a lot."

Rolland rolled onto his back to keep his distraught expression away from the child—freaking her out didn't seem like a good idea.

He took a few deep breaths and rolled back toward her. "What do you like to eat for breakfast?" he asked, trying to sound cheerful and friendly while knowing that whatever she replied, he probably didn't have in his kitchen.

He was itching to rush to his panic room to see if the self-proclaimed witch was held captive down there. Though if she truly were a witch, wouldn't she have freed herself and her daughter by now?

The kid was here... He could only hope he had sequestered the woman and not dispatched her. He couldn't wait to get an answer.

But first, he had to attend to this pint-sized problem standing in front of him.

"Toast is fine." She shrugged. "Or whatever you have."

Toast he could do, and this felt like a lucky break.

"I'm Camelia. What's your name?"

"I'm Roll—" he caught himself. "Rolly." He cringed at himself on the inside.

"Thank you for giving me Sharky."

Who the hell was Sharky?

"Who's Sharky?"

"The plush you gave me, silly," she said with enthusiastic exasperation.

"Right."

Camelia ran out of the room like the place was on fire. Rolland shot out of bed, hurrying to put on his pajama bottoms and a robe.

He didn't recall giving her a plush and was curious to see what the kid would produce. She came back in as fast as she'd left, holding a small stuffed shark, a stuffed shark Anna had given him at a Christmas gift exchange. His stomach dropped at the thought of having to part with a present from Anna.

"This is Sharky," she declared. "Do you like his name?"

Rolland ran a hand over his face. He couldn't get upset at the kid for giving her the stuffed shark, and he couldn't take it back, either.

"That sounds fitting." He struggled to keep his voice normal, free of strangled notes. "All right, let's bring Sharky downstairs. How about you watch cartoons while I make you breakfast?" He didn't recall ever faking this level of enthusiasm before in his life.

She followed him down the stairs like a puppy. He worked on convincing himself that she deserved Sharky and, as a grown-ass adult, he should get over it. And himself.

"Are you gonna bring Mommy some toast?" the little one asked. Why this kid—without her mother present, no less—wasn't traumatized at the sight of a scary-looking stranger was beyond him.

"You think Mommy would like some toast?"

"Yes."

"Okay. I'll get Mommy some toast too."

The kid obediently sat in front of Rolland's wall-mounted TV in his living room with the stuffed shark. He made toast as fast as possible, hoping food would keep her busy while he snuck down the stairs. But then he remembered kids could choke on food and he should be around while she ate to prevent any complications from this already complicated situation.

It took her a good fifteen minutes—who needed fifteen minutes to eat a piece of toast!?—during most of which Rolland groaned internally despite busying himself at his computer. His fingers fidgeted against the keyboard while waiting for updates. Several local news searches for a woman and daughter abduction produced nothing—thank God! And the live feeds of his security cameras also reported nothing but dead calm.

Earlier footage showed him bringing in a sleeping Camelia, and then her unconscious, blindfolded mother, but he didn't bring the woman back out. There was hope that she was still alive in the panic room, Rolland told himself as he deleted the incriminating clip from his hard drive.

Rolland looked at the kid. She was finally done eating, her empty plate balancing in her lap, and still engrossed in the cartoons.

Rolland slipped to the basement stairs and headed down, both heart and head pounding. The headache pills he had taken hadn't yet kicked in, but the suspense of what he would find down there was killing him even more than his throbbing headache.

CHAPTER TWENTY-ONE

Elenora had expected the apartment of Danika Tremblay, the missing witchcraft store owner, to have heavy drapes, a crystal ball, the mysterious vibe of a tea leaf reading room, and a corner devoted to herbalism. She got mostly the opposite.

The two-bedroom apartment was sparse and bright, had Ikea furniture, and suggested nothing remotely occult. The only plant in sight was a miniature cactus agonizing on the windowsill above the kitchen sink.

Moments after hearing of the woman's disappearance, she and Tom had met Alex at a nearby coffee shop to tell him about Serena's visit and show him the incredible video images she and Serena had produced of Rolland Carmichael. They figured this latest bomb would go over better in person.

The jury was still out on the impact.

Once again, Alex took everything in without interrupting, but he didn't hide his growing bewilderment. When they left the coffee shop to head to Danika Tremblay's apartment, he was still in shock. His solitary car ride to the missing woman's apartment must have given him enough time to chill, as he seemed less freaked out when he arrived.

The trio had come to the apartment on a hunch to look for signs that Rolland Carmichael might be involved. Since the woman's young daughter was also missing, they reasoned that if a kidnapping had taken place, the woman's home was a more likely place of abduction than her store, so it made sense to start there.

"Hey, Elenora. Shouldn't you be at home resting?" Detective François Lagacé, the missing persons lead investigator, asked her. He and his partner were on their way out.

"We were having lunch nearby when I got the call," Tom fibbed to nip the discussion in the bud.

Elenora appreciated his quick thinking. She was still rattled from her encounter with Serena, and left to her own devices, she might have unwittingly blurted out an inconvenient truth to their unsuspecting colleague. How much of her body language was already giving her away?

It was hard to not think about everything she'd heard and seen earlier in her living room. And while Tom concealed his turmoil well, she could still tell that he, too, was struggling to appear unaffected.

The morning's revelations had left Elenora feeling conflicted: hopeful that she might now get some help and answers regarding her new situation, but she found Serena's cautious attitude about approaching Rolland unsettling. The witch's assumption that he was an extremely dangerous man brought chills down Elenora's spine and sorrow to her soul. If an experienced, powerful, and knowledgeable woman like Serena had reservations, where did that put her, Tom, and Alex? And what could they possibly do to stop the guy?

Yet, here she was, trying to do her part and waddling around the place of this newly missing woman, brushing her thinly gloved hands—a precaution making things harder—over every surface, looking for clues to help stop the unstoppable.

Tom had suggested she stayed home to rest and call her if it looked like Rolland had been there, but she felt she had to come. Hearing that a little girl was missing hit close to home for Elenora. If there was a chance she could pick up anything on the disappearance of the mother and daughter, whether tied to Rolland or anyone else, she had to make the effort. She needed to do this, and besides, she would've gone crazy staying home by herself.

There was also a part of her that was curious to know if the shop owner had any genuine connections to the occult. The prospect of meeting a second witch was alluring.

Lastly, her own intuition told her that Rolland had something to do with this, and who knew what he would do this time. Would he kill both mother and daughter? Would he dare murder a child?

He had to be stopped. There was no doubt about that, but the actions needed to stop him worried her. If Serena was right and the man was acting under a foreign influence within him, they could be facing a perpetrator and a victim rolled into one. Would they be able to punish the murderer without hurting the innocent?

If they had to exorcise him or take whatever drastic measure to rid him of evil, would he perish alongside his monster? Or did he have a chance of surviving?

If he did survive, how damaged would he be?

From what Elenora gathered so far, Rolland had been

around and possibly dead inside for over a century. She knew that the human soul was resilient and could survive a long time in the dark. Sometimes the light inside someone almost vanished from harsh conditions but then rekindled and shone bright again. Brighter, even. And it was so beautiful when that happened. But sometimes, the light struggled for so long it eventually had no other option but to die.

Elenora thought of the glimpse of humanity she'd seen in Rolland's eyes and suspected there was still light within him, a will for his soul to survive. Perhaps he could be saved.

But how could she help save such a deeply damaged man, afflicted with supernatural darkness?

She wasn't trained for this.

"I know what I'm getting you for Christmas."

Alex's gravelly voice yanked Elenora away from her musings, and her eyes found him. He was showing her a deck of tarot cards he'd found in the top drawer of a credenza. He was trying to make her smile, though she could also tell he was still uncomfortable and making a big effort to act normal.

She gave him the biggest smile she could to reward him, and he responded in kind. She then resumed her tactile quest to find a trace of Rolland, going around the small apartment methodically.

Her sense of hope deflated with every room that yielded nothing. With every unsuccessful minute passing, her stomach tied itself into a tighter knot.

"How are you holding up?" Tom asked her. "I'll give you a foot rub when we get home."

"It's beyond frustrating that I've got nothing. I'm trying, I swear."

"We don't even know that Carmichael's involved. And

even if he was and had abducted them, it might not have happened here. That's a good chunk of unknowns. You can't beat yourself up for not trying hard enough."

"Hmm."

Elenora knew she was being irrational, but she couldn't help feeling that she was letting everyone down, including Rolland Carmichael, by not finding anything.

Pregnancy hormones for the win.

She couldn't wait to give birth, to meet her baby daughter, of course, but also for her body to go back to some kind of normalcy. The postpartum stage could also offer a special brand of crazy, but she'd have to worry about that later. She had reached her quota of worrying for the day.

"We're almost done. D'you want to sit?" Tom said.

Sitting sounded good to her feet, but what if there was one clue somewhere to be found, and she missed it because she chose to sit? There went her crazy train of thought again.

"How about some fresh air?" Alex suggested. "You can wait for us outside. It's nice out."

Fresh air sounded good, but she felt she should keep looking until Tom declared their time was up.

"Ele, you're being stubborn," Alex added, guessing what she was thinking. "There's no sign of breaking and entering or a struggle. It's unlikely that Carmichael was even here. We're just doing our due diligence. That said, maybe he got to them outside."

Right. She should get a head start on feeling for things outside. They had rushed to the apartment, and she hadn't paid attention to the staircase or the walkway outside leading to the building on their way in.

"Okay. Fresh air it is, then."

It had rained earlier, but it was now a gorgeous late October day.

Elenora's gaze swept around for clues of Rolland's past presence. The rain-soaked lawn was covered with colorful leaves, and a gust of wind sprinkled another batch of them over the grass. It wouldn't be easy to find anything.

She forced herself to take a deep breath, feel the crisp air enter her lungs, and be in the moment.

A subtle movement at her periphery caught her attention, and she turned to locate it. She searched but found nothing. It must have been a leaf dancing in the wind.

Another movement caught her attention, and again, she looked but saw nothing that could be at the source of it. She took a few steps toward the street to investigate.

As she reached the sidewalk at the foot of the walkway, a faint shimmering occurred to her right above the curb. She walked closer and found herself sucked into a vision.

It was night, and a car pulled up in front of her. A woman was at the wheel, and before she even turned off the car, a hooded figure opened the front passenger door, got inside, and ordered her to drive at gunpoint.

A hand landed on Elenora's lower back. "Ready to go?" a voice asked behind her.

Elenora jumped out of her skin. She'd recognized Tom's voice but couldn't help her knee-jerk reaction. At this rate, the jarring transport from a vision back to reality would give her a heart attack and be the death of her.

"Ele?"

"He was here! I think it was him." She pointed to the empty parking spot on the street. "Danika Tremblay came home, and a man with a hood hijacked her car. Told her to drive."

Tom and Alex looked at her expectantly.

"What else?" Alex prompted her when she didn't add anything else.

"It was dark. Night."

"You got a good look at him?"

"No."

"If it was dark, and he had a hood on, how do you know it was Carmichael?"

Hmm. "I guess I don't," she admitted, deflated.

"But you feel like it might be him?" Tom tried.

"Yes..." While her gut screamed it was Rolland, Elenora's logical brain convinced her she couldn't be certain.

"Your latest visions have been in connection to either the victim or Carmichael," Tom pointed out. "Since you just had a vision, unless there's another player involved, maybe we should assume it's him."

"Was her daughter with her?" Alex asked.

The daughter...

Elenora closed her eyes, trying to recall the insight. When nothing came to her, she focused on the color black and reminded herself that it had been night. From pictures, she knew what Danika Tremblay looked like, and she tried to transpose her likeness to her memory to jog it. But this didn't work.

She opened her eyes. "No, I don't know if her daughter was with her. It happened so fast, and the vision was brief."

She walked around in case a different spot on the pavement triggered the vision again. She went around the parking spot, too. Still nothing. She blew out a breath, the specter of frustration looming again.

"She's young. If she was in the car, she would've been in the backseat," Tom said.

"Right. I'll head out to her store," Alex called over his shoulder as he went around his car.

"Let's go too, Ele. You've done great," Tom said.

"Okay. Let's check out the witchcraft store."

"How about I drop you off at home?"

"But—"

"You've seen Carmichael abduct them here, and I doubt there will be more for you to find at the store."

"What if he passed by the store earlier to check her out, and I pick up something about his plan?"

Tom stood still for a moment, either considering her argument or looking for an ironclad way to rebuke it. "What if he thought about his plan while grocery shopping? Should we go around town canvassing every grocery store?"

"If you let me take a nap first, I'm up for it," she deadpanned.

Tom let out a groan. "If he's on the store's security footage or if you get a very strong hunch while resting at home, I'll bring you to the witchcraft store later."

CHAPTER TWENTY-TWO

Each stair leading to the basement brought Rolland closer to a heart attack. What would he find on the other side of the door? What kind of killing was he responsible for this time? And how would he get rid of a body in this neighborhood?

But the scariest question of all: how would he deal with Danika Tremblay's newly orphaned little girl? He may have lived longer than most people—if not longer than anyone who ever lived—but he would never be prepared for something like this.

He unlocked the door to the panic room and opened it. His breath hitched.

The woman was alive! She was flinching but alive. And she seemed fine, physically at least. She was sitting on the bed reading on Rolland's e-reader.

He was so very, extremely relieved.

But wait... Could this be a trap? What if the woman was indeed a witch and had waited for him to return to exact a horrible revenge on him?

Rolland studied the witch's moves, sizing her up, and noticed she was doing the same to him. They both eyed each other with matching deer-caught-in-headlights expressions.

"Is my daughter alive?" she asked him, her voice soft and submissive, her eyes averting his. She was genuinely worried about the safety of her child. She was no witch ambushing him. *He* was the monster.

"Yes—"

"Please don't hurt her!" she blurted out. "I will do anything to help you, sir, but believe me, I don't have magical powers. I'm so sorry if I mislead you. I'm so, so sorry—"

"Camelia's safe, and nothing bad will happen to her, I assure you," Rolland said, hoping to stop the woman's scared rambling. Her distress was affecting him to his core. He had to undo whatever damage he'd done.

"Are you hurt? Did I hurt you?" he asked apprehensively. She frowned, confused. Perhaps she, too, now wondered if this was a trap.

"I'm so sorry, Miss Tremblay, for any distress I might have caused you. I owe you a mighty apology for everything I have done. I... I have medical issues."

Right. That was it. A medical angle. Mostly a truth.

"I've had a horrible reaction to... A terrible interaction with—sorry, I don't need to bore you with the details. In a nutshell, I wasn't myself earlier. I had blackouts. I'm afraid I don't know what I did... I know that's no excuse! I just want you to know that I don't know the extent of the anguish I must've caused you, and for that I am truly and deeply sorry. I ask for your forgiveness."

The fake witch was listening, but she was still scared. His heart sank. He had traumatized her and no matter what he said, the damage had been done. Angst radiated from her and echoed deep inside of him. He must have been monstrous to her, maybe even her worst nightmare, and he couldn't help feeling rotten and responsible for his uncontrollable inner asshole, who had apparently decided to interfere with his plan and this innocent woman's life. What was he supposed to do now?

He felt faint. If he didn't fix things now, he would end up in prison because his inner asshole had terrorized Danika Tremblay because... Because he considered some half-baked plan while sick with a fever? Really?

Prison. Forever. Game over.

Hear that, asshole? An eternity locked up in a small room. No more Netflix.

Rolland halted his train of thought. Had he just provoked the jerk? Would it retaliate? Now was so not a good time for that.

He had never addressed his parasite directly before and didn't know what to expect. Would it answer him? Was there some kind of mental intercom linking his mind to wherever the creep lived? Is that how it knew of Rolland's desire to flush it? No doubt it knew a good deal about him by now, but how much?

Anyway, if you don't want to go to jail, I suggest you play nice and let me handle this, he thought for good measure.

His kidnapped guest cleared her throat and timidly said, "My daughter is fine? For real?"

"Yes. She had toast for breakfast and she's watching television."

Toast. He forgot to bring the woman toast like he told Camelia he would. He really was an awful human being. His heart sank a little deeper, reaching the ball of stress in his stomach.

Fix this!

He opened the mini fridge for a bottle of juice. He offered it to her, and she winced, as if expecting an assault.

She caught herself, straightened her back, and accepted the bottle with an unsteady hand, eying the seal before twisting the cap open. She took a sip. Her movements were slow and cautious. Was she afraid to trigger him?

"Do you remember how you got here?" He tried his best to sound friendly. Non-threatening.

With the guardedness of someone wondering if this was a trick question, she answered, "You got in my car and asked me to drive."

He'd been in her car... Rolland tried to recall getting in the woman's car, but his memory was vague.

"And you drove us here?"

"No. You asked me to pull over after a few minutes so you could drive. We stopped in an alley."

Disjointed tidbits of the previous night flooded Rolland's mind. An alley, yes. A dark one. He saw his hand pointing his old Derringer pistol—that had seen the Civil War and which he'd won in a poker game way back when—at a dumbfounded Danika Tremblay. He told her not to move while he went around the car.

He remembered yanking her out of her vehicle and putting her in the trunk, gagged and her hands tied. How he had done that was a mystery to him, but there it was.

As he sat behind the wheel, he spotted her cell phone in a tray between the seats and dropped it down a metal grate covering a manhole.

His recollection of the ride home was murky, but he remembered getting the car in reverse to park it behind his house with the trunk closest to the door.

Rolland covered his face with his hands in shame. "I'm so sorry about everything," he mumbled against the palms of his hands.

"I understand," she said.

Rolland brought down his hands and looked at her incredulously. Had he heard her correctly?

"No one needs to know about this," she added. "I'd be happy to move on if you'd like to move on too. No harm, no foul."

Despite her shell-shock state, her suggestion seemed authentic and devoid of malice or trickery. She didn't seem to be messing with him. Maybe she simply wished to get out of this bizarre predicament with no one hurt, as Rolland did. It wasn't hard to believe.

"I'd be very happy to move on too. How do you suggest we make this happen? What would suit you?" he said, trying not to get his hopes up.

Maybe it was the woman's survival and maternal instincts at work or perhaps she felt some empathy or pity for Rolland—or both—but the next thing he knew, they were upstairs in his kitchen drinking tea and strategizing the best way for Rolland to bring her and her daughter back to their home without getting him into any more trouble. She might not have been a real witch, but she sure knew how to work some magic in the organizational department to make them both come out on top. He was grateful for her creative thinking and her generous spirit.

Rolland would never forget the smile that lit the woman's

face when she was reunited with her very chill and very unharmed little girl. The grateful look she gave him convinced him he could trust her not to go blab to the police. She even gushed over the stuffed shark Rolland had supposedly given her daughter, playing it cool and making it sound like everything was well with the world.

"Isn't Rolly awesome?" Camelia asked her mother. He had set her up on an online video game with penguins on his laptop.

"Totally," the woman answered, matching her kid's enthusiasm. Rolland didn't even detect an ounce of sarcasm or dishonesty.

He and Danika then headed to the kitchen to discuss a plan. She was willing to go the whole hog to make sure she wouldn't be able to disclose his location under any circumstance, and that included the willingness to ride in her car's trunk again.

He appreciated her cooperation but was uncomfortable with having her in the trunk. He suggested she rode crouched on the floor of the front passenger seat, wearing his bedtime eye mask as a makeshift blindfold. He would take a convoluted route around the city to ensure Danika would be properly disoriented. They would then stop in that same alley, where he would say goodbye and let them drive back to their home.

Danika liked his plan and thought it would work. They decided to wait until after the sun had set, to head out under the cover of darkness.

Before they left, Rolland insisted on giving her some cash to replace her phone and an expensive bottle of wine as a token of goodwill, and she altered her car plate with white correction tape in case her car was spotted.

The plan went smoothly. When they reached the alley, Camelia was bummed to leave her new friend, and Rolland and Danika gave each other a high five before going their separate ways.

Rolland felt his life couldn't possibly be more bizarre.

On the cab drive back to his neighborhood, he rehashed and mulled over the unreal incident. He was so relieved his inner jerk-off hadn't made him kill Danika Tremblay and her lovely daughter. Why it had spared their lives, he didn't know. Perhaps it adhered to its own set of rules or moral code and only killed men. Some cold comfort, but Rolland immensely appreciated the fact he didn't have two more departed souls on his conscience.

He came up with a theory as to why he'd ended up kidnapping the fake witch instead of dispatching her: his creep must have figured out his plan to get rid of it with the help from someone with supposed occult abilities.

Flushing the darkness out of his system was the only way Rolland could finish healing himself—both outside and inside—and have a shot with Anna and at a happy life. The darkness, which had made his life hell for so long, didn't want him to be happy.

Ever.

And by sabotaging Rolland's plans of getting help against it from a fake witch—who could have gone to the police and have him arrested—it was trying to drive him insane or teach him a lesson, or both, so that he wouldn't be tempted to try getting rid of it ever again.

If the thing had parasitic qualities, like Rolland suspected, it would make sense that it tried to preserve itself.

That damn thing would be the death of him.

That is, if there *could* be a death of him.

A long time ago, while at the end of his wits and drowning in despair following the death of his brother and the killing of the Toronto quack, Rolland had tried to hang himself to put an end to the evil dictating a life he had stopped enjoying since his beating.

He ended up swinging in mid-air in the middle of his living room for hours, getting bored and hungry, cursing the fact that the rope would leave burn marks around his neck which, with his luck, might end up not healing, just like the repulsive scars on his face.

He hung from the ceiling all night and until the next morning, when he got the attention of a nosy street kid, who stuck his face in the front window to spy inside his place.

Waving like a madman while swinging around, Rolland had startled the bejesus out of the kid but managed to coax him inside. Luckily, the kid was carrying a knife and agreed to let Rolland use it to cut the rope in exchange for money.

This was the first time Rolland began to suspect that the thing lurking inside of him had prevented his death and had even more control over his life than he'd previously thought.

This also raised another dreadful question: if he couldn't die, was he immortal?

Rolland tested that theory on a few more frustrating occasions, escaping unscathed every time except for a few minor scratches that healed in an instant, unlike his facial scars.

If that wasn't a taunt...

CHAPTER TWENTY-THREE

After arriving home from Danika Tremblay's apartment, Elenora lied down for a bit, hoping for an energy-restoring nap. But her mind was racing too much to sleep, and she felt restless.

Adding to this, little heels or hands poked around her belly. The baby was due in a few weeks and had grown too big to swim around as freely as she used to. But poking, she sure could do. And jamming a foot up her mom's ribcage was a clear favorite.

With her thoughts on Rolland, Elenora absentmindedly caressed her stomach and chased after the pokes, gently pinching the tiny protrusions.

The baby shifted and Elenora's bladder sent a signal of distress. She dragged herself out of bed and went to the bathroom. As she washed her hands, Elenora caught her reflection in the mirror, and it reminded her of seeing Rolland's face in a mirror. How he'd seen her in the reflection as well.

Did he, too, see her in his mind? Or in his dreams?

That would be so weird.

But just because he, too, was paranormally afflicted, she couldn't assume that he also had visions or powers other than not aging.

Did he have other powers?

The question made her dizzy. As they tried to catch him, would they have to contend with other powers on top of everything else? What a horrifying thought.

Who and what are you, Rolland? What's going on with you?

As Elenora asked herself these questions while staring into her own eyes, she noticed the shade of her gray irises pale until they became almost white. And then an unexpected tint of baby blue appeared.

She widened her gaze and stiffened. She was no longer staring at herself but at Rolland...who was looking back at her with a bewildered expression.

"Who are you?" he whispered.

Just as stunned, Elenora took a moment to answer. "I'm Elenora. I want to help you, Rolland."

A flash of hope in Rolland's face quickly made way to a drastic change in his expression. His face hardened, and his eyes darkened.

Before Elenora could react, his arms shot out through the mirror, and his hands wrapped themselves around her delicate neck and squeezed. The swift and unexpected move caused her to stumble backward, out of the killer's reach. She let out the mother of all screams.

Survival mode kicked in. She dashed out of the bathroom and kept running. As she reached the landing, Tom and Alex were rushing up the stairs to her.

"Is it the baby?" Tom shouted, blanching.

"What happened?" Alex was just as irked as Tom.

"He's in the bathroom!" Elenora pointed hysterically to the master bedroom. Alex ran past her to the bedroom while Tom grabbed her in a fierce embrace. She collapsed into his arms and broke down into a violent round of sobbing.

Alex came out of the bedroom, gun in hand and visibly on edge.

"I didn't see him. Ele, did he come in through the window?" His brows were drawn together in manic confusion. They were on the second floor.

"The mirror," she said with a sniff.

"You saw him in the mirror?" Tom asked, perplexed.

Elenora nodded jerkily, still shaking with nervous sobs.

"Was he behind you, hiding in the tub?" Alex said.

She shook her head. "No. He was inside the mirror."

Alex stood a moment wondering before putting his gun away. He looked ready to call it a day.

"Please tell us what happened." Tom handed her a tissue.

Elenora blew her nose and worked on calming herself. Time was of the essence. She could have all the breakdowns she wanted later, when the killer was no longer on the loose. "I was washing my hands and wondering if Rolland Carmichael could see me in his mind, like I've seen him, and my eyes went pale—just like you said, Alex."

"Like in the kitchen at work?"

"Yeah. And then, in the mirror, it was no longer me. I was looking at Rolland as if he were standing right in front of me. He looked confused. And then he asked me who I was. I told him and that I wanted to help him. And his face changed, becoming evil. And then—" Elenora's voice became strangled as the very fresh and horrific memory of the very real assault resurfaced.

And then it dawned on her. "Oh my God, Tom, I gave him my name!"

Tom rubbed her back. "Shhh. What happened next, sweetie?"

Elenora refocused on the traumatic event. "And then, it happened so fast. He had his hands around my neck and tried to strangle me."

"His hands? How did his hands make it to your neck?" Alex's frown couldn't get any deeper.

"They burst through the mirror. I don't know how the hell that happened, but I sure felt his hands."

Tom leaned back a few inches and inspected her neck. His face fell. "You're bruised." He shook his head in disbelief, his face reddening with anger. "The bastard... This has got to stop."

"How'd you escape from him?" Alex asked.

"I fell backward, and he lost his grip."

Alex headed back to the bedroom, taking his gun out again.

Livid, Tom dialed Pierre. He explained to him what had just happened and asked him if he'd move in with them for the time being so that Elenora would never be alone. He would not let Carmichael endanger the life of his wife and child.

"He's gonna come?" Elenora asked, hopeful, after Tom hung up. She found comfort in the plan.

"Do you really think there's a chance he would not have agreed?"

Elenora couldn't remember Pierre ever turning her down. Of course, he would come.

"He's gonna bring Céleste too for good measure."

Céleste was a German Shepherd that Pierre had adopted when she retired from police work and her handler could no longer keep her. She was a lovely animal with terrific instincts. Knowing she would be around comforted Elenora even more.

CHAPTER TWENTY-FOUR

Rolland had barely set foot inside his home after dropping off Danika and her daughter, eager to put the heart-stopping incident well behind him, when he felt a strange pull. He was standing at his back entrance, about to take off his shoes, and found himself inexplicably walking down his long corridor toward the hallway mirror near his front door.

He felt strangely compelled to look at himself in the mirror. Was this his guilty conscience forcing him to take a good look at himself?

Staring at his face, he expected to feel remorse or have a revelation about the meaning of his meaningless life. Instead, his pupils caught his attention. The blue of his irises drained of color and became gray.

Was the fever coming back?

He noticed with a start that his reflection was no longer his. A woman with long dark hair and delicate features was staring back at him.

A woman he had seen in dreams before.

What was she doing in his house in broad daylight? Was he hallucinating?

"Who are you?" he whispered to himself.

His words stunned her, as if she hadn't expected him to address her.

"I'm Elenora. I want to help you, Rolland."

Hallucinating, it is. Otherwise, how would she know his name and that he secretly wished for help? Or was it his subconscious reaching out to him, trying to get his attention?

It didn't matter. Just hearing the word "help" was enough to give him a shot of hope, even if this was a god-knows-what-induced daydream.

He was about to ask the woman how she could help him, but everything went dark, and he found himself at his back door, taking off his shoes and struggling with mental whiplash. What the hell had just happened?

Rolland leaned a hand against the wall to steady himself and closed his eyes. What was happening to him now?

He touched his forehead. No fever that he could tell.

Maybe it was the acute stress of the impromptu kidnapping taking its toll. That would be understandable. His exhausted mind must have imagined this trippy little trip to the hallway mirror.

Rolland reopened his eyes, and his gaze landed on a trail of mud along the floor ahead of him, leading down the hall.

He had not imagined things.

His inner jackass was up to something again, and he had no clue what it was.

Rolland tried to go to bed early to harness the crazy, but being idle only made him more restless so he decided to go out. He desperately needed to clear his mind and let go of some stress before he lost it. He needed to shake off the image of Elenora, the mysterious woman from his dreams, who was now appearing in his hallway mirror—of all places—as well as the unsettling ominous feeling haunting him.

Who was she? What did she want? What did she know of him?

While he had no proof that the woman existed outside of his head, he had a gut feeling she was not a mere figment of his imagination.

She had offered him help... Had she really offered him help?

And then she vanished before Rolland had the chance to accept her help. No doubt the damn parasite interfering. She must have been reaching out to him for real if the vile thing felt the need to pull the plug.

Or was this just another elaborate mind-fuck?

A shiver ran down Rolland's spine, and he brought up the collar of his leather jacket. It was cold and windy, and he couldn't wait to arrive at the homeless shelter where he'd been volunteering for years.

As it was with morgues, shelters were a place where Rolland didn't feel like he stood out like a sore thumb. In fact, he felt like he belonged, and being able to blend in without being judged was a welcome respite. And he didn't have to bother with makeup. Not only was his destroyed face not a deterrent to the crushed and battered clientele of the shelter, but it also made him relatable. Approachable.

He wasn't scheduled to go in that night, but the Jeanne

Mance Mission always could use an extra pair of hands, and he desperately needed a distraction. Anything to prevent him from overthinking himself to death. The shelter was always a good place for him to clear his mind. Keeping busy and helping others grounded him and gave him perspective. It kept him away from his darkness.

Like Anna did.

She had a way of keeping the darkness away. And she would be there tonight.

At the thought of her and the prospect of seeing her soon, Rolland's heart skipped a beat. So many of his most cherished memories involved her. Like the day they met.

It was her first day on the team. She was studying to be a nurse and had shown up to help provide basic medical care to a group of homeless folks at a park. Rolland was already there, and she was so nervous—being young, and new and all—that she mistook him for a street person in need of care thanks to his rough appearance and his fresh-looking scars.

She introduced herself to him, meeting his eyes with a gentle gaze, and stood up on her tiptoes to inspect the marks on his face. Her eyes narrowed in concentration as she brushed her fingers over his cheeks, near his ancient wounds.

He was stunned. He hadn't been touched in ages, and it took him a moment to realize what she was doing. She was being so lovely and attentive; he didn't have the heart to stop her and tell her he was a fellow volunteer.

For the first time, he wasn't cursing his face.

Her presence and proximity stirred something inside of him—not the parasitic asshole part, thank God—but a longing for her touch and attention. A craving that was so unexpected for him but unmistakable. They were strangers, yet he felt a strong pull toward her.

"Hey, doc. Check this out." A drunk man stuck his face between Rolland and Anna, breaking the magic.

"I'll be with you in a sec, Lenny," Rolland said without taking his eyes off of Anna's face.

Lenny ignored his reply and lifted his shirt to show off an old knife wound underneath his ribcage.

Rolland turned his attention to him and looked at the scar. "Looks like it's still healing well. Is it bothering you?"

"What?" The man dropped his shirt and faltered.

"I don't see a problem with your knife wound, Lenny. It's not infected or anything. Is something else bothering you?"

Anna's gaze went back and forth between the two men. Her face reddened as the situation dawned on her.

Lenny turned around and left.

"Take care, man," Rolland called after him. Lenny gave him a thumbs up without turning.

"You're not here for medical care..." Anna's confused gaze took in Rolland's decrepit appearance.

"I am."

Her confusion deepened, and he quickly added, "I'm here to help with the first aid stuff. Not to receive it."

"Oh. *Oh*. Right." She blushed a deeper shade, her gaze skating from Rolland's red scars to his clothes once again, unsure if he was pulling her leg.

"I'm sorry, I thought..." She scrambled to find the right words.

Rolland grabbed the hem of his falling-apart hoodie and pulled on it to showcase all of its stained and faded glory. Looking down at it, curling locks of his unkempt hair fell in front of his face. He realized how craptastic he must have looked.

"You think I don't look the part? Are holes already out of fashion? Or does distressed chic only apply to designer jeans?"

He heard teasing in his voice. *Teasing.* Where had that come from? Teasing had long left his repertoire. But here he was...amused? And quipping? Did he even know how to do that anymore?

His quip got him a relieved smile from Anna, and right there, he made it his mission in life to make her smile. His own lips called up the boyish grin that had women fanning themselves in the salons of yesteryear and which hadn't graced his face since that golden era of his life.

Clearly, he was on a roll.

"What happened? How did you get the scars, if I may ask?" Anna asked Rolland once they were done treating their outdoor clientele and heading to their next location.

Very few people had ever dared or cared to ask him about the scars. Most people were too repulsed by them, by him, and avoided making conversation and eye contact. And of the few who had asked, they had done so to be polite, with a cringe ready to pinch their lips in anticipation of gory details. So, Rolland always gave them a superficial answer—which evolved with the times—like he'd been trampled by a horse or had fallen out of a moving tramway car or been hit by an electric fat bike.

Coming from Anna's sweet lips, the question had a different ring. In it, he picked up genuine interest, and he surprised himself by blurting out the truth.

"I was assaulted, beaten up, and left for dead."

Her eyes widened with shock. "Oh my God. Did they catch the guy?"

How could he answer that? "That was a long, long time ago. Everything is fine. No need to worry."

She laid a hand on his upper arm, and he wished she would never take it away. "I hope you at least got some good karma out of it."

His inner cynic scoffed at the notion of him having gotten good karma from the horrible ordeal, but the spike of bitterness was quickly eclipsed by a much better sentiment: he couldn't remember the last time someone had cared for him, and the intoxicating feeling rattled him as it radiated through him.

And then he fought it. He'd have to be careful not to get used to it. Not fall into that trap again.

But it was hard.

Anna had a calming and benevolent effect on everyone. A smile always ready to bloom on her lips, even through the hard times. She treated everyone with warmth and respect and lent an attentive ear to anyone in need of one, no matter how fucked up the speaker seemed. No matter how scruffy or repulsive. And that spoke loudly to Rolland.

Not only did he feel she didn't judge him, but she also seemed to genuinely appreciate his presence. His wit. When she laughed at his jokes, it filled his heart with a lightness he didn't know was possible.

His interest in her grew, and he soon realized the inevitable: he was smitten.

A gust of wind blew around his legs and up his jacket. He saw the building of the Jeanne Mance Mission up ahead. Only a block to go, a few more steps, and he would be there.

She would be there.

Welcoming. Anchoring. Soothing his badly bruised soul. She would make him feel like a good man again. Make him forget everything that was wrong with his life.

Rolland opened the service door at the back of the building. Entering the industrial-style kitchen, he breathed in a comforting smell of soup. His shoulders relaxed.

He scanned the room and spotted Anna chopping carrots. One of the new guys was buzzing around her. A little too close for Rolland's taste.

He felt a pang of jealousy but quickly caught himself.

He could not wish the man any ill.

CHAPTER TWENTY-FIVE

"I don't know if he can see you too, but I find the possibility intriguing," Serena said to Elenora. The two women stood with Tom, Alex, and Pierre in the cramped bathroom with the hazardous mirror.

Pierre had called Serena about the baffling mirror incident, and she showed up at the house at lightning speed to inspect it for paranormal activity. While she found a waning trace of Rolland's earlier presence, she detected no activity and concluded he was long gone. She also assured Elenora and Tom there was nothing inherently magical about the mirror itself and it wouldn't be prone to causing more undesired ghastly visits as long as Elenora avoided staring at herself in the eye while thinking about bad people. That last part also applied to any reflective surface, including utensils.

"So, this mirror is not some kind of portal to hell, and we don't have to burn the bathroom down or anything?" Tom said dryly, eliciting a smirk on Serena's pretty face.

"That's right. You're all good."

Elenora was happy to know that the mirror hadn't caused

the bewildering connection with Rolland, and she could sleep in peace in her bedroom without having to put a hammer to it.

That was the good news.

But the fact that she had somehow summoned evil in the flesh in her own home by staring at herself was a disturbing notion.

She walked out of the crowded bathroom, and everyone followed.

"You think I summoned him by staring at myself?" she asked Serena.

"As some kind of self-hypnosis? Yeah, that's what I'm thinking. So, please don't do that," the lively witch advised.

"What do you think made him jump at her throat?" Tom asked. "Ele said he was fine one moment and then turned nasty on her."

Serena pondered the question. "He freaked right after you offered to help?"

Elenora nodded.

"Right. Then, if my possession theory holds water, the spirit may have sensed you'd be able to help Rolland get rid of it and saw it as a threat to its existence. A spirit needs a host to have a physical presence in our world."

"So, it tried to strangle you to get you out of the picture," Pierre jumped in.

"When I offered Rolland help, I meant psychological support. Not an exorcism. It actually believed I could get rid of it? How?"

Tom shifted his weight, his face dark.

"Your guess is as good as mine," Serena replied. "But it

attacked you after you offered to help, so we should assume it sees you as a threat."

"With her visions, Elenora's already helped us identify Carmichael," Alex pointed out. "That in itself might be enough to freak it out. It doesn't want to give us any more ammunition against it."

Serena turned her olive-green eyes on Alex. "Good point. It wouldn't be too keen on that. It's made Rolland kill several times—that we know of—and commit only God knows what other atrocities for almost two centuries, and now Elenora's pissing in its cereal."

"Thanks for the visual," Alex sneered. He'd been eyeballing the witch with suspicion from the minute they'd been introduced moments earlier.

"Don't mention it." She offered him an amused grin.

"One thing for sure, we need to keep you away from him, Ele. He could have killed you," Tom said.

Elenora gave him a side hug. She could tell this was getting to him at a whole new level. "Don't worry, Tom, I'll be extra careful around mirrors."

"We can cover the mirrors and get plastic cutlery if we have to," Pierre added.

"But it's not just the mirrors and the cutlery. The guy's out there!" Tom was getting angry again. "We don't know what he's capable of, and now she's got a target on her back."

"If I may..." Serena said. "First, Elenora understands it's a form of self-hypnosis that caused the summon, not the mirror itself or any other objects. And it takes more than just a glance. She's safe in the house."

Elenora gave her an appreciative nod.

Serena went on. "And outside too. Because—second—as

long as no one makes a direct threat to the spirit's survival, I don't think it would want to attract attention, especially if there are witnesses or if it's outnumbered. So, Elenora, don't go dicking around in dark alleys all by yourself, and don't offer Rolland any help if you see him, and you should be fine. That's what my gut is telling me."

Alex raised an eyebrow at her.

"And my vast experience," she added for his benefit.

Tom let out an unconvinced huff, and Pierre said to him, "I'm here. Elenora won't be alone. Have a bit of faith."

"Right. Thanks for being here, Pierre. Appreciate it."

"So, what the hell do we do now?" Alex asked.

"Now, we keep trying to figure out as much as possible, except with extreme caution," Serena answered him before turning to Elenora. "When you saw Rolland at first, he seemed normal, correct?"

"Very briefly but yes. He seemed surprised but not evil. The opposite, in fact. He looked pleasant and hopeful."

Elenora could be wrong, given how taken aback she'd been by Rolland's sudden appearance in her bathroom mirror, and it all happened so fast, but her experience with similar matters told her she was correct.

"Okay..." Serena pondered Elenora's answer for a moment. "I think this confirms what we discussed earlier, that Rolland's soul is still around, but he's no longer in charge. It means we should assume we're dealing with good and evil all wrapped into one. It means we can't just throw in a hand grenade and call it a day."

"You mean we can't, in good conscience, shoot to kill when we find him?" Elenora felt a sense of hope rising inside of her.

Pierre's dog Céleste walked into the room, padded up to Serena, and nudged her hand. The witch glanced at the animal lovingly and petted her. "I missed you too, Cellie."

"So, when we find this guy, we have to play 'good victim, bad perp' because he's both guilty and innocent? Is that what you're saying?" Alex said, frowning.

"No, we're not to engage with him at all," Tom replied.

Alex shot Tom a look of disbelief. "In Elenora's case, I understand, but—"

Serena cut him off. "Tom's right. We know this thing is strong and dangerous, but we don't know the extent of its powers. Or how it would make Carmichael react in a physical confrontation. We can't risk pushing it into survival mode."

"Even if we outnumber him? In broad daylight? You just said it wouldn't risk getting attention." Alex came closer to Serena, towering over her.

She didn't let him intimidate her. If anything, she didn't seem impressed. Serena looked him straight in the eye. "I'm extrapolating based on past experiences and similar, documented behavior. But we don't know enough yet. We don't know its rules or its full strength."

"Alex, trust me," Pierre added with authority, "some of these assholes, you don't want to fuck with, even if you have an army."

Alex backed up a bit and crossed his arms in front of his chest, clearly not liking the conversation. "So, we play dead, then? Roll out the red carpet for that creep? Offer him a massage?"

"First, don't forget we're dealing with two beings here and the host is likely innocent. And no, you don't have to turn in your badge or your man card. If you find him, you report him to us and see if you can monitor him from a safe distance until we show up," Serena explained, her steady tone hardening with each word.

"Who the hell is 'we'?" Alex's voice betrayed his struggle to keep his cool.

"Serena and her colleagues." Tom gave Alex a warning look as his phone rang. He glanced at the number. "Gotta take this," he muttered and headed out of the bedroom.

"Your *colleagues*..." Alex said to Serena. "They've dealt with this kind of paranormal bozo before?"

"Let's just say that we've dealt with a variety of situations that have required very creative solutions."

"And that's all above board?"

Serena gave him a sassy smile. "It sure beats the alternative."

They stared at one another in defiance until Pierre broke the tension. "In the meantime, let's focus on talking to Carmichael's surviving colleagues," he said.

"Once we find them, yeah," Alex said.

"Claire-Lune retraced three of them."

Alex gave Pierre a blank look. "Someone already tracked down three unidentified guys from the 1940s?"

"Yes, my sister did," Serena replied.

"From a picture that she miraculously pulled out of her ass just this fucking morning?" Alex said through gritted teeth.

"Yes. She has a very talented ass."

"Unbelievable."

"No argument there. I, too, find it unbelievable that you're pissed because she's *helping* your case. How dare she, right? What a bitch." It was Serena's turn to be in Alex's face, and she seemed to enjoy every second.

"Well, if she's anything like you, I'm not sure she beat us fair and square," he mumbled, getting red in the face.

"Of all the things he could latch on..." She snorted derisively.

"It's not a competition, Alex," Elenora told him softly.

"I know, but it makes me wonder if us regular saps with a regular badge shouldn't just all retire and let them do their hocus pocus shit and catch all the bad guys with a snap of their fingers or whatever the hell it is they do." Alex now sounded more discouraged than angry, though some hostility still tainted his words.

"Yeah, because my brand of hocus pocus shit is just so damn effective," Elenora replied, just as discouraged.

"I didn't mean you, Ele. I'm sorry, it's just that..."

Serena ditched her abrasiveness, too. "Detective Bélanger, I very much wish a snap of my fingers could right all the wrongs in this world. I understand your frustration at our advantage in this particular situation but let me assure you it's far from always the case. And believe me, there are times when I, too, wish I could retire."

"Yeah, Serena's only got like 700 years of service left before she gets the gold watch," Pierre joked to add some levity.

Serena snorted again, but in amusement this time, and gave Pierre a huge smile. "That one will be a hit at the water cooler."

"Great news, bad news," Tom announced, returning to the room.

All eyes snapped to him.

"Danika Tremblay and her daughter are alive and well!"

"Thank God," Elenora said, relieved that mother and daughter were fine and Rolland hadn't made another fatal mistake. "What happened?"

"They came back to their apartment a few hours ago, and Ms. Tremblay contacted her sister, the one who reported them missing, and she phoned the station to call off the search."

"What's the bad news?" Alex asked.

"She refuses to talk about what happened. Lagacé went to see her, and she stonewalled him. She insisted it was nothing and apologized for wasting his time."

"She's scared to talk," Elenora said. "Maybe Rolland's holding a sword over her head."

"He knows where she lives, and she's afraid he'll retaliate," Pierre added.

"There might be more to it," Tom said. "Lagacé offered to take them to a safe place, and she refused."

"So, Carmichael's got eyes on her place…and threatened to do something if she left?" Alex tried.

"Or maybe my vision was wrong, and they didn't get kidnapped," Elenora said.

"But you've been right so far," Pierre pointed out.

"Elements of my dreams were right, yes. But how reliable are my visions? What if my subconscious made me see what I wanted to see because I wanted an answer?" she argued.

"Anything's possible, of course, but I'd say it's unlikely," Serena jumped it. "Does your gut tell you you're wrong about the carjacking?"

Elenora took a moment to be honest with herself. No, she didn't doubt her instinct on this one. She shook her head.

"Then trust yourself."

"Did Danika Tremblay deny that she and her daughter were kidnapped?" Alex asked.

"She refused to deny that they were kidnapped, and she deflected every time he tried to get a straight answer out of her."

"She doesn't want to lie but doesn't want to talk," Elenora theorized.

Tom looked at her. "I think Lagacé recognized that, too. He told her she should talk to you, and if she agreed to meet with you, he'd get off her back."

"That's perfect!" Elenora said.

"She hasn't agreed yet. He said he'll give her a call in the morning when she's had a chance to rest."

"Then let's hope a good night of sleep will work in our favor."

CHAPTER TWENTY-SIX

Elenora woke up to the smell of bacon. Despite the previous nerve-wracking day, she had a good night of sleep. Neither her overworked mind nor Rolland or the baby dared to interfere with it. Céleste slept on the floor next to her, guarding the space between the bathroom mirror and the bed. Maybe the dog's presence put Elenora's mind at ease and kept her worries and bad dreams at bay. She felt rested and energized, ready to take on a new day.

With Céleste at her heel, she went down the stairs, where Tom and Pierre greeted her in the kitchen.

"She's agreed to meet with you in the afternoon," Tom told her enthusiastically.

"Danika Tremblay? Wonderful." Elenora took the mouth-watering plate of eggs, bacon, and fruit Pierre handed her, thanked him, and sat at the table.

"If you're up for it, we could pay a visit to Carmichael's old colleagues in the meantime. See if we can get anything."

"Do we have appointments?"

"I think we should just drop by. I don't want to upset

them with police business ahead of time. There's no point in making them fret or giving them a heart attack."

Elenora liked the idea of visiting the old doctors, and they hit the road shortly after breakfast. Alex said he'd join them as soon as he could. He promised his mother he'd help her with yard work, a promise he had to break too many times already because of work.

On their drive to the first retirement home on their list, Elenora examined a blown-up version of the post-war picture of the doctors Tom had printed out at home. She studied it intently and swept her fingers numerous times over it, on the off chance that she'd get a read from it, but no visions came to her.

She analyzed Rolland's neutral expression just as many times, trying to guess his thoughts. His face was mostly blank, and he was nowhere near smiling, but his posture suggested he was relaxed and comfortable in the hospital environment and with his colleagues. His gaze conveyed he was at peace.

A time of inner peace, perhaps?

Her encounters with Rolland always seemed so extreme in the emotional department. Tortured or aching with soul-crushing sadness, or filled with hope, then downright murderous. It was hard to imagine him happy or simply content. Devoid of inner turmoil.

What is it like to live with so much torment for so long?

The visit to the first doctor at a senior home on the west side of town ended before it even began. The clerk at the reception told them Dr. Frenette was suffering from pneumonia and in no shape to have visitors. The man's memory was also mostly gone, and he had a hard time communicating on a good day, so they wouldn't have gotten much out of him, anyway.

As they headed to the second retirement home, Alex called to say he was ready to join them. Tom told him their visit to Dr. Frenette was a bust and where to meet them next. When they arrived at the second senior home, Alex was waiting for them near the entrance. Once inside, the trio was led to a welcoming communal space, where the residents could entertain visitors, and warned that Dr. Lamoureux suffered from Alzheimer's. There was no telling what his state of mind and lucidity would be.

A male orderly wheeled a delicate senior in a wheelchair toward them. The old man was well-groomed and dignified. His face lit up, delighted to have visitors, even if they were strangers.

The orderly crouched next to his patient, catching his attention.

"Dr. Lamoureux, these are the detectives I told you about. They have a few questions for you about something that happened a long, long time ago. So, it's okay if you don't have answers and there's no reason to worry, all right?"

The old doctor nodded. His vacant stare made it unclear whether he had caught everything he was just told. He just looked happy to be there.

Tom introduced himself, offering his hand to shake. "Good to meet you, sir. I'm Tom." He took the man's frail hand into his own and shook gently.

"Hello," the man responded.

"And these are my colleagues, Alex and Elenora."

Alex and Elenora followed suit and shook the man's hand.

"Aren't you a pretty thing," the man said to her, taking her in.

"You're quite the looker yourself," she replied, making him chuckle.

"What can I do for you, dear? Are you here for lunch?" he asked her.

Tom reached inside his jacket and retrieved a folded copy of the enlarged printout of the post-war picture.

The old man leaned forward to look at the picture. His face lit up again. "Those were the days."

"What can you tell us about those days?" Tom asked.

Tom must have been burning to jump in and go straight to the point, ask the man if he remembered Rolland. But a nurse had told them they had the best chance of success if they didn't rush the old doctor and asked him one simple question at a time. Prompting him to reminisce out loud to jog his fragile memory seemed like a good start.

"I sure had more hair back then..." Dr. Lamoureux nodded to himself and his voice trailed off.

After a long pause, Tom tried again. "This was after the Second World War. You worked in a burn victims' unit, correct?"

"Oh, yes. Burns and patching up soldiers in any way we could. Ah, good old Bugsy," he said, pointing at a man standing next to him in the picture. "He was a little crazy, if you ask me, but he had golden hands. He could do flap surgery in his sleep, I swear." He chuckled to himself.

"Sir?" Alex jumped in a little brusquely. He put a finger on Rolland. "Do you remember this man?"

The old doctor took a moment to bring his focus back to the picture and process Alex's question.

"Him?" He pointed at Rolland.

"Yes. Please tell us about him," Elenora said softly.

The doctor gave her a smile, still looking so tickled to have company. "Yes. That's Steve."

Elenora, Tom, and Alex exchanged a glance.

"Steve was a doctor?" Tom asked.

"Oh, no," the old man exclaimed. "He works here. In the kitchen. Makes the best potatoes."

The old man's memory was playing tricks on him. They'd been warned this could happen and shouldn't be surprised. Still, Elenora had high hopes that he could shed some light on the Rolland enigma. It was hard not to feel some disappointment.

"Do you play chess?" Dr. Lamoureux asked Tom. "You look like someone who plays chess."

Alex took in a deep breath and cracked his neck. "I've played in the past but not recently. And not very well. What about yourself, sir?"

The old man's eyes glazed over. "What's that, son?"

Alex's foot started to fidget.

"Do you play chess, Dr. Lamoureux?" Tom asked again patiently.

"Oh... I don't think so." A flash of confusion crossed his face before he turned to Elenora. "Have we met, miss? Aren't you a pretty thing."

Elenora leaned toward the senior and laid a hand on his. "We are meeting right now. And it's a pleasure."

Tom folded the picture and tucked it away in his jacket before signaling to the orderly that they were done.

"You take care of yourself now," she said to the senior.

"You too, dear," he replied.

As the orderly got hold of the wheelchair's handles, the old doctor said to no one in particular, "I wonder if he ever atoned enough."

"What do you mean, sir? Who?" Elenora touched his arm, this time to keep his attention from fleeting.

"The man in the picture," he replied, as if it was obvious.

Tom fumbled to get the picture back out. "Which man?" He crouched and held the paper picture in front of the doctor again. The doctor pointed at Rolland.

"He said he needed to atone?" Elenora asked.

"When they ask you why you wanted to become a doctor, many say, 'I want to help.' Or, 'I want to make the world a better place.' 'My father was a doctor...' But when people asked him, he'd say, 'To atone.' That always struck me. I'll always remember *that* about him."

"Did he ever say what he needed to atone for?" Tom asked.

"No. But the way he fussed over everyone, you'd think he committed every sin under the sun. Even when he saved them all, it seemed like it was never enough. The poor man." He shook his head with sorrow and drifted down memory lane again.

"Anything else you can tell us about him, Dr. Lamoureux?"

The old man lifted his head, and his gaze found Tom's. "Who?"

———✤———

"Rory *did* use to say that. Yes. I remember."

Doctor Sedgwick had a sharp glint in his eyes as he spoke, the memories fresh in his mind like they happened yesterday. He held the unfolded picture in his slightly trembling hands. "Yeah. It's something he used to say."

"Did he say what he needed to atone for?" Elenora tried.

The old man chuckled and shook his head. "No. He must've taken that to the grave. Or he's about to if he hasn't yet. Fellow didn't talk much. Kept to himself a lot. But his kindness and care for others spoke for themselves, and loudly so."

Doctor Sedgwick was lucid and spry for his age. He had welcomed Elenora, Tom, and Alex into the study of his small apartment in the Golden Square Mile neighborhood of the city. Even after living there for several decades, his place had kept its original character. His study had books from floor to ceiling, and there were piles of paper on his desk like the man was still running a practice. There was no doubt he liked to keep himself busy.

"D'you know if he had family? We are trying to retrace anyone related to him," Tom said.

The doctor thought for a while. "I don't think so. None that he'd mention. Actually, if memory serves right, he was always keen to work a double shift and in no hurry to go home."

Because he had no one to go home to and his work kept him from being alone with his pain, Elenora thought.

"Did he ever go out with his colleagues?" Tom asked.

"We had little time to socialize back then, as you can imagine. But yeah. He would join us for a pint. Wouldn't say much, and he'd nurse his beer—not the type to get crazy drunk, he was too serious and dedicated for that—but he still looked like he was fine to be there."

He wanted to remain in control.

The old doctor laughed. "Perhaps he should've let loose every once in a while. But overall, he was an esteemed colleague if you could look past his aloof demeanor and off-putting looks. That last part must have been hard for him. He must have felt for people looking worse than he did."

"Did he say how he got the scars?" Tom asked.

"Shrapnel, I think. He served in the war, you know. We'd tell him he was lucky to have survived, considering the facial damage he had. He'd just shrug and joked that he was impossible to kill." The doctor laughed again. "Yeah, he was an odd one, that's for sure."

"Your team was doing surgery. Do you know if he ever tried to have his scars corrected?"

"I don't think so. He didn't come across as the vain type. I don't think he cared about his looks all that much. But the techniques fascinated him, always keeping abreast of new technology. Come to think of it, though, the techniques at the time wouldn't have done his scars much good, I don't think."

"And today?"

"We have the means today, yes."

"Do you know what happened to him?"

"Hmm... He moved? To New York, was it? I think he considered a few places. I can't recall where he finally headed to." The man paused a moment. "I regret not having kept in touch. He sure was something else."

"You own a witchcraft store, correct?"

Elenora sat in a comfortable armchair in Danika Tremblay's living room, facing the woman. She looked tired and weary. Despite the effort she made to appear welcoming and amenable, Elenora sensed a heavy burden weighing on her.

The woman's sister sat next to her for moral support. Her brother-in-law, a large guy, leaned against the doorway, his arms crossed over his chest. *Security duty*. Danika Tremblay needed to feel safe right now, not threatened. Elenora had asked Tom and Alex to wait in the car while she spoke to the traumatized woman.

"A metaphysical supply store, yes," Ms. Tremblay replied stiffly.

"On your website, it says 'For all your occult needs.' Do you provide witchcraft-related services?"

Elenora made sure her voice was soft and devoid of judgment. Still, Ms. Tremblay did a double take at the question, as if someone working with the police could seriously ask her this.

She cleared her throat. "I'm a businesswoman, Mrs. Bello," she answered cautiously. "I don't have any kind of special powers if that's what you're hinting at. The products and services I offer at my store are for entertainment purposes, and I try my best not to make false claims. What people do with them or what they believe in is none of my business."

"Please call me Elenora... Did he think you had powers?" Elenora went out on a limb. She was unsure why that specific question popped into her mind, but it felt right to ask it.

The question took Danika Tremblay aback for a split second before she recovered. "I don't know who you are referring to," she said, looking away briefly before making eye contact again.

Elenora offered her a comforting smile. "I'm asking because we are looking for a man who might be interested in witchcraft. And since you own a metaphysical store, it seemed possible that he would approach you. That man needs help, and I want to help him."

Danika stared at her in disbelief, her mind racing.

Elenora sipped at her tea, giving the woman time and space for her to consider answering the question truthfully.

Danika started kneading her fingers together, and her brow creased slightly. Finally, she turned to her sister. "Can you and Dominic go make Camelia a hot chocolate in the kitchen?"

The sister's eyes narrowed. "You sure?"

Danika nodded.

The sister stood up slowly, unconvinced. "Just holler if you need anything. We won't be far."

She walked out of the room with her husband, glancing at Elenora over her shoulder before disappearing.

Once they were out of earshot, Danika breathed in sharply. "You're a social worker, right?"

"That's right."

"Working for the police."

"Indeed."

"Does patient confidentiality apply?"

Elenora knew where this was going. And as much as she would like to be able to offer the woman confidentiality, she couldn't make any promises. She leaned toward Danika as much as Aubrey allowed her.

"It can, but I'll be frank, it's a complex matter, with many gray areas. I think you can understand and appreciate why I can't promise you confidentiality."

Danika let out a soft huff, visibly disappointed.

"However, I can assure you that I have your best interest at heart, and I would not put you or your daughter in harm's way. I have that man's well-being at heart as well. I want to make sure he doesn't do anything harsh...or irreversible."

Danika winced, the words getting to her.

Elenora added, "My husband, who I trust very much, is a detective and he's on board. Nothing you tell me has to be broadcasted at large."

The woman squinted. "Is your husband Detective Lagacé?"

"No. You haven't met him."

A moment of heavy silence passed. Danika raked her throat. "Just so we're clear, I won't press any charges, no matter what, and I don't want to be badgered by anyone."

"Did Detective Lagacé badger you?" Elenora frowned.

"He...tried to be persuasive." Her voice wavered. "Anyway, this isn't about him. Look, I don't want to be lying to the police. I just want this to go away with no harm done."

"I understand."

"And I don't know where he lives, I swear to God, and even a polygraph would confirm that I'm telling the truth—not that I want to take one!"

Elenora reached for Danika's arm to stop her growing panic. She wished she could tell her that she knew about the kidnapping. That she'd seen it. That she also knew firsthand how utterly chilling Rolland Carmichael could be.

How brave she had undoubtedly been.

"It sounds like you got dragged into a very stressful and

complex situation. You might have feared for your life. And you did what you had to do to make sure your little girl was safe."

Bottom lip quivering, Danika gave her a bewildered look, as if Elenora had read her mind.

"You feel conflicted, and it's normal to feel conflicted. But you did the right thing. Whatever made this happen, it's not your fault. You don't own this. And I'm sorry you had to go through it."

Danika broke down in tears and let Elenora draw her into her arms.

"He became so scary when I told him I didn't have any powers," she blubbered. "I'm not a real witch. I mean, duh! But he got so mad. I've never seen anyone looking so mad in my life. I was sure he was going to kill us."

Elenora was still fighting the urge to share her own experience. Instead, she nodded and rubbed the woman's arm. "Danika, you must have been terrified."

Danika nodded vigorously and started hiccupping. "Yeah... Yeah. But he's not really a bad man. And he's sooooo young! He doesn't know any better. He's sick. He has medical issues—mental issues, sounds like? It's not his fault. He is sick, Elenora. It was all a misunderstanding. I felt it, you know. Deep down, I know it was."

"I know."

"Detective Lagacé thought I didn't want to talk because I'm afraid. But that's not it. I can't talk because—well, yes, I'm a little worried he could come after us again if I talked and he had other problems with his meds. I'm not stupid. But it's not that simple. Sending him to prison wouldn't help him. It would ruin him for the rest of his life. He..."

Her voice trailed off, and her expression tensed as something horrible dawned on her.

"Oh my God, that doesn't work either," she hissed, her eyes widening in panic. "I can't break my promise to him. I totally meant it. But what if he does this again to someone else? I don't know what to do. Someone has to help him. But I can't betray him."

"I want to help him, Danika. And so does my husband. This shouldn't be on your shoulders. Let me—let us take the burden away and take care of this. Take care of him."

"But how? Your husband's a cop. The police will know." Her eyes widened even more. "Oh my God, he's done this before. Or your husband wouldn't know about him, right? What kind of detective is he? Which department?"

Shoot. Telling her that Tom was homicide would not be a good thing. But neither was lying to her.

Danika picked up on Elenora's reluctance to answer her and must have guessed her dilemma. She started shaking.

"Danika, look at me," Elenora said softly, trying to bring her back to her and away from hyperventilation. "I, too, think he's not a bad man. *We* share your impression of him."

Danika's eyes found Elenora's and focused on her.

"We, too, want to help him. Please help us help him."

Reluctantly, Danika gave her a shaky nod.

"Would you like to hear what my husband has to say? Should I ask him to come join us?"

The woman nodded again, half-resigned, half-relieved.

Elenora took her cell phone out of her purse and texted Tom a three-letter code: *SCA. Sensitive. Come alone.* Short for "Bring an extra dose of empathy and ditch Alex."

"Why is he interested in witchcraft?" Danika sounded

calmer, but her fingers were drumming against her thigh. "You know what? Don't answer that."

"You've done the right thing. Never forget that, okay?"

"Okay."

A fit of little girl giggles of joy and carefreeness erupted from the other end of the apartment. The sound was a balm on Elenora's heart, and Danika's too, judging by the way her features relaxed at the sounds of glee.

Elenora felt movement in her belly, as if baby Aubrey were reacting to the delighted squeals as well.

May you never go through something like this, little love.

"How's Camelia doing?"

"She thinks the whole thing was a game. I'm so grateful he treated her well. Didn't touch one hair on her head." Her voice vibrated with emotion, and her eyes started watering again.

"She interacted with him?"

"Mm-hmm. He was great with her, if you can believe that. There's good in him, you know? There has to be."

Elenora nodded and asked, "May I see her?"

Danika wiped the budding tears from her eyes and called over her shoulder, "Camelia, dear! Come see mommy."

Tiny footfalls resonated down the hall as a knock sounded at the front door.

"That'd be Tom." Elenora struggled to get out of the over-stuffed armchair, and Danika stopped her.

"Don't get up. I'll get it."

Camelia came running into the room, and her mother intercepted her, swinging her around, causing more giggles. Danika gave her a fierce hug, from which Camelia squirmed free.

"Cami, say hi to Elenora. She's very nice," Danika said on her way to answering the door.

Hugging a plush shark, the girl stopped in the middle of the room and gave Elenora a shy smile.

"I like your shark. What's its name?"

"It's Sharky. He's a boy. Rolly thinks it's a good name."

"Rolly?" *Rolland.* "Is Rolly your new friend?"

Elenora studied the girl's body language, looking for signs of distress. The child nodded enthusiastically. So far, nothing suggested she had suffered a recent trauma.

Thank God.

Camelia's eyes danced with enthusiasm. "He gave me Sharky."

"Oh, that was so nice of Rolly to do that."

The girl took a few wiggly steps toward Elenora. "Sharky looks so soft. May I give him a hug?"

Camelia bounced the remaining steps to Elenora and offered her the plush. Elenora took it and made a show of giving it a big hug, turning her head down to shield her eyes from the girl. She also braced herself for a vision.

Sure enough, Rolland appeared in her mind, holding the shark. She had expected to see him with Camelia, but he was with a young woman in a nondescript room—a business setting? The place had Christmas decorations. The young woman had her back to Elenora. There was a soft smile on his face. "Isn't it the most adorable thing?" she asked him.

Elenora felt a tug on her arm, and the vision dissipated. Camelia wanted her plush back.

Recovering, she handed it back to her. "Sharky is adorable. Thank you for letting me hold him."

Camelia was staring at her with eyes as round as saucers.

Had she seen Elenora's eyes pale from getting sucked into a vision even though she tried to hide her eyes?

Before she could say anything, Camelia told her, "Bye," and pranced out of the room, carefree once again.

"Yes. That's him." Elenora overheard Danika say to Tom.

When Elenora and Tom left Danika Tremblay's place, Alex was waiting for them in his car. They rushed inside his vehicle to get out of the miserable weather and catch him up.

Tom had not learned all that much more than Elenora had, though Ms. Tremblay did confirm Rolland's identity when he showed her a cropped picture of him. And while she'd been willing to cooperate, she couldn't tell him anything about where Carmichael could be found since they had made sure she couldn't retrace him. Tom understood what they had done and believed her.

Elenora told Tom and Alex about Camelia's stuffed shark and what she'd seen when she touched it. She had mixed feelings about the vision—at once elated that it had occurred like she thought it might but bummed that it had yielded little information.

"If only I'd seen the woman's face, Serena could've done her image capture trick, and we'd have a visual. But no... I don't think I saw anything useful."

"Did you see her hair?" Tom asked.

Elenora thought so, but she blanked when she tried remembering that detail. A wave of frustration unfurled inside of her. She closed her eyes and tried to recall the vision.

Nothing came.

Ugh.

She heard Tom's soothing voice and felt his arm landing gently on her shoulder. "Perhaps don't try to remember a specific detail. You saw Rolland with a stuffed shark. It must have been quite a sight..."

It had indeed been quite a sight. Her mind briefly recalled Rolland with the stuffed shark—the surprising image was hard to forget. She saw a faint version of it but enough to catch more details before it became out of focus and disappeared.

"There was wrapping paper in his hands too, like he had just unwrapped the shark as a Christmas present," she said, keeping her eyes closed. Her voice sounded muffled to her own ears, and she wasn't sure if she'd said the words out loud or just to herself.

A Christmas present. He'd received the plush as a present and seemed happy. His happiness had struck her, and she remembered thinking that.

Another flash of Rolland with Sharky appeared in her mind. His unexpected smile at the plush and the young woman in front of him. He looked touched. The vision waned again. Elenora didn't chase it. Instead, she kept herself relaxed and focused on Rolland's emotions.

The present had moved him, there was no doubt about it.

It had meant something to him.

Warmth washed over Elenora, and she could feel how giddy Rolland had been at that moment. His gentle expression, his face, and the vision itself all reappeared in her mind in sharp focus.

She could see the young woman with as much clarity as the first time.

"Brown hair in a ponytail. Medium height. She seemed thrilled that Rolland liked the gift. She wore a t-shirt that said 'volunteer' on it."

"Does it say a volunteer for what?" Tom's voice made its way through the vision, quiet but audible.

Elenora took in the t-shirt in her mental image. She couldn't see a name. "Hmm... I don't see other letters. The t-shirt is gray, the word 'volunteer' is written in blue. There's a drawing on it of a woman with a long, pointy collar...like a historical figure."

"Like Marguerite Bourgeoys?" Alex tried.

"Yeah, but she doesn't look like a nun." The vision faded, and Elenora opened her eyes. The drawing seemed familiar, and she tried to place it.

A search on her phone jogged her memory. "The Jeanne Mance shelter," she said triumphantly.

CHAPTER TWENTY-SEVEN

"Rich, do you know this man?"

Elenora showed the cropped picture of Rolland to Richard, the manager of the Jeanne Mance Mission.

"Yeah, that's Rolland. Great guy. He's been working with us for a long time. Is he in trouble?"

"We'd like to warn him about something," Tom said in a friendly tone, choosing his words.

This was a delicate situation. Elenora had known and worked with Richard for years, and they'd handled a gamut of hard situations together. He was trustworthy, but now that they knew Rolland wasn't a beneficiary of the shelter but a fellow worker, they couldn't afford to give anyone at the mission so much as a hint that Rolland was a menace, even to an ally like Richard.

"Is he around?" Elenora asked. Since arriving, she had scanned the large dining room several times, watching the workers coming and going, and hadn't seen Rolland nor the young, brown-haired woman from her vision.

"I don't think he's scheduled until Tuesday night."

"Do you have an address for him?" Tom asked.

"Don't know if I have an address, but I have a cell number. Follow me."

If Richard didn't have an address for Rolland, a phone number could be a start—assuming it wasn't a burner phone—but not what they were hoping for. Calling him would be a surefire way of spooking him. Contacting the phone company for an address would likely lead to a fake address, considering his history. And tracking the phone itself would require a warrant and they didn't have a case to back up such a request.

"I'll just sit here for a minute," Elenora called after Tom. With one hand on her belly, she pointed to a chair with the other to tell him to go without her. Tom acknowledged her request with a quick nod, and he and Alex followed Richard down a corridor.

Elenora sat even though she didn't need a break; she wanted to be on the lookout for the young volunteer from her vision. This spot gave her a good view of the main entrance and the large dining area, where rows of tables and chairs were neatly lined up. It was too early for the dinner service but mouth-watering aromas wafted in from the kitchen.

They hadn't checked the kitchen.

Elenora stood up and took a few steps before a contraction struck her. The shooting pain stopped her dead in her tracks, rooting her in place. She grabbed hold of the back of a chair for balance and tried not to attract attention.

It's just a Braxton Hicks. Come on... You can do this.

She waited for the wave of pain to ride through her and subside, grunting mildly.

Holy cow. These contractions were supposedly milder than the real thing. She couldn't fathom that thought. She resumed her trek to the kitchen, wondering how much time she had until the next round of pain.

The room was filled with equipment, workers, and volunteers. Her gaze swept around, taking in the eclectic mix of people chipping in, from the student to the homemaker to the businessman on his day off. Her eyes landed on a woman of average height, with long brown hair. She could be the young woman who had gifted Rolland Sharky.

"Can I help you?" a young man peeling potatoes asked Elenora.

"Hi. I'm Elenora. Please tell me, the young woman stirring a pot over there, with long brown hair... What's her name?"

The kid turned around to look. "Anna."

"Could you please tell Anna I would like to speak with her?"

"Uh..." He frowned, hesitant. He noticed her very pregnant state. "I guess? Just a sec."

"Thank you," she called after him as he went to talk to Anna.

The young woman looked Elenora's way, her turn to frown. She handed her wooden spoon to a fellow cook and came over. "Hi. Jacob said you want to talk to me?"

"Yes. Hi. I'm Elenora. Can we go speak over there?"

Elenora led Anna to a table in a quiet corner of the dining room. "I have a peculiar question to ask you," Elenora said. "Rolland Carmichael..."

At the mention of Rolland's name, Anna blushed, and she couldn't help a small smile. "What about Rolland?"

"Did you ever give him a stuffed shark?"

The puzzled look on Anna's face said it all. "Yes...?"

"Do you know where he lives, by any chance?"

Anna's smile turned cautious. "Why would you like to know?"

Elenora picked up on Anna's protectiveness of Rolland. It pleased her to know someone cared for him, but the girl would also not give away his location easily. Behind Anna, she saw Tom and Alex approaching. She looked at Tom inquisitively—had they gotten what they needed?

He gave his head a curt shake and lifted his chin at Anna.

Elenora returned her attention to Anna, knowing that Tom would get her silent request to stay away, since she didn't invite him to join them.

"Anna, I won't beat around the bush. I'm a social worker, working with the police. If I told you Rolland was in trouble..." She showed the girl her work badge and let her statement sink in.

"Oh my God, what happened to him?"

"He is fine right now. But we suspect he could be a danger to himself. And it would be very helpful if we could reach him without scaring him off."

Anna silently took in what Elenora was saying.

"I help people deal with tricky situations so that they can nip trouble in the bud. Rolland is a terrific man. I want to help him."

"And to do that, you need me to tell you where he lives?"

"That would help a lot."

Anna squirmed in her seat. "I don't know if I can..."

Elenora guessed Anna's dilemma. "You're afraid you'd be betraying him. And you're wondering if my intent is honest and good for him."

"Nothing personal. I'm just having a healthy bit of skepticism. Comes with the territory," Anna replied, letting her gaze travel around the shelter. There was no edge in her tone, just the right amount of prudence.

"I understand."

Elenora waved Tom and Alex over. "This is Detective Tom Madigan and Detective Alex Bélanger. They can vouch for me, as can your coworker, Richard. Tom, Alex, this is Anna. She's a friend of Rolland's."

"Anna," Tom and Alex said in unison, giving her a nod and flashing their badges.

"What happens if you don't find him?" Anne asked, eyeing the three of them.

"Then we'll be back here on Tuesday before his shift and hope nothing bad happens in the meantime," Elenora answered truthfully but omitted to mention that they'd have a witch in tow and God knows who else if they had to come back to the shelter for Rolland. They'd probably have to evacuate the place, too.

"And believe me, I'm not trying to sound dramatic."

Anna chewed on her bottom lip, looking like she wanted to trust Elenora, but something held her back. "Can I think about it?"

"Certainly." Elenora was used to keeping her disappointment in check whenever someone couldn't be rushed. She gave her a card. "If you change your mind, get in touch anytime. I mean it."

Anna took the card and stood up.

"Yo, Mrs. B!" A booming voice coming from a stocky young guy with a volunteer t-shirt and heavily tattooed arms caught their attention. He made a beeline for Elenora, coming at her with open arms and a broad smile that ate up half his face.

"Francesco!" She stood and accepted the hug. "You look good!"

Elenora had met Francesco a few years ago when he was a street kid enmeshed in an impossible gang situation and an even worse family dynamic. They had developed a surprising rapport, and now he emailed her occasionally and every Christmas.

Anna observed their joyful reunion with a sharp eye.

"Because I *am* good." Francesco's gaze dropped to Elenora's belly. "And I see you've got an arts and crafts project going on."

"I sure do."

"When are you due?"

"Three weeks."

"Awesome sauce. You're gonna be one hell of a mom."

"Frank!" a woman called from the kitchen. "Get your tush back here!"

"Duty calls. Great seeing you, Mrs. B. Stay out of trouble." Francesco winked at her as he took a few steps backward.

"I can't promise you anything. Great seeing you too."

"I should get my tush back there, too." Anna pulled her cell phone out. "Look, I don't know Rolland's address, but I remember the neighborhood, and with Google Maps, perhaps I can recognize his house."

———⁓———

Anna had directed them to a quiet street in the borough of Little Burgundy, lined with older houses from the Victorian era. Most of them were majestic and well kept.

At the top of the street, Tom slowed, and Elenora spotted the house that matched the image and address Anna had located for them. It was a two-story Victorian Greystone row house loaded with architectural details and charm. It blended in well with the other houses.

It was late afternoon and already dark, given the time of year, but no lights were on at Rolland's place.

Tom drove past the house and around the block, stopping at the entrance of a narrow alley behind the block of homes. They had a clear view of the back of Rolland's house, and from that perspective too, it looked like nobody was home.

They turned around, drove once again in front of the house, and parked farther down the street. Alex, who had been following in his car, stopped behind them.

Tom killed the headlights and engine. A moment later, the back door behind Elenora opened and Alex hopped in.

"Pierre should be here any minute," Tom filled him in. "He said Serena's running late, but she'll come as soon as she can. He reminded us to stay put until she gets here."

"I'll try not to ignore her arrogant recommendation," Alex replied.

Elenora pulled her sun visor down to glare at him in the mirror.

"Just kidding, Ele," he beamed her an exaggerated grin. She flipped the visor shut in response and shook her head.

Tom's eyes spotted something in the rear-view mirror. "Here he comes."

The other back passenger door opened, and Pierre slipped into the car. "Howdy."

"Hey."

"Hey, Pierre." Elenora turned as much as she could to greet him.

Crackling with nervous energy, he squeezed her upper arm, eyes darting around both sides of the street.

"So, the house with the green door over there, is it?" He craned his neck to give the house a good look and whistled. "Not too shabby, eh?"

"Yeah, we'd love a place like that," Tom said over his shoulder.

"No driveway, though," Alex pointed out.

"No, but there's a parking spot in the back," Tom said.

"You're right."

Silence ensued in the car, and Elenora's mind wandered to how lucky they'd been to have found Anna and how focusing on Rolland's emotions about Sharky had relaxed her mind and allowed her to recall the vision. Was that the key?

A contraction snuck up on her, pulling her away from her thoughts. She looked out her window as she winced, determined to keep the pain to herself. She didn't want to distract Tom from the task at hand, nor risk him sending her home.

This was the fourth contraction she had in the past hours, and they were getting nasty. Still, they were too inconsistent to be the real deal. She had gone to the hospital the week before with similar contractions, and it had been a false alarm. They were so close to intercepting Rolland and putting a stop to his destruction, and hopefully helping him too. Now was not the time to give in to false labor and let it screw everything up.

"Is it okay if I take a bit of a walk?" she asked Tom, trying to sound nonchalant. At his starting frown, she added, "I think it would be good for the baby. I've been sitting a lot today."

"It's awfully cold outside," he countered.

"Just for a bit."

"I'll go with you," Pierre volunteered. "If we head away from the house, that'd be all right, no?" He looked at Tom for his approval.

Alex got out of the car. "Go drop them off on the next street over. I'll keep an eye out," he told Tom.

Tom turned on the car. "The Braxton Hicks are back?"

"With a vengeance, it seems. I must have pissed someone off royally in a previous life to be worthy of this kind of stellar timing."

Tom let out a chuckle, part amusement, part nerves. "D'you want me to—"

"I'm good, Tom. Really," Elenora tried to sound convincing. She couldn't engage Tom's overprotectiveness right now.

The car turned into the next street and stopped, letting her and Pierre off. "Elenora, if there's anything. *Anything*," Tom emphasized.

"If there's anything, Pierre's right here with me." She gave him a bright smile and closed the door. Undeterred, Tom buzzed the window down like he wanted to argue.

"We'll keep you posted," Pierre said, putting his arm around Elenora's shoulder.

"All right, fine. See you soon." Tom abdicated, buzzed the window back up, and drove off.

As the car turned the corner, Elenora let out a sigh of relief. She was now free to endure some agony in peace. She sucked a giant breath back in as a mother of all contractions hit her.

"Hang in there. And tell me if you need to rush to the hospital," Pierre said.

She took a few labored steps. "Hopefully, not before she's ready to come out for real. Come on, Aubrey. Chill out, girl."

Her experience with the previous false alarm had been taxing. After setting foot at the hospital and being admitted, examined, and monitored, the damn contractions had thumbed their noses at her and started receding, becoming further and further apart instead of progressing. She had no desire to repeat the experience. She would put up with these, even if they hurt like the dickens.

Except this one—argh! —this one was a real mofo.

Elenora grabbed Pierre's arm and stopped walking, doubling over in a failed attempt at curbing the pain.

"Breathe, luv," Pierre said softly.

Elenora struggled to curb the pain with her breathing.

"Are you all right, miss?" A male voice called near them.

Elenora grunted and took great effort to lift her head to tell the concerned stranger that she was fine.

She felt Pierre stiffen next to her.

The man in front of them dropped his grocery bags and approached them with an assured gait. "How far apart are they?"

Rolland was standing in front of them. Her shock of recognizing him rivaled the intensity of her contraction.

"You?" he said, bowled over as recognition also dawned in his pale blue eyes.

He knew about her? Elenora stilled. *Do not engage!* She could hear Serena's voice loud and clear in her head.

What was she to do? She hadn't sought Rolland out, but there he was anyway. Right in front of her.

Her mind raced. She had to keep going and hope Rolland would just let her be.

"When are you due?" he asked.

"Three weeks," Pierre answered for her, sounding cool and collected. At least *he* wouldn't be ruining this operation or putting them in danger.

Another unbearable pain shot through her, and she couldn't help let out a strangled moan. And then, as if things couldn't possibly get any worse, she felt a liquid warmth between her thighs, soaking up her pants.

No...

No, no, no...

NO!

"I think my water just broke," she hissed quietly at Pierre, hoping that Rolland wouldn't hear.

"I'll call an ambulance." Pierre whipped out his phone.

"Wait! No." She grabbed his arm holding the phone. "Not necessary. Let's just walk to the car and bring me in. It'll be fine."

Getting an ambulance could make Rolland hang around too long, and the more time they spent in his presence, the more they risked setting him off. She would crawl to the hospital on her knees if she had to, if that meant keeping Aubrey far away from him.

She forced herself to look up at Rolland and tried not to grimace as more pain paralyzed her. "Thank you for your assistance, sir. We'll be good. Have yourself a good evening."

"Where are you parked?" Rolland asked, looking concerned and having none of this nonsense. Just like Pierre, he too kept a cool head and acted like this was not his first time.

She remembered he was a doctor, after all.

"Just around the corner," Pierre answered, giving Elenora's arm a little squeeze. Was he asking her to play along?

"Ma'am... Elenora, is it?"

"Yes..."

Rolland briefly shook his head in shocked disbelief. "Elenora, please allow me to pick you up."

CHAPTER TWENTY-EIGHT

This had to be one of the strangest nights ever.

First, before Elenora could protest, Rolland had scooped her up in his arms and carried her swiftly to Pierre's car like she weighed nothing.

And then, she could have sworn the baby's head was already coming out, and she said as much. Everything became a blur of sights and sounds as she swam in and out of various states of consciousness.

She vaguely remembered sitting awkwardly on the edge of an armchair in a living room as Rolland delivered Aubrey. Tom held her hand, reminding her to breathe, while Pierre told her she was doing great. Alex stood at the edge of the room, observing from afar.

She could also swear Rolland had guided Tom in cutting the umbilical cord with scissors after instructing Pierre on how to sterilize them in his kitchen.

A centuries-old murder suspect had delivered her baby. In his house.

It sounded like a strange dream. Or a bad acid trip that had miraculously ended well.

Elenora was now holding her perfect little girl, bundled in a vintage blanket, on their way to being checked at the hospital. She was exhausted but elated. Aubrey had survived her rocky journey inside and out of her womb, unscathed.

And Rolland hadn't killed them.

"He just vanished?" Elenora asked Tom, who was sitting next to her in the back seat of Pierre's SUV, while Pierre drove.

"Looks like it. One moment he was there, and the other he wasn't. Alex looked away from him for a nanosecond to glance at the baby, and that's all it took," Tom said, staring adoringly at his new daughter. "We found the back door unlocked."

"He must've figured out who you were."

"Yeah."

"And Serena?"

"She must have arrived by now," Pierre said, glancing at the time on the dashboard. "She'll help Alex look around the house, throw a few detecting spells around. Should be interesting."

"It's so weird that he would just leave his house with a bunch of strangers in it."

Elenora brushed a finger over one of Aubrey's chubby cheeks. Did she look like her? Or would she take more after her dad? Would she grow up to look like the little white-haired girl from the courtroom? What about her temperament? Elenora suspected she'd be a warrior.

"He must've thought that disappearing was a better

course of action than sticking around. He figured out we were cops and he's got something to hide," Tom said.

"You think he's aware of the crimes he...helped commit?" Elenora asked.

"He ran. He must know something is wrong on some level."

They rode in silence for a moment.

Elenora took another long look at her daughter's sweet and innocent face. She had waited for this moment for so long and desperately wanted to savor it. But she also couldn't help the pang of sadness and anxiety she felt for Rolland. The man had helped her and now he was on the run because of it, probably distressed thinking the police were after him.

She'd hoped she could help him when they finally got to meet without triggering the darkness inside of him. He needed help. She should have been the one to help him. Instead, he acted selflessly, putting his neck on the line for a stranger and her newborn daughter's safety.

And now that he knew they were on to him, they might never find him again.

Despite mom and baby doing well, the doctor at the hospital asked them to stay overnight. Once they were set up in a room, Tom got in touch with Alex to know what he and Serena had found at Rolland's house.

Since Rolland had willingly brought them in, they figured they could do some discreet snooping, despite the ethical gray area. Serena also argued it was for Rolland's own good. The more they knew about him and his current state, the better chance they'd have of saving him.

Unfortunately, despite Serena's magic, they found nothing incriminating other than faint traces of dark vibes, which meant diddly-squat in a court of law. There were hints that Rolland had been alive for nearly two centuries, but that also was not a crime.

They found his panic room, and it was squeaky clean. Perhaps they could find a fingerprint belonging to Danica Tremblay if they looked hard enough, but proving she'd been there wouldn't do much for their case at this time.

Alex did a live video tour of the home on his phone for Elenora and Tom, focusing on elements she had seen in her visions. The stone-walled basement. The wooden desk. The letters and restaurant flyers. The daguerreotype.

They matched exactly.

Alex and Serena had hoped to find papers, credit card statements, or other ways to retrace Rolland, but there were no indications of where he might have gone.

The trail was cold.

CHAPTER TWENTY-NINE

Despite the harsh, icy wind whipping at him as he flew down the highway on his old motorcycle, Rolland had chosen to head up north to his little secluded cabin in the Laurentians. He needed to hide without fear of being found, at least long enough to gather his wits and try to understand what the hell had just happened.

One moment he was heading home with some groceries, looking forward to a quiet evening in front of the TV. The next, he was running into *her* and taking charge in a lightning-fast baby delivery. And then, he had to abandon a home he cherished and to which he'd probably have to wait decades before he could return. If ever.

What in the actual hell?

When the woman—Elenora was her name, as she confirmed it—had appeared in his hallway mirror, he suspected he would see her again. But he could never have imagined it'd be under this kind of life-altering, screwed-up circumstance.

He had so many questions for her and had longed for a

chance to talk to her without interference. But today's encounter had been the polar opposite of that. They had barely exchanged a few words, and most of them had been about guiding her to give birth.

It had been a few decades since Rolland had delivered a baby, but he could have proceeded with his eyes closed. His experience had been in conditions so much direr than those of modern days.

He had seen and done it all, except delivering a mysterious woman he vaguely knew and with whom he felt a strange connection, under the watchful eyes of her detective husband and his colleagues, a breath away from being arrested and no doubt being thrown in jail to rot for crimes he never truly committed but to which he was undeniably tied.

If he ended up in jail, he would never see Anna again.

The thought strangled his heart.

This was all speculation since the three men accompanying Elenora had said nothing to confirm his suspicions. But the way the big and burly one—Alex, was it?—kept a hawkish eye on his every move had given Rolland reason to believe he was in a force of some kind. The man's entire demeanor screamed cop. And while the older man seemed less wound up and more approachable, there was also something in his eyes that said he was observant and taking in everything.

How the hell did he get involved in this? And why did he let them into his home?

This last one was a rhetorical question. Rolland knew very well why.

When Elenora said she felt the baby's head, he couldn't abandon her to give birth on the sidewalk in near-freezing weather. They were so close to his place; he didn't have to think about it twice. What he hadn't seen coming was that Elenora's husband and Alex would appear out of nowhere and join them.

They'd appeared out of nowhere.

That was the first thing that clued him in that something strange was going on beyond his unexpected encounter with Elenora. They surely didn't conveniently appear out of nowhere. They had been there, waiting for him to come home. They were onto him because Elenora must have known something about him, and they were there to talk to him or coerce him or arrest him. It was hard to think otherwise. Their presence seemed contradictory, though. He felt a benevolent vibe from Elenora, and yet she showed up with cops at his door?

Trying to figure out their motives made his head hurt, much like the delivery itself.

It happened so fast, as if the baby had decided to come out the moment Rolland had shown up. It had briefly crossed his mind that Elenora might be a witch who provoked her own delivery to catch his attention, but that seemed so far-fetched, and she looked to be in real pain. He nipped this harebrained theory in the bud.

And then there was the baby. Little Aubrey. Another puzzling piece.

She looked like a normal baby, and Rolland didn't think she could have orchestrated her own birth to coincide with his presence, but there was something special about her. He could feel it. When Elenora pushed her out, and he took her, he felt an unexpected warmth travel from her to him, reaching into his core. He couldn't explain the odd, yet pleasant sensation, just that he had felt it, and even now, it lingered inside of him.

What did this mean?

What did any of this mean?

Rolland suddenly felt exhausted.

Fortunately, the sign for his exit appeared up ahead. He looked forward to balling himself up in front of a fire in his cabin and forgetting about the whole world on the other side of his door.

CHAPTER THIRTY

"If you ever encounter Rolland again, tell him you have a message from an old friend and show him this video. It's a spell that should freeze up his inner jackass for a while. Think of it as like a spiritual stun gun."

The day after Aubrey was born and Rolland escaped, Serena had prepared a video recording for Elenora, Tom, Pierre, and Alex. On camera, she had recited an incantation meant to subdue Rolland's inner demon temporarily if any of them came across him again. The digital spell would hopefully work and give them time to react and deal with him so he wouldn't get away this time should Serena be unable to get there fast enough.

While no one was blaming her, the witch still felt responsible for Rolland slipping through their fingers, even though her showing up late at his house had been out of her control.

"And this is gonna work?" Alex inquired with suspicion.

"We *hope* it's gonna work. But ideally, we won't have to try and find out in the first place," Serena replied.

Despite the untested efficiency of the recorded incantation, the digital ammunition brought them some reassurance. They hadn't heard from Rolland and didn't know what to expect next. Would the vile spirit make him retaliate and hunt them down to *deal* with *them* before they could get to him? Serena thought the possibility was real. Rolland had fled, no doubt feeling threatened.

And so they waited, on their guard, expecting a sneak assault at any time.

Weeks went by with no sign of Rolland.

Pierre had extended his stay with Céleste at Elenora's and Tom's place.

While Tom was taking time off work to help take care of his newborn, he still did some work from home on the Rolland front. He, Alex, and their team at work kept investigating and monitoring the city, the province, the country—traffic cameras, police reports, local news—on the off chance they would have a breakthrough, but nothing new came up.

Serena and Claire-Lune were also doing their best to find something.

A week after Rolland dropped off the face of the earth, his friend Anna from the Jeanne Mance Mission showed up in Alex's office at the station, demanding answers. What had they done to Rolland? He had not come to work since their visit and was nowhere to be found. She blamed his disappearance on their intervention.

Faced with Anna's fiery pain and obvious care for Rolland's well-being, Alex got in touch with Elenora and Tom to decide how much they should tell the girl. They did an impromptu videoconference with her, telling her the disclosable parts of what had happened that night, from the bizarre sudden baby delivery to Rolland's gracious help to him leaving before they even had a chance to have a real talk.

Anna must have believed their sincerity. She backed down but asked to be kept in the loop when they found him.

Despite the circumstances, Elenora was glad to be reminded that she wasn't the only one to care about Rolland's welfare. Now, if only they could find him.

During this unnerving period of suspicious calm, Elenora was as sleep-deprived as ever and did her best to adjust to her new role of mother to an adorable infant who slept sporadically and often battled her over breastfeeding.

Aubrey was a tranquil yet feisty little thing. With every new day, she looked more and more like Elenora had pictured her. Her full head of black hair from birth was getting lighter fast and already a light chestnut brown. Would her hair eventually become almost white in her toddler years?

Elenora and Tom brought Aubrey to see her grandmother Muriel a few times. Muriel's reaction to the baby had been unsettling, if not downright creepy. Now, her usual dead gaze would come to life upon seeing the little one and latch onto the baby with a disturbing intensity, to the point Elenora wondered if her mother would attack her newborn if she could. They had to space out the visits for Elenora's sanity.

Otherwise, Elenora was over the moon to be spending time with Aubrey, but she also felt postpartum depression lurking around the corner. Or maybe it was the constant stress of the unsettling possibility that Rolland's inner evil would return to dispatch them. If it did, could they battle it and win?

Everything felt so surreal.

Her nerves were frayed, and her mental health hung in a precarious balance. To feel proactive, she absorbed all the information she could find on handling postpartum depression and demons. Nothing beat reading up on baby blues, possession, and exorcisms between two diaper changes.

At least, save for the cocky little twerp at the bottom of the river occasionally crashing her otherwise uneventful dreams—presumably to remind her of his pestiferous existence—her sleep had been wonderfully ordinary. Suspiciously or not, premonitions had left her alone. And while it would have been beyond convenient for a dream to reveal Rolland's whereabouts, Elenora certainly didn't need to be shown cryptic images of other deaths or strangers in distress on top of everything else going on.

She savored the marvelous absence of visions, the welcome psychic reprieve, giving little thought to the potential return of her troubling abilities. She had no mental or emotional real estate left to worry about them.

The status quo drastically changed the week before Christmas.

It was a beautiful, quiet winter night. Holiday decorations and colorful lights brightened the streets. Fat, cottony snowflakes fell from the sky, muffling the sounds outside. The atmosphere lent itself to drinking hot cocoa and mulled wine by the fire.

It was a little past nine o'clock. The house was calm and cozy. Tom had stepped out to help his team on an unrelated case, and Pierre had taken Céleste on her evening walk.

Elenora was home alone with Aubrey, who had just finished nursing. The little one was already asleep, but she kept rocking her and studying her, enjoying some well-deserved peace. Elenora loved that time of night, when everything was muted and calm. She would soon head to bed but not before taking her sweet time and thoroughly enjoying the moment.

And then she heard something. A shuffling. Footsteps?

The noise seemed close by, on the second floor, where she and Aubrey were.

She stopped rocking and strained her ear to listen. Was it their older home creaking in protest, sounding like footsteps? Or was there someone in the house?

How could there be someone in the house?

If it were Tom or Pierre, she would have heard the front door open and close. The sound of boots thumping off snow or the swishing of a winter jacket being shed and put on a hanger. Footfalls on the staircase.

But she had heard none of that.

Elenora slowly stood up and put Aubrey down in her crib. She scanned the room to find a weapon so she could go investigate the sound.

It was probably nothing.

A movement caught her attention in the cheval mirror in the corner of Aubrey's room. In it, she saw a dark, tall silhouette. It came closer and her breath caught.

Rolland?

He was in the mirror, staring at her with dark, paralyzing eyes. Would he cross the mirror again to get to her?

His hands reached for her, and panic rose inside her.

She sensed a presence behind her, and before she could move, hands slid around her throat.

Rolland was no longer just in the mirror; he was right there in the room with her, hell-bent on strangling her.

Elenora struggled, clawing at his hands to make them loosen their grip. She had learned self-defense techniques over the years and broken up fights involving much bigger opponents. She'd been assaulted, too. But nothing could have prepared her for this. Rolland's grip on her throat was tight and brutal. She could barely breathe or think.

"You won't be saving him," a low and guttural voice whispered into her ear. Chilling and inhuman. Elenora was no physical match for a man this size, let alone one possessed by only God or the devil knew what.

Still, her motherly instinct to keep her daughter safe kicked in, and her body thrashed around like a wildcat, determined to put up a good fight.

While flailing, her legs kicked Aubrey's crib. The baby made a noise, a peep announcing an imminent crying fit on the horizon.

No, no, no, no, no...

Shush, Aubrey. Don't cry!

Elenora felt Rolland loosening his grip around her throat. She gasped for air and stomped on his foot the hardest she could.

His long fingers resumed their death grip. His arms encaged her tightly to restrain her and squeeze the life out of her.

Elenora felt light-headed. When would Pierre come home?

Please come home!

The room swam.

Aubrey squeaked again. And the squeak quickly evolved into a cry, then a full-blown wail.

Elenora felt Rolland stiffen. His fingers stopped squeezing. His grip loosened again, and his arms went limp. She stumbled forward, gasping and struggling to recover her breath.

What was his plan now? What sadistic game was he playing? Did he step back so he could swing at her and strike her with force?

She ducked out of the way and readied herself for an attack. But as she turned to face Rolland and assess him, she saw he'd fallen to his knees, his hands gathered behind his head, as if giving himself up to be arrested.

He was weeping.

"Please make it stop," he said in a meek voice, confused and wild-eyed.

"Rolland?" She croaked, her throat raw.

"I mean you no harm, Elenora, I swear!" he said with alarm. "I don't know how I got here. One minute, I wished I could talk to you, and now, here I am in—" His eyes searched the room. "Your house? I'm so sorry, I really don't mean—I'm unarmed!"

His attention shifted to the crib, as if finally noticing that Aubrey was wailing. He dropped his voice to an urgent whisper. "I didn't mean to wake her. I'm unarmed. Believe me. I'm so sorry."

"It's all right, Rolland," Elenora replied soothingly. "Is it okay if I pick her up?"

"Of course."

Without turning her back on Rolland, Elenora reached

for her crying daughter and rocked her in her arms. She kept a sideways glance at the intruder as she hummed a lullaby. She gestured to the rocking chair, offering it to him. He went to sit in it.

Elenora paced around the room, Rolland's apologetic stare following her. He was keeping still, his hands clenched together on his lap, afraid to move.

"There's something I'd like to show you on my phone. I'm going to reach for it, okay?" she said to him over Aubrey crying.

He nodded again.

Elenora slowly slipped her phone out of her robe pocket. She angled it toward him so he could see she wasn't calling anyone. He looked at her, puzzled, as she searched for Serena's video and cued it. She handed him the phone.

"An old friend of yours has a message for you."

Rolland took the phone, and his eyes widened.

Please work. Please work. Please work.

Elenora held her breath while pacing with Aubrey—who was quieting down—eyeing Rolland discreetly. While she was hoping for the best, she stayed on high alert and prayed that Pierre would walk in the door any second now.

Rolland was thrown aback to see Serena and frowned in confusion, but his features quickly relaxed as the witch's soothing words had a hypnotic effect on him. Dazed, he stared at the phone for a while after the video ended.

He looked up at Elenora. His face calm, relieved. Almost serene.

"How are you feeling?" she asked him.

"It's the weirdest thing... Like a tremendous weight has been lifted off my shoulders."

She smiled. Serena's spell must have worked. But how long would it hold?

"Would you like some tea? Or scotch?" She offered him, taking her phone back.

"Tea would be lovely, thanks."

"Let me put her down."

Thankfully, Pierre and Céleste came back home minutes after Elenora had started making tea. Being left alone with an evil spirit lurking, sedated or not, had frazzled her nerves. Now that Pierre was back, if Serena's theory was right, the spirit was less likely to manifest itself and attack while being outnumbered.

Their remaining challenge was to not provoke it until Serena showed up.

Pierre kept a trigger-free, neutral conversation going with Rolland, from weather to sports to science. And Céleste helped, too. It turned out that Rolland was a dog lover but felt like he'd be a horrible person to take care of one and thus never had one. He enthusiastically petted Céleste, who acted normally with him. She must not have picked up anything unusual about the spiritual state of their special, unexpected guest. Elenora took that as a good sign.

The conversation not only kept the spirit at bay, but it also seemed to put Rolland at ease with them, though a glimmer of sorrow never left his eyes. Twice he tried to apologize to Elenora for what he'd put her through, and both times she assured him she knew he wasn't at fault before promptly changing the subject. Serena would arrive soon, and Elenora didn't want to tempt fate in the meantime.

The front door opened, and Tom and Alex came rushing in. Tom's face welcomed an extreme amount of relief when he saw the trio peacefully sitting at the kitchen table.

Rolland shifted in his seat at the sight of the two men.

"How's the baby?" Tom whispered to Elenora, hugging her from behind her chair.

"Still fine and still asleep."

Tom let out a deep sigh before turning his attention to Rolland. "Mr. Carmichael," he greeted him with a cordial tone.

"Sir." Rolland eyed him nervously.

"We didn't have the opportunity to properly introduce each other before," he said, holding out his hand. "Please call me Tom."

"Tom. Rolland." They shook hands.

"We didn't get to thank you properly for the delivery either."

"Don't mention it. It was a privilege."

"You remember Alex?" Tom pointed to his partner. Alex took a few cautious steps and offered his hand.

"Alex," Rolland said, taking Alex's hand. After they let go of the handshake, Rolland brandished his hands up in surrender, waiting to be cuffed. Elenora gently brought his hands down. He gave her a quizzical look.

The doorbell rang, and Pierre stood up swiftly, sending his chair scraping behind him. "That would be Serena."

CHAPTER THIRTY-ONE

"It really is you!" Serena squealed as she laid eyes on Rolland.

"Miss Barton?" Rolland said, as bewildered as when he'd seen her in the video message. He gave her a little bow, as if his muscle memory brought him back to the last time they'd met.

"In the flesh. And it's Winston now. But still Serena. *Always* Serena."

"Noted... How we meet again after all this time, my dear Miss Winston, is a baffling miracle." He reached for her hand and kissed it. Old habits really died hard.

"I agree." She pulled him into a hug, taking him by surprise. "You've been through so much. And please don't *Miss Winston* me. Times have changed."

"They sure have and thank God for that."

They took in one another, hardly believing what they were seeing. Rolland broke the spell first. "I am delighted to see you, though I suspect this is not entirely a social call... Also, I didn't quite decipher your video message to me."

"You mean this?" She positioned herself in front of Rolland, locked her eyes to his, and recited the incantation from her video.

Once again, Rolland visibly relaxed at the words and took a moment to react. "Yes. That. And it's just as cryptic the second time around."

"How do you feel now?"

"Even lighter than before."

"Great. That should give us some time."

"What did it mean, what you said? My Latin is a little rusty."

"It's a message to whatever's possessing you, so it doesn't go all jackass-in-the-box on us. It also means we want to help put you out of your misery."

Rolland's face lit up with surprise and hope.

Serena turned to the others, her gaze traveling from one person to the next. "I spoke to Claire-Lune and Wren. They think we should all meet at Rolland's place since there are remains of dark energy there and we don't want to leave any loose ends or have it spill out somewhere else, uncontained. So, plan A: we assess what crawled up his ass and see if we can banish the crap out of it."

"I see you've picked up modern-day lingo just fine," Rolland quipped. "And I also have a cabin up north. I've been staying there lately."

"Good to know. We'll smudge it later for good measure."

"So, the plan is to poke the bear?" Tom asked.

"Pretty much."

His face fell.

"And what's Plan B?" Pierre petted Céleste absent-mindedly.

"We'll figure out Plan B and any other letter if Plan A fails." When no other questions came, Serena said, "Okay then, let's get going."

"Are we absolutely needed for this?" Tom gestured at Elenora and himself. He was never one to retreat from anything, which made his question even more surprising. "We have a baby to think about."

Serena looked away in thought.

"As much as I would like to help, it sounds risky and way out of our league. Out of mine, anyway," Tom pleaded with a hint of shame. "Pierre, am I overreacting?"

Pierre stroked the stubbles along his chin. "Well, I've seen the girls tackle spirits before and my money's on them. But, yeah, there are risks."

Serena added, "Pierre's right, things can always go sideways, and I think we've got this one, but I'll be honest. This case is particular, and Elenora has a strong and unique connection to it. I have a feeling her singular gifts could very well make a difference in putting an end to this madness for good."

"There's no way you can permanently sedate the spirit, like you're doing now?" Alex asked.

She shook her head. "It would adapt and get past the spell. We need a permanent solution. Otherwise, it might come after Elenora again. And after what happened tonight, it seems there's no lock strong enough to keep it from getting to her."

Rolland buried his face in his hands, and Pierre laid a hand on his shoulder in solidarity. "Don't blame yourself."

Elenora blew out a breath. Tom took her hand to get her

attention and said, "How about I stay with Aubrey, and you decide whether to go? I'll support your decision."

She knew what he meant, what *this* meant, and the gravity of the situation hit her hard: she was free to go with them and fight the good fight, and should anything serious—lethal even—happen to her, their little one wouldn't become an orphan. Tom had always been the one with the higher risk job. Until now.

This was unfamiliar territory, and the stakes gave her vertigo.

She found herself at an emotional crossroads. She yearned to help Rolland more than anyone else she'd ever helped, but she also wanted to stay with her daughter and let them deal with it.

"I'm so sorry for putting you through all this and in this impossible situation," Rolland muttered to her, his gaze sincere and pained.

"I don't want to pressure you," Serena told her, "but if it helps, Pierre's been around this block before and can take you away to safety if things go south."

"For sure. And I can bring Céleste, too. She's an old pro," Pierre confirmed, studying Elenora. He drew her into his arms for a fatherly hug and told her, "I'm proud of you no matter what you decide."

Serena glanced at her watch.

Elenora's gut twisted into a tighter knot. Deep inside, she felt guilt and a strong pull to stay home with her newborn. If she went, this would be the first time she'd leave Aubrey, and the intervention presented risks much different from what she was accustomed to.

Working with the police, she was no stranger to the notion that any intervention could turn sour. Danger was a part of everyday life, both for her and Tom. They had signed up for this. But this case was far from a typical intervention. This one had elements of unnatural instability and something straight from hell thrown into the mix. Who knew where that could lead? Who knew what kind of devastating effect their actions could have as they tackled a murderous spirit? A demon?

But even worse, who knew what kind of devastation it could bring if they failed and it came back for her? If their actions fell short because Elenora's special skills and strengths were not there to tip the balance in their favor?

If their intervention failed because she stayed home?

They couldn't fail.

She couldn't allow another close call with evil like she had in the nursery.

The best and only way to protect her daughter might be for her to take part in this crazy mission despite the risks. She had to do this for Aubrey's sake.

Guilt would have to wait.

Elenora, Serena, Pierre, and Alex followed Rolland to his kitchen for him to make a pot of tea. They had some time to kill before their reinforcement arrived.

The room at the back of the house was eclectic. A Wi-Fi-enabled electric pressure cooker tucked in a corner of the worn wood countertop mingled with a huge stove from the 1940s. Some of the décor could have come straight from a museum. The flowery wallpaper was probably original to the house, which must have been built in the second part of the 1800s, and Elenora wondered if the pigments contained arsenic.

The previous and very brief time she'd been in this house, she hadn't made it past the front room and didn't have the opportunity to take a good look amidst the fuzzy chaos of her childbirth. But she was all eyes now. There was something breathtaking about the room despite its lack of unity.

"I gather you're a collector," she said to Rolland.

"You're being generous. I'm more of a historical hoarder," he replied, pouring tea in mugs. "Grab a cup, everyone."

"Shall we retire to the drawing room?" Serena asked tongue-in-cheek, reaching for a dainty teacup.

"Drawing room? That's what's been missing in my life," Alex muttered, fighting an eye roll.

"For the record, I haven't called it that in ages." Rolland led them to his living room at the front of the house, where heavy velvet burgundy drapes framed majestic-looking windows. Here too, the wallpaper was vintage and the furniture from a long-gone era.

Elenora sat on a fancy armchair, and her gaze swept the vaguely familiar room. This was where she had delivered Aubrey, but it was more than that. She'd also seen bits and pieces of it in a dream.

This was where Delphine had passed.

Birth and death.

Making the connection between the two events gave her an odd but not unpleasant feeling. She simply couldn't quite put her finger on it.

Then again, seeing Rolland's place in person—without being in the throes of childbirth—was a bit of a shock for her, perhaps the origin of her funny feeling. It had been one thing to see parts of it in her mind and a different feel when Alex had given her a virtual tour with his phone. And being here again was something else, too.

The place was like a time capsule, and Elenora picked up on so many vibes—good and bad—she felt an intensity she had rarely felt before. She feared that if she let her fingers roam around the room, she could get sensory overload.

"Was this your place when we first met?" Serena was taking in the room with a light frown. "It looks familiar, but I didn't think you lived in this part of town."

"No. Delphine lived here, after she married this man... His name eludes me. A nice guy, that one," Rolland answered.

"Léandre...something, was it?"

"Right. Léandre Leblanc."

"Léandre Leblanc, yeah. That's right. Awfully nice guy. Unfortunate breath. How did you end up in her house?"

"When she was older and he and her entire family were gone, we...reconnected."

"You re-entered the salon society?" One of Serena's brows shot up in doubt.

"God, no. I came across her at the Ursulines Hospital. She was terminally ill and wished to spend her last days at home. I helped her make that happen." Rolland's voice hitched. "When she passed, she left the house to me. I offered to purchase it from her, but she refused. She had no one else to leave it to and didn't see the point in taking money to her grave."

"But your name is not on the deed to the house, is it? We would have caught that," Tom asked from Pierre's cell phone, which was propped up on a small table so he could be present via video conferencing.

"No. The house is currently under Rolland Deschamps. For practical reasons."

"To stay under the radar," Tom said.

"Let's say it proved useful."

Elenora searched for the antique tapestry settee on which Delphine had lied down in her dream, and she found it in a corner of the room. Curious, she headed for it. Despite her earlier resolve of keeping her hands to herself to avoid sensory overload, she couldn't help wondering if touching the settee would trigger the same vision she'd had.

She kneeled in front of it and laid a hand on the right arm where Delphine's head had been. A rush of physical pain and a mixture of strong emotions swelled inside of her. She was sucked into the dream she'd had, except now she was experiencing it from a much different perspective. She saw Rolland holding her hand as if she, herself, was the one dying. She was inside Delphine. She *was* Delphine.

Rolland's face was devastated, his gaze on her intense with pain. Elenora was transfixed by his presence, the pain, and the affection and admiration Delphine had for him.

Someone lifted Elenora's hand away from the settee, bringing her back to the present.

"Are you okay?" Alex was crouching next to her, his eyes filled with worry.

"Yes." A tear ran down her cheek and she wiped it. She found Rolland staring at her with wild eyes. "She was so grateful you were there for her in the end, taking care of her. She loved you very much," she told him softly.

Rolland's face filled with infinite sadness. It took him a moment to ask in a choked-up voice, "Was she at peace?"

"I think so."

Feeling remnants of the acute pain and emotions from the vision, Elenora touched her sensitive stomach and couldn't help wincing.

"Is she still here? Did she not move on?" Rolland asked, panicked, in reaction to her grimacing.

"I don't know."

"She suffered so much before she passed."

Elenora closed her eyes and searched within herself for the answer to reassure Rolland, but she simply didn't know. She put her hand back on the little couch and strained herself, but she got no more insight.

She shook her head, disappointed. "I'm sorry, Rolland. I don't know."

"Hold on." Serena crouched next to Elenora, elbowing Alex out of the way to touch the settee too.

"You can see spirits?" Elenora asked.

"No, but I can feel their energy sometimes. Let's see if we can get something, together."

"Okay."

Serena put her free hand on top of Elenora's, connecting herself to her like she had previously. Under the witch's touch, the room darkened and everyone else vanished. The colors drained in a surreal fashion. Elenora looked around and knew without hearing words that Serena was guiding her, asking her if she saw or felt anything spiritual.

Delphine's lifeless body appeared in front of her, lying on the couch. She was transparent, like she'd already started transitioning to an ethereal state. Her eyes were closed and her features at ease. She was hovering a few inches over the plush cushions of the settee.

Elenora reached a hand toward the old woman, and it slid through her. This time, she felt no pain or powerful emotion. Only relief and light-heartedness.

The translucent vision of Delphine departed and Elenora told Serena in thoughts that all she felt was light-hearted and the feeling had waned and disappeared, along with the specter. A clear reply from Serena in her mind explained this meant that Delphine had moved on.

The light came back from the lamps around the room, restoring colors to their muted evening shades, the way they'd been a moment earlier. Rolland appeared on the other side of the settee, his eyes glued to the two women, expectantly.

"She's not suffering, Rolland," Elenora heard herself say to him. "I think she passed away peacefully and moved on." She turned to Serena for validation and got a proud nod from her.

"You heard me correctly," the witch confirmed with a grin.

It amazed Elenora that she didn't imagine Serena's voice in her head and that she saw and felt Delphine's departure, too. She suddenly felt privileged and honored to be privy to a most intimate and sublime moment, that of a soul leaving this world in a state of serenity.

Rolland's reaction to her confirming Delphine's peaceful passing also made a deep impression on her. If she was being honest with herself, she had to admit this aspect of her new powers was intriguing, thrilling, and oddly satisfying. She could begin to understand Pierre's enthusiasm and giddiness for these peculiar interventions.

This was special, and she had a front-row seat.

"Ele, are you okay?" Tom inquired from the cell phone.

Her nod got interrupted by a knock at the front door, and two women walked in. One was the spitting image but an older version of Serena, and the other one was tall and willowy, with shoulder-length, curly black hair and a mocha complexion. Both seemed in their late forties.

Pierre greeted them keenly. "Claire-Lune. Wren. It's been a while."

"It's been too long, Pierre," Claire-Lune replied, giving him a hug.

"Agreed," Wren said next to her, waiting for her turn.

Pointing at her doppelgänger with silver-stranded auburn hair, Serena said, "This is obviously my sister Claire-Lune—"

"Aren't you supposed to be twins?" Alex interrupted her, suspicious.

"We are. But I'm comfortable showing my natural age, without a glamor. Unlike some." Claire-Lune gave her sister a teasing smile.

"It's not that simple, and you know it," Serena scoffed. "Plus, it's come in handy to play mother-daughter at times."

Alex's frown deepened with their explanations. Pierre patted him on the shoulder. "We'll explain later. It's all good."

"And this is Wren." Serena continued her introduction. "We've been friends a very long time and through so much. She's like a sister to us."

"Out of curiosity, when you say, 'a long time,' how long are we talking about?" Tom asked from the cell phone.

"Let me guess: they met at the Salem witch trials," Alex said dryly.

"We met in—when was that, Wren? Around '92?" Serena said. Wren wiggled her hand to show it was indeed around then.

"1992 or 1692?" Alex asked.

"Try 892," Wren replied with sass. There was an elegance to her, warring with a glimmer of mischief in her eye.

Alex's eyebrows shot up past his hairline, making Serena and Claire-Lune chuckle.

"They're messing with you," Claire-Lune said. "We met around 1992. And thankfully, we were on this side of the border when the trials happened."

Alex shook his head, as if he now lived in a constant state of disbelief. "Do you have vampire blood too? Are you immortal?" he asked Wren.

"No. What you see is what you get. I'm forty-five and owning it."

"Good for you."

"All right, folks." Serena clapped her hands. "We better start dealing with Rolland's pressing matter so he can finally enjoy life again and stop terrorizing everyone else's."

"I don't know about enjoying life, but not having to worry about killing people anymore is a goal I can strive for," Rolland said.

Knowing the drill, Pierre went to the windows to close the drapes and said to Claire-Lune, "I suppose you'll be putting up a perimeter spell."

"Already done."

"Of course." Pierre noticed Alex looking at them, trying to follow. "It's like a shield around this place to contain whatever's about to go down," he explained.

"So the neighbors don't call the cops?" Alex caught on. Pierre nodded.

Serena turned to Wren. "Since we'll be rattling its cage, could you please focus on maintaining the taser spell on it?"

"You got it."

Serena's gaze traveled to Elenora, and she said, "Wren's the one who came up with the spell to subdue the entity. She's marvelous with spells. We're in good hands."

"Looks like she did a great job." Alex's praise surprised everyone.

"Thanks," Wren said to him.

Serena turned to her sister. "Lunie, please focus on keeping Rolland physically stable."

"Restraining him and watching for medical foul play?" Claire-Lune said.

"Yeah."

"Medical foul play? That doesn't sound reassuring." Rolland paled.

"We want to be ready for any kind of physical reaction, both knee-jerk and plain jerk."

Rolland answered by sucking in a sharp breath.

Serena went around him, assessing him. She focused her attention on the scars on his face and ran a finger over the biggest one. "This is the most they've ever healed?"

"Yeah. They haven't budged since 1847, when I got the fucker's teeth into my gums."

On the way to Rolland's house in Pierre's SUV, Serena had dared asked Rolland a few questions about his state, and that had led to him explaining his theory about his "parasite" and the teeth in his mouth from a foreigner presumably named Oliver.

"The beating broke several of my teeth, and I had to replace them," he'd told them, sandwiched in the back seat between Serena and Alex. "I made myself a pair of dentures, but the tools and technology back then...long story short, the horrible contraption hurt so much and one drunken night—I'm honestly not sure what happened or how it happened—but I ended up shoving some of a dead stranger's teeth right into my gums. And that's when the trouble started. The first murder happened on that very night."

"That explains so much now," Elenora said, turning to look at him from the front passenger seat.

"What do you mean?"

"The teeth. We tried to make sense of them."

"You knew about the teeth?"

"I've *seen* teeth, yes."

"So, you think those teeth were cursed or something?" Pierre asked Rolland while driving.

"Something along those lines."

Rolland had gone on to tell them how he'd tried to get rid of the teeth to stop the evil within him. And when that failed, he'd tried to get rid of himself but had miraculously survived his various attempts.

"Did you ever try to have the scars corrected?" Serena was now pacing in front of Rolland while interrogating him in the living room.

"Yes. Over the years, I've tried several things and surgeries, including experimental techniques that I've performed on myself."

*The scalpel in my vision...*Elenora thought.

"Did any of your attempts make any progress, even just temporarily?"

"Yes. A skin graft did a bit, but the next morning, my face had rejected it completely and gone back to this." He pointed at his scars. "Which didn't make any sense. I mean, rejection can be expected, but I had made other incisions, and those healed just fine. It's as if my body refused to have anything done to the scars. And then the same happened with early laser surgery. It took a few hours before reverting, but they came back. It defies all logic."

"It sounds like the parasite doesn't want you to do any healing, physical or emotional. It wants you permanently scarred," Elenora pointed out.

"That sounds about right."

Serena's attention went back to Rolland's face, and she seemed to consider something. "Hold still," she said before whispering a string of words while gliding her index finger over the biggest scar once again. But this time, the scar healed under her touch, leaving no trace at all but fresh and beautiful skin. A soft, collective gasp echoed in the room.

"I'll be damned," Alex mumbled.

"Trust me, you don't want that," Rolland replied dryly, touching his cheek. His face twitched, and the scar reappeared at the same place, looking the same as before.

"It's confirmed. We're dealing with a nasty little fucker," Serena declared. She cradled Rolland's face with her hands. "My poor friend, I can only imagine the torture you've been going through all this time... Now, please hold still again and look into my eyes."

Rolland did as he was told. Serena's stare became intense and bore deeply into him. She narrowed her eyes, deepening her focus even more. She muttered more words that were impossible to hear or decipher, until she groaned and took a step back.

"Too much interference?" Claire-Lune asked.

"It's slick. A parasite indeed. I can't seem to latch onto it. It keeps evading me."

The three witches exchanged pondering glances.

"Perhaps Elenora could help you see it?" Pierre volunteered. All eyes in the room snapped to him.

"Would that be dangerous?" Tom's apprehensive voice came from the cell phone.

The three witches exchanged more glances.

"Can't you just use some kind of *magic* to see him?" Alex asked, the word "magic" catching in his throat.

"No, I can't," Serena said defensively. "We wish, but no. We don't have a gift of sight like Elenora does. Witches all have strengths and weaknesses."

Elenora gave Serena a distraught look. "You think I'm a witch?"

"I'm not saying you're a witch," Serena backpedaled diplomatically.

Despite Serena's denial, was witchcraft somehow at the root of her gift? Elenora didn't know how she felt about that.

"Would you please try to help me see it?" Serena asked her nicely.

Elenora got a hold of herself. *One problem at a time.* "What do you have in mind?"

"We do like we did with the settee, link ourselves to one another and Rolland. See if you can get a mental image of the spirit. Anything to help us figure out what—who—we're dealing with."

"That sounds logical and reasonable." Also chilling and

intriguing. She was getting mixed messages from her brain and her instincts. But overall, she felt compelled to accept.

"You don't have to do this," Tom reminded her.

Elenora wandered up to the cell phone. "I know, Tom, but I feel like I should," she told him softly.

"As long as you're comfortable with it. But the moment you no longer are..."

"I know. Don't worry. They've got my back."

Alex pulled out his gun and asked Serena, "Would this help at all?"

"A gun might work or not. We'd know only after the facts," she said.

"I brought this for good measure." Pierre brandished a taser gun. "I know Claire-Lune and Wren are restraining him, and I would never question their efficiency, but how about we also restrain him physically since we have the luxury? Tie him to a chair? That can't hurt, right?" Pierre said.

"Good point, Pierre," Wren agreed.

Alex whipped out his handcuffs while Pierre went to fetch a chair in the next room.

Serena looked at Rolland. "You won't mind too much?"

He shrugged, but weariness spread over his face. "Whatever helps keep everyone safe from me."

Rolland sat on the chair that Pierre produced behind him and said to him, "There should be rope in the little shed out back. The key's hanging by the back door."

"Got it." Pierre took off to fetch the rope.

Within minutes, Rolland was tied up like a stick of salami to the chair in the middle of his living room. "Now what?"

"Now, you brace yourself and try not to fight back," Serena replied, her tone all business-like.

She did one last visual assessment of Rolland before saying, "Alex, please have your gun handy, but just in case, all right? Only if things get really ugly."

"Define 'really ugly.' I suspect we have very different definitions of 'really ugly,'" he replied.

"Okay... If you feel like the apocalypse has been unleashed, then count to ten. And if you must shoot, please don't shoot to kill if at all possible."

"Just a friendly reminder that I don't seem to be killable," Rolland said.

"You may seem immortal, but even immortality is not always forever. As for physical indestructibility, there's often a weakness somewhere," Wren explained.

Alex pinched the bridge of his nose.

Serena placed herself in front of Rolland and waved to Elenora to come stand next to her. "Ready?"

Elenora wasn't sure if she was ready, but her own comfort didn't matter right now. She was eager to make this happen and move on. She did, however, brace herself for horror to be unleashed inside her mind. The parasite had been a nasty piece of work so far. She didn't expect to encounter a boy scout. "Ready."

The witch yanked her cell phone from her jeans' back pocket and placed her hand holding it on Rolland's shoulder.

"Let's try to record this," she said to Elenora, taking her hand with the other. "When I say 'Go,' touch him on the shoulder too and see if you get anything."

"What if I touched his teeth? Wouldn't that be a more

direct conduit to the spirit? I might get a better mental image."

Serena looked impressed. "Would you be comfortable with that?"

"Won't he try to bite her?" Tom barked from the confines of the cell phone.

"I'll keep his teeth clenched shut," Claire-Lune told Tom.

"All right. Let's get this show on the road. Whenever you're ready," Serena said to her sister over her shoulder.

Claire-Lune's fingers made subtle movements, and Rolland's lips parted, curling enough to give Elenora access to his teeth.

Neat trick. Eerie but neat.

Elenora leaned toward Rolland, bringing fingers to his mouth.

Okay...here we go.

CHAPTER THIRTY-TWO

Elenora's fingertips landed on the enamel of Rolland's teeth. She barely had time to clear her mind as the rapidly flickering images bombarded the black canvas she had just begun picturing.

Bright and bold, they spun around her, immersing her in them.

Memories. Very bloody memories.

They flashed by at breakneck speed, tossing Elenora from one to the next. Too fast for her to make sense of them. However, she could tell that blood—oozing or spraying—was a common denominator, as was the overwhelming sense of hatred and self-loathing she could feel forcefully in every part of her soul.

A blood-curdling scream and a sharp bark brought her back to reality, back to Rolland's posh living room.

She felt arms wrapped around her and realized the scream was coming from her. All eyes around the room, including Rolland's and Celeste's, were on her.

"Elenora?" Pierre whispered in her ear. "I got you. We got you. You're safe. Breathe."

Elenora's breath was jagged. Pierre's comforting presence convinced her frayed nerves that she wasn't in danger.

"Wow, that was something else," Claire-Lune said. She looked at her fellow witches. "Did you feel that?"

In a state of utter stupefaction, Wren barely nodded.

Also in shock, Serena was frantically busy on her cell phone. "Hell, yeah. That was intense. I'm surprised that any of it translated."

"You captured *that*?" Claire-Lune asked in awe.

"Can you believe it?" Serena turned to Elenora. "Did you see clear bits or was everything all chopped up?"

"All chopped up. It was way too fast to see anything," Elenora replied, recovering. She felt slightly dizzy, but at least the room wasn't spinning.

"Okay. Let's see if we can make anything out of this."

"Slowing down the images might give us something," Claire-Lune suggested.

They all huddled around Serena's cell phone, angled at Rolland to include him. Pierre held his own cell so that Tom could also see the images.

Played at a very low speed, the insights from Elenora's mind revealed a sequence of tableaux from the early 1800s, depicting a variety of murders carried on by the teeth's previous owner. He obviously hadn't cared to distinguish between men and women, young or old. Anyone seemed fair game to him. A sick method emerged in the killings: he would strangle the victims and made them bleed in various ways.

Everyone in the room was transfixed by the atrocities that had flashed in Elenora's mind. Expressions of disgust and horror spread across faces. Once the last images ended, the room was dead silent for a moment.

"*Game of Thrones* has nothing on that guy. What a peach," Alex said, venting his revulsion and eyeing Rolland.

"Play it again," Wren asked while Elenora went to sit on the settee. She had seen and felt more than enough.

"Do you regret doing this?" Pierre sat next to her.

She took a moment to consider her answer. "Not if it allows them to deal with him in the best possible way. But I might need therapy."

Pierre chuckled and gave her a bear hug. "We all might need therapy."

"You did great, Ele. I'm proud of you," Tom said from Pierre's phone. Elenora took the device from Pierre and brought it to eye level. Tom had the rattled look of a first-timer getting off a roller coaster.

"Thanks. I really hope it helps. How's Aubrey doing?" she asked for both their benefits. He must have felt helpless watching her go through this, and she wanted to distract him. She also needed to remind herself she was doing this for their daughter. The thought of her little girl gave her a warm feeling that eased some of her stress.

"She's sleeping like a brick. The one night you're not here to catch up on sleep, of course."

"Of course," she laughed.

"What do you make of all this?" Alex's booming voice brought Elenora's attention to him and the witches, who were shaking their heads over Serena's cell, still baffled.

"You see here, how he slit his own wrist?" Claire-Lune said to Alex, pointing at the video.

"Yeah."

"It's so dark it's hard to see the surroundings, but this looks like an inverted cross. I get the vibe of an attempt to summon the devil."

Serena and Wren nodded at Claire-Lune's assessment.

"So, the devil's involved?" Alex pinched the bridge of his nose.

"In some way, probably, yeah. But it gets...different," Serena said.

She tapped her cell phone screen. "See right here? This woman he's strangling? She looks like she's trying to put a curse on him. Except she's thrashing around so much, she has little control." The three women exchanged concerned looks.

"You're saying she might be a witch?" Alex guessed.

"You're getting good at this," Serena said, meaning it.

He gave her a blank look and went on, "And her spell might have failed, is that it?"

"Failed or, worse, gone wrong," Wren replied.

"Meaning?"

"Well, the spell—whatever it was meant to be—might have gone differently than she intended," Claire-Lune explained. "A wild card curse, if you will."

"So, basically, we don't know what it can do, and it could be nastier than the one she intended," Wren said.

"But wait, there's more," Claire-Lune added humorlessly. "It could have gotten layered on top of whatever arrangement that blowhard made with the devil, further complicating things."

"And this makes it even harder for us to detangle this already impossible mess," Serena said. "It's like trying to defuse a bomb, but someone dumped honey and cereal on the wires for shits and giggles, and now ants are crawling all over them."

Alex blew out a breath. He looked so done. "So, a goddamn spell gone wrong on top of some deal with the devil?"

"Yeah. To kick things up a notch," Serena said. "But there is a silver lining. I spotted a few reflections in the footage. We got a colleague who might be able to identify the asshole. It wouldn't hurt to know who we are dealing with, past a first name and the knowledge he was bad at poker."

"Will you still try to banish the spirit?" Pierre asked from the settee. "You guys are pros at that."

Elenora wondered how much experience Pierre must have had with Serena and the supernatural to make such a statement. She suspected they would have so much to talk about when things were back to normal.

"Yes, because it's worth a shot. But don't hold your breath," Serena said before crouching in front of Rolland. "How are you holding up?"

"I feel like crap, and I have an urge to punch things, but it's all for a good cause," he deadpanned.

Serena examined him once again and then stood up. "All right, next round?" she asked everyone.

"What's the next round?" Alex said, slipping his gun out of its holster. Pierre had his taser ready. Elenora stayed on the settee, observing from a distance, with Céleste sitting in front of her in a protective stance.

"How about we start with a basic banishment spell and see how it reacts to it? And then crank it up if necessary?" Wren suggested.

"Sounds good," Claire-Lune agreed.

The next twenty minutes were a blur of incantations that seemed to have little effect on Rolland. But whenever his reaction became a cause for concern, from his eyes rolling to the back of his head to him levitating with the chair, Elenora retreated to the next room with Céleste on her heels and watched from the doorway, holding her breath and ready to run.

And then, the epitome of all reactions happened.

As Wren furiously mumbled a spell at Rolland, his body started to shake, and a glow appeared around him. It became more solid, and the likeness of the murderer emerged from it, a sentient spectral presence seeping from Rolland. The spirit's facial expression was nasty and unsettling, his lips twisted in a scowl. His ugly gaze took in everyone in the room and seemed to promise retribution. Elenora recognized the dead stare that had haunted her visions.

It discharged a violent pulse that sent everyone flying backward.

The witches lost their hold on it, and Rolland's body battled against the restraints, loosening the ties keeping him in place.

Alex was the first to recover and had his weapon back on Rolland within seconds. He gave Pierre a wavering look, asking him what to do. Pierre held up his hand, urging him not to shoot.

The witches struggled to regain their senses while Rolland's body was getting closer to being free from the rope.

Elenora felt a pressure against her throat, as if invisible hands were wrapped around her neck, tightening their grip. Her fingers let go of Pierre's cell.

This can't be happening.

She wanted to convey her distress, but an invisible force prevented her from moving. Her larynx hurt. Her lungs burned.

"Ele, are you okay? What's going on?" Tom's panicked voice escaped from the cell phone, which had landed screen side down on the floor.

Céleste emitted a low whine. Pierre gave her a signal, and she leaped in front of Rolland, growling to get the spirit's attention.

Pierre snuck around the edge of the room, up behind Rolland, and tasered him. Rolland's body and the spirit jerked against the unexpected shock.

Claire-Lune pointed her hands at him and recited a spell with a strained voice. It seemed to decrease the spirit's vigor. The life-threatening pressure around Elenora's neck eased and then vanished.

Serena and Wren joined the other witch's efforts, and the spirit let out an eardrum-piercing scream before worming itself back inside its host.

Rolland let out a loud gasp, as if he'd just emerged from under water. He struggled to grasp where he was, his bewildered gaze skating around between the people in the room.

"Did I hurt anyone?!" His eyes zeroed in on Elenora and implored her for an answer. "Who did I hurt?"

"Everyone's fine, Rolland." She rasped, taking her hand away from her sensitive neck. Giving him a guilt trip would not help.

He broke down, a nervous fit of sobs taking over him.

"Don't lose hope. We'll find a way." Serena said to him. A few tears rolled down his cheek, along one of his scars. But then the last tear halted. And rolled back up the cheek and into his eye.

"Holy shit," Alex said under his breath. "D'you all see that!?"

Rolland's face went from anguished to eerily calm.

"Oh, hell no." Pissed off, Serena cupped his chin and tilted his head up to line his stare with hers. "Look into my eyes." Her voice was growly and commanding.

Rolland's gaze darted around, avoiding hers.

Wren and Claire-Lune flicked their fingers at him.

Rolland's gaze struggled before snapping to Serena's eyes, an unseen force making him look back at her. She recited the sedation spell, picking up the pace. Rolland's stare grew defiant as a deadly glimmer appeared.

Claire-Lune and Wren joined in on the incantation, matching Serena's tumbling words to battle against the ornery spirit.

Rolland's gaze changed again, draining itself of the evil pushback. His shoulders slumped, his body becoming limp as the spell finally took effect and forced him to relax. His head lolled. He was more sedated than he'd been previously. Serena untied him.

"Is he really under control now?" Alex asked warily.

"Yeah. This time. But the spell's already less effective. There might not be a next time. We need to dislodge the fucker, *stat*, and banish it before it gains the upper hand."

Silent tears fell from Rolland's eyes. These didn't recede, and against his sedated expression, they gave away his existential fatigue.

Elenora wrapped her arms around him, inviting him to cry on her shoulder. The way he hugged her back—his limp arms trying to cling onto her for dear life, the soft tremors of his sobs overflowing from his tired soul—she knew he hadn't been given support in ages, and that broke her heart. He'd been on his own, dealing with the darkness all by himself. How terrifying and devastating that must have been.

"That light that came from him earlier, was that magic? Does that asshole have better magic?" Alex asked Serena reluctantly, as though he dreaded the answer.

"Not necessarily. It felt like the spell-gone-wrong might have mirrored some of our interventions and bounced them back at us. That's my guess."

"So, if you don't do that again, it can't just blast us again?"

"That's right. Hopefully."

The tension in Alex's shoulders eased a little.

"But that could be just the beginning," Claire-Lune said, getting Alex's hackles back up.

Pierre clasped a hand on his shoulder. "The upside: when we get the little bastard, you'll taste a brand-new kind of satisfaction. Trust me." Alex shot Pierre a look heavy with doubt that any kind of satisfaction was worth this ride from hell.

"So, plan G?" Claire-Lune asked her fellow witches.

"Geoff?" Wren replied.

Serena thought for a moment. "Yeah. Let's bring him to Geoff."

CHAPTER THIRTY-THREE

Geoff's office was an upscale, high-tech medical and dental cabinet catering to those with supernatural predispositions. Charts and illustrations, ranging from vampire dentitions to various shifter physiologies, adorned the walls of the waiting room, where Elenora and the gang waited for their host to be ready to see Rolland. Alex's eyes scanned the posters, becoming more perplexed as he took in the bewildering information.

Pierre reconnected with Tom via his video-conferencing app.

A prickly-looking little man appeared in the door frame. It was well past midnight, and Geoff hadn't appreciated being yanked out of bed for their emergency. He pushed his glasses up his nose, shot a quick glare at Serena, and disappeared back inside the next room muttering about her owing him big time and a bag of bagels.

Serena clasped her hands and said cheerily, "Excellent. He's ready to see us."

They followed her to a large room containing various

medical equipment. Claire-Lune guided Rolland, who was still under the sedation spell and shuffling his feet. Céleste stayed put in the waiting room.

Perched on a stool, Geoff motioned to Rolland to take a seat. The witches, Elenora, Pierre, and Alex stood back, watching.

"So, Rolland," Geoff said gruffly. "Serena told me what she thinks is wrong with you, but I'd like to hear it from you. Starting from the beginning, what happened?"

In a slurring monotone, Rolland told the doctor the highlights of his predicament, from being beaten up to the hell-grade dentures he wore to getting involved in medicine and trying to fix himself to being plagued by horrific nightmares and the fear that he committed horrible acts against his will, without ever being certain.

Elenora listened to every word of a story she mostly knew by now, but it still moved her. Rolland was being succinct, sticking to facts, while still telling a lot. He must have rehashed all these turning points so often in his life, in his never-ending quest to understand what was wrong with him so he could put an end to the evil.

For Elenora, it had only been a few months since her own inexplicable changes had happened, that she'd been trying to understand what was wrong with her and done this kind of mental synthesis, too, albeit on a much smaller—and non-lethal—scale. She craved getting answers and couldn't imagine rehashing her thoughts on the matter for years, let alone centuries.

That would be maddening.

She felt Rolland's pain in a whole new way.

Once Rolland was done with his tell-all, Geoff said,

"Serena told me what you've all tried so far, and I agree that the next logical step is to go to the root of the problem and check out those infamous teeth."

Geoff rolled his stool closer to Rolland and unceremoniously shoved a few fingers underneath his lips, moving them out of the way to inspect his teeth. "Open up." After some poking around, he commanded that only Rolland follow him to another room for a scan.

After a few minutes of busy silence, they heard Geoff exclaim, "Holy mother!"

Elenora caught Pierre biting back a smirk as they all rushed to the imaging room, which had a CT scan behind a glass wall. On this side of the wall, Rolland towered behind Geoff, who sat in front of several monitors that showed various angles of Rolland's insides, from his head down to his chest. They showed his teeth and their roots.

The freakishly long roots had grown downward into his body. Exceptionally thin, they had entered his jugular and traveled all the way down to his heart, around which they were wrapped tightly.

Even to a medically untrained eye like Elenora's, it seemed like any attempt at yanking the teeth by force would have a devastating effect on Rolland's heart.

"That's gotta be a first." Geoff's previously annoyed expression had morphed into one of wonder and bafflement. "I don't know what to say."

The entire room—including Rolland, who had a muffled look of terror on his face—stared at the screen. Claire-Lune turned to Wren, breaking the silence. "How about a spell to loosen up the roots around the heart?"

Wren shook her head. "They're there, most probably, to

serve as collateral. I'm afraid they would constrict and strangle the heart in reaction to any kind of probing. And that could be fatal..."

"If it kills me, it might die along with me," Rolland pointed out, his voice still sluggish, but his mind sharp enough to keep up with the discussion. "Would the parasite take that risk?"

"That's a fair point." Wren conceded. "Perhaps it wouldn't be fatal but certainly painful. If the fight it put up earlier is any indication, I would expect a nasty reaction. It would find a way to damage you just enough to keep you alive and in check."

Alex muttered to Pierre, "I can't wait to go back to our usual garden-variety psychos. This shit's too messed up for me."

"It'll grow on you," Pierre grinned.

Wren studied the monitors with a concerned focus. "Ultimately, it's your call, Rolland. I can try detangling one root gently while we observe the progress on the scan. We'll see the reaction, but..." She didn't seem to know how to finish her sentence.

"For what it's worth, this seems too risky even for me. We risk making Rolland a vegetable, and then who knows what the asshole will do without a conscience to slow it down." Serena let her head fall between her hands. "Geoff, any ideas?"

They all turned to the doctor. His eyes were scrutinizing the images, his mind racing. His expression was as despondent as hers. "I... Let me think."

Claire-Lune's phone chimed. She glanced at it and brightened up.

Serena perked up. "What's up?"

"Oliver Barlow. Jeb says he's on the list but a no-show."

"English, please?" Alex said.

Pierre jumped in with excitement. "It means that Mr. Barlow, our cantankerous guest, has indeed struck a deal with the devil, hence he's on the list. But since he's in this room, he hasn't reported to hell after he kicked the bucket."

"The no-show part?" Alex tried.

"The no-show part." Pierre turned to Claire-Lune. "Did I miss anything?"

"You still got it." She gave him a smile.

"Okay, but concretely, what does this mean?" Alex's hand rested on his gun.

"Concretely, we now know he's not a demon sent from hell, unless there's a glitch in their system," Serena explained. "As suspected, this is a peculiar situation. We can assume the witch's curse went wrong and put a wrench in Barlow's plans."

"Jeb says we should go to him," Claire-Lune said carefully, watching for her sister's reaction.

Serena pinched her lips in annoyance. "We haven't tried everything... Wren?"

"We've tried everything," Wren said with dejection. "I'll need time for new spells."

"Reena..." Claire-Lune tried coaxing.

"We don't have enough for a case," Serena snapped.

"Why don't we let him be the judge of that?"

"He can *judge* all he wants, that won't give us hard evidence, Lunie."

"Right. But then he could—"

"He could what? Pull a case out of his ass? And then cowboy his way through it?"

The two sisters glared at one another.

"You got a better idea?" Wren asked politely, making Serena groan.

"Translation?" Alex's irritation matched Serena's.

"Our colleague Jeb wants to make an appeal," Claire-Lune started explaining.

"An appeal to whom?"

"The Gray Court."

Pierre added, "Or as they like to call it, the Devil's Bureau."

CHAPTER THIRTY-FOUR

"They will ask you to sign a non-disclosure agreement," Serena said flatly to Elenora and Alex from the back seat of Pierre's SUV. It was close to two a.m., and they were escorting Rolland to a mystery location to meet a man named Jeb, who supposedly had a long-shot solution. Judging from Serena's reaction—she'd been quietly fuming since they decided on this course of action—the plan was a hairy one.

"You can't accuse them of taking themselves too seriously," Alex mumbled sarcastically.

"They have to."

A moment of tense silence filled the car before Alex craned his neck to glare at Serena, who was sitting on the other side of Rolland. "Can you tell us who *they* are?"

Serena shrugged dismissively.

"Let me guess: they're gonna mess with our brains on the way out." Stress and weariness tended to sharpen Alex's edginess.

"Only if you don't sign the NDA." Serena gave him an abrasive smirk.

Alex scoffed.

From the front passenger seat, Elenora ignored their bickering. She, too, was eager to find out where they were going. After seeing Geoff's cabinet and what the three witches were capable of, maybe she was getting closer to answers about her own situation. She felt some apprehension but mostly curiosity. Maybe she was getting used to this, maybe she was adapting. A few months ago, she wouldn't have thought that possible.

"We are going to the OPO," Serena finally said.

"That stands for Off-Path Office," Pierre added, proudly in the know.

"Some kind of special case division?" Alex said. "Or are we stuck in a cheesy B-movie?"

"Oh, there's nothing cheesy about the OPO." Pierre could barely contain his excitement.

"Is it affiliated with any police force?" Elenora asked.

"Surprisingly, yes. It's a national policing entity that operates way under the radar on cases of very singular natures," Pierre replied.

"So, you've already dealt with cases that?" Elenora looked at Pierre, even more intrigued about the past double life he seemed to have lived.

"Let's say I had the eerie pleasure of working with them on a few occasions. They do have good people over there with very open minds and some unorthodox tactics." He grinned.

A soft moan rose from the back seat.

Elenora twisted herself to glance at Rolland. He looked a little green around the gills. Wren had come up with an additional restraining spell to slap on top of the existing one so the feisty spirit wouldn't try anything funny on the way to the OPO. It seemed to be working.

As if picking up on Rolland's subdued misery, Céleste, who was riding at the very back of the SUV, had laid her head on his shoulder.

Elenora stretched her arm to pat Rolland's knee. He answered with a faint smile.

"We're almost there," Serena grumbled.

An abandoned industrial building came into view. Pierre turned into its pothole-plagued parking lot, the vehicle bumping around as it headed toward the back of the building. Pierre was right: there was nothing cheesy about the OPO. "Derelict" and "in a hopeless state of disrepair" would be much better ways to describe it.

"*This* is the place? I need to renew my tetanus shot." Alex huffed.

"Just be patient," Pierre replied.

The SUV beamed its headlights on a rusty garage door covered in old graffiti. By the look of it, it hadn't been used in forever and was probably rusted shut.

"You're shitting us, right?"

"Ye of little faith."

They inched forward slowly as Pierre buzzed his window down, stuck his head outside, and waved. The door opened smoothly, and the vehicle drove down a ramp leading to a high-tech underground parking lot, with small lights above each space pointing out the free ones in green.

Alex surveyed the surroundings, dumbfounded.

They parked and walked to an elevator tucked in a corner, noticing several security cameras along the way.

"Why do witches need security cameras? Don't they have

crystal balls for that?" Alex's tone had moved from exasperation to genuine curiosity.

"There aren't just witches working here," Pierre said.

"Is there anyone like me here?" Elenora perked up, hope budding inside of her.

"With your expertise? Not at the moment," Serena replied, her tone warmer for Elenora.

Her "expertise." That sounded so much better than "nightmare-inducing curse." It was amazing how a single word could make one see things differently.

"The closest one's in Toronto. And he's quite busy."

They entered the fancy elevator, and a guard with jet-black, slicked back hair appeared on an LCD screen. "Hey, Serena. Pierre! Long time no see. Welcome back!"

"Thanks, Vince. It's good to see you. How are you?"

"I'm good. We'll have to catch up. Where to, Serena?"

"Hey, Vince. Fifth floor, please."

"You got it."

The screen shut off, and the elevator headed up to the fifth floor.

"Is he a vampire?" Alex whispered.

Serena narrowed her eyes at him. He gestured to his hair to justify his question.

"No. He's Italian."

"Are there vampires here?" Alex continued, earning him an eye roll from Serena.

"Jesus! Obsessed much?"

"What? It's a legitimate question!"

"Fine. We got a floor full of 'em. I'll take you to it, and you can spend the rest of the night."

"You have a full floor!?"

"She's yanking your chain, Alex," Pierre said, fighting off a grin.

"What about this Jeb guy? What is he?" Alex tried.

Serena took a long and noisy intake of air through her nose. "He's a permanent pain in my ass."

Pierre laughed. "She means he's a descendent of Osiris and has been reincarnating for ages. He should be around making her life miserable for a very long time."

"Thanks for the reminder."

An amused smirk appeared on Alex's lips. "Let me guess: he's your ex?"

In response, Serena lifted her eyes to the top of the elevator and stared at it, making Alex chuckle.

The doors opened on a floor that was the antithesis of the exterior of the building. The place was clean and had a vibe of understated opulence.

Large windows in perfect shape—while they had seemed broken from the outside—let in faint, blueish light from the moonlit mid-December night. The warm amber glow from wall-mounted sconces illuminated original brick walls and wood beams, bringing an appealing historical touch to an otherwise modern space. It had the feel of a Silicon Valley tech start-up from the 2000s, with snack stations offering Belgian chocolates and Mariage Frères teas. The spaces were a mix of hipster coworking areas and welcoming private offices.

A tall blond woman with soft curls spotted Pierre and headed their way. "Detective Deveraux, it's been a while."

"It's because it's *retired* Detective Deveraux now, Dr. Brent." They both seemed happy to see each other.

"Elenora, this is Dr. Meredith Brent. She's a paranormal

psychologist," Serena said cordially, her mood lightening considerably. "Doctor, this is Elenora, the gifted woman I told you about."

"Elenora, it's a pleasure to finally meet you. Serena finds you quite intriguing."

"Damn right, I do."

"Perhaps you'd like us to have a chat sometime?" Dr. Brent offered.

The kind but unexpected invitation took Elenora by surprise. "I suppose. I do have a lot of questions."

"I bet you do. Tell Serena when you're ready, and we'll make it happen." Dr. Brent turned to Pierre, "And you, don't be a stranger." She waved to the group and left.

"A paranormal psychologist... I don't recall our guidance counselor ever mentioning *that* as an option," Alex said dryly.

"Wait until you meet Jeb," Pierre replied.

"What does he do?"

"He works with the devil's advocates."

Jeb lit a few candles in his large, yet cozy office as he described to Rolland, Elenora, Pierre, and Alex what they were about to attempt to help Rolland. Wearing a t-shirt and a tie, he seemed like a laid-back, hip surfer-dude type, one Elenora would never have mistaken for a high-powered attorney. But on their way to the man's office, Pierre had told them he'd overturned hundreds of curses and deals with the devil. If that wasn't the definition of high-powered...

"Look at it like it's a video conference," Jeb explained to Rolland.

Serena, Claire-Lune, and Wren, who already knew about the workings of the Gray Court, hung out on a couch at the back of the room, Céleste lying at their feet.

"In a nutshell, our bodies will stay in this room—mostly," Jeb went on, "but our minds will meet one of their clerks on a spiritual plane."

"This sounds very abstract. Will you be able to see him? The clerk?" Elenora asked.

The plan, as far as Elenora understood it, was for Jeb and Rolland to meet an emissary of the devil and lodge a complaint to nullify any dark dealings responsible for Rolland's unfortunate and convoluted predicament and get them to take the parasite away from him. Their argument was that Rolland had nothing to do with any of the nasty spirit's shady deals with third parties, and he shouldn't be held responsible for them nor have to uphold the end of any bargain.

The plan seemed at once logical and completely surreal.

"Yes. In fact, it will feel like we're physically there with him in the room, just like we are here, because we partly will be. This makes the meeting more concrete but also makes us more vulnerable. Psychological warfare is a specialty of theirs." Jeb turned to Rolland. "In other words, don't let the clerk psych you. If we stick to the business at hand, all should be well."

"How are you going to dial into this virtual meeting?" Tom asked from Pierre's cell phone, back in video-conferencing mode and sounding as fascinated as ever. "The candles?"

"Oh, no. I just like the mood they provide to the room, along with the smell. It's jasmine. No, Serena and these other lovely ladies will help establish and maintain the connection."

Sitting in a club chair next to Rolland, Elenora noticed him fidgeting, no doubt growing nervous.

Jeb addressed Rolland again. "When we're there, let me do the talking, all right? No matter what he says or does, don't argue back. Try not to attract attention. And be prepared to be short-changed. Fairness doesn't exist where we're going. Are you sure you want to do this?"

Rolland gave Elenora a wavering glance. She answered him with a supportive smile. "You're incredibly strong. You've already won impossible battles against this evil inside you. You're an extraordinary man. You deserve a better life."

"With all due respect, Mrs. Bello, I'm afraid it doesn't really matter what he deserves," Jeb said softly.

"Okay. But this man has been living in hell for too long." Elenora's voice was also soft but betrayed her need for justice. "In my humble opinion, any shot at him gaining a better life is better than not taking a chance."

"What if the clerk gives him a death sentence to void the contract? It's a possibility. Rolland knows it's a risk."

Upon their arrival, Jeb had conferred with Rolland to make sure he understood what was at stake and to evaluate if he was willing to take the risk and give this a serious shot. Jeb had then excused himself briefly to build a case in record time.

"Death would be a relief," Rolland said.

Elenora reached for his hand and gave it a squeeze before letting it go. Rolland's eyes lit up with gratitude and got a little misty.

"Rolland, I just want to make sure you're going in with

eyes wide open," Jeb added.

"What are the odds of this working? Him getting a fair deal if there's no fairness?" Alex asked, invested.

"Well, it's worth a shot, but let's put it this way: nothing can ever be taken for granted when Satan and his minions are involved," Jeb replied.

"If they are fickle or don't have morals, then what prevents them from giving you the worst, cruelest possible deal?" Elenora tried to understand.

Jeb smiled. "Ah, yes. This is the fun part that makes this bewildering treaty we have with them possible. Of course, evil would be satisfied with everything being evil all the time. As far as they're concerned, there's no such thing as too much chaos and cruelty. However, plain evil across the board is not sustainable for anyone, them included. They thrive on corrupting the innocent. If everything is evil and they run out of innocence, it's game over for both sides, not just the good guys."

"Like the food chain in an ecosystem, they need one another. They need balance," Tom said from the phone. Alex shook his head in bafflement.

"That's right. Of course, it's slightly more complex than that. But in a nutshell, yeah. There needs to be a balance for life on earth to go on," Jeb confirmed.

"Are you limited in the number of cases you can present?" Elenora asked.

"There are quotas, yes, and all the OPOs have to pick their cases judiciously. But more importantly, the cases that have a chance need to involve the total innocence of the requesting party, like Rolland here, who got sucked in against his knowledge. Whereas if someone were to enter an agreement with some knowledge, then it sucks to be them. We have no power to erase all evil just by pleading that evil was involved. There will always be evil."

Jeb's watch beeped as the door opened, and a petite blond woman in a paramedic's uniform walked in, closing the door gently behind her. "Hey, Juniper. You're right on time."

"Hey, Jeb," she replied and headed for a seat in an empty corner of the room, as if she didn't want to disturb anyone. She seemed to be about Elenora's age and of calm demeanor. An observer.

Jeb silenced his watch and said, "All right. We better get at it. The clerk on duty is expecting us soon and we don't want to be late."

He reached for a file folder on his desk and stood near Rolland, while the three witches stood up and came closer.

"What do I need to do?" Rolland asked.

"Nothing much. Just remain seated and don't fight it," Serena said with a professional tone, deliberately avoiding eye contact with Jeb. In contrast, Jeb's gaze often landed on her.

"Okay," Rolland said, glancing at Elenora for reassurance.

"Take a few deep breaths and keep your breathing in mind if you start to feel anxious," Elenora suggested to him.

"Okay." Rolland took in a long breath.

"Are you ready, Rolland?" Serena asked him.

"Let's get this over with."

Serena recited an incantation. Rolland shot one last look at Elenora. She instinctively reached for his arm. Jeb saw her hand land on Rolland's arm, and his eyes widened.

"Don't—"

CHAPTER THIRTY-FIVE

It took a moment for Elenora to grasp what had happened to her.

She'd touched Rolland's arm to comfort him when everything went dark around her, and it felt like every sound was sucked out of the room. A sudden, drastic change in the air pressure made her ears ring. A warm breeze caressed her face.

And then here she was, in a dark room without walls with Rolland and Jeb. The three of them were sitting in plushy chairs facing a desk.

Was this the Gray Court? And if so, what was she doing there?

She wasn't supposed to be there.

Oh God, would her presence hinder Rolland's case? Her heart sped up.

A man appeared before them out of thin air. The clerk, she presumed. He looked human, and she wondered if that was his true face or just a show for their benefit. She felt eyes on her and turned to meet Jeb's gaze. He looked calm and raised his hand slightly to tell her to let him handle this. She gave him a subtle nod.

The clerk sat at the desk without acknowledging them. "What do we have here?" he muttered to himself, perusing papers in front of him, looking bored.

"Oh yeah, *that* clusterfuck. I've been wondering when it'd come up." He let out a frustrated sigh.

He finally looked up and acknowledged Jeb. "Jeb."

"Stefan."

Stefan's gaze moved to Rolland. "Rolland Carmichael, I presume?"

"Yes."

Stefan's stony gaze moved on to Elenora, and he frowned. "And you are?"

"Allow me to introduce Mrs. Elenora Bello," Jeb said. "She's a psychic social worker who's been collaborating with us on this case, helping us understand to the best of our abilities before presenting it to you. You know how much we value your time, Stefan."

Jeb's smooth ass-kissing seemed to do the trick and divert Stefan's attention from the fact Elenora had no business being there. She concentrated on keeping herself still and not giving the clerk any reason to look at her, listening intently as Jeb pleaded Rolland's case. He recited all the facts that were known to them, every detail they'd managed to piece together.

From Elenora's insights into the parasite's psyche that Serena had recorded, a colleague of hers named Ethan found out more about Oliver Barlow—the spirit's former human form—a murderer from Britain. He was convicted of several murders during his life and served time in a handful of prisons but escaped each time. However, neither Ethan nor the trio of witches nor any other colleague succeeded to identify the suspected witch or was able to figure out the curse she had put on Barlow. Jeb's case held together with bits of scotch tape and a lot of hope.

Still, Jeb came across as confident, convincing, and to the point as he pleaded the case, highlighting the known and indisputable facts.

"Stefan, the bottom line is, what we have here is a second-hand deal. Plain and simple. My client inherited it unwillingly, without his knowledge or consent. Had he known that the owner of the teeth was cursed and in such a confusing spiritual state, he would not have acquired them."

There was a pause. Stefan stared at his papers, pondering.

"But your client didn't inherit the full deal, correct? Unlike Mr. Barlow, who sold his soul to the devil, Mr. Carmichael still has full ownership of his soul. So why bother?" Stefan countered.

"Technically, he does, but barely. Full ownership would mean that he'd have a choice to reject the unwelcomed actions Mr. Barlow's spirit imposes on him at his whims. But we both know and recognize this is not the case. As it is, Mr. Carmichael must put up with the immoral actions of Mr. Barlow and has no recourse in preventing them, which interferes with his own free will and the ownership and morals of his own soul. Mr. Carmichael strongly objects to murdering on Mr. Barlow's behalf."

Stefan graced them with an eye roll, as if Rolland was being such a prima donna for not embracing murder.

Jeb went on, "And my client is stuck in a vicious circle, unable to move on since he's immortal—"

"Yeah, that part looks like a...goddamn glitch," Stefan said with annoyance, one brow raised in incomprehension. The moment the words were out of his mouth, he looked like he regretted letting them slip.

A glitch? Was this guy serious? Rolland had been living several lifetimes of misery because of a so-called glitch in their twisted system?

Elenora took in a slow breath to temper her rising outrage.

"It looks to us like that glitch, as you called it, was introduced by a witch's curse gone wrong when Mr. Barlow strangled her," Jeb said.

Stefan's eyes widened in surprise. He seemed to wonder how Jeb could possibly know that. His gaze flicked to Elenora before he regained his stiff composure.

Jeb added, "The actions of this witch, with whom my client had nothing to do, are yet another set of actions from a total stranger that has interfered with the full ownership of his soul, despite his will."

The clerk let out a frustrated grunt. Under normal, real-life circumstances, Elenora imagined he'd be backed into a corner. Jeb's arguments felt solid and warranted for Rolland's situation to be rectified. But here, who knew where this could go from there.

"You know, Jeb, a deal's a deal. The original owner of the teeth died without fulfilling his end of the bargain," Stefan said, bad faith leaking from his every pore.

"Stefan... You're arguing my case for me. Mr. Barlow couldn't—and won't be able to—remit his soul to your boss until he ceases clinging to my client's body. Hence, releasing my client from any ties to Mr. Barlow's deal with your boss would allow completion of Mr. Barlow's bargain with him," Jeb said with a voice of honey. Elenora could tell he was struggling not to appear smug.

But Stefan seemed unimpressed and unready to budge, which didn't make sense. Didn't he want to collect Barlow's soul and call it a day?

"In the end, my client should not have to bear the brunt of any of this, and we would like to terminate this unlawful agreement once and for all. In return, you finally get that soul that was promised to you and get to reconcile your books," Jeb added to nudge the clerk toward the right decision.

Elenora felt Rolland tense in anticipation, and she caught herself in time before she gave him a pat.

Don't move a muscle.

They held their breath while waiting for Stefan to speak. He was taking his time, and it was torture.

Torture.

Jeb had mentioned psychological warfare. That was probably what this guy from team evil was going for.

Stefan rubbed his chin, as if brewing an idea. Perhaps wondering if he could add another layer of wickedness into the mix.

"Interesting," the clerk mumbled at last.

He stared at Rolland for a while, then shuffled through the papers in front of him, pretending to study Rolland's unfair situation. Elenora was getting more convinced he was doing this for show, to keep them on pins and needles for the fun of it. *His* fun.

Stefan let out a long sigh. "Gee... I dunno."

Elenora glanced at Jeb and noticed the cool dude stiffen. That couldn't be good.

"You know, the timing's not all that great..." Stefan shrugged, scratching the back of his head, making it sound like the decision was out of his hands.

Jeb's face hardened, and Elenora's insides flipped.

"You're hoping for a two-for-one..." Jeb accused the clerk with barely veiled contempt. "You're going for the long game, hoping that Barlow will eventually wear my client down. Well, I'm pretty sure no amount of eternity will ever give Mr. Carmichael a taste for killing. You're not gonna turn him."

Stefan shrugged again and put up an air of nonchalance, but Elenora detected a sting. He didn't like being called out. "You don't know that. Humans are influenceable," he said. "You give them enough time, enough rope..."

Jeb scoffed.

If Elenora understood this right, this evil minion was toying with a man's life. For what, a quota? To suit his whims? To satisfy his need for cruelty? All of it? The jackass! The nerve.

Anger filled her, and it must have shown on her face. She realized the clerk was staring at her. "Something you'd like to share?" he asked her blankly.

Oh. Crap.

She lowered her gaze to escape from the unsettling coldness of the eyes boring into her. "No, your Honor," she answered, schooling her voice to keep her anger and fear out of it.

"Just Stefan," Jeb whispered to her. His voice sounded steady, but she imagined him cursing her in his head. She was worsening an already awful situation, digging their collective grave a little deeper when she wasn't even supposed to be there.

"Stefan, sir. I didn't mean to interrupt. Please accept my apology."

"No. You look like someone who's dying to say something. I'm all ears." His sadistic delight was palpable. If only she knew the rules of this perverse game.

Elenora had helped conduct tricky negotiations before, but this was in a league of its own, a league that had no use for the well-being of the parties involved. Whenever appropriate, she'd try to find a concession that her party could make. Sometimes it was easy, sometimes it was near impossible. But most humans understood the principle of give and take.

Here, there was just "take" as far as she could tell.

"I don't have all day." Stefan sounded annoyed, forcing her to give him something.

Something that won't further deteriorate Rolland's chances, no matter how meager they seem.

Something he wouldn't miss...

And then it came to her: immortality.

Rolland didn't care to live forever and was ready to die to put an end to his nightmare. And if Stefan took Barlow's spirit from Rolland, then the witch's curse—which they assumed was the cause of Rolland's immortality—would most likely leave with Barlow and no longer affect Rolland. So, if the spirit left, immortality would be lost regardless.

Hence, sacrificing immortality would be a false concession for Rolland.

She just had to make the jerk clerk buy the appearance of a concession, convince him of having the upper hand. Unless he knew what the witch had done and called Elenora's bluff. But like them, Stefan didn't seem to fully understand the witchcraft at play, and he might not know that Rolland's immortality came from the curse. Jeb hadn't disclosed the fine prints of his client's endless existence.

Stefan might buy this.

It was worth a shot.

"Stefan, I was respectfully wondering... Maybe you would consider a concession from Mr. Carmichael to sweeten the deal in your favor?"

Stefan perked up. "What kind of concession?"

She pretended to be reluctant.

"It pains me to even suggest this, as it would hurt our client. But what if you take his immortality to teach him a lesson? You know how us humans are, wanting to live forever. This would be a high price to pay, but Mr. Carmichael might consider it."

Ugh. Elenora hated the taste of those twisted words on her tongue. But when in Rome... This was the only language this guy seemed to understand. She could feel bad later.

Stefan steepled his fingers under his chin, studying the situation. He seemed to like what he heard. "Well..." He glanced at his watch and stood up. "Gimme a sec." He vanished.

Was this a good sign? Had he fallen for it? Or had he called her bluff and was now angry and on his way to concoct something even more horrible?

"Is this normal?" Elenora asked Jeb in a whisper.

"It's not abnormal."

"What do you—" She wanted to know his thoughts on what she had done, but he brushed an index finger over his lips, urging her to stop talking. He acted cool and detached but also seemed hyper-aware. Was the clerk still in the room? Were they being watched? Was this a test?

"We have a new deal to propose," the clerk's voice echoed against invisible walls right before he reappeared.

Elenora stilled and braced herself for this new deal.

"We are listening," Jeb said.

"As you know, life is unfair, and everything has a price. So, here's the deal. We will take back Mr. Barlow's soul and free Mr. Carmichael of any remnants of it. And as proposed by the missus over there"—he pointed at Elenora—"we will take away your client's immortality as a processing fee for our trouble. AND..." The clerk paused for effect, and they could hear his taunting metaphorical drumroll of triumph.

"Mr. Carmichael will also return to the physical state he was in right after his beating."

That last bit brought a vicious, self-satisfied smile to his face. "And to celebrate the full recovery of his humanity— since it's all so important to you—we forbid the use of magic to help the healing. Take it or leave it."

The surprise addition was a cruel and unnecessary injustice to make Rolland suffer more than he needed to, and Elenora wanted to shout that the acquisition of the teeth happened well after Mr. Carmichael had started to heal. But she bit her tongue and forced herself to keep a blank expression to not derail the precarious offer that was on the table. An offer that, while not entirely fair, would still give Rolland back his humanity and a chance to live the rest of his life in relative normality, what he wanted all along.

This felt like a big win.

"Mr. Carmichael, do you agree to this?" Jeb asked him.

Rolland gave him a curt nod. Elenora imagined he'd be holding his breath until the ink on the deal was officially dry.

"All right. Then, sign here," Stefan said, pushing a pen and a piece of paper on the desk toward Rolland.

Rolland took the pen and started to sign. The moment the last stroke of ink landed on the paper, his body started jerking uncontrollably, and he fell to the ground.

Elenora rushed to his side. With horror and helplessness, she witnessed Rolland's physical state degrade before her eyes. He was reacting to invisible blows, as if the beating from centuries ago was reenacted in real time with unseen assailants.

A spray of teeth and blood came out of his mouth. Agony and distress contorted his face as bruises bloomed on it.

Oliver Barlow's spirit appeared in a trail of smoke. It shrieked and writhed as it was forcefully being pulled out of Rolland's body. But it wouldn't go down without a fight. The spirit anchored itself and budged no further, stretched in mid-air between an invisible force and Rolland, who was balled up in pain, struggling to remain conscious.

Stefan let out an exasperated sigh and went around his desk to get physically involved. His arrogant confidence that he'd control Barlow quickly turned into a grimaced struggle as the spirit fought back. Stefan got hold of the smoke as if it were material, but then it slipped through his fingers and started to seep back into Rolland, pissing Stefan off.

"Why, you...little...heathen... I'm gonna. Show. You. Who's. Boss." He grunted each word.

Elenora held onto one of Rolland's arms and legs to keep him from thrashing around and hurting himself even more. Jeb came to help her stabilize him while glaring daggers at

Stefan. "I swear to everything that is unholy, Stef, if we lose him, we're both gonna regret it."

Without breaking his hold on the rodeoing spirit, Stefan returned a daggered glare on Jeb. "No need for threats!" After a few precious seconds, he added, "Fine. Call in your cavalry. But no healing!"

"Serena!" Jeb shouted. "Send in Wren and Junie!"

Wren and Junie materialized in the room, their eyes already on Jeb, waiting for his instructions.

"Wren, sedate Barlow. Junie, stabilize Rolland. Pain management only."

"No healing magic!" Stefan barked at Juniper.

"Yes, I got that part," Juniper said under her breath as she assessed Rolland's gnarly condition. She placed a hand on his shoulder, and her touch appeased him. She whispered words to him, and he closed his eyes, his jagged breathing becoming more normal despite Barlow jerking his body around.

Judging from the weird shade of gray on Stefan's face, he was redoubling his efforts to get Barlow out. Wren started an incantation that seemed to help as the spirit became slightly less reactive. But it wasn't enough. It still had plenty of fight left in it.

"Why don't you call for backup?" Jeb asked Stefan. He received a disdainful look from the clerk in return.

"I'm *not* calling for backup."

Jeb shook his head. "Stubborn a..." His frustrated mutter trailed off. "Serena, send—"

Claire-Lune appeared before her name came out of Jeb's mouth. He didn't seem surprised to see her appear this fast or that she naturally picked up Wren's incantation mere seconds after her abrupt arrival. The spell started making a difference, extricating Barlow from its host inch by inch.

Before long, Stefan gained the upper-hand and yanked the spirit out of Rolland. In a sizzling hiss, the smoke previously known as Barlow dissipated with one last scowl.

"He's gone?" Jeb asked Wren.

"Yes," Stefan said curtly. Jeb ignored him, his eyes on Wren as she crouched near Rolland and hovered a hand over his body, scanning.

"He's gone," she confirmed.

"Great. Serena, bring us back," Jeb said, and everything went dark again.

CHAPTER THIRTY-SIX

Elenora found herself back in Jeb's office, she and her new colleagues in the same positions as they'd been seconds before: Claire-Lune stood nearby while Elenora, Juniper, Wren and Jeb kneeled by Rolland, limp and unconscious on the floor, looking like he'd just been in a severe car accident.

Alex looked on in horror. Pierre looked grim but not surprised. "What happened?" he asked Jeb.

"The bastard jumped the gun," Jeb muttered, livid.

"What do you mean?" Alex said.

"As part of a deal and as punishment, the clerk insisted that Rolland return to his physical state when he was beaten up—don't ask. They all hold Ph.Ds. in creative logic. But Rolland's state shouldn't have changed until we were back. Stefan's making us pay for forcing his hand. He's quick to turn anything and everything into a pissing match to remind us they can fight dirty. But this was low, even for him." Jeb turned to Juniper. "How is he?"

"He's hanging by a thread. I put him in a temporary coma

to ease the pain and to survive transport. But that's it. No healing magic, as douche face demanded."

"So, you guys can't fix him here?" Alex asked.

"Sounds like that's part of the deal," Pierre replied.

Jeb took over with an explanation. "Correct. You will need to escort him to a hospital and tell the staff you found him beaten up in an alley or something. The OPO will supply the ambulance and play along, but we can't be further involved to respect the terms of the new deal."

"Fuuuuck. Those people have issues," Alex huffed out.

Jeb clasped a hand on Alex's shoulder, making him wince. "You don't know the half of it."

A man wearing a paramedic's uniform like Juniper's entered the room with a gurney and swiftly wheeled it next to Rolland. "This is Hassan, a fellow healer," Juniper said to Elenora and Alex. "He will help us with transport."

They greeted the newcomer while he and Juniper placed Rolland on the gurney. When they were done, Wren hovered a hand over Rolland's inert body, once again scanning for something.

"Didn't she do that already?" Elenora asked Serena in a hushed tone.

"She's using a more advanced detection spell to double-check no molecule of Barlow's slimy ass was left behind. But she's also checking that darling Stefan didn't gift us a Trojan horse. So, basically, she's really making sure they're keeping their end of the bargain to a T."

"Do they ever renege?" Alex asked.

"Not usually. As evil as they are, they have no incentive to waste their own time with us coming back to them and crying foul. But we always check."

"Better safe than sorry?"

"When evil is involved, you gotta," Jeb replied.

"He's good to go," Wren declared. Juniper and Hassan started wheeling Rolland carefully out of the office. Jeb invited Elenora, Alex, and Pierre to come along.

"What will happen to Barlow's soul?" Elenora asked him as they followed the gurney.

"It's gonna burn in hell like it should've been all these years. And I have a feeling they're gonna crank up the heat on this one."

Elenora tried to follow the logic. "But, with the murders it committed through Rolland, it did the devil's work. Shouldn't it be rewarded instead of punished?"

Jeb chuckled. "You'd think, eh? But no. Barlow did do very bad, punishable things, probably to ingratiate himself with the devil and try to buy his soul back. The way he clung to Rolland suggested he didn't want to go to hell."

"But he was just buying time, no? Wasn't he heading to hell eventually, anyway?"

"When someone who sold their soul arrives in hell, they have no choice but to submit, because their free will is stripped from them as a part of the transaction. Now most criminals are feisty pains in the ass—even for Satan—so he's too happy to make a bargain with them prior to their arrival."

"Criminals who still have their souls can rebel in hell?" Alex was all ears, fascinated.

Jeb nodded. "Power struggles are frequent. Torture comes in handy."

"So, if Barlow was trying to recover his free will, in a way, he was trying to trick the devil..." Elenora said.

"Looks like it. But here's the thing about messing with the

dark side and thinking you can outsmart the devil. It doesn't matter what you do. In the end, you just can't win."

It was agreed that Pierre and Alex would ride in the ambulance with Juniper and Hassan to accompany Rolland to the hospital while Elenora and Céleste headed back home to Tom and Aubrey in Pierre's SUV.

Elenora dozed off in the living room with baby Aubrey sleeping in her arms, waiting to hear some news, when Pierre called from the hospital. Tom put him on speakerphone.

"Everything's going smoothly. Juniper made it so that her pain-management coma spell would wear off once Rolland was safely hooked up to the medical equipment, and her painless transition worked as planned. Rolland regained consciousness minutes ago. He's alert and remembers what happened. His body's in horrible shape, but he gave us the biggest grin. I don't think I've ever seen someone this happy, and relieved, and grateful. It was very touching."

"I'm so happy to hear that, Pierre." Elenora's heart swelled.

"I think Alex even got something caught in his eyes." Pierre chuckled.

"Yeah, he's a big softie underneath it all," Tom replied, also amused. "How's Rolland going to be? What did the doctor say?"

"Lots of broken bones, cuts and scrapes, and half his teeth have fallen out," Pierre said. "But he's stable, and his primary organs weren't critically affected. They cleaned him up, and the painkillers are working, and he's already looking better.

He says that thanks to modern technology, this time around feels like a walk in the park compared to what he went through the first time."

Elenora was elated to know that Rolland was truly out of danger, not only physically but spiritually and emotionally as well. Obviously, a big part of her was relieved to no longer have an evil murderer after her and her family. But right now, she was mostly thrilled that a man who'd been through so much adversity and unspeakable horrors was now free to live life on his own terms.

He could live, now. Simply live. Something he hadn't been able to do for nearly two centuries.

That was big.

"It must be weird for him to relive the same medical recovery but with vastly different technology. I can't even imagine how rough people had it back then," Tom said.

"He said he could barely afford minimal care back then, so yeah, this is night and day." Pierre's sentence ended with a yawn.

"Come home, Pierre. He's out of danger, and we can all use some sleep," Elenora said.

"Alex and I are getting in a cab as I speak."

"We'll probably be in bed when you get here." Elenora stood up slowly to not wake up Aubrey.

"Yeah, don't wait up for me." After a pause, Pierre added, "You know what he said? We brought him to the Ursulines, right? It's the same hospital he'd gone to the first time, and he thinks he's on the same floor. He might even be in the same room. How weird is that?"

Elenora got goosebumps. How weird indeed it would be if that were the case.

"Anyway, when the nurse kicked us out, I told Rolland we'd come see him."

Elenora looked forward to seeing Rolland's progress and discovering the man he truly was—the man he was always meant to be—now that his crippling supernatural burden was gone.

How bizarre and exciting a situation this was. Never in a million years could she have envisioned being a part of such a singular journey. She wondered if her own paranormal journey would end with this resolution or if this was just a chapter.

The first of many?

More goosebumps crept over her skin.

CHAPTER THIRTY-SEVEN

The more Rolland studied the shapes and patterns of the cracks in the ceiling, the more he became convinced he was indeed in the same hospital room as before. He didn't know what to think of that.

Was it fate warning him to not get too comfortable? That he may no longer be subject to someone else's whims, but he was still firmly in fate's grasp? That he'd never truly be in control of his own destiny?

Ugh.

That would really suck.

Or perhaps it meant that his troubles had come full circle, and he was now free to live according to his own will.

He chose his second explanation instead of thinking there was a brand-new metaphysical tyrant in town to replace the previous one in ruling over his life.

So here he was again, under the same ceiling but in much better physical shape and in a vastly different state of mind. Better food too.

Way back then, he had come so close to dying, and when Delphine had walked in and plunged a metaphorical knife deep into his back and through his heart, he knew the life he had known was over.

But boy, had he ever underestimated how over it would be.

Here he was, and once again, a previous life was over. One he was so happy to leave behind. Despite the aches and pain, he felt so light. A little scared of the unknown, sure, but also filled with an overwhelming sense of peace. Like he was given a clean slate.

For one thing, he was no longer running and hiding.

Legally, he didn't know what would happen to him. Would he have to serve time? If he had to, then so be it. It would be a temporary discomfort, and then he'd be done paying for someone else's sins. He had nothing to hide anymore, and the dark urges—the real prison—seemed gone for good.

He never thought he'd be free again, and the prospect of being his own man without horrific repercussions was at once elating and daunting.

What would he do now? Who would he be? What would it feel like to age again, to become older? To know that he would eventually die?

He'd have to be more careful when he jaywalked.

The thought made him chuckle, and the chuckle made him wince, having triggered a sharp pain that shot through every corner of his body, but in his mouth in particular. His gums were so sensitive. His tongue could feel the holes where his missing teeth once were and the teeth that were left teetering, on the brink of falling out. He'd have to look into implants or dentures or whatever other options he'd have now. But surely, they would all be free from evil.

It was so nice to have good options, he told himself, feeling drowsy.

He closed his eyes and drifted to sleep.

***

Rolland's eye caught movement in the doorway. Elenora was poking her head in the room, offering him an authentic smile. "Hey, there!" There was a bit of a squeal in her voice. She seemed really happy to see him.

Rolland had wondered if she'd pass by and hoped that she would. He was dying to talk with her and thank her properly for everything she had done for him. She'd been there for him when he was at his ugliest, but somehow, she'd been able to see through the evil and believe he was salvageable and worthy of rescuing. She had taken incredible risks to stand by him.

What if things had gone horribly wrong when she summoned him in the mirror? Or when he appeared in baby Aubrey's room? How could she still have wanted to help him after his own hands had tried to strangle her and almost succeeded—twice?

He would be grateful to her forever.

"I'm nominating you for sainthood," he tried to say to her, but the words came out a bit garbled. Damn teeth. Or lack thereof.

She caught his drift and let out an airy laugh. "I think I've had enough dealings with heaven and hell stuff for now. Let's not tempt fate."

Rolland smiled, thinking it probably came out as a grimace that made him look even scarier. He gave her a thumbs-up to make sure she didn't think he was in more pain than he truly was.

Her smile grew even wider before sobering as she took in his condition. Most of his body was in a cast. He looked like a mummy with a black-and-blue face.

"I can't imagine the pain you must've felt the first time, without proper medical care."

Rolland nodded and lifted his chin at the television set. "No cable back then."

Elenora barked out a laugh, and her delightful presence made him feel so warm inside. Along with the absence of darkness. It sure felt good to no longer suffer the oppressing and relentless influence of evil.

"How's the tiny one?" he asked.

"She's awesome. Sleeping much better already. It makes such a difference."

"I'm glad," he said, and he was. "She's special."

"Yes. But not too special, I hope." Elenora's face darkened a shade.

Rolland remembered the strange current that had gone through him when he held the baby after her delivery. Seeing Elenora's concern about Aubrey being special, he kept this puzzling piece of information to himself. For now, anyway. There was no need to make her worry. Perhaps he'd ask Serena what she thought about it if he ever saw the kind witch again.

He heard a gasp from the doorway and looked.

"Oh my God!" Anna was standing there, a look of horror on her face, her hand covering her mouth.

Seeing Anna looking at him like this ripped Rolland to shreds. Panic spread inside him, the pain of an impending heartbreak surpassing his current physical agony. He wanted to scream. This couldn't be happening. Not with Anna.

She wasn't meant to see him in this state, even more monstrous than usual. He had wanted to heal first, then go back to the shelter and pretend that nothing had happened. Tell her he'd been away, taking care of a long-lost cousin or something. That would have been the plan. A perfectly good plan.

Until now.

Now she would find him so repulsive she'd never be able to look at him in the eye again. Or look at him, period.

He had lost his chance with her.

His heart broke more with each step she took toward him, her face in shock as she took him in. She would see the damages up close, turn around and run straight out of his life.

Like Delphine had.

Except this was so much worse. It hit him how much more Anna meant to him than Delphine ever had. He loved Anna, and he could not survive having his heart broken again, not in this cruel way. Not now that he was finally given a real chance at healing and having a life.

And just as a seed of rage at the unfairness of it all budded inside his soul, Anna sat next to him, and her expression of shock turned to deep concern. She let out a deep sigh of relief. "I was so worried I'd find you on your deathbed."

Her eyes briefly went to Elenora, who was sitting by

Rolland on the other side of the bed, before she turned her attention back to him and unleashed a torrent of words.

"I mean, Elenora insisted that you'd be okay, and I so wanted to believe her. But I was still worried sick. She said she couldn't tell me more—she said it would be your story to tell. And I respect that. You can tell me when you're ready. If you want to. But for some reason, I've just had this dreadful feeling haunting me ever since you've been gone. So, it's been tough not knowing. You have no idea how relieved I am. I thought you were gone forever. I was so scared I'd never get to see you again."

Her passionate words hung in the air, and Rolland wondered how much damage his hearing had sustained from the recent beating. Or maybe he was hallucinating again.

Anna laid a lingering kiss on his forehead, one of the few patches of skin that wasn't in a cast. Rolland couldn't believe he was feeling the sweet touch of her lips, let alone what she'd just said.

"Would it hurt if I touched your hand?"

He shook his head, and she smiled, putting her hand over his. He couldn't help a few tears from escaping.

"You must hurt everywhere. I'm so sorry."

If only he could tell her that these were tears of joy. "I'll be fine," he croaked. "Don't feel sorry for me."

"Can I feel angry then?" Dropping her voice, she added, "Unless you got hit by a truck, I can go kick someone's ass real good. Just say the word."

Rolland let himself chuckle softly, careful not to wince.

"Did your husband or Detective Bélanger get whoever did this?" Anna asked Elenora, a glimmer of hope in her eyes.

"Let's just say that justice has been served," Elenora replied with a smile.

When Rolland was discharged from the hospital, Elenora, Tom, and Pierre came to bring him home. He couldn't believe their generosity.

He was also overjoyed to see that Anna was already at his place, ready to welcome him with butternut squash soup simmering on the stovetop. She had made sure the house was ready for his convalescence at home, including a full fridge.

She had volunteered to play nurse to Rolland. Since she was a nursing student, she had solid arguments that made it hard for him to decline her offer. He craved her presence and wanted her near him more than anything. But he didn't want her waiting on him hand and foot. Spoon-feeding him. Giving him sponge baths in his grotesque state. Not the most alluring way to attract someone.

He argued that he'd be much more comfortable paying someone to do such thankless tasks. She retorted his excuses were lame, and it would take much more than that to make her go away. Besides, she could convince her school to accept the experience as an internship. Would he dare deny her the opportunity? She had said this facetiously. He knew she wasn't the type to go for emotional blackmail.

Rolland caved in, and Anna turned out to be even more wonderful than he already thought her to be. Every day, he was filled with love and gratitude and falling for her a little more. And he felt like she, too, had a growing appreciation of him.

From a medical standpoint, Rolland's convalescence mirrored his previous one as far as natural progression was concerned, minus a great deal of pain, both physically and emotionally.

One thing tugged at his heart, however: the frequent reminder of his long-gone brother Rory, who had been the one to fuss over him the first time around. He missed him more than ever.

Rory would have loved Anna. And she would have loved him.

Another shadow darkening Rolland's rebirth was keeping his past from Anna. The closer they grew, the more he felt like he was lying to her. This weighed on him, and he felt it hindered their budding intimacy. He had lived with secrets and lies for far too long and was tired of it. He wanted to share everything with her and let her in entirely. But he feared the repercussions of telling her everything.

He feared losing her.

Every time they watched a show with paranormal elements—of which she was a fan—he burned to tell her about his own experience, how he knew for a fact that witches were real and that life in the Regency, or Victorian, or Edwardian eras was in fact like this or that. He wanted to tell her about Rory. He wanted to no longer feel like he was deceiving her.

But how could he possibly tell her he was born in 1820 and had once been made immortal and possessed by a malevolent spirit who had forced him to commit murders on its behalf? But he was fine now, really, because an emissary of the devil had taken the evil douchebag back in exchange for Rolland's immortality and the sadistic joy of crippling him once again with an impressive beating that landed him in the hospital. Please pass the salt, darling.

Not exactly a casual topic of conversation.

But a conversation *would* have to happen. While Anna was not a snoop, she lived in his museum of a home and was bound to come across something he'd have to explain. Fortunately, she kept proving herself to be discreet, trustworthy, and very open-minded, enough for Rolland to test the waters.

"Do you think there's such a thing as magic?" he asked her, perched on top of crutches. He was helping her unpack groceries as best as he could, despite her insistence that he didn't need to.

"I'd like to think so," she replied matter-of-factly. "And if not, then how could we explain Charlie managing to finally get off the street—and stay off—after so many stints in rehab and sleeping outside in winter? He managed to rebuild his life. If that's not magic, I don't know what is. So, yes, I guess I do believe in magic."

She gave him an impish smile.

"One could argue that Charlie's case was a miracle, not magic," Rolland said teasingly.

"What if miracles are a subset of magic?" she countered.

"You got me there." He couldn't help smiling. That woman. "So, you'd be okay if magic existed..."

"I'd be fascinated."

"How about possession? Do you think someone can be possessed?"

"You mean like the people struggling with inner demons every day at the shelter?"

Anna's answer surprised Rolland. She was right. Most of the men they worked with waged serious internal battles, often acting on impulses that were not entirely their own but were caused by a variety of illnesses or addictions. Often both. These men and women were just as devastated as he had been. Past a certain point, there was no reason to quantify or qualify that kind of misery. Just because most of them hadn't killed another person didn't make their suffering any less.

"I hadn't looked at it that way."

He couldn't help gazing at Anna with admiration. She had such a fresh and kind perspective on life, on people. It never ceased to amaze him.

"Why are you asking about magic and possessed people? Are we having company for dinner?" she asked wryly, making Rolland chuckle.

"No, but perhaps we should."

She surveyed what they had bought at the store. "Does someone who's possessed eat for two? I think we could wing it."

Mulling over Anna's reaction and outlook on life, Rolland became convinced that if there was one person in the world who could handle the kind of revelations he was itching to make and keep a cool head, it was her. But first, he would give Elenora a call and ask her what she thought of him telling Anna the truth. She already knew how he felt about keeping his past from Anna, and it couldn't hurt to get her opinion.

That very evening, he waited for Anna to leave for her biology class and dialed Elenora.

"I think coming clean would be very freeing," Elenora said. "At least in my limited experience. Before I told Tom and Alex, I was so nervous and convinced that they couldn't handle it."

"Yeah, but you never killed anyone," he pointed out.

"True. But neither have you, if you think about it. I can vouch for you and the situation if you think that'll help."

"I'd love that. But if you get involved, you might end up exposing your own gift."

There was a brief silence on the line before Elenora answered.

"You know what? I don't plan on broadcasting my disturbing skill set to the world, but in your case—and to support you, your new life, and your happiness—I'd be willing to make an exception. And from what I've seen, Anna adores you and she's worthy of trust."

"You think she adores me?" Rolland's heart made a flip.

"I think she does."

Rolland savored that notion. "So...any idea what I should do next?"

"Perhaps we should talk to Serena. She must have experience with mind-blowing reveals of this nature."

"Good thinking."

"How about I talk to her and get back to you?"

When Rolland hung up the phone, he was confident that the two women would find the right way to help him deal with his challenge.

A few evenings later, they all met at Rolland's place over dinner, with the mission of helping him unveil his troubling secrets to the woman he was now convinced was the real love of his life.

Serena had suggested a Plan B in case Anna freaked out beyond salvation. She would cast a memory spell and gently erase the dinner-gone-wrong from the young woman's memory, making her think she had dreamed the encounter.

Rolland started his declarations during dessert, looking nervous as hell and his voice wavering. "Anna, you mean the world to me, and I want you to be a part of my life as much as you are willing to be."

"Shouldn't you be on one knee for this?" she teased him.

"Hmm. No, I think I should be sitting for this..." He cleared his throat. "At any rate, before my knee has healed enough to support me, I must share some heavy secrets with you."

"I gather Elenora and Serena know and are here for support?" she said, fully attentive and receptive.

"Indeed."

Rolland hesitated to go on, and Anna jumped in, looking him in the eye. "Are you a wizard? Or did you use to be possessed? Or both?"

Rolland choked on his sip of tea. "Wow, you really do pay attention."

Anna grinned. "Well, you seemed rather invested when you broached those topics the other day. So...how warm am I?"

Serena went straight to the point. "Long story short, I'm the witch," she said, gesturing to herself, then to Elenora. "She's psychic. And Rolland used to be possessed, but he's all good now."

Serena's straightforward reply stunned Anna momentarily, but her eyes quickly narrowed, trying to gauge whether their guest was pulling her leg. Her gaze returned to Rolland, who was pale and quiet, eyes filled with worries. Anna stood up and opened her arms to give him a hug. He wobbled to a standing position to welcome it.

"You're not upset?" He mumbled into her hair.

"Why would I be upset? Granted, I'm not sure what this all means, but if it's happened to you, I want to hear about it. Even though it sounds terrifying."

"It was...intense," he murmured, holding her tight. He couldn't believe how well this was going. "And overwhelming. I don't know where to begin."

"Why don't you start from the beginning?" Anna coaxed him.

Rolland nodded and took a deep breath. The beginning. All right. He invited her to sit back down and did the same.

"I was born—" An idea struck him, and he turned to Elenora. "Could you please go get the daguerreotype from my desk in the basement?"

"With pleasure." Elenora stood and left the room, Serena following her.

"You've got a daguerreotype?" Anna seemed impressed. "I mean, I can see you're quite the collector, but aren't those rare and expensive?"

"It was expensive, but it's priceless."

A moment later, Rolland held the precious picture of him and Rory, taken a few years before the beating. Both brothers looked dashing and serene despite their neutral expressions. Their brotherly bond was also apparent.

"That's you?" Anna asked him, with a confused frown.

"Yes. And my brother Rory." Emotions caught in his throat.

Anna admired the picture. "Wow. So well made. You could swear it's an original. Where d'you have it done?"

"It *is* an original. My friend Charles paid for it. He was very generous, and his family was loaded. Whereas Rory and I were the exact opposite," he said with a bittersweet smile, already down memory lane. He was overjoyed to finally be able to tell her about his dear brother and his own life before it had taken a severely wrong turn.

Anna's initial surprise quickly morphed into rapt attention, seemingly willing to go along for the ride, no matter how fantastic it sounded. She hung onto Rolland's every word as he told her about his birth in 1820 and his humble beginnings, his friendships—including meeting Serena—even mentioning Delphine. Her eyes were round with fascination, and she didn't interrupt him—perhaps afraid to break the magic.

But despite Anna's awesome receptiveness, Rolland knew it was a lot to process and didn't want to push her.

"How are you feeling so far? Do you have questions?" he asked before telling her about the beating, knowing there would be no turning back from the darkness they were about to enter.

"I don't have words...but you bet I will have questions, for the next decade or so, and I will want you to tell me all of this again. It's so very amazing and a lot to take in. But I'm dreading the bad part I know is coming, that might explain your scars. And the whole possession thing... I don't know how literal you're being about that, but it makes me nervous. I feel *you* growing nervous. Maybe we should rip that bandage off?"

Nothing got past her. He loved that so much about her.

"So, who's up for a round of whiskey?" Serena stood up.

"I'm buying." Rolland made a circling gesture around the table jokingly. The witch smiled at him and, walking behind him on her way to the kitchen, she gave his shoulder a squeeze.

Anna reached to grab Rolland's hand, and her touch gave him courage.

"When I first mentioned possession, you made the very apt observation that it was like the folks at the shelter battling their inner demons and not being aware of some of their actions. You remember that?"

"Mm-hmm."

"Please hold on to that thought." Rolland's eyes were pleading.

"Okay."

Serena came back with glasses of whiskey and handed them around before taking her seat. Rolland was tempted to down his glass but refrained from doing so. He wanted to remain level-headed, as he'd only get one chance to tell his story properly to Anna.

He glanced at Elenora, who had offered him to help break the news of the inadvertent murders when he'd get to it, and she gave him an encouraging nod to proceed.

"Also, please keep in mind that this has a very happy ending," Rolland said to Anna before launching into the retelling of the grisly night that would change his life.

At the right moment, Elenora took over the telling, explaining to Anna how she found out about Rolland and telling her side of the events, emphasizing that he'd been like a hostage inside his own mind and body.

Unsurprisingly, the grim revelations shook Anna to her core. The young woman's eyes had gone wide—and stayed wide—during the entire account. But she stayed there, sitting with her back straight at Rolland's dining room table instead of running for the hills, screaming. She looked deeply concerned but for his well-being more than anything else.

When all was said and done, Rolland told her softly, "I so much wish none of this was true, and I hope this will not affect our relationship. I hope you won't see me as a monster."

"Oh, Rolland, don't say that. Please don't even think that. I'm there for you," Anna replied, as if any other course of action would be unacceptable.

Rolland's heart was full that evening. He still couldn't believe the support and acceptance he was getting after two centuries of lonely battles with himself in the shadows. He was healing nicely, both on the inside and on the outside.

Serena pointed out that his facial scars seemed less pronounced than they'd ever been. Rolland made some calculations and realized that, in this parallel recovery, he was now past the stage where he had implanted the stranger's teeth into his own gums, back then, and he said so.

"So, this is uncharted territory," Elenora said. "Perhaps the scars will heal entirely this time."

"Or if you have laser surgery, it should take, now," Serena added.

Anna's hands got hold of his face and she turned him toward her. She brushed fingers over the scars, much like the first time they met, studying them. "They're hardly noticeable. It's your decision, but I think they give you character. They *show* character. You've been through hell and back, and these are a testament to your very singular journey. Your impressive triumph over evil."

Anna understood. Truly understood. A wave of relief washed over Rolland at the thought she wouldn't be holding his past against him. She was accepting him as he was, including the truly ugly parts. And she was right. The scars were a part of him. And with the way she looked at him, he realized he no longer cared to have them removed. They no longer mattered. It even felt right to keep them as battle scars.

It had taken him only almost two centuries, but he was finally proud of who he was and who he had become.

He couldn't wait to see what the future held for him, with Anna at his side.

CHAPTER THIRTY-EIGHT

"He's running a bit late," Serena said as she hugged Elenora by the coffee shop counter and kissed her on both cheeks. "My word, your cheeks are freezing!"

While April often brought pleasant weather in Montréal, it also liked to remind people it was still early springtime. Today was one of those days.

"And judging by how warm yours are, you've been here a while. Am I that late?"

"Nope. You're right on time. I just like having some time here all by myself. To think. Relax." She fake coughed and added, "Gawk at Gavin."

Elenora shot a discrete glance at the male barista manning the espresso machine. Mid-thirties, tall, dark, and handsome, no doubt Serena's type. She grinned. "Nothing wrong with a little gawking."

"That's what I keep telling myself."

Elenora had been so happy when, the week before, Serena invited her to meet with her and Rolland over coffee. The invite had come when the witch phoned Tom to update him on what the OPO had done to help close and classify Rolland's case. File it away for good.

The OPO had contacted the precinct, with which they had worked before—an interesting little fact that Elenora, Tom, and Alex were surprised to learn. There was a hush-hush agreement between the two entities for jointly handled abnormal cases.

In Rolland's case, Claire-Lune had created a report that Mr. Oliver Barlow of Great-Britain—she even included his last known address in Kent from 1847—had been accused and found guilty of the murder of Dr. Réginald Haché. Which, in essence, was the truth.

The file with the hard-to-believe information—how could a criminal from the mid-1800s have killed a surgeon living in the twenty-first century?—had been added to the police's database to close the case, with a repelling "spell of disinterest"—Wren's words—on it to discourage anyone from digging it up. On the surface, save for the spell and the file's unbelievable data, it all looked kosher. And it helped that Haché didn't have a family to question the information or ask anyone to dig deeper. Even Alex had to recognize that, technically, this was brilliant and as legal as it could get given the extraordinary circumstances.

Gavin called their drinks, bringing Elenora's wandering mind back to the cozy little coffee shop, and Serena rushed to the barista to pick up their order.

The man squinted at one of the cups and said, "Serena?" before looking up at the witch with a brow raised, clearly teasing—he could barely hold back a grin.

"You'd think after my twelfth cup today, you'd remember

my name," she teased back with feigned outrage. "You should have your short-term memory checked."

Gavin chuckled and returned to the espresso machine. Serena grabbed both cups, handing Elenora hers. Over her shoulder, she said to Gavin, "I'll be back soon. Perhaps the next drink will do it."

"I'm here till four."

The two women headed to a table near a window that Serena had claimed as hers with her classy gray coat that clashed with the beaten-up college-student backpack she had with her today.

"Remind me to ask you someday about how that whole dating thing works for you with, you know, your skills and having been around for so long," Elenora said, slinging her purse strap over the back of one of the free chairs.

"You want to know how many courtships and liaisons I've had throughout the centuries?"

"That'd be interesting to know."

"How many years do you have?" Serena joked as they both sat.

"As many as needed. But I have more pressing questions if you don't mind."

"Shoot."

Elenora dropped her voice. "Were you born a witch?"

"Yes. My sister and I were born witches."

"When did you find out about your skills?"

"Very early on. My parents were witch and warlock, as were most of my ancestors, so there were no surprises there. The absence of power would have been the surprise."

"Do you think *I'm* a witch?"

"I honestly don't know."

"Is one necessarily born that way, or can you become one?"

Serena shook her head. "I don't know. Your visions started when you got pregnant, right?"

"Yes, aside from that odd episode as a child, as I told Anna. But I remember very little about it."

"Right. Then what about Tom? Did he ever have visions himself? Or anything out of the ordinary?"

Serena's questions took Elenora aback. "Why are you asking about Tom?"

"It seems that your powers started, or were triggered, or heightened when you became pregnant. When you welcomed some of his genes..."

"Huh." The thought that Tom could have anything to do with her powers had never occurred to her.

"Tom's got great intuition and empathy. But not at a supernatural level, I don't think. I'm sure he would've mentioned something by now."

"And no one in his family?"

"I'll have to ask. We'd have to check. To be honest, he seemed genuinely dumbfounded when he found out about me, so I'd be really surprised."

"And he's still floored when he sees you at it. I've noticed. He looks very impressed."

That made Elenora smile. Tom never hesitated to let it show that he thought she was awesome.

"I wished I had someone in my life who was *that* impressed with me." Serena's gaze wandered toward Gavin, who was now wiping a nearby table.

"I find you very impressive, if that's any consolation."

Serena beamed at her. "Thanks."

They sipped their beverages in silence for a moment.

"Would it be so bad? If you turned out to be a witch?" Serena asked. "I mean, it's just a word. A label. We're all individuals. Like me, you'd still be you. You with an unusual gift, but still you. Things have already changed for you, and there's no turning back. So, why let a word worry you?"

Serena was right. Things had already drastically changed for her and so far, she had come out of it alive, and more. Different, obviously, but she'd survived an impossible ordeal and even helped save a man who might not otherwise have been saved and might have kept on taking lives. Instead, she got to have coffee with him and hear the joy in his voice and see a newfound passion for life in his kind eyes.

Thinking about Rolland's new life brought her so much happiness. Having had the odd privilege of helping him made her feel like her mission in life had deepened.

So, what was bothering her?

"Maybe I fear change," Elenora said. "The good old common fear of the unknown. But I have to admit that as scary and traumatic as the visions have been, they've also allowed me to do things I would never have thought possible. Good things. And I am grateful for that."

"If you had the chance at a clean slate, like Rolland, would you want your powers to go away? Now that you know?"

Hmm.

"Honestly, as much as I'd rather not suffer the bad parts of it, I'm not entirely sure I'd want to go back."

How bizarre that she was now thinking this, after so ardently wishing for the powers to go away and leave her alone. Let her be normal. "Ha. Imagine that."

Serena smiled. "It's all very normal. I totally hear you about wishing there was no bad side. After all these years—centuries—really, I still have a hard time coping with some consequences of my own skills."

"Really?"

"Of course."

"Have you found anything that helps you cope?"

"Talking with my sister. But therapy, as well. Meredith at the OPO can be a lifesaver when I fly off the handle and Claire-Lune's had enough of my shit."

Elenora chuckled. "That's the psychologist I met?"

"Yeah. And I assure you, she has seen and heard everything."

"And that's coming from you?"

"She's been around even longer than I have."

"She doesn't happen to be a vampire, does she?" Elenora asked with an impish grin.

"Maybe..."

"No!"

"Just don't tell Alex," Serena said with a matching grin.

Elenora laughed, shaking her head. "Wow. I can't even..." She sobered. "Just wow. It must be something else being in your shoes. Yours and hers. And just about everyone's at the OPO."

"Well, it must be something else being in yours, too. The glimpses I got of your power... My God, girl. That's some cool shit!" Serena's enthusiastic candor made Elenora laugh again. A frank, clear laugh. The witch was good for her.

"Is it cocktail o'clock already? You guys sound suspiciously merry," a male voice said behind them, catching their attention. "What'd I miss?"

Rolland had changed even more since Elenora had last seen him at his great "coming out to Anna" soirée. Physically, he had recovered most of his original good looks, minus the two faint scars that he still left alone. They did give him character and a hint of mystery. The centuries-old dark shadows under his eyes from a perpetually tortured state of unrest were mostly gone too.

But his handsomeness was not the reason he was stunning. A light shining from within him gave him an irresistible charisma, an air of benevolence and serenity. He looked like a happy young man. He looked so young now, like decades had been shed from him.

"We were just pondering on existential angst and waiting to grill you," Serena said tongue-in-cheek.

"My favorite topic!" he replied jovially, with a hint of sarcasm.

"You look well. How's Anna?" Elenora asked.

"She's up to her eyeballs with schoolwork but otherwise good. And I will soon be joining her. Did Serena tell you?"

"Didn't get to it yet." The witch turned to Elenora. "Geoff accepted to take Rolland under his wing so he could expand his medical knowledge even more."

"Isn't that awesome?" Rolland was grinning from ear to ear.

"Totally!" Elenora matched his grin.

"Don't just stand there. Go get your drink!" Serena ordered him, giving him a playful shove. Rolland gave her a military-style salute to show he would not argue and headed to the counter.

"And say hi to Gavin for me."

Rolland raised an eyebrow. She waved her hand around

dismissively. "Never mind," she added with a smirk.

"Peace of mind sure suits him," Elenora said, hearing pride in her voice.

"It does. You did great," Serena replied.

"It was a team effort."

"Yeah. But you believed in him when he looked unredeemable. You stood up for him. And he knows it."

"Thanks for saying that. And for being there for me."

"Anytime." Serena took a sip of her drink. "I mean it."

Elenora followed her lead. Her insides warmed up from the silky sip of heavenly latte and the fact that she knew her new friend meant it. It crossed her mind that with her career, the pregnancy, and now a newborn, she hadn't made time for friendship in a while.

Rolland came back with a chai, and they caught each other up with their news. Baby Aubrey was teething. Serena was considering adopting a cat but worried it was too cliché. Rolland wanted a dog. To Elenora's delight, Serena and Rolland reminisced about the not-so-good old days before electricity. They had such a good time, they vowed to get together again soon.

On their way out the door, Elenora remembered something that had caught her attention on her way to the coffee shop. She parked a few blocks away, and while heading there on foot, she had felt a "warm chill" go through her, if there could be such a thing. The sensation was odd, and she'd been meaning to mention it to Serena.

"Does that ring a bell?" she asked the witch.

"Well, chills are often felt when there's a spectral presence. But a *warm* chill?"

"Where were you when it happened?" Rolland asked,

growing curious.

Elenora looked down the street to where she was parked. "Somewhere down there. I didn't pay attention to where I was exactly. Just what I felt."

"Let's walk you to your car and tell us if it happens again," he suggested.

The trio headed down the sidewalk until Elenora stopped in front of a neglected vacant lot. "I think it was around here."

"Are you feeling anything now?" Serena asked, her eyes on her.

Elenora waited for the weird chill to happen again, but she didn't feel anything peculiar. She closed her eyes to tune her awareness, to pick up any subtle hint.

But she felt nothing.

She smiled and reopened her eyes. "I must have imagined it. Perhaps it was the wind. Do *you* feel anything?"

Serena shook her head. "No, but I don't reliably feel spirits. So don't take that as a sign of anything."

Rolland cupped his hands around his mouth and called toward the lot, "Mary!?"

"What the hell are you doing?" Serena whistled between her teeth and gave him the evil eye.

"Perhaps good old Mary has a message for me," Rolland said, amused. "Mind you, we didn't part on the best of terms. You might want to park somewhere else next time."

"Mary?" Elenora had a feeling she wouldn't be as amused as him.

"As in Mary Gallagher?" Serena tried.

It dawned on Elenora that Rolland was referring to the famous prostitute in the late 1800s who had been beheaded.

Her ghost was rumored to make an appearance every seven years on the anniversary of her unfortunate demise, holding her severed head against her hip.

"Oh, come on," she whispered.

"Mary, this is Rolland Carmichael. If you can hear me, I'd like to apologize. I had no business being harsh with you. I take back what I said." A smirk appeared on his lips. "Except the part about you being stubborn."

Serena elbowed him in the ribs. "Sweet Jesus, don't antagonize her! Do you still have a death wish?"

"She used to tease me about being more stubborn than her. I don't think she'd lose her head over this," Rolland said, fully grinning.

Serena groaned.

"I assure you, Mary could take it as well as she could dish it."

"Back then, but now? People change..."

"At the risk of sounding heartless," Elenora said with growing alarm, "if it is her, there's nothing I can do for her. Maybe someone from the OPO? Dr. Brent, if she needs to chat?"

Serena and Rolland took in Elenora's panicked look. Serena gathered her arms around her and pulled her into a hug. "You're still frazzled and it's normal."

"I'm sorry I made light of this. I didn't mean to cause you distress—" Rolland started.

"Rolland, I'm not trying to make you feel bad. I just..."

"You're just not ready for another roller coaster ride so soon?" Serena volunteered.

"Yeah. I think I've had enough thrills to last me a lifetime."

"Well, for all it's worth, I've got your back if you ever got shoved on another ride," Rolland said.

"And you won't be able to get rid of me either, girlfriend," Serena added. "Let's get you to your car." They walked the rest of the block in silence, with their arms hooked together.

As they crossed the street, Serena said, "I apologize, Ele, but I have to ask. Rolland, when you said you didn't part on good terms with Ms. Gallagher, did you have anything to do with her...?"

"Her death? Oh God, no!"

"Not even your ex-inner-asshole?"

"No. Thank goodness, no. I was at a medical conference in Philadelphia."

Serena let out a sigh of relief. "Just checking."

"I understand."

They reached Elenora's car and shared hugs before heading their separate ways.

Driving home, Elenora tried to repress the memory of the warm chill and focus on her time spent with her new friends at the coffee shop. They made her feel fuzzy—in a good way—and energized, and she believed them when they said they'd have her back. If only that simply meant being there for the *normal* ups and downs of life—like going out for coffee or a beer, having the occasional trivia night, celebrating birthdays. Not dealing with paranormal threats.

But what was the point in fretting and expecting the worst? She had a loving husband and an adorable baby girl waiting for her at home.

Should the visions come back...she would deal with them then.

For now, she had moments of her own to cherish.

THANK YOU FOR READING!

Elenora, the gang, and the little boy at the bottom of the river return in *Trapped Souls*.

Curious to know what happened to Tim, Pierre's childhood friend? Find out by reading *Shade of Evil*, a short story prequel featuring Pierre as a budding detective. You can get it for free when you sign up for my newsletter or buy it from your favorite retailer. Visit www.jacinthedessureault.com to subscribe.

If you enjoyed this book, please consider leaving a review.

A THOUSAND THANKS

I'd like to thank my wonderful husband—my white knight. His love and relentless support made this book possible.

Thank you to my awesome parents, family, and friends for your encouragement. It means the world to me.

A special thanks to my friend Catherine for the teeth-related inspiration.

And last but not least, thank you, Nadene, Bettina, and Gloria for your astute feedback and enthusiasm.

ABOUT THE AUTHOR

Jacinthe Dessureault writes paranormal mysteries and humorous fiction. She is a big fan of lemon meringue pie and of the silly antics of Boonie and Jackson, her family's two adorable lop buns. She lives in Montréal, Canada with her husband and daughter.

HER BOOKS

Elenora Bello Paranormal Mysteries
Shade of Evil (short story prequel)
A Sinister Gift

Humorous Fiction
Igloo High (young adult)